THE DOG ROSES

RESOLUTION

DAVID H. MILLAR

TITLES BY DAVID H. MILLAR

CELTIC HISTORICAL FANTASY/FICTION

The Conall Series

Conall: The Place of Blood: Rinn-Iru

Conall II: The Raven's Flight: Eitilt an Fhiaigh Dhuibh

Conall III: The Sisters: Na Deirfiúracha

Conall IV: A Brace of Eagles: Snaidhm Iolar

Conall V: Retribution: Díoltas

The Dog Roses Series

The Dog Roses: Na Feirdhriseacha

The Dog Roses: Resolution

The Blood Queen Series

The Blood Queen: A 'Bhanrigh Fuil

Brianag

The Dog Roses
Resolution
DAVID H. MILLAR

The Dog Roses: Resolution is a work of fiction. Apart from obviously historical figures and places, all names, characters, and incidents are either the product of the author's imagination or are used fictitiously. Any resemblance to actual persons, living or dead, establishments, events, or locales is entirely coincidental.

A Wee Publishing Company, LLC
HOUSTON, TX, USA
http://www.aweepublishingco.com

Paperback ISBN: 979-8-9865756-5-0
eBook ISBN: 979-8-9865756-6-7
Library of Congress Control Number: 2024902822

A Wee Publishing Company, LLC, Houston, TX

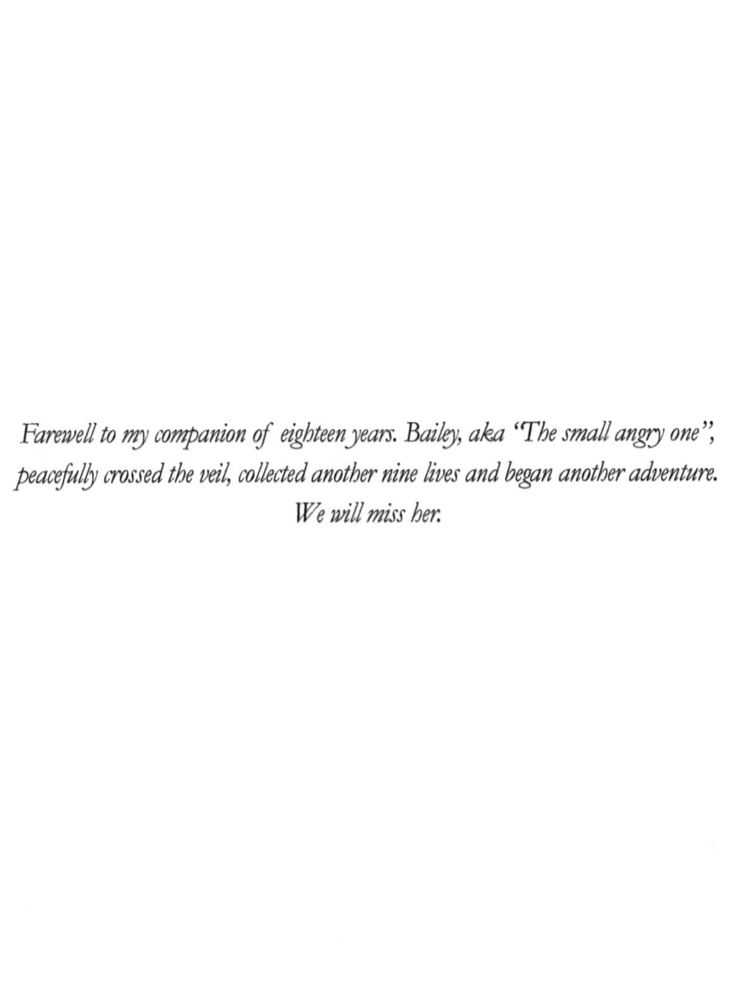

Farewell to my companion of eighteen years. Bailey, aka "The small angry one", peacefully crossed the veil, collected another nine lives and began another adventure. We will miss her.

ACKNOWLEDGEMENTS

The process of writing, publishing, and marketing novels is a team sport. Often, it is arduous, especially when faced with a blank page for days or weeks, and sometimes, it is inspiring. A good sense of humour and a bottle of Irish whiskey within reach are always essential.

I am always very appreciative of the international cast that comprises Team Millar. Thanks to my editors (Kahina Necaise and Cecily Blench from The History Quill/Fabled Planet), my cover designer and internal formatter, Ida Jansson, Amygdala Design, and my patient map illustrator, Chaim Holtjer.

Lastly, thank you to my beta readers: authors Judith Fullerton, Jolie A. Reynolds and Brendan Sullivan, Chris Hurt, Lauren Millar, and Susan Robitaille.

CONTENTS

GAELIC PRONUNCIATION

There is a global fascination with all things Irish. After the initial glow, probably from Guinness or whiskey, they face the obstacle of an unpronounceable Irish language—Gaelic!

The story uses Gaelic (some ancient) for many proper nouns (people and places). Do not be dismayed! Consider the English kings and queens in Bernard Cornwell's *Last Kingdom*, the elves and orcs of Tolkien's *Lord of the Rings* and even many characters in George R. R. Martin's *The Game of Thrones*. Many hardly trip off the tongue.

I advise pronouncing the Gaelic in the way that gives you the most pleasure. That is what I do! However, I have provided a guide to the most frequently used names in the novel below. Hopefully, this will ease the pain.

IRISH

Ailill Mac Máta (**AHL-il** mak MAWta)

Aillean (**AL-yan**)

Aoibheann Ni Neill (**AY-veen** NEE-ul)

Aodán Mac Conall (**AY-awn** mak KON-ul)

Aodh Mac Aodh (**AWD** mak-AWD)

Aoife Ni Cináed (**EE-fa** nee-KIN-awd)

Báine (**BAWN-yuh**)

Barra Mac Conall (**BAR-a** mak KON-ul)

Beacán Ó Cathasaigh (**B'YAG-awn** o-KAS-akh)

Bláithín Ni Neill (**BLAW-heen** nee NEE-ul)

Bran Mac Labraid-Loingsech (**BRAN** mak LA-ra-LING-shek)

Brighid Ni Conall (**BREED** nee KON-ul)

Brónach Ni Ciar (**BRO-nakh** nee

Calman Mor (**CAL-man** MAWR)

Cairbre Mac Ailill (**CAR-bryeh** mak AHL-il)

Cass Mac Cináed (**KASS** mak-KIN-awd)

Ceara (**KYAR-a**)

Cet Mac Ailill (**KET** mak AHL-il)

Cináed (**KIN-awd**)

Ciar Ó Róich (**KEE-a** o REE)

Conall Mac Gabhann (**KON-ul** mak GAWN)

Conchobhar Ó Deargáin (**KRU-hur-o-var** o-

Cúan Ó Neill (**KOO-awn** o NEE-ul)

Cúscraid Mac Conchobar (**KOO-skri** mak KRUH-who'r)

Danu Ni Conall (**DAH-noo** nee-KON-ul)

Daráine Ni Sláine (**dar-AWN-yeh** nee- SLAWN-yah)

Draighean (**DRYNE**)

Dubhgall Mac Rónain (**DU-gal** mak ROON-an)

Eithne (**EN-yeh**)

Fainche (**FINE-kha**)

Flann (**FLAN**)

Glaisne Mac Aodh (**GLASH-neh** mak AWD)

Gobán Ó Cuilinn (**GUB-awn** o QUILL-un)

Íar Mac Dedad (**EER** mak DAY-da)

Iarlugh Ceann-Laith (**EER loo** KEEN

Iobhar Mac Brighid (**EE-ver** mak BREED)

Lonán Ó Neill (**LUH-nawn** o NEE-ul)

Maine Athramail (**MAN-yeh** AH-raw-mal)

Medb (**MAY-ve**)

Messin Corb (**MES-in** CURB)

Móirne (**MORN-yeh**)

Mongfhionn (**MUNN-yung**)

Mórrígan Ni Cathasaigh (**Moe-rig-gAHn** nee-KAS-akh)

Neamhain Ni Fearghal (**NYAV-in** nee FER-ul)

Nuadha Ó Dubhghaill (**NOO-a** o DOO-l)

Óengus Dubdétach (**ENG-gus** DUB-day-takt)

Olcán Ó Dubhan (**UL-cawn** o DOO-awn)

Onchú Ó an Cháintigh (**UN-choo** Awn HAWN-tyg)

Órlaith Ni Óengus (**OR-la** nee ENG-gus)

Rós (**ROS**)

Sláine Mac Sláine (**SLAWN-yah** MAK SLAWN-yah)

Tadhg Ó Cuileannáin (**TYG** o QUILL-an-awn)

Tanaí Mac Bran Loingsech (**THAN-ee** mak BRAN LING-shek)

Teachta (**TAK-ta**)

Torcán Ó Dubhghaill (**TURK-awn** o DOO-l)

Uallachán Ó Dubhghaill (**OOL-akh-awn** o DOO-l)

Úna Ni Onchú (**OO-na** nee UN-choo**)

SCOTTISH

Carmag Mac an t-Sionnaich (**KAR-ah-mak** mak an-CHUN-ich)

Gràinne Ni Fearghal (**GRAN-yuh** nee FER-ul0

Iasg (**EE-ask**)

Mòrag Ni Artair (**MOR-ak** nak ASH-ter)

Ruairidh Mac Carmag (**ROO-uh-ree** mak KAR-ah-mak)

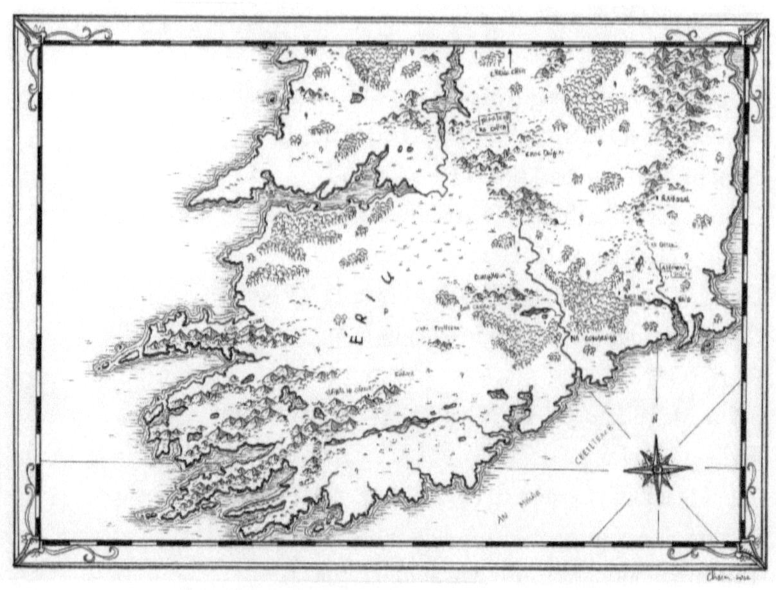

CHAPTER 1

383 B.C.—Summer—Caher Conri

The heavy oak doors of *Caher Conri*'s Great Hall slammed against its stone walls. Across the entrance strode Aoife. A single thick black braid swung furiously. It was a good representation of her mood. Those who stepped in her path melted away at the icy stare from lapis-blue eyes. Although just eighteen summers old, Aoife's reputation as a warrior had few rivals.

Yet it was not only Aoife's gaze or mien from which those in the hall recoiled. No, their eyes were drawn to the bloody spear gripped in her right hand, and the object spiked on it. Mutters of "The Hag!" and "Shite!" were interspersed with retching from those with weaker stomachs. Brighid and Báine rose as she approached the high table. Burly shield-men made to intervene, but Báine's raised hand dismissed them.

Aoife mounted the black granite plinth and placed the spear on the table. The act was reverential, not angry. Yet when she spoke, her eyes held Brighid's gaze, and her tone promised retribution. "Did you order this?"

Spitted on the spear was the head of a child, no more than two summers old. Limp ribbons of long blonde hair, matted with blood, hung from the small skull. The face, frozen in death, reflected the horror of the baby's last moments.

"Children, mothers with babies in their bellies, young boys, and girls were violated, gutted, and their heads mounted on spears. I saw fifty such as this in the settlement northeast of Caher Conri." Aoife's eyes sharpened. "It was the same community you railed against for their stubborn support of your sister, Danu."

Ashen-faced, Brighid gripped the oak table for strength. *How can I be held responsible for this?* Yet she knew her propensity for terror gave licence to such actions. *The strategy worked for my ma.* That thought ended abruptly with the vision of Mórrígan's awful face and the voice in her head.

"I do not kill babies or sanction rape. Never think of me as a partner in your crimes. Danu and you disappoint me and hurt your father. The Goddess and the Law require justice and reparation. Who will pay your debt?"

Rocked by the condemnation and the promised retribution contained within it, Brighid's nails cracked as her knuckles whitened. *I'm going mad.*

"Answer Aoife, did you approve this?" Her lover's voice snapped Brighid out of her momentary confusion. Báine's bearing threatened violence… but to whom? The smoke-white cheeks of the commander of Caher Conri's riders flushed an angry red. In her eyes, Brighid saw the remaining threads of their relationship severed.

"I may have mentioned that the community needed to remember which queen it served. I never gave any order." Brighid's excuse was weak, and her voice trembled. "It was to be a warning—a slap to an unruly child's arse.

"Who did this? I want their names. I will dispense justice for the dead," responded Aoife. Brighid's involuntary glance toward the exit was followed by a panicked scuffling and doors slamming shut. Aoife had her answer.

"Seize the disloyal *bitseach*—bitch. Bind her. Throw her in the dungeons," shrieked Brighid. No one in the hall moved.

"Why don't you strike me down with your powers?" A spiteful smile twisted Aoife's lip. "But you can't. The *Aes Sídhe* gave them and took them away. The Goddess removed your authority. Even Uallachán was not as vulnerable as you are now, and you know his end."

"Enough!" roared Báine.

"Yes, kill the bitch for her insolence," snarled Brighid.

"No! She is my family. Her words are intemperate…" Báine pointed to the baby's head. "…but she is in the right. Touch her, and you lose her chariots and my riders. You have already lost me."

White-faced with fury, Brighid snapped, "They are my chariots and my riders."

"Are you confident enough to test your claim?" asked Báine.

With a shriek of diminished power, Brighid fled the room.

✳✳✳

Aoife's satisfied expression was short-lived when Báine said, "You should be more respectful of the queen, and this should have been dealt with in private. We have more than enough problems without adding to their number." The young warrior dipped her head to hide eyes that could never lie. They said she disagreed with one who was closer than a sister.

As she walked away, Aoife rubbed the small wolf sigil above her eyebrow. Recently, she had turned eighteen. Since then, the design began to throb, and her dreams were filled with wolves and hunting. The visions were frightening, but only because of the side she took.

CHAPTER 2

Autumn—Lugudunon, Gaul

The vibrancy had departed from ice-blue eyes. In its place were anger, despair, and disappointment. A father who hitherto was proud of his daughters, Conall Mac Gabhann, seemed diminished as he chewed on the bitterness of the reports.

The accounts were from those he trusted, giving Conall no route to disregard them as jealous gossip. The *Rí Ruirech*—King over Kings—and ruler of *Clann Ui Flaithimh*, a tribe he had founded and nurtured into greatness, slumped on his throne.

Conall's *rígan*—queen—Mórrígan, sat beside him. The deep green eyes of his hand-fast partner, more widely known as *An Fiagaí Dorcha*—the Dark Huntress—smouldered with fury. The dark, curling symbols swathing her body throbbed with power, begging for release. Had anyone but her offspring caused her partner such pain, they would have suffered a terrible death. She put a hand on her childhood love's arm and squeezed.

"We will find a way," said Mórrígan.

Lost in thought, the sole occupants of the cavernous Great Hall awaited their guests.

***

The autumn sun dipped its head to the fortress of Lugudunon as it slipped below the horizon. The *ráth*—fort, its glacial white walls bathed in gold and red, stood as a shimmering symbol of power in Southern Gaul. The stronghold was the centre of Clann Ui Flaithimh. The tribe's government had long been entrusted to Conall and his queen, Mórrígan.

Conall and Mórrígan's *Chomhairle*—Council—and guests, including their sons, Barra and Aodán, were seated at the high table in the Great Hall. Both young men—Barra was twenty-four summers old and Aodán twenty-six—looked distinctly uneasy. To describe the mien of those around the table as solemn was an understatement. The assembly also included Mongfhionn and Draighean of the Aes Sídhe, which added to the ill omens.

"I hope this is not about anything we did," said Barra in a low voice.

"I don't think so. We've been pretty good recently, and we settled the border dispute with the *Arverni* as well as expected," replied Aodán. Yet Aodán's voice held an uncharacteristic smidgen of anxiety, which did little to quell his younger brother's rising apprehension.

Silence fell as Conall stood and nodded to Mórrígan's brother, Beacán. Chosen to brief those assembled on the events in *Ériu*, the clann's renowned assassin looked distinctly embarrassed. He had assumed the burden of Brighid's and Danu's behaviour, and his voice held tones of grief and defeat. After his delivery, Beacán sat down, head in his hands. Not even the squeeze of his arm by his hand-fast partner, Iasg, gave any comfort.

"This is not your fault and will never be laid at your feet," said Conall, rising to his feet. "My daughters have humiliated their family and disgraced our tribe. Enemies mock us. They were sent to deliver our people from the tyranny of Uallachán and the *Connachta*. Instead, they became despots. Elected to serve the people, they oppress them."

Conall paused and sipped on a cup of water. He grimaced. It tasted as bitter as wormwood. He glanced at Mórrígan, who dipped her head, knowing what he was about to say. "For the sake of the people of Ériu and Clann Ui Flaithimh, Brighid and Danu must be held accountable. There must be a reckoning for the foolish paths they have chosen."

Mother and father looked at Aodán and Barra before Conall addressed the Chomhairle again. "My sons will travel to Ériu. With my authority, they will assume the throne of Ráth Na Conall and the leadership of the clann in that domain. They will use whatever tactics are necessary to accomplish their mission." Conall looked at Draighean. "The Sídhe has informed me that, with the Goddess's permission, she removed your sisters' powers. That should make your task less hazardous.

"You will travel with an army of one thousand, chosen by myself and your mother. Lonán Ó Neill will act as your counsellor to support you, especially in battle tactics. Pay attention to his counsel, but remember, my authority is vested in you. You are the *ríthe*—kings—and only you will bear the responsibility and consequences for your actions. Your days of princely freedom are over."

"The Hag's tits!" gasped Barra. For the first time that day, Conall smiled.

"Your uncle, Beacán, has asked to accompany you." The brothers' sighs of relief were unhidden but quickly crushed. "I have refused his request. He deserves time with Iasg and their family. Triremes from Pytheas and quinqueremes from Dionysius have been secured. A fleet and your warriors are being assembled in *Massalia*."

✱✱✱

As the last person departed the Great Hall, Mórrígan turned to Conall. "I disagree with this decision," said Mórrígan. "The treason of Lonán's brother, Cúan Ó Neill, taints him and is not easily washed away. Blood is blood." Mórrígan sighed heavily as if not wanting to put her thoughts into words. "Also, it is widely known that Lonán is bitter at being passed over for higher office due to his age and the injury received at the Battle of Allia."

Mórrígan paused. "He needs a staff to walk, Conall. How can he protect Aodán or Barra?"

Conall's tone was brusque. "Lonán has been a faithful servant and a great warrior. His job is not to protect or to command but to provide counsel."

"Shall I list the number of times you allowed compassion to place enemy blades at the throats of our loved ones and people?" retorted Mórrígan. "Lonán is no *fidchell* player, and his diplomatic skills are limited to how quickly he can unsheathe his sword."

"I have made my decision." Conall's tone was unduly curt, if only because he knew his weakness and the truth in Mórrígan's words.

"We are king and queen, Conall. You are not a dictator, and I am not just your hand-fast partner." It was The Mórrígan who spoke, and Conall flinched.

"What do you propose?"

"Tisiphone."

"An assassin."

"A protector."

"For whom?"

"For those who are of our blood."

***

"Let me be clear. Your mission is to bring peace to our domain." Conall looked sternly at his sons. "Danu and Brighid are our daughters and your sisters. Reason with them. Threaten them. Judge them. If needed, bring them back in chains."

Conall paused. "However, never underestimate them. Even without their powers, Brighid and Danu are formidable and battled-tested."

***

Outside the Great Hall, Barra turned to his brother. "The Hag, Aodán, if this is taking responsibility, I'm not sure I want it or the price we may have to pay. Brighid and Danu are our sisters. Also, they never listened to us when we were younger. Why would that change now?"

A perturbed Aodán nodded. "Our ma and da have sent us. That must count for something... and we have an army."

"The Connachta had twenty thousand warriors, which didn't do them much good."

"No one said this was going to be easy," said Aodán.

✳✳✳

Lonán Ó Neill retained one sentence from Conall's orders: "*Your mission is to bring peace to our domain.*" To him, the subtext was crystal clear, and he smiled knowingly. Furthermore, a successful mission would give him his rightful place in Clann Ui Flaithimh.

He turned to Aodán and Barra. By reputation, Lonán was a man of few words who did not suffer fools. He smiled, which was a rarity. "From boys to kings in less than a sunset," rasped Lonán. "Don't worry. I have a cycle of the moon to whip you into shape… or kill you." With a belly laugh, the mountain of a man turned about, grasped his staff, and hobbled away.

"I don't think I've seen him so happy in a long time," said Aodán.

Barra nodded. "That's what worries me."

CHAPTER 3

382 B.C.—Summer—Niúig

Oar blades slashed the surface of the bay's calm waters as the chevron of triremes and quinqueremes glided towards *Niúig*'s ancient jetty. Lonán's concern was whether the wooden structure at the bottom of the cliffs would last until the men, women, horses, and supplies were unloaded.

He turned to face Aodán and Barra. "You have met your *ceannairí céad*—leaders of one hundred. They are experienced warriors, and you should listen to their counsel. Still, you are here in the Rí Ruirech's place. Conall's authority is channelled through you, and you will be held responsible for decisions, not them." The burly warrior chuckled. "When we disembark, you will take charge of your men and women… for better or worse."

Aodán looked at his brother, dipped his head, and addressed Lonán. "Barra is a much better cavalry tactician and horseman than I. He will take command of the two hundred riders and ten chariots." Lonán nodded in agreement. "I will command the shield-wall." Aodán hesitated. "And the *Cinn Péinteáilte*—the Painted Ones."

Lonán chortled. "Those are tough *tuilithe*—bastards. I advise you to get better acquainted with their leader, Ruairidh. He's the son of Carmag Mac an t-Sionnaich, so that should give you an idea of whom you're dealing with."

"Shite!" breathed Aodán. "As to the ballistae and defences, Barra and I have decided to put the Roman, Decimus Augustus, in charge. He comes highly recommended by Cúscraid, Gaius, and Aulus."

His lack of a clear leadership role irritated Lonán, but he kept his thoughts to himself. *I know what needs to be done.* Instead, he said, "Good. It is time for both of you to start issuing orders. I suggest you convene a meeting of your captains once we have ensured our safety from attack."

*∗∗

She was the outcome of the brief coming together of an Etruscan sailor and a Greek whore. As a child, she never knew her father. Likely, if he knew of her existence, he had no ambitions to accept the role.

Her mother was inattentive rather than neglectful. Often the victim of ill-chosen and brutal clients, the lady's journey meandered through drunkenness and disease to eventual madness. Perhaps her fall from Massalia's Temple of Apollo onto the rocks below, whether deliberate or accidental, was a mercy.

The young girl's career progressed by design from thievery to prostitution. At fifteen summers, she was the whore over whom men and women fought and lusted. Gold was her guide. While still an early adolescent, she transformed into an assassin everyone feared.

Tisiphone's name meant "voice of revenge" after one of the Greek Furies; perhaps the gods preordained her future. She upgraded from harlotry and stealing to assassination and spying seamlessly. Yet addicted to the ephemeral desire in men's eyes, Tisiphone could never give up whoring.

Standing on the prow of the quinquereme, Tisiphone enjoyed the feeling of her long white chiton and chestnut-brown hair whipped into a corona by the sea breeze. A sharp pain in her belly—a memory from the knife wound inflicted in the back alleys of Massalia—caught her breath. She smiled and whispered, "Thank you." Her appreciation was for Mórrígan's brother, Beacán.

Pytheas, the Greek merchant and Conall's business partner, although that did not come close to the totality of his activities, had a fondness for Tisiphone. That said, it was never carnal. She was the daughter he never had. Thus, perhaps in a moment of prescience, he prevailed upon Beacán to watch over her. Tisiphone touched the puckered ridge of the scar where a knife had almost ended her. Beacán had saved her from bleeding out in the shit and waste of a Massalia backstreet.

Tisiphone was used to the back alleys and drinking dens of Massalia, so she wondered if she could adapt to the mountains, vast forests, and lush meadows of Ériu. She sighed. Sadly, men's and women's desires rarely changed. Now twenty-six years old, age had increased Tisiphone's sensual beauty. Her allure was as much a weapon as her blades and donated a brief edge in a fight. With her skill with a knife, it was all she needed.

***

A cough behind her surprised Tisiphone. She turned and smiled at Lonán. While her domain was the shadows and dark arts, Lonán, by reputation, was an efficient killing machine on the battlefield. Yet something else lurked in the warrior's eyes. *Was it residual pain from his injury or thwarted ambition?* Still, what man or woman does not have secrets after a certain age?

"We will disembark shortly," said Lonán. "You will be the first of us into battle. I have selected your companion." Tisiphone thought him presumptuous but smiled. She was more than capable of stating her argument, but likely, there would be more serious battles to fight. "He's a young man called Teachta and wet behind the ears, although he has a sharp mind." Lonán chuckled. "Go easy on him."

***

Lonán watched Tisiphone collect her horse, a rose grey, and companion and depart the ship. He sent a quick prayer to the Goddess for her safety. Then he inhaled deeply. His senses quickened at the cries of the seabirds and the scents of hay and peat fires. A large raindrop on his muscled arm and the skies beginning to cloud over made him laugh aloud. Some things never changed in Ériu.

He had grasped the opportunity Conall offered him. Yet not to visit

Ériu and see his family, who lived in the far north in the lands of the *Ulaid.* Many had likely been killed in battle or died of disease or old age. Lonán was a plain-spoken warrior, disinterested in politics. His lineage and links to the nobility of the Ulaid meant little to him.

Since his return from Rome, the fifty summers old veteran had been repeatedly passed over for elevation. Indeed, he had been advised to retire with a whore to his farmstead in the Liga Valley. Younger rivals, without injury, were preferred to him. To no avail, he had challenged and killed several to prove his utility. It grated on his self-esteem that his talents were constrained to minor skirmishes, and most were sympathy appointments with no real danger.

The veteran recalled the pain in Conall's eyes as he described Danu's and Brighid's descent into lawlessness and tyranny. He knew that kings often left their true desires unsaid. Thus, Lonán read between the lines, and his mind interpreted and completed Conall's meaning. His mission was to bring "peace to our domain" and to restore balance in Southern Ériu.

He would accomplish his king's command, no matter the cost. If that meant the deaths of Danu and Brighid, that was a price and a burden for which Lonán was prepared.

CHAPTER 4

Autumn—Ráth Na Conall

Ten summers ago, the defeat of the Connachta by Danu and Brighid was met with wild celebrations. The kingdom of Southern Ériu and its people enjoyed peace and security… for a time. Music and laughter, not fighting and dissension, filled Ráth Na Conall's square. Trading ships from the Great Sea nations brought prosperity. The land produced bountiful harvests.

Five summers later, it had gone sour. The glimpse of *Mag Mell* on earth vanished in the wake of Brighid's and Danu's incessant arguments and the inevitable acrimonious schism. The people were left bitter, divided… and afraid. The lush farmlands surrounding Ráth Na Conall became barren.

At whose feet did the blame lie? Who was the bigger bitseach?

***

Danu visualised Brighid sitting on Caher Conri's throne. She wondered if her sister was lonely, too. Did her heart feel as hollow? However, pride would not permit Danu to accept partial responsibility or take the first step towards reconciliation. *It was Brighid's fault, and she should make the first move. She was impulsive and immature and could never be a queen.* Yet Brighid was a queen, and who was to judge the more successful?

A striking woman of twenty-seven summers, Danu stood and pushed the carved wooden throne backwards. The scraping noise had the beneficial effect of silencing her audience's loud and discordant chattering. The shouted *"Get out!"* instantly emptied the room. The rígan's moods and punishments for disobedience were well-known. Mutterings of "Tyrant" were numerous but kept at a level just above that of thought.

Ráth Na Conall's queen looked along the long table and saw empty seats. Only two remained from her Chomhairle: Cináed, the Civic Leader and Flann, her aged battle commander. Flann's eyes told of his deep disappointment. Danu chose to believe this was directed at Brighid, but that was disingenuous.

Cináed looked permanently unhappy, which irritated Danu. However, his demeanour was understandable. Cináed's family had chosen different queens. His son, Cass, served in the garrison at Ráth Na Conall and his daughter, Aoife, chose Caher Conri and Brighid's forces. That said, everyone knew Aoife's choice was due to her deep friendship with Báine and not loyalty to Brighid.

The farming communities and Cináed blamed the *rígana*—queens— for the land's troubles. They deemed it cursed by the Goddess because of the twins' rift. People could not work the farms, and they fell into disrepair. Many turned to thievery and banditry to feed their families.

Given his age and precarious health, Flann constantly reminded Danu that he should not be the garrison's commander. Yet she had no one experienced enough to take his place. More than that, she trusted Flann.

Everyone has deserted me. The whiny tone made Danu grind her teeth. Disgusted by his nieces' bickering, their uncle, Beacán, had turned his back on them. He, Iasg, and their sons and daughter returned to Conall and Lugudunon. Danu's lip trembled. *What has he told my da and ma?*

Aoibheann Ni Neill, Danu's former battle commander, and her family had boarded the same ship. The excuse that she wanted to spend time with her sister, Bláithín, was partially valid. However, Danu knew Aoibheann wished to be far from the siblings' squabbling and the memories of her lover Conchobhar's death. The Roman, Aulus, pleaded other duties and returned to Lugudunon.

Former allies and friends distanced themselves. Fainche returned to *Curraghatoor*, taking half of Ráth Na Conall's riders with her. She now commanded Curraghatoor's cavalry. Eithne, the hand-fast partner of Onchú Ó an Cháintigh, the Rí of Curraghatoor, fell ill and crossed the veil. Rumours that Onchú and Fainche were close grew like weeds. Danu growled. Curraghatoor had two hundred riders and a larger garrison than Ráth Na Conall. Once a valued advisor, she increasingly perceived Onchú as a threat.

After a period of close relationships with Ráth Na Conall, Aodh Mac Aodh had shaken his head, given the twins a piece of his mind in his typically blunt manner, and turned his back on them. He resumed *Clárach*'s historical neutrality and self-interest. Furthermore, and perhaps perceiving a future threat, Aodh significantly upgraded Clárach's defences and doubled its permanent garrison.

In a repaired and strengthened *Cnoc Duíginn*, the new king Sláine Mac Sláine's relationship with Brighid flourished. This was partly due to Sláine and his sister, Daráine, aiding Brighid's escape from the invading Connachta and Uallachán.

The remotest ráth of the former alliance, Sláine remained grateful for the protection of Brighid's riders and paid for her services from the output of Cnoc Duíginn's silver mines. Yet Sláine was wise enough never to take sides. As such, he offered an open communication channel between the twins. So far, that had never been called upon.

Danu scratched at a crumb lodged in her cleavage. The act brought memories of a furious Draighean. The Sídhe had accused the rígana of betraying their mother and father, Mongfhionn, the Aes Sídhe, the Goddess, and their tribe. At Draighean's final address to the Chomhairle, she advised its members to cast the queens out.

Still, Draighean's parting slap was to diminish the images and powers of *Na Feirdhriseacha*—the Dog Roses. They were little more than pale shadows of their former glory. The link between the sisters was sundered, leaving the rígana truly alone. Additionally, the mystical curling designs swathing the twins' bodies had faded until they were unremarkable. Danu had tried to paint the sigils to maintain appearances, but mysteriously, the dyes never held.

Formerly a quiet and introspective, if somewhat cold, young woman, Danu responded by choosing strategic pragmatism as her guide. Having lost the powers given to her by the Goddess and the Aes Sídhe, Danu turned to her remaining assets—her beauty and rational mind.

Since the sundering, Danu's reputation grew to rival the famed Medb of the Connachta, whose "friendly thighs" were legendary. Courted by kings, Danu used her cot to seal treaties. *Am I little more than a striapach—a whore?* A son, Tanaí, and daughter, Órlaith, from different fathers outside the bonds of hand-fasting, shouted, "Yes!"

Uncomfortable with her train of thought, Danu fled to her private chambers.

✳✳✳

The door creaked open, and Danu glanced up, angry at the disruption. Her demeanour instantly changed when Órlaith, aged five summers, entered, holding her brother Tanaí's hand. Tanaí's nurse, for he was three, was dismissed.

"You did not break fast with us, Ma." Órlaith's accusation, full of righteous chastisement, also showed disappointment. Her lip trembled when she said, "We missed you."

"I am very sorry, I missed you too, but sometimes queens have clashing priorities." It was a stupid excuse; Danu knew it… and so did Órlaith.

"Are we not a priority, Ma?"

Danu felt as if a knife plunged into her heart. Tears streamed down her face as she fell to her knees and opened her arms. "I love and need you; you are my priority above all others, and everything I do is for you."

The chamber door opened again, but this time Flann entered. He flinched at Danu's glare and wished he did not have to interrupt the family, whose embraces seemed to tighten with each step he took. "I'm sorry. You are needed in the Great Hall."

✳✳✳

Danu watched a tall young man stride down the central aisle. He stopped a respectable distance from the raised platform and bowed from the waist. A wave of Danu's hand indicated he should speak.

Teachta coughed to clear his throat. "My queen, a half-cycle of the moon ago, a fleet of triremes and quinqueremes entered the bay of the *An Bhearú River*. Over a thousand warriors, comprising a mix of shield-warriors, Cinn Péinteáilte, mounted warriors, chariots, ballistae teams, and supplies, disembarked at Niúig. As I departed to report, they were strengthening Niúig's abandoned ringfort."

The envoy paused as if not wanting to add to the unwelcome news. "The banners and flags on the fort's walls bear the colours and emblems of Clann Ui Flaithimh and its Rí Ruirech." With a bow, he took a step backwards.

Flann looked at Cináed, shook his head, and muttered, "Conall."

Danu's face blanched, and she twisted her fingers in rising anxiety. Where her father, Conall, travelled, so did her mother. Danu had no desire to face their anger and disapproval. *What should I do? Perhaps I should warn Brighid.* Her lips curled into a calculating smile.

The Hag, no! Perhaps I can lay the blame on my sister. Danu turned to Flann and Cináed. "I will retire to my chambers to consider my reply to this information." With a nod to the messenger, Danu added, "You are dismissed but remain within the fort. There may be a response to your news."

✳✳✳

Flann turned to step away from the table, but Danu put a hand on his forearm. "Have any strangers entered Ráth Na Conall recently?" Flann tugged on braided whiskers that had lost their lustrous blue-black sheen and were liberally sprinkled with white. He shook his head.

"No one of consequence—a whore looking for business and the

17

usual farm labourers hoping for work. Both will be disappointed." Flann paused. "You suspect spies?"

"Why not? Assessing our strengths and weaknesses would be a sensible first step before negotiation—or confrontation."

"We are unprepared for a battle or even a lengthy skirmish." Flann took a deep breath and held Danu's gaze. "If our visitors are Clann Ui Flaithimh warriors, few in Ráth Na Conall will fight them. Your conduct has not engendered loyalty among the army or the people. How full is the treasury? You may need to purchase a substantial force of mercenaries."

"Let me worry about that," snapped Danu. "In the meantime, check all who have entered the ráth over the past cycle of the moon."

Flann dipped his head. About to walk away, he stopped and turned back. "My eyesight is not as sharp as it once was, but I cannot recall having seen that particular messenger previously. Have you?"

"The Hag, no!" exclaimed Danu. "I was more concerned with the content of his message than his appearance. The Hag! Perhaps the first piece on the fidchell board has already been moved. Find him and throw him in the dungeons. We can apologise later if we're wrong."

* * *

Outside the Great Hall, the envoy flicked flakes of early snow from his shoulder and walked quickly across the square to the stables. He exhibited no panic and smiled as he passed a young woman wearing a clean, well-worn léine.

Her raiment did little to disguise her beauty or the swell of full, firm breasts. Brown eyes sat in a field of honey-almond skin. Thick tresses of dark hair tapped her arse cheeks as they rose and fell with the upward roll of her hips. Her feet were tiny, and she wore neither boots nor *bróga*.

"Perhaps some smudges of dirt on your cheeks." He smiled, speaking in a low but clear voice. "Here, the people's skin is the colour of milk below the cream."

"Thank you," she said, walking past the messenger without breaking her step. At a suitable distance between them, Tisiphone remembered Lonán's words and smiled. "A clever and observant young man, indeed."

CHAPTER 5

Caher Conri

Brighid awoke from her dream, screeching, "*No!*" Tears streamed down her face, and her cot was soaked with sweat. Ten summers had passed. Yet the vision of Caher Conri's courtyard littered with the bleeding bodies of forty horses and the hate in their riders' eyes haunted Brighid. *I said I was sorry for sacrificing the horses, Báine. It was the only way we could retreat. Yet you have never forgiven me. Would you rather I lost the riders as well?*

Shortly after her cry, the bedchamber door flew open, crashing against the wall. In swept Báine, followed by two burly guards. After a quick survey of the room, the men were dismissed. "The usual nightmare?" asked Báine. Brighid nodded. Care and concern filled Báine's eyes, but also distance. *Where is the love, the intimacy we shared?*

The room used to be their bedchamber, but after Aoife's confrontation, Báine removed her belongings and moved out. *Why? Have I changed so much that you no longer find me attractive? That bitseach, Aoife, is to blame. Her whisperings about unity have caused you to doubt me.* Báine looked sharply at Brighid as if reading her thoughts. Brighid's cheeks reddened.

"You need to speak with a Druid," said Báine.

"I thought I had you to confide in." Brighid's lip trembled.

"That was a lifetime ago when I thought I knew you. It seems we were both mistaken. I will send servants to stoke up your fire and put fresh straw in your cot." With a dip of her head, Báine turned and exited the room.

Terrified by the nightmare and wounded by her lover, Brighid's heart pounded, yet not her dog rose. The bloom had slept for five summers. Without colour or form, the petals were little more than a charcoal smudge between her breasts. In the light of the log and peat fire, Brighid looked down and shook her head. *I'm going mad.*

Báine had remarked on the change when they last lay naked together. Intermittent sharp pains deep in Brighid's chest made her gasp and appeared to support the observation. A ring of thorns had sprouted around the faint shadow of the rose.

The bitseach! This time, Brighid referred to Draighean. The Sídhe had removed their feirdhriseacha and powers. Were the thorns more retribution? Has Danu suffered the same transformation? *I hope so.* The merest thought of Danu was enough to divert Brighid's musings.

Her lips twisted into an ugly sneer. *It's all her fault. She never wanted to share the throne with me.* Humiliated and unwilling to suffer Danu's disregard and mockery of her ideas and recommendations, Brighid took her riders and fled Ráth Na Conall. To her credit, she took this road only after several summers of continual arguments.

Misplaced hubris arose in Brighid's breast. *My sister's a striapach. I earned my kingdom through battle and blood, and my army is feared throughout the southwestern lands. My wealth and power are built on raiding the settlements to the north and those who do not support me. I did not bend over to be mounted or lie on my back and spread my legs.*

Yet the Goddess was not in the mood to allow Brighid to wallow in self-justification. The queen fell to her knees, clutching her head. The memory of the baby's head on a spear filled her sight and stabbed her heart. *I am evil.* In her heart, Brighid knew she and Danu had become what they had fought against—tyrants.

A tear rolled down Brighid's cheek and fell with a soft plop into the cup of spring water. She was alone, and she hated that most of all. Furthermore, the twins had no Connachta invasion to force them together this time. *Our kingdoms are a mess. Are we only together when we're at war, Danu?*

***

Five sunsets after departing Ráth Na Conall, Teachta awoke in a camp in the forest beyond Caher Conri's defensive berm and a half-day's canter from the promontory fort. Still wrapped in his *brat*, he slapped his arms and legs to encourage his blood to flow less sluggishly in his veins.

Without Tisiphone, the campfire would have died instead of radiating a welcome heat on a cold autumn morning. She had already departed and would ensure he reached Brighid's stronghold safely. Once he was inside the fort, only words would protect him.

Although only a few summers older than he, Tisiphone was more worldly. Her skills with blades and stealth were beyond what Teachta could ever hope to achieve. Many said she rivalled the talents of Beacán, the clann's greatest assassin. The envoy knew she would have disposed of any in Ráth Na Conall tasked to follow him.

He shivered as he shed the heavy woollen brat and dressed. After feeding his horse, the messenger munched on wild berries and drank spring water while considering his next audience.

***

The contrast between Caher Conri and Ráth Na Conall was stark. Although substantially diminished, Danu's hillfort remained a centre for the community's social, business, and religious activities. It resembled a smaller version of the Connachta's *Chrúachain* or the Ulaid's *Emain Macha*.

The clang of artisans' hammers, the thuds of wooden looms weaving plaid cloth, and the grinding of corn between quern stones lent an air of normality. Bread baking on iron griddles, meat roasting over open fires, and stews simmering in black cauldrons added mouth-watering smells to Ráth Na Conall's ambience.

According to Tisiphone, the most complimentary description of

Caher Conri was an army encampment—rough, fractious, and not the place to put down roots or raise a family. As he walked his mount across Caher Conri's courtyard to the stables, the envoy also sensed an atmosphere of dread.

The messenger was well briefed on the history of Caher Conri and the depravities successive kings had visited upon their subjects. *It should have been razed to the ground, and its stones crushed and thrown into the sea.* He prayed to the Goddess that Brighid had not travelled down that path. By all accounts, Brighid preferred bloodletting, force of arms, and terror to keep an iron grip on her kingdom. *Is she much different from her mother, Mórrígan?*

✳✳✳

The doors of the Great Hall opened. Teachta took a deep breath and stepped across the threshold. Striding down the central aisle of the chamber, he detected the taint of cruelty swirling in the air. The fine hairs of his nape stood up, and he wished Tisiphone was at his side.

Teachta groaned softly and gave a wry smile. Most messengers had short lives. Praying that he could hold to his story long enough to escape that fate, the young man put on a mantle of confidence and straightened his shoulders. Head held high, he walked the final steps towards the throne. Stopping a diplomatic distance from the plinth, he bowed deeply.

"I have travelled from the east to bring news, which I trust you will find informative," said Teachta in a voice he hoped concealed his anxiety.

"The east, you say. From *Ráthgeal*, perhaps," said Brighid, leaning forward. The envoy smiled knowingly, and Brighid chuckled. "Perhaps your king has no desire to be seen to favour certain rígana. Given my past dealings with Ráthgeal, it is a wise posture." Emerald eyes held the messenger's brown gaze. "Come closer."

Several paces from the throne, the young man stopped and bowed again. "Your skin colour intrigues me. Mine used to be like that, but only when I lived in Southern Gaul. You cannot be from Ériu, north or south; your accent holds traces of other lands and peoples. How is that so?"

"You are very observant, my queen," replied Teachta. With a practised flush of embarrassment, he smiled broadly. "I have wealthy parents who continue to support my education and travel to far lands, including the Great Sea."

Brighid looked to Báine and laughed. "We have a wastrel or an adventurer before us. Neither are particularly commendable." Returning to the messenger, Brighid said, "Your current choice of occupation comes with its hazards. Few messages are welcome. Tell me yours and discover what your fate may be."

"A fleet of ships recently sailed into the bay of the An Bhearú. Over one thousand warriors—shield- and mounted warriors, Cinn Péinteáilte, chariots, and ballistae teams, with supplies and horses, disembarked. The quinqueremes immediately turned about and set sail, likely for a safe winter refuge in *Northern Aremorio*. Five triremes remained." The young man paused and indicated a jug on a nearby table. "May I?"

He continued after a short dip of Brighid's head and several long sips of cool spring water. "Thank you, my queen. The warriors immediately began to reinforce the old ringfort at Niúig. The riders and chariots patrol the surrounding landscape." At the mention of Niúig, Aoife's eyes widened, for she had been born in that community. She glared at Brighid.

Curiosity alighted briefly in the envoy's eyes, but he dismissed it. He had a job to do. "The banners erected on the walls of the ráth had the colours of Clann Ui Flaithimh." The messenger paused for dramatic effect. "…and your father, Conall Mac Gabhann. The *scíatha*—shields— had a swooping black raven on a field of red."

"Does my sister know of this news?"

Teachta considered lying, but Brighid had a sharpness to her demeanour, which suggested it would be a poor choice. He bowed and answered, "I am but a lowly messenger and my master gave me a list of those who might be interested in this information. I visited Ráth Na Conall five sunsets ago." At Brighid's narrowed eyes, he said, "I also am to visit Clárach, Curraghatoor, and Cnoc Duíginn."

Brighid smiled, and the young man relaxed. "Your master is shrewd." Then she turned to Aoife. "See that the envoy and his mount are well-fed. If he wishes a cot for the night, arrange that, too." Again, she turned to the messenger.

"Thank you for your report, although I sense some missing elements. Likely, that is part of your king's future negotiating tactics. No blame will be assigned to you for any omissions."

* * *

A wave of Brighid's hand dismissed the emissary. As he crossed the Great Hall's doorway, Brighid turned to Báine. "He is as honest as most diplomats can be but likely has not told us the full story. Have him followed. I wish to know how much of his tale is truthful." Báine nodded but, instead of moving away, stood firm. At Brighid's raised eyebrow, she spoke.

"You should speak with Danu," said Báine.

"No!" snapped Brighid. Her cheeks flushed hotly at Báine's suggestion and the implication of her words.

Yet Báine stood firm. "This is a situation that concerns both of you. Caher Conri cannot face a shield-wall of that size and origin. United, there may be a chance of resisting or negotiating terms.

"Their riders and chariots outnumber us, and the Cinn Péinteáilte have few rivals in forest battles. The sea no longer protects us because they have ships that can outmanoeuvre and surround us. What if the kings of the South unite against you? You have made more enemies than friends.

"Neither you nor Danu has your powers. There is no Sídhe to support you; the Goddess has turned her back on you. You and Danu lie on a cot of nettles and thistles grown by your own hands."

Báine rested a hand on Brighid's arm but quickly withdrew it when she flinched. In a harsher tone, she added, "Those who returned to Lugudunon will have reported on Danu and your recent history as queens. It will not have been complimentary. Your ma and da may have landed at Niúig, and you know why.

"Do you propose to go to war with them? Will you force them to kill their daughters? You know your parents. They think firstly of the clann and will not shrink from what needs to be done."

Caher Conri's garrison commander paused and, in a voice full of sadness, said, "For the sake of those who follow you, speak with Danu. Unite and negotiate terms. I will stand at your side." Brighid's eyes brightened but quickly dimmed when Báine shook her head. "No, I will not order my riders and Aoife's chariots into battle against Conall and Mórrígan." Báine took a deep breath and exhaled slowly. "Those with memories of your folly and their dead horses will not fight."

Brighid recoiled as if Báine had slapped her face hard. "Leave me. Now." The tone was curt, yet Báine understood the turmoil roiling Brighid. This, however, was not the time to indulge Brighid's naïve dreams of a great kingdom.

***

A short time later, Báine and Aoife stood silently in the courtyard and watched the sun drift towards the horizon. They looked at each other and spoke one word. "Shite!"

"Will you stand with her?" asked Aoife.

"Perhaps dying with her is the best resolution to our relationship. If the Goddess is merciful, we will meet in Mag Mell." The deep sadness and torment in Báine's voice broke Aoife's heart.

"You expect a baby killer to enter Mag Mell?"

"Without proof, I do not accept that Brighid sanctioned the atrocities."

Aoife shook her head and said, "She is the rígan." She flinched at the pain in Báine's eyes and swore retribution on the one who caused it. In a less terse tone, she said, "Perhaps you are right. When I track the tuilithe down, we will have our answer."

CHAPTER 6

Winter—Cnoc Duíginn

The ríthe of Clárach, Cnoc Duíginn, and Curraghatoor gathered to celebrate *Samhain*. Early winter winds and light snows swept the ráth's ramparts as the kings sat round a long oak table supping beer and wine from pottery vessels. Onchú rubbed a thick finger along his cup's stem and mused that the chalice was a good measure of the clann's social and economic progress.

Troubled countenances, not pre-festival jocularity, were the rule as the kings pondered the flood of news gleaned from various sources. Most reports conflicted and were little more than gossip. Some were blatant fabrications from those seeking to benefit from muddied waters. Only those from longstanding informants were taken seriously.

A good proportion of disinformation could be traced to Caher Conri and Ráth Na Conall. Caught off-guard, the queens quickly fought back by spreading gossip and innuendo, casting doubt on anything originating from Niúig. Their strategy was uncoordinated but had one common objective. To stall for time.

The rígana needed time to prepare their defences and to recruit allies and mercenaries. Still, Danu and Brighid kept only a few close advisors fully informed. Even the most loyal were threatened with harsh punishment and retaliation on their families should the truth emerge. No army confronted them, yet the queens were besieged.

***

"What do we know?" asked Onchú, dipping his head to Sláine.

Sláine, who sat opposite him at the centre of the table, smiled. On Sláine's right was his sister and counsellor, Daráine. Seated on Onchú's right side was Fainche. Although visibly pregnant, she insisted on travelling with her hand-fast partner. On Onchú's left sat Aodh of Clárach. Brawny sentinels stood behind each king and queen and along the walls of the Great Hall.

"We know nothing. It's all farfetched rumours and likely derives from the *bitseacha*—bitches. They are plotting something and wish to catch us off-guard." Aodh's tetchy tone spoke of his disappointment in the queens.

"If that is the case, they have succeeded beyond their expectations." Onchú's dry tone made his irritation with his fellow kings obvious. "We know nothing because whoever has landed at Niúig has thrown a ring of iron around their activities. No scout has got past the riders and chariots and remained alive. Rumours of an assassin more skilled than Beacán are rife."

"Curraghatoor has mounted warriors. Why haven't you broken through?" challenged Aodh. His question was aimed at Onchú, but an angry Fainche answered.

"Because none of us wants a war with Conall and Mórrígan," snapped Fainche, impatiently twisting the thin black braids in her ash-grey hair. "Furthermore, the likelihood is that whoever has landed at Niúig is a greater threat to Danu and Brighid than us. From what I know of their ma's and da's reputations, they are unlikely to be happy with their daughters."

Aodh snorted. "And what will they do? Take a switch to their arses, scold them, and pack them off home? Family is family. There will be no punishment. Danu and Brighid will return to Gaul, and we will be left to pick up the pieces." Aodh's tone was as bitter as the fruit from *An Chaithne* trees.

A cough drew their attention to Daráine, the youngest of those present. Daráine was a striking young woman. Tall and slender with hazel-green eyes, she was twenty summers old—four summers younger than her brother, Sláine. The Goddess favoured Daráine, sparing her the generational curse of pock-marked skin, although not the random patches of thin hair.

Yet what made Daráine's appearance arresting was not the ample breasts for which the women of her clann were famed. No, rather than suffer the indignity of encroaching baldness, Daráine had shaved her head. In doing so, she immediately added an exotic trait to her bearing.

Undaunted by those at the table, Daráine said, "It strikes me that those at Niúig are accomplished fidchell players. That is unsurprising, for we know Conall's reputation for strategy." Raised eyebrows greeted Daráine's statement. She grinned. "Have they not drawn together three ríthe who have not met in almost five summers?"

Daráine chuckled, and it sounded like spring water tumbling over stones. "Sláine and I are always delighted to see you, but when did we last celebrate Samhain? And why now?" Daráine smiled sweetly. "Indeed, would anyone here be surprised at a timely knock on this chamber's door?"

"I would not."

"The Hag's arse!" Onchú looked to his shield-man. "Stand ready." Then he turned to Daráine and Sláine. "How many additional guests should we expect?" Underneath Onchú's irritation was admiration. Sláine and Daráine had undoubtedly inherited their father's diplomatic skills and network of spies and connections.

✳✳✳

Teachta strode into Curraghatoor's Great Hall. In his wake were Aodán and Barra, followed by Lonán. As a sign of good intentions, Aodán and Barra chose not to be flanked by their usual hard-muscled shield-men, although they had not foregone armour and weapons.

Tisiphone, dressed in a loose-flowing, diaphanous white Greek chiton, continuously circled the party. However, like a drifting cloud in the skies, she managed to give the impression of not moving at all. She was also the most lethally armed among the small group.

Her long hair had been braided and lay in coils atop her head. The pins that held the style in place doubled as long, slender blades—likewise, the jewelled clasps, which secured the chiton on her shoulders. Broad gold wristbands concealed short spring-loaded knives with edges coated in poison. The most conventional of her weapons were the sheathed daggers strapped to her thighs. Before entering the Great Hall, she teased Lonán that other weapons were concealed in more intimate areas.

A cough returned the high table's attention to the messenger. "I have the honour of presenting the sons of Conall Mac Gabhann, the Ríthe Aodán Mac Conall and Barra Mac Conall. The tall man is their counsellor, Lonán Ó Neill, and the winsome lady is called Tisiphone."

"Ríthe," snorted Aodh. "By whose authority? A king who lives in Gaul and hasn't been seen in Ériu for over twenty summers. A man whose meddling in our affairs has always produced trouble and whose daughters are little more than tyrants. Take your army and return to Conall. We will serve justice on the rígana."

Aodh glared at Lonán. "As for this 'gentleman', he has more scars on his face and limbs than Onchú and I combined."

"Perhaps you would allow me to address the kings," said Lonán, seeing Aodán and Barra bristle at insults, which were not entirely without foundation. "I will use simple words to aid their understanding." At nods from the brothers, he looked at each king present and addressed Aodh.

"Brave words for men who have spent five summers scratching their fat arses while the people of the South suffer. Spare me your sanctimonious tattle. *You* could and should have resolved this, but instead, you scurried back to your *rátha*—forts—and cowered like mice.

"Danu and Brighid saved you from the Connachta when they were little more than adolescents. They deserved your honest counsel and a hard kick in the arse when needed. *You* failed them. It was you who made them tyrants."

An astonished Barra looked at Aodán, who dipped his head. Not once since they departed Lugudunon had Lonán defended Danu and Brighid. Indeed, both suspected Lonán's preferred solution was their sisters' heads in hessian sacks.

"We tried to persuade them that their path was unwise," said Onchú. Yet he recognised the weakness in his words.

"Obviously, you didn't try hard enough," said Lonán.

Aodán and Barra looked at each other and grudgingly appreciated Lonán's surprising clarity and verbal onslaught. "I think I have a much better appreciation of Lonán's diplomatic talents, brother. They are reminiscent of our da," muttered Barra to Aodán.

"Yes, like in battle, he takes no prisoners," said Barra.

"We have enough men to see you never live another sunset and then remove the bitseacha," snarled Aodh, ignoring Onchú's wary and disapproving looks.

"Brave words from a man who would never see Clárach again." Lonán's words were ominous, and his tone unemotional. His demeanour gave no hint that he could not carry out the threat. Aodh's shield-man, the son of his former shield who had crossed the veil five summers ago, tensed. His hand rested on his sword's hilt.

"Bluster and words with no meaning," responded Aodh.

"There are beautiful forests around Curraghatoor. I think pine, oak, and some alder," said Lonán. Onchú's eyes narrowed, and he glared at Aodh to stop adding fuel to an already roaring fire.

"Your observation is correct. Yet your admiration of our landscape is not the message. Is it?" asked Onchú. Lonán smiled.

"Please, no," muttered Aodán and Barra, rubbing palms over the pommels of their swords.

"If any harm comes to the kings or their retinues, everyone inside this ráth, save Sláine and Daráine, will next greet each other in Mag Mell."

Aodh opened his mouth, but a raised hand from Onchú curtailed his words. "In the woods, two hundred Cinn Péinteáilte await. All are direct descendants of the Forest People of *Northern Albu*. When facing these warriors, I have yet to see anyone win a battle in the trees. Barra's riders stand ready to intercept the few who might evade the Cinn Péinteáilte."

Lonán dipped his head to Onchú. "As for those in this room…" Using the argument's diversion, Tisiphone had noiselessly positioned herself within striking distance of the high table. "It is said that Beacán Ó Cathasaigh, whose reputation, as you know, is understated, stands in Tisiphone's shadow. I very much doubt any of you would survive the lady's attentions.

"Indeed, as I said, the only ones guaranteed to walk free and unharmed from this chamber are Sláine and Daráine. They are young yet have shown more common sense than kings who should know better."

"You will die," rasped Aodh. He was shocked at Lonán's great belly laugh.

The iron grip of his shield-man on his shoulder and a whispered, "On this ground and at this time, you cannot win this fight, my king," forced Aodh to remain seated.

"Do you think that worries me? Look at me. I am a cripple. I have no fear of the *bean-sídhe*. Indeed, I welcome her." Lonán looked at Aodán and Barra. "However, I prefer my younger companions live many more summers."

An ominous silence descended on the room and lingered until Lonán spoke again. "Do we unsheathe blades and let the *mná sídhe* loose or put them aside? Surely, we can sit around this table like adults, eat and drink, and agree on a plan to bring peace and order to this land?"

Lonán nodded to Aodán who said, "Here is what my brother and I propose."

***

As the servants guided Cnoc Duíginn's guests to their chambers, Aodán turned to Barra and grinned. "Strike quickly, brother, for this assembly will only be together for two more sunsets, and only the Goddess knows when you will next meet her."

"What?"

"It is usually considered impolite to spend an evening staring at your hostess's tits," said Aodán.

Barra reddened. "Was I that obvious?" Aodán nodded. "Shite!"

"I'm quite jealous. Daráine did not seem to have any objection to your attention."

***

Hearing a soft knock, Daráine smiled and walked across the chamber. Her face fell when she opened the door to find her brother standing there. Sláine chuckled. "May I enter?" Daráine dipped her head and pointed to a small table and carved chairs.

"Were you expecting someone else?" Daráine's cheeks flushed. "I am not unobservant. Even when deep in our discussion, Barra's eyes barely ceased his admiration of you." Sláine paused, and Daráine sensed his discomfort. "He appears to be a good man and has a powerful family." Sláine inhaled deeply. "Our clann is small, Daráine, and survival depends on the alliances we broker."

"Is this conversation going somewhere, *brother*?" Daráine's tone sharpened, and her eyes narrowed.

Sláine gulped, and his Adam's apple bobbled. "I would not stand in the way, should you and Barra decide to ummm… get together."

"Let me make this clear, *brother*. Our father's wish was that we rule as king and queen. I am not nor ever will be a piece on the fidchell board to be moved and traded for advantage." Daráine stood, walked to the door, and opened it. "Goodnight, Sláine. Your heart is good, and you love your people and me. Therefore, I will consign this conversation to the garbage where it belongs. Have I made myself clear?"

Sláine nodded, mumbled, "Sleep well," and exited the bedchamber.

Simmering with anger, Daráine paced her room for what seemed ages before she calmed down. She breathed deeply and smiled. "You're an eejit, brother," she murmured. Yet Daráine loved her brother and would never hold his stupidity against him. "Men!"

Daráine looked at her cot while she removed her day clothes. She always slept naked. A wood fire roared in the stone grate, and the room was pleasantly warm. Her toe touched the wood of the bed frame. A thought was followed by an image that made Daráine's cheeks redden. Her heart's steady beat increased rapidly.

"The Hag! What room did I put you in, Barra?"

Barefoot, Daráine padded to the wall opposite her chamber door and pushed on a stone. A section glided open, and she smiled. Cnoc Duíginn was riddled with secret passageways.

CHAPTER 7

Cnoc Uisnigh

The death of Maine Athramail, Rí Ruirech of the Connachta, and the humiliating defeat of his army at the hands of Brighid and Danu did not end the tribe's misfortunes. The rout precipitated an opportunistic invasion of the clann's lands and the siege of the stronghold of Chrúachain by the northern Ulaid. Thus, Cet, the newly confirmed Rí Ruirech, had no choice but to focus on defending territory rather than continuing his brother's aggressive expansion.

However, when Fate slams one door shut, the Goddess opens another. Thus, and perhaps for the first time in memory, the warring ríthe and clanns within the Middle Kingdoms of the *Mhór Midhe* saw an opportunity. Generations of the tribe had been despised, looked down on, and preyed upon by their more unified neighbours.

In the wake of the Connachta's defeat and the chaos that followed, rather than bickering and fighting, the nobility of the Mhór Midhe gathered in *Cnoc Uisnigh*. The hillfort and tribe's civic centre rose from the bog surrounding it. The ráth boasted long sight lines, such that no enemy could approach undetected.

The territory of the Mhór Midhe lay at the heart of Ériu. It was a barren landscape dominated by vast, flat bogs, many of which had dried out due to the cold and harsh winds. Recently, green shoots and new growth appeared on the trees encircling the wetlands. It brought hope that the frigid conditions witnessed by many generations were ending.

Perhaps the marshlands would become wet and productive again.

A tribe of bandits, mercenaries, and slavers, the Mhór Midhe blamed their unsavoury traditions on economic necessity. The tribe was sustained by plundering its neighbours for cattle, people, and gold. Kidnapping for ransom or sale was a thriving business. However, if the marshes unfroze, the clann's ancient pursuits of peat harvesting and mining for bog gold could re-emerge.

Yet only the Goddess knew whether the Mhór Midhe would cast off generations of callous brutality and disregard for human life. The tribes around them could not foresee a viper turning into a worm.

***

"This would be an opportune moment to remove many of my ene-mies," said Messin Corb. The Rí Ruirech's hand hid his mouth as he spoke softly to his shield-man. Once again, he shifted his arse cheeks to ameliorate the spreading numbness and wished he could do likewise with his brain.

Messin's aside referred to his fellow ríthe and the nobles seated around the long table. That said, their natures dictated that the thoughts and murmurings of those present were likely the same as Messin's. Still, the rising babble likely had more to do with his guests' arses be-ing stabbed by splinters from the recently constructed rough wooden benches. Grand meetings at Cnoc Uisnigh were infrequent. The king was parsimonious, and carpenters were rare among the Mhór Midhe.

Unity remained a distant dream for the Mhór Midhe. Yet the prom-ise of power and wealth fosters strange alliances, especially when faced with a fragmented and weakened enemy. Messin stood and announced, "Friends, we have gathered to celebrate Samhain."

Derision and laughter greeted Messin. "However, we also have an opportunity to discuss. The southern kings and queens are divided and in disarray. This is the time to crush them and take their lands and wealth. The rígana rule as tyrants… just like us." That his words pro-voked cheering rather than protest proved Messin's point.

"It is common knowledge that Brighid and Danu have lost their powers and no longer have the support of the Aes Sídhe. The Goddess has spurned them, and they are vulnerable. As for the other kings, when the queens' heads hang from our belts, we will attack and conquer them, one ráth at a time."

Messin surveyed his audience with the predatory stare of a buzzard. His amber-yellow gaze was unnerving. Still, Messin knew the colour of his eyes had changed in concert with the growing expansion of his belly. He knew the recent swelling was not due to overeating. Indeed, the clann's oracles prophesied that the once great warrior had only a few seasons to become a legend. The momentous news was rewarded by the Seers' demise.

"I have heard Conall and his queen, Mórrígan, have landed with a large force at Niúig and reinforced its defences." The speaker was Calman Mor, the Rí of the *Magh-Breágh* clann. He was thirty summers old and the most successful raider among the Mhór Midhe. His demeanour was almost Druid-like, yet all knew his reputation for brutality was well-deserved.

"I have heard the same, Calman Mor," said Messin. "I have also heard that Conall is a god and Mórrígan a goddess. Neither is likely to be true." Laughter rippled through the assembly. "They are flesh and bone like us and can be killed with steel." Messin stood and thumped the table with his massive fists.

"What I propose will not be easy. Battles will be fought, and many seated around these tables will die. For those who survive, the *seanchaithe*—storytellers—will write great poems about your victories. Your sons and daughters will look at you with pride and follow your example. The time of the Mhór Midhe has come." Raucous shouts and cheers ascended to the rafters. Messin had given them a vision, and they desired it.

"Who will be my battle commanders?"

***

Calman was delighted to be far away from the political squabbling at Cnoc Uisnigh. He and two others had been given Messin's approval to launch the first waves of attack on the southern hillforts.

Readying his army of one thousand warriors was not problematic since they were preparing to attack one of Messin's closest allies' hillfort. Long before the meeting at Cnoc Uisnigh, Calman had decided he had tarried enough. It was time to challenge Messin for the throne of the Mhór Midhe. The upcoming invasion of the South delayed but did not supersede his ambition.

Thus, Calman was the first to begin the Mhór Midhe's campaign. Blessed by ground hardened by winter winds and freezing weather, his warriors marched southwest towards Caher Conri and a confrontation with Brighid. In Cnoc Uisnigh, Messin had the dubious honour of forging a Mhór Midhe alliance between the remaining kings and chieftains.

Let Messin sort that pack of arseholes out. As much as Calman disliked Messin and saw himself on the throne of Cnoc Uisnigh, he admired the king's political astuteness. Without that, the campaign would never be more than a series of large raids. Messin's task was to build an army of twenty thousand, an invasion force to conquer the southern kingdoms and hold the territory.

Only one thing gave Calman any anxiety. He had never fought mounted warriors. Indeed, of his army, only he rode a horse and uncomfortably at that. Calman slipped his feet from the girth loops, swung his leg over the horse's broad back, and dismounted. His shield-man strode forward and walked alongside him.

"Once we cross the tall stones at the border, kill everyone in the farmsteads and settlements in our path—no exceptions. Our men and women may rape and desecrate whomever they want, but before we move on, everyone must die. We cannot take prisoners for ransom or sell them as slaves. We kill, burn, and move."

The hefty shield-man would have smiled, but thick scars and a poorly set jaw from a fight in his youth did not allow the emotion. Instead, he opened his mouth, showing how few teeth remained, and dipped his head.

CHAPTER 8

Cnoc Duíginn

Brighid entered Cnoc Duíginn's Great Hall cautiously, accompanied by Báine. Aoife had declined to make the journey, pleading "other duties". Báine sighed. Her young friend relentlessly pursued the warband who slaughtered the small community. In this, she had been successful. Half of the lowlifes were dead; most were executed by staking.

Yet Aoife's success made completing her quest more challenging. The remainder of the band, dreading retribution, had gone to ground. Aoife received information on their whereabouts just before Brighid, and she departed Caher Conri. Báine sighed again. How could she stop Aoife's thirst for revenge from blighting her life? Báine glanced at Brighid. *If only you would learn that lesson, too.*

A sharp look from Brighid caused Báine to refocus on the purpose of the visit to Cnoc Duíginn. Sláine's message all but demanded their presence, and that was worrisome. He and Daráine were usually much more diplomatic. Following the envoy from the east and Clann Ui Flaithimh's forces landing in Niúig, the timing raised Brighid's suspicions. This time, Báine thought Brighid had every reason for caution.

***

"Welcome, come closer. Sit and eat," said Sláine, pointing to a table laden with food and drinks. Daráine sat on his right side as usual, and of the two, she appeared to be the most composed. Ten paces away stood an attractive young woman whose choice of dress and colour seemed to blend perfectly with the wall tapestries. She gave the impression of being a servant, yet Brighid's instincts sensed a viper ready to strike.

"Watch the 'servant', Báine. I doubt she is what she seems." Brighid's voice was low and whispered in Báine's ear. It was the closest she had been to Báine in several cycles of the moon. Her scent fostered a torrent of roiling emotions that Brighid fought to control. *I need a clear head.*

The pitch of Sláine's welcome held a hint of unease, making the fine hairs on Brighid's neck stand. *What is going on? Has Sláine joined my enemies?* Paranoia seized Brighid's mind. "I am always delighted to visit with Daráine and you. Although usually, there is more warning and less urgency in your invitations," said Brighid.

"Is there something serious to discuss? The land is rife with rumours. Perhaps you have facts rather than gossip. That would be welcome." Brighid dipped her head in the direction of the young woman. "However, let's start with introductions. Who is she? I suspect she is not what she purports to be."

A quick flutter of panic in Sláine's eyes and reddened cheeks convinced Brighid her suspicions were well-founded. Sláine glanced from his shield-man to Daráine and, finally, to the young woman. Daráine's smile widened to show her teeth. A worldly smile from the unknown guest matched it.

"You have embarrassed the king, if unwittingly." White teeth flashed as plump, raspberry-pink lips parted. "My name is Tisiphone. As for my purpose, in your language, I'm a striapach." Brighid's eyes widened. Taken aback at the unexpected and forthrightness of the response, her cheeks flushed pink.

"It's not often a whore attends such meetings," said Brighid.

"I'm a very special whore…" Tisiphone stepped forward and smiled at Sláine. "…and I am very persuasive." The sultry huskiness in Tisiphone's voice left little doubt about her claim. Báine blushed, although not from embarrassment. That she appeared unable to wrench her eyes from the striapach did little to improve Brighid's mood.

"Why are we here, Sláine? Is it so serious that it could not wait? Winter is upon us."

Happy to be on firmer ground, Sláine said, "My informants tell me that Messin Corb and the Mhór Midhe are gathering an army together. The Connachta are weak and have withdrawn to defend their traditional borders. The Ulaid have had their fun, and the usual bribes of cattle and gold have encouraged them to return to their homes beyond the Black Pig's Dyke. Therefore, the Mhór Midhe see an opportunity."

"I fail to see why that should be of interest to me. They can raid the Connachta lands to their hearts' content," said Brighid.

Sláine shook his head. "Their objective is not the Connachta." Hazel-coloured eyes narrowed, and Brighid saw a hardness in them and… disappointment. "They see a southern kingdom divided against itself and rival queens who hate each other. They watch rígana, who have lost the support of the Goddess and the Aes Sídhe, rule by brute force or bedchamber intrigue. Messin knows the southern ríthe will not lift a hand to support or save you… or Danu. Thus, they see kingdoms ripe for the picking."

"The Hag's arse!" gasped Báine.

"You, Brighid Ni Conall, Rígan of Caher Conri, Messin has deemed the weakest and, therefore, the easiest to conquer. An army of one thousand led by a brute called Calman Mor departed Cnoc Uisnigh five sunsets ago. He will be at Caher Conri's gates in a half-cycle of the moon.

"Two similarly sized forces follow in his wake. Calman's orders are to rape, pillage, and burn every farm and community in your domain. He probably wants Caher Conri as his winter refuge. In the meantime, Messin is raising an invasion army. I suspect he will attack around *Bealtaine*."

A sip of cold water revived Sláine's voice. He scratched his pâte and watched dry skin flakes fall to the table. When Daráine touched his forearm and said, "Tell her everything, brother," he dipped his head.

"Calman is a tyrant who has known nothing but raiding all his life. His father before him and his before that were the same. He is a monster who places no value on human life. He fears neither death nor the Goddess. He has no honour and makes that a weapon against those who have."

Sláine's eyes held deep sadness. "He sees you and Danu as despots and no different from him." The blood drained from Brighid's face as she gripped the oak table.

"Do you have any good news, Sláine?"

"Neither Calman nor any of the Mhór Midhe have experience fighting against mounted riders." Brighid looked at Báine and smiled, but any euphoria was short-lived when Sláine said, "You have less than one hundred riders and a handful of chariots. Yes, you have mercenaries, but how many will fight when faced with Calman's army? What happens when the other two armies join Calman? Can Caher Conri withstand a long siege?"

"Caher Conri's walls are strong," snapped Brighid.

"I recall Flann, Iasg, and fifty shield-warriors successfully scaled Caher Conri's walls to rescue children from Uallachán's dungeons. Do not underestimate Calman or his warriors. He is an animal but like a wolf, not a boar. His fighters rank among the best spearmen in Ériu."

"Perhaps you would like me to run away," growled Brighid.

"That is one option and may spare the lives of your warriors, if not your people. There are other choices, but you will like them even less." The glint in Sláine's eyes made Brighid pull a dagger from its sheath. "Brighid, do you know Daráine and me at all?" Sláine looked at Tisiphone and shook his head. "If I wanted you dead, you would already be in Mag Mell."

Brighid caught the glance and faced Tisiphone. She shrugged. "I never said I was just a whore," said Tisiphone. Brighid caught her breath. The steel in the attractive female's voice was wrapped in wool. It reminded her of someone. *But who?*

"War is marching towards Caher Conri, Brighid. Sláine and I think you should meet with Danu," said Daráine. At the anger in Brighid's eyes, Daráine shrugged. "Your other option is to take your best warriors and journey to Niúig. Ships await and will transport you safely to the port of Massalia. From there, you will be escorted to Lugudunon and your parents' judgement."

***

A disheartened Sláine turned to his sister and Tisiphone as Brighid stormed from the chamber. "That went as well as I expected. Brighid will neither run nor accept help. Perhaps for her, a glorious death would be a welcome end."

"But not for those she should protect," said Tisiphone. "Will we get a better response from Danu?"

Sláine shook his head. "I doubt it. Both sisters inherited their father's stubbornness, if not his love for his people. Brighid is impulsive, and Danu is pragmatic. However, both are proud, and that madness will not allow either to ask for help… especially from each other."

"Because of the Mhór Midhe, we have little time to resolve this situation as Aodán and Barra had hoped. You have had time to assess Lonán and know he has no love for the sisters." Tisiphone's tone sent shivers along Sláine's spine while Daráine bit her lip.

Sláine shivered. "I pray the Goddess will guide the rígana."

***

Midway between Cnoc Duíginn and Caher Conri, Brighid pulled sharply on her reins. The ride had been at a gallop, and the black horse whinnied in protest. Brighid patted its velvet shoulders and whispered, "Sorry." *That's the first time Brighid has apologised to anyone in a long time.* Báine raised an eyebrow in anticipation of an explanation.

"The whore, Tisiphone. I've seen or heard of her before. Have you?"

Báine flushed and shook her head. "I think I would have remembered her." Báine coughed as if to clear her throat but could not quite

disguise the soft huskiness in her voice when she said, "She is quite…
arresting." Báine thought for a moment. "Oddly, her skin tone is similar
to the young envoy who visited us, and her accent is similar to the Greek
merchant, Pytheas."

"Shite! It can't be. They would never do that to me."

"The Hag's arse, Brighid. Does it always have to be about you or
Danu? I've never known two sisters so self-absorbed." That Brighid did
not instantly shout and rail at her words alarmed Báine. "What is it?"

"I remember my uncle, Beacán, telling me about saving a young,
almost dead Greek striapach. She was one of Pytheas' best informants
in Massalia."

This time, Báine's tone was laden with annoyance. "Pytheas had an
eye for a beautiful young woman. So what? It's not that unusual, especially for wealthy older men."

"No. You don't understand." The anguish in Brighid's expression
startled Báine. "My uncle told me the striapach was an accomplished
assassin even at fifteen summers. He thought she would become better than him. I remember her name now… it was Tisiphone." Brighid
gulped as if needing air, and tears streamed down her cheeks.

"Our parents have sent an assassin to end Danu and me."

Báine shook her head and pulled Brighid into her arms. "I can't believe that. There must be another explanation. She could have killed you
in Cnoc Duíginn."

"Perhaps the sharp edge of an assassin's blade is the best I can expect… or deserve, Báine. At the least, it would be a quick death. I sense
that Tisiphone is an efficient rather than a sadistic bitseach." Deep in
thought, a silent and sober duo rode through the gates of Caher Conri
as sunset cloaked the sky in ambers and reds.

CHAPTER 9

Ráth Na Conall

At Cnoc Duíginn, an unusually forthright Sláine accused Danu of putting the southern kingdoms in grave peril. Sláine informed her that thousands of the Mhór Midhe were already marching toward Caher Conri. An invasion-sized army would arrive around the festival of Bealtaine.

Later, in her private bedchamber, Danu sat, head in her hands and shoulders slumped. *What can I do?* Emotions overwhelmed the queen, blocking a retreat to pragmatism. She stood and paced the small room, twisting her fingers and wringing her hands.

I need to get control. Her thoughts were in turmoil, and sharp pains stabbed her chest. The ring of thorns seemed to have become more solid, and their impact deeper in her chest. *Is this Draighean's perverse revenge? Does Brighid suffer likewise?* For once, Danu's concerns were not solely focused on her troubles.

She thought of Órlaith and Tanaí and wept. *Will I be the cause of my children's deaths?* Danu's mind was simultaneously numb and in disarray, making her unusually indecisive.

What about Brighid? That she cared shocked Danu. The folly of the schism with Brighid gnawed at her mind, and she could not ignore it this time. "Rut the Hag's arse," she muttered through clenched teeth.

Without the feirdhriseacha, she had no idea how severe Brighid's predicament was. *My sister could be dead and her head on a spear. Or worse, captured and repeatedly violated, and I wouldn't know. What have we done, Brighid?*

That she attributed blame to both Brighid and herself took Danu's breath away.

Yet there were benefits to losing her powers. Danu would never feel or suffer the agonies of Brighid's death, and neither would she die in sympathy. No one could lay the circumstances at her feet. *You're a selfish, cold-hearted bitseach!* Danu's mind screamed the accusation. Unable to bear the truth, she collapsed to the dirt floor.

✳✳✳

"Are we agreed on the plan?" asked Aodán.

Aodán glanced at Barra, Lonán, and Tisiphone. The group sat around a campfire within sight of Ráth Na Conall. Barra nodded immediately, but Lonán and Tisiphone were reluctant to concede. "Well?" Aodán's question was aimed at the battle-scarred veteran and the assassin. Barra dipped his head to Aodán, signalling he should continue.

"Only as a last resort will my sisters be harmed. Under no circumstances are they to be killed. They will be judged fairly under the Law of the Gaels and will compensate those they have harmed. *We* will have your oath on this, or you will be escorted under guard to Niúig. There, you will await a vessel to return you to Massalia."

Lonán exhaled. He disliked taking any option off the table. Still, he understood that Aodán and Barra would do anything to rehabilitate their sisters. *The foolishness of blood ties.* Danu and Brighid had taken a wrong path in the brothers' minds and could be redeemed.

To support them were generations of Gaels and thousands of *Brehons* and Druids. All would testify that the *Fénechas*—the Law—demanded punishment, atonement, and the payment of an *eiric* to the wronged, not death. Executing the twins was anathema to the brothers, and the Law supported them. To Lonán, death was the perfect solution.

Lonán knew the brothers suspected, correctly, that their parents had not been entirely forthright with them. Barra and Aodán were young but, having observed tribal politics since their youth were not stupid. Still, Aodán had asked for his oath and that troubled Lonán. Once given, would his honour allow him to break it?

Lonán shook his head. "No." Aodán's and Barra's hands dropped to their scabbards. "Are you sure you can kill me? Stay your hands. I propose a compromise. Exile. Your sisters will be cast out of Clann Ui Flaithimh. During their journey, they should seek guidance from the Goddess regarding how they can make amends."

Barra scowled at Lonán but signalled his consent to Aodán. Annoyed at Lonán outmanoeuvring him, Aodán put his mind to determining what loopholes he could use to aid his sisters. Grudgingly, he said, "I agree." He turned to Tisiphone. "And you, my lady?"

Tisiphone smiled. "I am far from being a lady and am flattered you consider the word of a whore and assassin may last longer than the time taken to speak the oath." She inclined her head. "For what it is worth, you have my oath." The looks of relief on Aodán and Barra's faces touched Tisiphone. "However, Calman's horde may already occupy Caher Conri, and Brighid may have crossed the veil."

"True. None of us anticipated the precarious situation we find ourselves in or the constrained time to reason with my sisters. Yet by the same logic, when Danu and Brighid stepped across Ráth Na Conall's gateway, could they have predicted they would have to confront and defeat the might of the Connachta? Their experience may prove vital for us."

"They had the Goddess, a Sídhe, and their powers on their side," grunted Lonán, unwilling to concede to Aodán's logic.

"I believe the Goddess has a plan for my sisters." Aodán looked at Lonán. "It is not death by your…" Aodán looked at Tisiphone. "…or an assassin's blade." Eyes widened at Aodán's frank accusation. Tisiphone smiled as if welcoming the honesty, but Lonán glowered.

"Get some sleep. Tomorrow's conversation may not be as pleasant as this one," grumbled Lonán. He wrapped his brat around him and soon was snoring.

"How are we supposed to sleep? An avalanche makes less noise than him," grumbled Barra.

***

"Can we do anything to help Brighid?" Danu's question stunned Cináed and Flann.

Flann shook his head. "We have a score of riders and no chariots. Most followed Brighid. Ráth Na Conall's garrison is half-strength, so we can hardly spare men to reinforce Caher Conri. Besides, it would take seven sunsets for shield-warriors at a hard march to get there. When they arrived, they'd be exhausted and outnumbered." Flann held Danu's eyes. "I'm sorry. It is too late. We can do nothing except prepare ourselves for an attack."

"What do you say?" asked Danu, and instantly flinched. Cináed's eyes burned with anger at Aoife's peril. Furthermore, he made no effort to conceal who he held accountable. "You have likely killed my daughter. Do you now wish to see my son dead? Will *you* explain to Ceara how you sent our children to their deaths? The land has rejected you. The people have rejected you. Leave us. Can the Mhór Midhe be any worse than you or your sister?"

Anger flared in Danu's eyes, and she hissed, "Oh, things can and will get much worse under the Mhór Midhe. With Brighid and my help, you avoided slavery once. You will not under the Mhór Midhe. If you cannot contribute sensibly to this discussion, get out of my sight." The door slammed as Cináed stormed from the room. Danu's shoulders slumped at the helplessness of her situation. However, further discussions were curtailed by a loud banging on the chamber doors.

Breathless, Cass, Cináed's son, burst into the room and gasped, "An army is at our gates!"

"Shite!" exclaimed Flann. "I did not expect the Mhór Midhe so quickly."

Cass's long black braids swung as he vigorously shook his head. "You don't understand. There's an army of almost two thousand. Of that, over half bear the banners and colours of Clann Ui Flaithimh and your father. By their flags, the remainder consists of contingents from Clárach, Cnoc Duíginn, and Curraghatoor. The South has risen against us. Ráth Na Conall's garrison is already divided."

The young warrior snorted in disgust. "The mercenaries have fled through the southern gate."

✳✳✳

Danu reached the eastern gateway in time to hear a loud bellow from a man she remembered well. *He has aged, although not his voice.* "In the name of Conall Mac Gabhann, Rí Ruirech of Clann Ui Flaithimh and Rí of Ráth Na Conall, stand down. The sons of Conall, Aodán and Barra now govern this fort and its domain. The rígana Danu and Brighid no longer have standing in the clann. Lay down your arms or prepare to fight."

On the walkway, Flann scanned the garrison. Many had arrived with him ten summers ago and looked to him for guidance. He turned to Danu. "Over half of these shield-warriors are loyal to Conall. I will not ask them to betray their oath."

"Did they not swear an oath to me? Does that mean nothing? Are all oaths worthless?" Guilt reddened Flann's face.

Danu faced the army at her gates. "Lonán Ó Neill, it has been long since you bounced me on your knee. At your advanced age and state of health, I thought you long retired, tending your vines and a whore in your cot. Yet it seems you have not avoided the folly of old men."

Lonán glowered at Danu, but her gaze had turned to her brothers. "Are you tired of border skirmishes in Gaul and seek to play kings for a while? Believe me; no throne is to be desired." A smile broke out on Danu's face when she spied and pointed to Tisiphone.

"*She* is the only honest one among you—the striapach who mysteriously arrived at the same time as the messenger. My uncle, Beacán, spoke highly of an assassin who was also a striapach. I assume that is you." Danu's lips thinned. "Should I thank you for not cutting my throat, or would that be precipitous? Where is your companion? I found him quite personable."

Danu returned her focus to Lonán. "A simple knock on the door would have sufficed. For the moment, you are welcome. Enter."

✳✳✳

The atmosphere in the chamber was heavy with unspoken thoughts and disappointment. Danu looked at Aodán and Barra. *I have made an enemy of my sister. Why not my brothers?* Danu fought not to visualise her ma's and da's faces and shivered at the prospect of her mother's wrath. She and Brighid had lost their powers, but Mórrígan's grew stronger with age, as did her propensity for vengeance.

"I suppose it would be futile to ask you to return to Lugudunon."

"We are long past that option, Danu. You have lost your people and powers and may have lost Brighid from what we hear." Danu flinched. Lonán looked at Tisiphone and then at her. "Do you also wish to lose your life?" The implication was unsubtle.

"Ráth Na Conall will fight if I command it." Danu looked at Aodán. "Is that what our parents want? Their problem daughters in Mag Mell?"

"That is unfair, and you know it. Be the queen who cared and fought for her people. Surrender Ráth Na Conall. You are alone and cannot prevail against us and definitely not against the Mhór Midhe. The kings of Clárach, Cnoc Duíginn, and Curraghatoor fight alongside us, not you. They have no faith in you." Deep pain filled Aodán's voice, and the chamber fell silent.

"The Connachta horde thought Brighid and I could not win, Aodán, but we did."

"You stand alone, Danu. Brighid is not with you. Neither is the Goddess nor the Aes Sídhe," said Aodán.

Danu sipped her cup of water. "It is a brave man who speaks for the Goddess or the Aes Sídhe. Perhaps I have misjudged your valour, brother... or your self-pride. What of Órlaith and Tanaí? Will you guarantee their safety?"

"Surely you can't think that we would harm our niece and nephew," interjected a shocked Barra. *What causes Danu to contemplate such vileness*

52

from us?

"*You*, perhaps no…" Danu glared at Lonán. "…but *he* would kill them if it suited his purpose. I see it in his eyes." Lonán's only response was the glimmer of a smile. "As for her…" Danu then looked at Tisiphone. "Who knows? Gold is her master, but whose coins are in her pouch?"

"Órlaith and Tanaí will become mine and Aodán's wards until we return to Lugudunon. There, they will be in the care of their grandparents," said Barra.

Danu rose from her seat and smiled thinly. "So, that is your plan. To return to Gaul and abandon the kingdom to the Mhór Midhe. What of your responsibility to the people? Do your 'allies' know of your treachery? Regardless of what title you have been given, you remain princes, not kings." Aodán and Barra recoiled at the slap, and their cheeks flushed.

Silence descended as Danu wrestled with her thoughts. "And me? What is to be my fate?" She looked at Tisiphone. "An assassin's knife in the dead of night?"

Lonán shook his head. "Your brothers forced Tisiphone and me to swear an oath." The warrior held Danu's gaze as he pronounced, "At sunrise, you will be banished from Ráth Na Conall and declared an outcast of Clann Ui Flaithimh. The Goddess will decide your fate."

Blood drained from Danu's face, and she gripped the solid table for fear of fainting. Green eyes deepened until they were almost black, and those at the table glanced nervously at each other. Were the rumours false? Barra nudged Aodán. "Are we sure her powers are gone?" He received no answer save a troubled look.

"So, you chose cowardice," hissed Danu. Aodán and Barra winced at another insult. Danu looked at Tisiphone and said, "You would have shown some compassion by letting her cut my throat."

"I thought so, too," growled Lonán.

"Perhaps, Lonán, my brothers have no stomach for kingly decisions.

On the other hand, you know the sentence is a meandering path to the same end." Danu straightened her back and squared her shoulders. "I want two sets of armour, the weapons of my choice, and three horses, one of which will be one of the smaller chariot mounts. You will also provide food for five sunsets and a small pouch of gold."

"You're hardly in a position to make demands," retorted Lonán.

Obsidian eyes grabbed and held Lonán's gaze. "I will give you a war if you want. Ráth Na Conall's walls are strong, and I still have those who will fight to the death for me, especially if they perceive injustice."

"Agreed, sister," said Aodán, glaring at Lonán.

"Good. Now, get the Hag out of my way. I have goodbyes to make and a sister to find." Aodán and Barra's eyes widened at Danu's final words. Had they misjudged her?

As Danu strode from the chamber, it seemed to those gathered that Danu looked like a queen again. Lonán took Tisiphone to the side and, in a low voice, said, "Follow Danu. You know your orders. Do what you must."

Tisiphone slapped away Lonán's hand. "Do not assume you know my orders or who pays me." Lonán's eyes widened at the rebuke. "I will follow Danu, but only because it was always my plan."

***

"I must go away for a short while." Danu's eyes were red from crying at the pleadings from Órlaith and Tanaí to stay. Finally, and reluctantly, she relinquished their embrace.

Turning to face Órlaith, she said, "I want you to listen carefully and remember my words. After I have departed, go to your uncles and repeat them. Is that clear?" Órlaith nodded, and Danu bent down and whispered in her ear.

"Be brave, Órlaith. Tanaí, look after your sister. I will return."

***

The gates of Ráth Na Conall swung open before dawn, allowing dancing eddies of snow to enter. The usual squeal of iron hinges needing grease was absent. Only the soft crunch of hooves in the frost-covered earth and snorts from the small string of horses disturbed the pre-dawn silence.

From the foothills of the *Na Comaraigh* mountains, west of the hillfort, came a cry of *kraa kraa* from the lone raven elected to mark Danu's departure. A long, ululating howl from a single wolf followed it. Those inside the fort shivered, but not from the cold.

At the bottom of the hillfort's path, Danu paused and turned around on her thick *diallait*—horse blanket. Her heart was heavy. Saying goodbye to her children was the hardest thing she had ever experienced. Her eyes misted over, and tears streamed down her cheeks. Then her jaw set, and the obsidian gaze glinted with tongues of fire.

"Your mistake was to take my children from me." Danu tugged on the reins, and the mount set off northwards at a fast canter.

"She looks prepared for war, Aodán," said Barra, watching from the walls.

"I agree, but who with? The women in our family are fond of the dark arts and bloody retribution."

* * *

As Aodán and Barra descended the walkway, the western gateway opened, and a grey mare cantered out. Tied to its tail was a chestnut bay, carrying an armoury on its back. Like Danu, the horses skirted the foothills of Na Comaraigh. Riding had never been a skill in Tisiphone's quiver because there was not much call for the expertise in the back alleys of Massalia.

Yet she had become proficient under the watch of Clann Ui Flaithimh's veteran riders. More than that, Tisiphone discovered that she enjoyed riding immensely and, having chosen a mount, had developed a surprising affection for the horse. With a black winter cloak billowing behind her, she increased the pace to a gallop. She could not let Danu get too far ahead.

CHAPTER 10

Caher Conri

Aoife's chariots chased the last remnant of the murdering tuilithe for three sunsets across the snow-covered lands northeast of Caher Conri. The blades and *creta* of their *carbaid*—chariots—were covered in the blood, bone splinters and gore of the previous group brought to justice. She shouted, "*Ionsaí*—forward!" and her vehicles fanned out in a long skirmish line.

Silhouetted against the morning skyline, the slaughterers of women and children stopped their retreat on the crest of the hill. Some turned around and appeared to run or ride towards Aoife's chariots. "What's going on? Why have they stopped?"

The grizzled driver had been in many battles, but his voice's timbre was one of genuine surprise. "I have no explanation."

Mystified, Aoife shook her head. "Perhaps the futility of their flight has dawned on them." The driver snorted in disbelief. "We will greet them as they deserve," said Aoife. The morning's snow flurries presaged heavier falls, but the ground was hard. With banners flapping, the chariots charged. Aoife had no pity for the warriors, only sadness for the horses they rode.

Spinning scythes dismembered limbs; thrown javelins and darts punched holes in flesh. The rout was quick and final. All that remained was to cut the throats of the injured before beheading them. Aoife grimaced and muttered, "Sorry," as she looked into the sad brown eyes of another horse before plunging a long knife into its heart.

Weariness overwhelmed Aoife, and she dropped to her knees. It seemed an age since she had begun her quest for justice or when her long black tresses were not lank with grime and sweat or matted with blood. *I probably have lice.* A shout from nearby caused Aoife to look up and see her driver signalling furiously.

"Why isn't she dead?" snapped Aoife.

"You need to listen to what she has to say."

Blood seeped from the stump of a leg cleaved below the knee. As the rider's heart faded, the pulses of arterial blood became fewer. Aoife sensed the *bean-sídhe* hovering over the soon-to-be corpse. A hand weakly signalled Aoife to come closer. She looked warily at the miscreant, but the chariot driver shook his head. "She has no weapons." Even when Aoife bent almost to where her ear touched bloody lips, the voice was faint.

"Go to the ridge. An army approaches."

The voice faded, the woman's breasts ceased to rise and fall, and the bean-sídhe screamed. Aoife looked around and spotted the rider's horse. A head was tied to its girth strap. The sight was rare but not uncommon among Gaels. That it belonged to another small child was the obscenity. "Your death was quick, and that was more than you deserved, bitseach!"

"Take me to the top of the hill," said Aoife to her driver. The snow-covered ridge had a long, gentle incline, presenting no difficulty to the hardy horse team. When they reached the crest, Aoife exclaimed, "Shite!" Several thousand paces to the north, a large column of warriors was easily seen against the white background. They marched steadily in the direction of Caher Conri.

"We need to warn Caher Conri," said Aoife. *What have I missed when I was tracking these bastards?* Panic made Aoife's heart pound, and the wolf sigil above her eye throbbed. She prayed to the Goddess for Báine's safety.

***

The news Aoife brought was unwelcome but apparently unsurprising. She gasped in disbelief at Báine's and Brighid's stoicism as they summarised the meeting in Cnoc Duíginn. "Great, an army of the Mhór Midhe will be at our gates in two sunsets. Our only escape is eastward, but wait…" Aoife glared at Brighid, "…you're not welcome in Ráth Na Conall. Furthermore, another and possibly bigger army of your ma and da likely marches towards us."

"Rut the Hag! Could this get worse?"

"I was hoping for constructive suggestions, not sarcasm. Is that too much to ask?" The weariness in Brighid's voice and the fingers that constantly tapped the table caused Aoife's and Báine's brows to furrow. "What is our strength? Can we withstand a siege? Should we strike first?"

"The garrison is divided. Rumours about the landing in Niúig have caused disunity. Soon, there will be well-founded gossip about the Mhór Midhe." Báine smiled faintly. "The Greeks have a legend about being caught between Charybdis, a treacherous whirlpool, and Scylla, a horrid man-eating, cliff-dwelling monster. It would appear we have our version."

"I did not know you were versed in Greek tales," said Brighid. The remark was intended to be humorous but came out snide. Annoyed with herself, Brighid bit her lip until the metallic taste of blood made her grimace.

"There's a lot that you don't know about me," replied Báine, "…and likely will never know."

Brighid's cheeks flushed. "I'm sorry. I don't seem able to do or say anything these days without causing offence or harm." Brighid's shoulders slumped. She constantly envisioned the baby's head on Aoife's spear, and Mórrígan's repudiation played repeatedly in her mind. *Have I delivered my kingdom into the hands of a butcher? None will come to my aid… not even my sister. What would you do, Danu?*

Báine and Aoife exchanged startled glances. This version of Brighid was vulnerable and indecisive. It was an improvement on her typically autocratic, angry demeanour. However, the transformation came at the worst possible time.

"Snap out of it, Brighid. Your warriors need leadership—good or bad. We cannot allow our chariots and riders to be caught between the outer berm and Caher Conri's walls…" Báine gulped to restrain the bile rising in her gorge and cursed herself for what she was about to say, "…like the last time." Aoife stared open-mouthed at Báine. Cruelty was not in her friend's nature.

Reminded of her folly, visions from yet another recurring nightmare flooded Brighid's thoughts. Green eyes glared at Báine, and a mask of fury settled on her face. She stood still momentarily and then deliberately turned her back on her commanders.

Báine and Aoife watched, mesmerised, as a calloused hand moved slowly downwards. First, it stroked and then grasped the polished blackthorn hilt of her sword. Báine braced herself when, with a whisper, the sword cleared its fleece-lined sheath, and Brighid rotated to face the duo.

"Oh, my ma's tits!" exclaimed Aoife.

Báine did not know whether to fall on her knees and beg for mercy or rush forward to comfort Brighid. Her third option was to unsheathe her sword and defend herself. Instead, she stood rooted to the spot, dumbfounded. Brighid's eyes were as black as night.

"Are you well?" asked Báine.

A puzzled Brighid looked at Báine. She inclined her head and seemed bemused at the sword in her hand. "What's happening? Are we under attack? Did I faint?"

"The Hag's bony arse. Your eyes. Look at your eyes," exclaimed Aoife.

"I can hardly look at my own eyes, Aoife." Brighid gazed at a white-faced Báine. "Please, tell me what is happening."

"Your eyes are black, obsidian as when you had your powers. Have they returned?" Green shoots of hope sprung up in Báine's voice.

Brighid looked at her arms and chest. The curling sigils and feirdhris remained faint shadows and dormant, and the ring of thorns more defi-nite. "A cruel jest, I think. Neither the Goddess nor the Aes Sídhe fa-vours me."

Since the twins' cleaving, Brighid's posture had gradually become stooped as if she carried an onerous burden. Now she straightened up, squared her shoulders, and inhaled deeply. As she left the chamber, Brighid turned briefly. "I have fences to mend with my sister, yet it may already be too late." The spoken words startled Brighid, as did the reali-sation that she was not complete without Danu.

Aoife looked at Báine, who stood speechless. "Is this madness?"

"I hope not, Aoife. I hope not."

✱✱✱

A surprisingly refreshed Brighid greeted Aoife and Báine the following sunrise. For once, she had slept without nightmares. The obsidian gaze had gone, and her eyes gleamed like polished emeralds. "I will speak to the garrison. Please have them assemble in the Great Hall."

Apprehension, fear, and confusion were written on the faces of the shield-warriors and riders gathered in the chamber. When Brighid rose from the throne and walked around to stand before the high table, another element was added… dread. The queen's frequent and rapid-ly changing moods were infamous. As was her propensity for picking scapegoats to blame for her failures.

Brighid coughed, and the chamber fell silent. "You have heard the rumours and gossip. Here is what I know. An army of over one thou-sand Mhór Midhe warriors will reach the outer berm on or before *meán lae*—midday—on the next sunset. We do not have the numbers to de-fend the earthworks or Caher Conri's walls." Mutters of "Shite!" and various curses involving the Hag trickled through the congregation.

A sip of spring water and Brighid resumed. "A cycle of the moon ago, an army of over one thousand, which my father and mother may lead, landed at Niúig. It is certain that they, too, will march on us. We can expect no help from Ráth Na Conall. Apart from my sister's issues with me, she has as much to fear from that force as I do."

Her hand trembled as Brighid lifted the cup to drink again, and water splashed the table. She inhaled to steady herself as she placed the vessel on the table. "We cannot win against either army… but we might give one of them a bloody nose. I will ride out on the next sunrise to meet the Mhór Midhe. Whether my riders follow, I leave to your conscience."

Brighid smiled sadly and spoke again. "I have not been a good queen and have poorly led my people and warriors. For that, I am sorry. Still, perhaps I can be a true rígan for a few sunsets." Brighid paused to weigh her words. "Ráth Na Conall will not welcome me. The stronghold will, however, open their gates to you."

As if summoning strength, Brighid inhaled and exhaled slowly. "I thank you for your service and release you from your oaths of loyalty. May the Goddess go with you." Discordant rumbles of "No" and mutters of "It's a trick" percolated through the crowd.

"However,…" The sceptics in the audience rolled their eyes. Brighid chuckled and added. "…before that, I have one final order. Before battle commences, my shield-warriors will set fire to Caher Conri. You will leave the Mhór Midhe tuilithe nothing but ash."

A cheer rose but fell silent when Brighid said, "Then you will descend the southern walls and make your way to Ráth Na Conall along the coastal paths. Caher Conri cannot be defended against such numbers. As you will recall, we took it with far fewer warriors. I will not throw your lives away. This is not a request. It is my last command."

Brighid looked at Báine, Aoife, and the chariot teams and riders. "As for my cavalry and chariots, the choice is yours. Leave now and ride for Ráth Na Conall or follow me in a battle the *seanchaithe* will write songs about." Brighid raised her cup and laughed without moderation. It was a sound unheard of in many summers. "If I were you, I would ride for my sister's hillfort, for there is only death where I go."

Pausing as if to consider something that had just occurred to her, Brighid addressed Báine. "At the end of this gathering, please select a score of riders to gallop to the other headland forts. They must be warned and told of the Mhór Midhe and my decision. After completing that task, they should take the message to those farmsteads and communities within the peal of a bell."

To stunned silence, Brighid descended the plinth and walked to the heavy drapes behind the throne. Pulling the tapestry aside, she exited the room through the concealed doorway.

"What should I do, Báine?" asked Aoife.

"That is a decision I will not make for you. I have loved Brighid and perhaps still do. I will not let her stand or die alone." Báine embraced Aoife. "You have a family at Ráth Na Conall. Go, be with them."

"You are my family." Aoife bit her lips until they bled. She wanted, and needed, to tell Báine about her nightmares and the throbbing sigil. *How can I? I'll wait until I see her again.*

***

"The bitseach!" Calman cursed Brighid as his army entered the plain northeast of the promontory fort. Yet he could not restrain the glimmer of a smile at the rígan's ruthlessness. It was a tactic he would have employed.

Ribbons of black smoke drifted upwards, smudging a surprisingly clear winter sky. Yet it was not just Caher Conri. Every headland fort was ablaze, as well as farmsteads and settlements. It would be a harsh winter for his warriors unless new food sources could be found.

***

In Ráth Na Conall, guards opened the door of the small meeting room and ushered in Órlaith. By her side was her brother, Tanaí, whose hand she gripped firmly and protectively as older sisters do. Those seated around the table looked up.

The girl looked like a smaller version of Danu; the boy, with deep blue eyes and a chin ready to set, strongly resembled his grandpa, Conall. "Welcome. You have a choice of knees to sit on," said Lonán. His smile was forced, but Aodán and Barra reached out their arms, smiling broadly and expectantly.

Órlaith shook her head, making her auburn tresses fan out. She held Lonán's gaze with all the solemnity which a child her age is naturally expert. "My brother and I were wondering if you knew when our fathers will arrive."

There was an instant straightening of shoulders and sharpening of eyes. In one sentence, Órlaith had commanded everyone's attention. "Forgive us, Órlaith, things have been quite disorganised recently. Please explain." Lonán's demeanour spoke of unease.

Órlaith smiled, and Barra chuckled. He detected a "Got you!" in his niece's expression. "Before our ma departed, she told us she had sent messengers to my and Tanaí's das and that they would come for us. Tanaí is, after all, the sole male heir to his da's throne." She chuckled as if sharing a jest. "I'm just a *banphrionsa*—princess."

"Darling, who is your da?" asked Barra, dreading the answer.

"My father is Óengus Dubdétach." Órlaith smiled proudly. "He's a rí of the Ulaid and a commander of the *Cróeb Ruad* warriors."

"The Hag!" muttered Lonán, covering his mouth so only Aodán and Barra could hear. "I know of him and his kin. They're all vengeful bastards. The good news is they're at least a cycle of the moon's hard march away. More likely, perhaps even several cycles since they would have to fight their way through several kingdoms.

"The bad news is that the Ulaid have been seeking an excuse to expand south of the Black Pig's Dyke. Danu has just handed them the perfect cause. Who wouldn't enlist to rescue a king's daughter?"

Aodán rubbed his chin and smiled at Órlaith. "And who is Tanaí's da?"

"His father is Bran Mac Labraid-Loingsech, Rí Ruirech of Ráthgeal."

"The Hag's arse!" uttered Barra and then quickly muttered, "Sorry," to Órlaith. To Aodán and Lonán, he said, "He's a lot closer and has, by far, the largest army of any of the southern ríthe."

"He's also kin to Messin of the Mhór Midhe," added Aodán. "Thank you for explaining, Órlaith. I am sure we will soon hear from your das." He smiled and nodded to the servant who accompanied the children. "It is almost meán lae. Please take Órlaith and Tanaí to where their food has been prepared." Órlaith smiled at Aodán, curtsied, and turned to her brother.

"Come, Tanaí. It's time for food, and then you need to nap."

Outside the doorway and beyond the ears of the guards, Órlaith faced Tanaí and grinned. "I think I said all our ma wanted. Now, let's eat and play."

* * *

"Is this your sister's revenge?" Lonán glared at Aodán and Barra.

"It seems you underestimated Danu. You gave us advice based on inadequate information," said Aodán. "Like our da, Danu has a talent for the long game. And as with Medb of the Connachta, her alliances were well-chosen if negotiated uniquely."

Lonán's face flushed angrily, and he scowled at the admiration in Aodán's voice. Barra sat back in his seat, clasped his hands behind his head, put his feet on the table, and howled with laughter. It was precisely how his adopted father, Torcán, would have reacted.

CHAPTER 11

Caher Conri

Beyond the spine of rock concealing Caher Conri and before the landscape became a sprawling plain, a narrow strip of densely forested land followed the rocky coastline. At its centre was a well-rutted trail used by the local farmers and traders who served the promontory's forts. The coastal forest was five hundred paces at its narrowest point.

Here, Brighid's black mare ripped and slowly chewed tufts of grass. The act expressed the horse's boredom, for she had been well-fed. Bejewelled gold tack glittered in the sunbeams that penetrated the canopy. Threads of gold, matching the colour of Brighid's highlights, were woven into the mount's braided mane and tail. Chainmail protected its head, and a mail blanket rested on its shoulders.

Brighid shifted her arse on the thick, gold-fringed, crimson diallait. The horse sensed her impatience and whickered. Brighid smiled and patted its broad shoulders. "I don't think we will have long to wait, my friend."

At the first signs of the dawn sun, Brighid had exited Caher Conri alone and unseen. She now waited at the coastal choke point. A utilitarian iron helmet sat atop her head. It was smooth and unembellished, except for the red foxtail hanging from its acorn-shaped knub. A moulded boiled-leather cuirass with iron scales stitched between its layers sat over a short-sleeved chainmail tunic resting on her hips.

Brighid's short-hafted, double-bladed axes hung from two loops on an ornately carved, broad leather belt held together by a fist-sized gold, silver, and bronze buckle. A sword, forged in the style of a Greek xiphos, was sheathed in a wooden scabbard hanging from the belt. An array of knives in smaller sheaths were its companions.

On Brighid's arm, she carried a smaller version of Clann Ui Flaithimh's waisted oval battle shield with its red background and swooping raven. Strapped to her back was a bow stave. Two quivers of black-shafted arrows were tied to the mare's girth strap, as were two blackthorn-shafted maces. Javelins and heavy darts were in sheaths strapped to the horse's flanks.

Below her belt, Brighid wore red and black plaid *triubhas*—trousers—tucked into calf-high, soft boots laced up with leather thongs. Patches of chainmail protected her thighs; layers of sheepskin were lapped around her ankles and hid more blades. Brighid Ni Conall, Rígan of Caher Conri, was determined to make the Mhór Midhe pay a heavy price.

The child-like cries of seabirds made Brighid grin. "You better not shite on me," she threatened. The waters on her left filled Brighid's senses with the salty tang of sea air and the smell of rotting seaweed. Another sound, like wind chimes, caught her ears. Curiosity made Brighid turn around. She grinned stupidly and barely held back the tears.

"Did you think I would let you fight alone?" Báine cantered alongside her beloved. Arse-touching braids of white hair swung as she turned on her diallait and waved. "I've brought friends." One hundred riders galloped from the forest and took positions behind their queen and commander.

"This is an excellent choice of position. What's our strategy?" asked Báine.

"Kill everyone and try not to die," said Brighid.

Báine dipped her head. "It's a good plan."

"Aoife?"

"She will make up her mind, but honestly, I'd prefer she travelled to Ráth Na Conall." Báine looked around the forest. "This is not a battleground that favours chariots."

Brighid nodded. "I agree on both points."

* * *

Calman's column was two hundred men wide and five rows deep. Several hundred paces ahead of the main body ranged a score of scouts. He grumbled at being forced into the narrow coastal forest but knew he had no choice. It was the only path to Caher Conri unless he scaled the mountains.

The trees were younger than those in the ancient woods. Hence, they were closely spaced. Calman perceived that as an advantage if he was to fight mounted warriors. Chariots, he dismissed. *That would be folly.* Screams of agony sounded ahead of him. His warriors tensed, ready to rush forward. Snarled rebukes from Calman and his chieftains stopped them.

One hundred paces further down the trail, Calman found his scouts. All were bound to trees, gutted, and their throats cut. Some had been castrated. "The rígan does not give quarter or mercy. That is agreeable to me." Calman turned to his shield-man. "Move forward quickly but not foolishly. Kill everyone."

* * *

"From the noise, they're not trying to hide from us," remarked Báine.

"Are the preparations complete?"

Báine nodded. "The horses are tied five hundred paces to our rear. Each rider has chosen their stand and has two quivers of arrows. They can fire six arrows for every ten breaths."

"With the Mhór Midhe breathing down our necks, that's not a long time, either for loosing arrows or retreating to the horses," said Brighid.

"True," replied Báine and then grinned. "Although we do have other surprises for them. The last ones to run for their horses will remove the ribbons marking our escape paths. If we had mountain goats instead of horses, we could climb the mountainside and show the Mhór Midhe our bare arses before escaping."

"I'll bear your suggestion in mind."

"Sarcastic bitseach!"

***

Six thousand arrows fired by shadows which moved quickly and silently through the trees are impossible to defend against. Especially when you have no experience of that type of warfare. By the time Brighid's last arrow had been loosed, half of Calman's front rank sprouted black shafts. Of that number, a quarter would never rise again. The red and white fletches fluttering in the breeze marked where the cord tying the spirit to the body had been severed.

Calman swore loudly and felt blood trickle down his cheek. He had dodged the missile, quivering on his shield. However, its mate ripped a deep gash in his right cheek and took a bite out of his ear. His shield-man, a warrior Calman had known since childhood, lay with an arrow sprouting from his forehead. "Spread out!" he bellowed. "Do not run in straight lines. You are the best raiders of the Mhór Midhe. Use your brains."

Yet tempers rise in the heat of battle, and sober thought is often the first casualty. Spears held at waist height and gripped in calloused hands, the Mhór Midhe charged after Brighid's retreating riders. Screams of pain followed the dull crack of snapped bones as the short stakes hidden in the calf-deep holes pierced feet. More men and women cried out as they ran into patches of forest debris liberally sown with iron thistles.

"Rut the Hag!" shouted Calman in frustration. "Will they ever fight face-to-face?"

***

"I detest those iron thistles," said Brighid.

Báine's grim expression told that she agreed with the sentiment. "Mount up!" she roared and smiled at the cheers. Mounted warriors are never complete without their horses. "Do not engage. Attack and retreat. Use your ranged weapons first."

An intricate dance took form as horses and riders weaved in and out of the trees. The mounts snorted as knees, reins, and phrases guided them. Each warrior's touch was deft and light because their horses knew them well. At twenty paces, javelins were loosed, raising more cries from Calman's fighters.

As the missiles left their hands, the horses were already wheeling around in preparation for another attack. The action was repeated six times until the throwing *sleánna*—spears—were exhausted. Then Brighid's cavalry switched to heavy darts. Yet, as with the spears, each rider only carried six.

* * *

A ruthless leader fond of violence, Calman was also astute and observant. Correctly assessing Brighid's warriors had a limited number of arrows and throwing weapons, he bellowed, "Push forward!" Calman, however, had not counted on fighting man and beast. Brighid's horses were every bit as, and, perhaps, fiercer than their riders. As the Mhór Midhe closed on their enemy, bony hooves crushed skulls and caved-in chests.

Yet, unlike Brighid's riders, Calman had no affection for horses. His roar of *"Spear the horses!"* drew curses from Brighid and Báine's warriors. Still, the Mhór Midhe deserved their reputation as fearless and expert spearmen. They slowly and steadily pushed Caher Conri's riders back, thrusting and stabbing at their mounts' heads, throats, and shoulders. Not even chainmail could protect the mares forever.

Horses fell, and riders were swarmed and speared, but not without reply. Brighid's riders slashed faces to the bone with long-bladed swords. Heads were reduced to a pulp with flanged maces that quickly had strings of flesh and clumps of hair hanging from them.

"We're being pushed back. Soon, the forest will widen, and we'll be surrounded," shouted Báine. Her shoulder shuddered as she cleaved another skull in two, and she grimaced at the pinkish-grey brain matter released, splattering horse and rider. Yet it added little to the gore already covering them. Báine's leg and arm muscles ached, but that was the least of her problems. Pain stabbed her legs, her triubhas were ripped from countless spear slashes, and she felt the blood-soaked material stick to her legs.

Alongside Báine, Brighid wore a frightening mask of blood. The axes she wielded dripped blood from the many warriors she had sent to Mag Mell. Yet their edges were dull from the constant chopping and hacking at the enemies surrounding her. "More like clubs than blades," she growled. Looking up, she saw more Mhór Midhe before her and the horns of their bull formation stretching out to enclose her riders.

She looked at Báine. "Better we end this fight on open ground," said Brighid and bellowed, "Retreat!"

✳✳✳

Between Caher Conri's high earthworks and the forest was a broad strip of land cleared of trees. It was a killing ground designed to thin a besieger's force and weaken its strength. Over half of Brighid's riders were dead; those remaining burst onto the land and galloped towards Caher Conri's berm.

To the east, the foothills of the mountains rose gently, but there was no path forward for horses on its steeper slopes and snow-capped peaks. The land to the west was even more inhospitable. Brighid knew no riders would desert their friends again and looked at Báine. She knew her lover's thoughts, smiled, and nodded.

"We should position ourselves as far east as we can. Let the bastards exhaust themselves running to meet us." Brighid smiled grimly. "Any edge is better than none." Shouts from the forest told Brighid that the Mhór Midhe would soon break from the tree line.

At the foothill, Brighid turned to face her riders. "We have hurt Calman's horde and his pride. Let us show him how warriors of Clann Ui Flaithimh die." Roars of defiance rose, and the riders settled their favourite weapons in blood-stained hands. Horses snorted and stamped the dirt.

Báine looked at Brighid and thought of better times, soft kisses, and shared cots. Deep blue eyes misted as she reached across and put an arm around Brighid. "I love you, Brighid. I have one request. Find Danu. She is the dog rose's flower, and you are its thorny stem. One cannot thrive without the other."

Brighid's eyes widened, but she dipped her head. She started to speak, but a kiss on her lips stopped her. "I am sorry, my love and queen. Live long and remember me. We'll meet again in Mag Mell." Confusion filled Brighid's eyes, but not for long. Báine's fist caught her on the chin, knocking her from the horse.

As she hit the frozen ground hard, two riders bound her wrists and ankles and dragged her over the snow to a small copse. As she struggled to clear her mind, Brighid realised Báine had taken her horse. Her weapons lay several paces away. "The bitseach! I am betrayed."

Moments later, over the clash of steel, Brighid heard Báine bellow, "Protect your queen! Form a guard around me. Kill the Mhór Midhe tuilithe!" Brighid wept with guilt as she watched Báine take her place and charge Calman's warriors with the last of her riders. With a heavy heart, she watched Báine's white plaits swirl as she fought and then saw them disappear.

* * *

It took Brighid from meán lae to sunset to cast off her bindings. Injuries from the forest battle only permitted her to half stumble, half crawl to where Báine had fallen. Her stomach heaved at seeing her riders' naked, bloody bodies and their horses strewn over the grass. The bodies had not been beheaded yet. As Brighid crawled to the corpse with long white hair, she was thankful for that.

With bare hands, bloody nails, and a broken dagger, Brighid dug in the frozen dirt. She wept unceasingly for her lover and the times spent in each other's arms. Then she cursed herself for being a stupid bitseach and her foolish coldness. Before the last handful of dirt covered Báine, she snipped a lock of her lover's white hair. Tears cascaded like a waterfall. "Haunt the bastards, my love."

As the sun slipped below the horizon, Brighid, soaked in her lover's blood, rose slowly from the dirt. Her eyes were obsidian, and her chest throbbed faintly. The cry started low from deep within Brighid and bubbled like a spring to her mouth. When she opened her mouth, it became a thunderous, ululating cry of grief and promised retribution.

Calman stood on the smoke-blackened ruins of Caher Conri's northern wall and shuddered. He looked at his shield-man and said, "That is a declaration of war and a vow of vengeance. It seems we were deceived, and the Rígan of Caher Conri lives. Get this fort ready for attack." As he turned away from his post, Calman shook his head.

"What have I awoken?"

***

In the northern foothills of the *Bod Carraig* mountains, Danu tugged on her horse's reins. It stopped, and she dismounted. She did not know why, but the compulsion was too strong to resist, as was the long howl of grief that rose from within her breast.

"I'm so sorry, Brighid," she said, tears streaming down her cheeks.

Hidden nearby in the trees, Tisiphone waited and watched, uncertain what made Danu stop or prompted the unnatural howling. *Is she a daughter of Apollo Lykaios, Lord of the Wolves?* Spellbound, Tisiphone watched Danu grab the reins and prepare to remount her black mare. She held her breath as Danu paused and turned around.

Tisiphone shivered as if someone had walked over her grave, for Danu's eyes gleamed black, and it seemed they looked deep into her. "Shite!" Yet, while Tisiphone was unnerved by Danu's eyes, the knowing smile on Danu's lips concerned her more.

***

In Ráth Na Conall, three men felt an irresistible compulsion, perhaps from the Goddess. Lonán, Aodán, and Barra stood on the ramparts. Carried on a westerly wind, the first undulating howl from Brighid was faint, if unmistakable. The second from Danu was much louder and much closer.

"Shite! What have we awakened?" asked Aodán, echoing Calman. None of his companions was brave enough to answer.

***

"You have unfinished business; you must go back," said Mongfhionn.

Talk of *The Mounds* or the underground Halls of the Aes Sídhe is often accompanied by visions of dark, dank, earthy tombs. Yet nothing could be farther from the truth. The inhabitants were demigods, not cave dwellers. Thus, the room chosen by Mongfhionn was spacious but felt intimate. No light sources could be seen, yet there was no lack of illumination. The Aes Sídhe's traditional immunity to heat and cold meant the issue was irrelevant. The décor was understated yet elegant and, above all, comfortable.

"No," replied Draighean. "It is none of our business how they treat each other. Humans are short-lived, so how bad can the consequences of their actions be? No, we should remain neutral and not interfere in the affairs of men."

Mongfhionn smiled. "That is puzzling, Draighean. What explanation do you have for the anomalies in your wards' recent behaviour?" Draighean's ruby eyes narrowed, and it seemed to Mongfhionn that the Sídhe's usual pastel-pink colouring had deepened, if only on her high cheekbones.

Bluff was Draighean's only defence. "What do you mean?"

"Is it your claim that Brighid's and Danu's natural eye colour is black *and* green?" Mongfhionn's eyebrows were raised in scepticism.

"Bitseach!" Then Draighean smiled, and that set Mongfhionn's senses tingling. "You have been visiting the humans, too."

Mongfhionn nodded. "I have a long history with Conall and Mórrígan, and they prevailed on me to keep a watch on the twins."

"But not to interfere!" exclaimed Draighean triumphantly.

"No, I told them I would not intervene because they are *your* wards and responsibility." Mongfhionn watched Draighean's shoulders slump. "Guide them, support them, or kill them. Just finish what you started. That is your *geis*."

CHAPTER 12

381 B.C.—Winter—Bod Carraig Forest

Burdened by unrelenting guilt, Brighid staggered and crawled eastward for three sunsets. *What is there for me in this direction?* Yet it was away from the scene of Báine's death. She would rest and gather her thoughts when she reached the tip of the Bod Carraig mountains. Still, Brighid's strength was already at a low ebb. Her mind was as numb as her fingers and toes, and her wounds constantly broke and wept.

She sobbed. *I will die here, alone, and no one will know.* There would be no pyre to blaze brightly or anyone to honour her life. *What would they celebrate? Who will remember me?* She had no sister, partner, or children to shed tears for her. Brighid shook her head and growled defiantly. *I refuse to die until Báine is avenged.* Cold tears ran down her cheeks. She brushed them away with bloody hands, bowed into the wind, and stumbled a few more paces.

The tree's gnarled root stubbornly stretched to feed beyond the forest line. Hidden by the snow, Brighid did not see the tendril until it was wrapped around her boot. Her ankle twisted painfully, and, hands flailing, Brighid pitched forward.

With her mind and body frozen, it was doubtful if Brighid felt her head strike the rock or the trickle of blood flowing from her temple. *I'm sorry for failing you again, my love.* Brighid's mind shut down, and she embraced unconsciousness.

***

Immune from the cold—it was, after all, her domain—Draighean watched Brighid fall. Yet the Sídhe chose not to interfere. *I need to know if they are still sisters. Still Na Feirdhriseacha.* In her mind, she watched Danu's small string of horses struggle in the deepening snow. Sharp ears picked out the anguish in Danu's voice as she begged her mare and forced herself to keep going forward.

Draighean felt Danu's despair as her body demanded rest from the storm and saw her eyes strain against the gloom. The Sídhe smiled as Danu asked the Goddess to preserve Brighid's life. It was likely the twin's first honest prayer in many summers. Danu's tone told Draighean she was losing hope. Perhaps this was how it should end for Brighid… in a snowy tomb. The tribe's seanchaithe would love the poignancy, the tragic ending.

The Sídhe snorted, and so did her black mare. *Bloody Gaels.* Where would they be without their love of tragedy and vengeance? Draighean huffed. Probably conquerors of the world. She shook her head. *I do not have enough proof that they deserve a second chance.* Yet Danu's grief was reason enough for Draighean to act, and she did.

***

The beat thumping faintly in her chest startled Danu so much that she almost fell from her horse. The sensation was strange yet familiar, like an old friend returning from a long journey. It took Danu several moments before her eyes widened, and she gasped, "Brighid!"

Horror's tentacles seized Danu's heart. "*No!*" She felt Brighid's life ebbing and sensed the bean-sídhe was close. "No, bitseach! You will not have my sister," she shouted. Brighid's heartbeat was a waning beacon. Convinced of its direction, Danu cajoled her mare forward. The horse was tired, almost spent, yet did not object, for it sensed Danu's urgency.

This is the place; I'm sure of it. Danu dismounted and whirled round and round. Yet all she saw were endless mounds and hillocks of snow-covered rocks and fallen trees. Brighid could be anywhere. *I cannot and will not lose you, Brighid, but you must help me.* She felt Brighid's pulse grow weaker as if saying, "Goodbye," and screamed, "*No!*"

The low, mournful howl of a wolf startled Danu. "The Hag, not this too," she muttered, sweeping her sword from its scabbard. It was a massive beast with black fur. When its head turned to face her, its eyes glowed red and held Danu's gaze without flinching as if it knew her. With a bark, the predator turned and dashed into the forest.

Danu staggered to where the wolf had stood and prayed to the Goddess that she was not deceived. Frantically, she scanned the area with eyes raw from the glare of the snow and strained by night. That it was a cloudy night did not help Danu. She simmered in frustration and looked upwards. Perhaps the Goddess heard her prayer. The cloud hiding the sleeping moon drifted in a transient breeze, and the landscape became starkly illuminated.

Brighid's hand looked like a wax candle planted in a snowdrift, and as Danu held it, it felt like an icicle. Cursing the fading heartbeat, Danu dug with her hands until she felt Brighid's torso. *The Hag, she's so cold.* Her hands became as numb as Brighid's, and her nails were cracked and bloody. Yet she could not risk her daggers. Alongside Danu, her mare pawed at the snow as if understanding the urgency.

Finally, Danu reached under Brighid and released her sister from the snow's grip. Breathless, she cleared snowflakes and ice from Brighid's face and hair. Despair overwhelmed her. Was she looking at a frozen statue of her sister? Danu's tears cascaded like a waterfall, splashing Brighid's face. Over and over, she repeated, "No, no, no. I'm sorry, Brighid."

The teardrops pounding her eyelids caused Brighid's eyebrows to flutter. "Do you intend to drown me, sister?" Brighid's voice was faint and slurred.

"Bitseach," said Danu and embraced her sister, hoping to share the warmth of her body.

"Perhaps you now wish to crush me," whispered Brighid.

"Bitseach! Frighten me like this again, and *I* will kill you."

***

The snowfall loosened a few of the stakes in the farmholding's perimeter fence. Thus, it needed to be repaired. Predators looking for food would not refuse the opportunity. Nuadha rested from his duties, leant against a stake, and surveyed the farmstead. It had improved substantially since he first stumbled across the abandoned premises after his banishment.

The three wattle and daub roundhouses, with steeply thatched roofs, were fully repaired, as was the wooden barn. The sounds of contented animals—they had a handful of cows and two horses—made Nuadha smile. The horses were sturdy, if not of the best quality. He cleared enough trees for several small fields, which he planted with corn.

A small patch was set aside for onions and wild leeks. He even found a crab-apple seedling in the forest and transplanted it. The tree's fruit was small and tart, but the sweetly scented pink and white blossoms were pleasant to rest under.

Nuadha chuckled at how naturally he said "they". His companion, a sylph-like young woman, had stumbled into his "home" after falling on her arse into a pool of sleet and ice. At the time, he had, with reservations, agreed to her staying for several sunsets. Ten summers later, she was still here.

Occasionally, he suggested she move into the middle-sized roundhouse for more privacy. Each time, she shook her head. The trauma of losing her family had faded but not gone away, and she feared losing Nuadha. They were an odd couple but comfortable with each other. He was forty summers, and she twenty-three. They never had rutted… they needed companionship. Besides, females had never been his first choice. She would disappear for a few days if needed but always returned.

A shout from the roundhouses pulled Nuadha from his musings. He watched his companion grab her bow stave and climb the middle building's thatch to gain height. Nuadha bent slightly and gripped the smooth shaft of an axe. It was the same tool he had used to kill his brother, Uallachán. He turned in the direction she pointed.

Three horses emerged from the forest and walked down the dirt track towards his gates. They were led by a tallish female—at least Nuadha assumed the figure was a woman by the dark cloak and hood. Her steps were unsteady, as if she had travelled far in bleak conditions. A figure slumped over the shoulders of the mount whose reins she held, and it looked as if they were tied to the mare. *Are they a prisoner, ill, or injured?*

"May we enter? My sister is severely injured and has been exposed to the cold for too long. I fear for her life. Warm shelter for a few sunsets would be appreciated," pleaded Danu.

Nuadha's eyebrow arched as recognition dawned on him. "Is it irony or poetic justice? A former king asked to help the queens who judged him and are now outcasts like him."

"You!"

Nuadha dipped his head and beckoned to his companion. She had refused to take her arrow from the bowstring and glowered at Danu. "We have guests in need of attention. If you take their horses to the barn, I will help carry the injured one inside."

"I can pay," said Danu.

"Insult me again, and, injured or not, you will not be welcome in our home," snapped Nuadha.

* * *

Tisiphone was glad Danu and Brighid found shelter, although she wasn't sure why that should make her feel pleased. She knew them by reputation as two wilful queens. The assassin set up camp carefully to avoid detection and to provide a good observation spot. On the one occasion when Danu left Brighid's side to breathe fresh air, the queen had looked directly in Tisiphone's direction. Worse, she had imperceptibly dipped her head and smiled.

"I know your orders and the conflicts you manage and am impressed by your subterfuge. Lonán believes your goals are his. Aodán and Barra are suspicious but

have yet to discern your true mission. If needed, you will kill without mercy to maintain the deception. The voice startled Tisiphone, if only because it seemed disembodied. A knife appeared instinctively in her hand.

"The game has changed, Tisiphone. This is not Massalia, and those you watch are more than they seem. The time fast approaches when you will need to choose a side."

"Who are you? Show yourself, coward, and we will see who can play this game better." Tisiphone whirled around several times, sweeping her dagger before her. She did not know the forests but knew the darkness; it had always been her home and refuge.

The belly laugh was unexpected. *"I like you, striapach. Yet that is not enough. If I cannot trust you, I will end your life, which would be a pity after you cheated death in Massalia."* The voice became sterner. *"There is no Beacán to rescue you, and the Goddess reigns in this land, not Apollo. Rest, Tisiphone, we will speak again."*

Tisiphone's sharp hearing heard a soft rustling around her camp. When she sensed that whoever had spoken had departed, she sighed and returned to her campfire. The heat seemed warmer, and the need to hold her heavy cloak close was not as urgent. She shook her head and muttered, "I live and kill in the real world, spirit."

Although not unpleasant, the peal of laughter from deep in the forest made Tisiphone shiver. *"What would be the sense in you freezing to death and us never meeting? Sleep well, striapach."*

In the morning, Tisiphone awakened at dawn and looked around. "Shite!" Surrounding her camp was a hedge with unseasonable flowers blooming. Beyond that, the snow had piled up to form a protective barrier. "Apollo's cock! I'm losing my mind."

She heard a low and husky voice in her head. *The shrub is called Draighean, as am I.*

CHAPTER 13

Ráth Na Conall

"The envoy from Ráthgeal awaits an audience—*impatiently*," said Flann. He stood alongside Aodán, Barra, and Lonán. All were shrouded in heavy woollen cloaks lined and trimmed with thick wolf fur. Ráth Na Conall's former battle commander was more forthright than usual and walked with a lighter step. Everyone in the hillfort knew Flann had been delighted to cede his position to the kings and assume an advisory role.

It was sunset, and the small group stood on the wooden walkway, which had been cleared of snow. Sensing menace from multiple directions, they looked to the west, the north, and the east. Only the seas to the south gave any relief. They had triremes at Niúig, so who could attack them on that flank?

One portent held their attention on this and previous dusks: the howling from the forests. A single wolf had started the phenomenon as Danu departed the hillfort. Soon after, another predator, then one pack, and others joined the chorus. To the survivors of the massed wolf attack on Ráth Na Conall during the reign of the queens, the howling resurrected terrible memories.

None in the fort knew that the wolves' songs were in sympathy with the rígana. However, many believed it, and that was enough to cause disquiet. Lonán was a straightforward and perhaps unimaginative man sceptical of gods and demigods. He argued that the howling was nothing more than the northerly winter winds rushing through the trees.

Few in the fort were convinced; apparently, neither were the wolves. As each sunset approached, the predators began their nightly refrain. And in Ráth Na Conall, the belief grew that the rígana led the chorus. An irritated Lonán faced Flann. "Give Bran's messenger a comfortable room in the Great Hall and see that he is fed and given refreshments. Send a whore to him, if needed. Tell him we'll receive him at meán lae."

Aodán looked at Barra and then Lonán. "We do not need to make an enemy needlessly."

"We have Tanaí. Ráthgeal will do what we want," snarled Lonán.

"Our nephew is our blood, and that of our da and ma, not yours. He is not a piece on a fidchell board to be used and cast aside." Aodán glared at Lonán. "You would do well to remember that. Leave us."

The angry, staccato tapping of a staff on the walkway's timbers echoed around Ráth Na Conall's courtyard as Lonán hobbled away. Barra turned to Aodán. "He is a man searching for a purpose and a sword forged for battle. That is his nature. If we wish to confront him, we should be prepared to kill him."

✳✳✳

The ambassador from Ráthgeal was a tall man with a back as straight as a spear shaft. Aged about forty summers, his long, braided hair and whiskers were copper-red and showed no steel threads. The ceremonial crimson brat he wore was slung with a flourish across muscular shoulders. His stride was determined, and his demeanour confident. The scars on his face and hands suggested that diplomacy was not his primary duty.

As Flann predicted, the envoy was furious at being ignored. He served the most powerful king of any southern kingdom, which deserved respect. Thus, his face undiplomatically looked like thunder as he walked the central aisle of the Great Hall's main chamber. He stopped ten paces from the high table.

The tradition of ambassadors is to be courteous and to bow to their hosts, especially if they are royalty. Bran's envoy stood like an oak tree, unmovable and unyielding. There was not the merest hint of respect for those before him. Aodán rose, opened his arms, and smiled. "Welcome to Ráth Na Conall. I am…"

"I know who you and your brother are—usurpers and whelps who cling to the glories of their mother and father. Conall and Mórrígan earned their status and wealth through battle and shrewd alliances. Your sisters, whom you had the temerity to cast out, defeated the armies of the Connachta. They deserved their thrones. What have you, or your brother, done to gain my king's respect?

"The main armies of the Mhór Midhe will be at your gates by Bealtaine. An advance force led by Calman Mor slaughtered the garrison at Caher Conri and every community around it. None survived. Three thousand warriors use Caher Conri as their winter camp."

Aoife gasped, "No!" and was led sobbing from the chamber by Cass.

"What is the 'ríthe's' strategy? Perhaps you will use your fleet and scurry back to Gaul." Scorn permeated the ambassador's every word. Aodán's cheeks flushed at the accusation, and he scowled at the insult. Yet, tripped up by Barra and his words, Danu had levelled the same charge. Lonán's seat scraped over the wooden floor, and his sword began its journey from its sheath.

"Sheathe your sword and resume your seat, Counsellor," rasped Aodán.

The laugh from the ambassador was as much a surprise as a relief. "Counsellor…" snorted the envoy, "…he is as much an advisor as I am a messenger."

"Perhaps you would enlighten us to your name and rank. Then we can discuss the true purpose of your visit," said Aodán.

The emissary dipped his head, although that was more in agreement than respect. "I am Gobán Ó Cuilinn, Commander of the armies of Bran Mac Labraid-Loingsech, Rí Ruirech of Ráthgeal."

"A spy," grunted Lonán.

"My role depends on my task," replied Gobán, "as does yours."

"And the purpose of your visit, besides assessing our strength? I would have thought a delay would suit your activities," said Aodán.

"I knew your strength long before I entered the ráth. I have been in Ráth Na Conall on other occasions."

"Likely on bedchamber duty," murmured Lonán.

"As to why I am here. Is it not obvious? You hold my king's son hostage. I wish to see him immediately to confirm his good health. Following that, we will discuss arrangements for his travel to Ráthgeal."

"He is our nephew and is a guest, not a hostage," said Barra through gritted teeth. Barra was Conall's son, although his mother was Mòrag, a Cinn Péinteáilte queen. Thus, while Barra inherited Conall's pragmatic demeanour, he was very much his mother's son. And neither she nor her hand-fast partner were known for their patience. Hence, there was a limit to his, and it fast approached.

"A 'guest' in his home. He has more right to be here than any of you," retorted Gobán, relishing Aodán's and Barra's uncomfortable miens. "Has Tanaí asked when his father will come for him?" Reddened cheeks gave Gobán his answer. "If you wish to be kings, you should learn to lie without blushing." Gobán adjusted the clasp on his brat. "I will see Tanaí *now*."

"That is acceptable. Then you can report to Bran that he is happy with Órlaith, his sister, and will remain here until winter has passed. Travelling at this time of the year is hazardous. None of us wishes to put the boy in danger… do we?" Aodán held Gobán's gaze without flinching.

"It is agreeable, but only because it is what I anticipated. However, know this: Calman is a brutal man. Yet, he pales in comparison to me. Harm one hair of the child's head or refuse to let him go to his father when requested, and I will bring Ráthgeal's armies to your gates. Every man, woman, and child in Ráth Na Conall will be slaughtered. In Mag Mell, you will not need to worry about the

Mhór Midhe."

As Gobán strode towards the doorway to the children's quarters, Lonán turned to Aodán and Barra. "I like him."

Barra rolled his eyes and muttered, "I wonder why?"

CHAPTER 14

Nuadha's Roundhouse

Danu tried to smooth Brighid's long auburn hair and attempted to remove the hardened gore from the blood-stained braids. She failed miserably. She smiled at Brighid's thin blonde braids and wondered if her silver highlights could be woven similarly.

The sight of Brighid's wounds and her broken and bloody nails made Danu sob. She sighed and continued to gently spread salve over Brighid's injuries. Her sister had not risen from the cot in three sunsets. *Perhaps she does not want to live. Could I blame her?* Who had suffered more?

Yes, she was forced to leave her children, but they were alive and likely being spoilt by Aodán and Barra. Danu's cheeks flushed in anger. *They belong with me. The land will run with rivers of blood unless they are returned to me. Stay out of my way, brothers.*

Danu sniffed the air, and her nose protested. *The bitseach needs a bath and a change of clothes!* She dipped a bathing cloth in cold water, wiped Brighid's face and let it rest on her forehead. *I love my children, even if they come from political necessity.* Yet Danu had never known the love that Brighid had lost. There would never be another Báine to hold and comfort her sister. Danu trembled. She feared which Brighid would eventually rise from the cot.

Not for the first time, Danu cursed the removal of her powers. Still, what had guided her to Brighid? Hope arose in her breast that perhaps all was not lost forever. Danu tamped down the expectation, inhaled deeply, and stood up with a groan. The cot was low, and the roundhouse had little in the way of stools or benches. So, she sat beside Brighid's bed on the dirt floor. Danu stretched several times to release cramped muscles.

Nuadha looked up from the room's only table. "You look pale and sickly and will be useless to Brighid if you become ill. Go outside, ride your horse, get some fresh air. We're isolated. I doubt anyone will discover you." He laughed, and Danu thought it sounded like a man contented with his lot. "Until recently, it was quiet around here with few visitors." Nuadha paused and scratched his whiskers. "Have you considered your future?"

Danu shook her head. "That can wait until Brighid recovers. The winter gives us time. Thank you for extending our stay." A wry smile perched on her lips. "Maybe the Goddess hasn't totally deserted us." Pulling the hide covering aside, Danu stepped across the entrance and into the yard. Instantly, she was assaulted by unseasonably bright sunshine and blue skies. Both intensified the monotonous glare of a landscape blanketed in unspoiled snow.

"We're being watched."

The disembodied voice startled Danu, and she whirled around, looking for its source. A giggle made her glance up. Swathed in a heavy wolf fur, Nuadha's companion sat on the thatch of the middle roundhouse. Long blonde hair rose and fell in the breeze, and her cheeks were attractively pink. The young woman gripped a bow with an arrow already nocked and ready to fire.

"Are you any good with that bow?"

"I'm the best in the forest." She laughed at her jest and flicked the wolf fur. "It got me this."

"I'm impressed. What's your name?"

The young woman thought for a while as if trying to remember something unused for a long time. "Rós. My name is Rós." Saying the name aloud disturbed her, and Danu saw her lip tremble. *She may have a sadder story than Brighid and me.*

"I think it is time that I spoke with my shadow," said Danu.

"I'll watch. She's well within my kill range."

Danu dipped her head. "Thanks."

✳✳✳

Tisiphone sat in the tree and scratched an arse cheek, which was steadily approaching numbness. That was unsurprising. She had taken up her position on the bough after she had broken her fast, and it was now midday. Brown eyes watched Danu crunch across the yard and enter the barn. A while later, Tisiphone's brow creased. *That's a long time to feed and water horses.*

Her senses on high alert, Tisiphone scanned her surroundings. Pert ears twitched like a mountain lynx, and she strained to detect the slightest noise. Only the soft thump of snow falling from branches and the shuffling of small animals searching for food broke the silence. Too late, Tisiphone's fine neck hairs stiffened.

"I don't think we've been formally introduced. As you know, I am Danu Ni Conall, and you are…"

Only the grip of shapely but muscled thighs on the branch saved Tisiphone from an embarrassing tumble into the snow. That she had been so easily discovered bruised her ego. She sighed and climbed down. "You're good, very good. Very few can move as silently as me," she said, brushing snow from her clothing and boots.

Danu smiled. "You're not in Massalia. You are the Greek my uncle Beacán rescued, aren't you?" Tisiphone nodded. "The meadows and forests are my domain. I would likely be out of my depth in the streets of that city."

Tisiphone shook her head. "That I very much doubt. My name is Tisiphone."

"You have been shadowing me since I departed Ráth Na Conall, and know I saw you. Thus, I have a question. What sense is there in freezing your arse out here? You could be in the warmth of the roundhouse and still watch Brighid and me. I can recommend the food." Danu pointed to Rós. "She is an excellent archer and hunter."

"That she is. I have watched her hunt." Danu's offer was tempting, especially for one used to the warm climate of the Great Sea. Tisiphone looked around and shook her head. "Thanks, but I would feel safer in the open."

"If that is your wish. However, I should point out that I found you, and if she was well, my sister likely could, too. Also, if you are acquainted with our customs, you will know that once seated in our homes, our Laws of Hospitality require us to protect, not harm, you." Danu chuckled. "Of more relevance, those goosebumps will only disappear with a warm fire."

Conceding reluctantly, Tisiphone asked, "May I put my horses in the barn first?"

"Of course. They'll probably meet old friends in there."

***

"Are you going to drown me in tears? Better you had left me to the embrace of the snow, sister." The voice was weak and croaked, but the irreverence made Danu smile, and she wiped the tears from her eyes.

"One who has been rescued from the bean-sídhe might show a little gratitude," said Danu.

"Has that ever been our custom?" asked Brighid.

Danu shook her head, and tears again threatened to burst the dam. "Perhaps that's our problem. We fight well together but are easily defeated and wound others when we battle each other."

"Báine…" Brighid choked on the word. "Before she was murdered…" Danu's eyebrow lifted at Brighid's choice of words, but she said nothing. "…Báine said you were the flower, and I was the thorny stem of the dog rose. Both parts needed each other to live."

"She was very wise," said Danu.

"Can we change?"

"I hope so. We've hurt many people who once loved and relied on us." Danu leaned over and kissed Brighid on the brow but could not prevent the tears from splashing Brighid's eyelids. "Sorry."

Brighid's cracked lips attempted to smile. "I can get used to it."

Danu's proximity to Brighid made her nostrils crinkle, and she blurted, "You stink!" Brighid looked suitably embarrassed. "Is there warm water to bathe Brighid?" Danu asked Nuadha. "The rainwater in the barrel is frozen solid, and I don't think she'd survive a dousing in the river."

"I'll warm water…" said Rós, "…and can help with the bathing if you wish." Rós looked into Brighid's eyes and blushed. Nuadha's eyes smiled at the matching pink flush on Brighid's cheeks.

∗∗∗

Several sunsets later, Brighid looked around the roundhouse and then at Danu. "Is this a meeting of old enemies? Have you negotiated a truce or peace agreement? If so, that is a remarkable achievement, sister." Brighid looked and sounded much better, following more rest and warm food.

Still shaky on her legs, Brighid took Danu's advice and rested in her cot. However, she insisted on sitting and leant back on a pile of furs. Her original bed was deemed beyond redemption and burned, which was a relief for all in the roundhouse. Thus, Brighid surveyed the occupants of the roundhouse on a fresh bed of straw and reeds scented with meadowsweet.

Danu chuckled and nodded to Nuadha. "This is Nuadha's and Rós' home. They could have turned us away. We are, after all, banished, and they place themselves in jeopardy by letting us rest and heal. Be nice."

"And the whore who specialises in death?" asked Brighid, staring at Tisiphone. At Danu's perturbed look, she added, "We met in Cnoc Duíginn. Poor Sláine was quite embarrassed when she introduced herself as his striapach." Brighid giggled, and Danu wondered if her mind had fully recovered. "However, Daráine looked amused. That one has hidden depths." Brighid paused her reflection and looked at Tisiphone. "I hope Sláine paid you well."

Tisiphone laughed and dipped her head to Danu. "She's getting better." Returning to Brighid, brown eyes held emerald ones without flinching and threat from either woman. "Truce?" Brighid nodded, although there was a wariness in her gaze, which did not go unnoticed.

"You are an assassin held in high regard by our uncle, Beacán." The statement by Danu held no animosity, and Tisiphone nodded. "What is your mission? Who pays your fee? You had several opportunities to end Brighid and me, yet have not done so. Instead, you settled for observing us."

"I never reveal my clients' names or their orders. A pouch of gold seals my lips. If you employed me, would you not wish the same?" Tisiphone paused and pursed her lips as if not wanting to reveal confidences. "I will tell you that your brothers are not my clients. They were also adamant that no harm should come to either of you… or your children. Others were not as unambiguous."

Brighid's lips parted in a crooked smile. "I think, sister, we should not fear a knife in the back at night. I think she would come at us from the front in daylight."

Tisiphone smiled and murmured, "Thanks." A perplexed look appeared on her face, and she looked uncertain whether to ask the question that perched on her tongue. With a sigh of resignation, she glanced at Danu and then Brighid.

"Who is Draighean?"

"The Hag's tits! How do you know that bitseach?" asked Danu. Brighid looked anxious, and Nuadha considered ending his hospitality.

"So, she is real, not my imagination," said Tisiphone.

"That depends on your definition of 'real'," said Brighid. "But how do you know of her? You're a Greek, not a Gael!" Brighid looked at Danu, unsure of how much to reveal. "She is a demigoddess—a member of the Aes Sídhe. Danu and I were Draighean's wards until we had a 'disagreement'."

"The bitseach took our powers away," growled Danu.

"The Goddess and she gave them to us, Danu, and we became tyrants. We deserved it, and both of us paid a terrible price." Brighid choked on her words, and her eyes misted over. Danu, upset at Brighid's brutal honesty, fidgeted on her stool. "Again, how do you know of her?" asked Brighid.

"I think we had a conversation in the woods three or four nights ago. The ring of blackthorn around my camp was a nice touch."

"The Goddess preserve us, Danu. She's here."

Danu inhaled and nodded. "Perhaps that explains how I found you. Have you not felt 'different' recently?" Danu looked down. "I had thorns where my feirdhris used to be. They disappeared when I found you."

Brighid peeked under her fur, and her eyes widened. "Shite! You're right. Mine has gone, too and the awful chest pains. With all the recent events, I hadn't noticed." Brighid looked at Danu, suddenly unsure. "What do we do now?"

"We wait. She will come."

✳✳✳

No member of the Aes Sídhe can resist the opportunity to make a grand entrance. Danu's words were the perfect segue. As the winter sun dropped below the horizon, the roundhouse's entry covering was flipped aside, and Draighean stepped across the doorway.

The Sídhe's pastel-pink skin became pale blue as day became night. Long fingers grasped and threw the black cloak's hood from her head. A mass of long tresses, black as night, tumbled over her shoulders. The perfectly spaced, thin red braids highlighting Draighean's hair were coordinated with full crimson lips and fingernails.

Draighean opened her lips to reveal flawless white teeth with possibly too many incisors. "Will no one offer me a seat? I have come a long way." The Sídhe chuckled, and Brighid groaned.

"The Goddess, please, no. A Sídhe who makes jests."

CHAPTER 15

Caher Conri

Calman walked the smoke-stained stone ramparts of Caher Conri and swore. His new shield-man and second-in-command followed a pace behind. Calman looked out on the white landscape. Apart from drifts against the stronghold's walls and berm, the snow remained calf-deep. "It could be worse," he muttered.

Through squinting eyes, he regarded the charred ruins of anything that could burn. Most of the ramparts had collapsed, and the few surviving walls were permanently weakened when their wooden braces became ash. Some of his warriors had died, buried under rubble, after choosing the wrong place to set up a temporary shelter. "Who needs such eejits?" he asked, spitting a lump of phlegm over the smoke-stained wall.

Building new shelters for his men and the two thousand who had arrived recently proceeded as well as expected. However, Calman had executed one of the two ríthe who led the new additions. The man spread rumours of Calman being outfoxed by a woman. Few were surprised when he disappeared. Calman's intolerance of dissent was well-known. The rí's corpse would be found with its throat cut when the ice and snow thawed.

The rising volume of complaints of hunger from the army irritated Calman. There was little he could do about it or to prevent the disease and infection which inevitably would follow. He was already resigned to losing a quarter of his army by the festival of *Imbolg*. "Bitseach!" he shouted into the northerly winds sweeping over Caher Conri's walls.

Still, Calman was forced to acknowledge the effectiveness of Brighid's strategy. His army found the smaller headland forts empty of supplies and burned to the ground. Likewise, within the sound of a bell's peal, communities and farmholdings had been stripped of food and set alight. Putting their faith in the Goddess to keep them safe, the population and warriors of southwestern Ériu fled east to the Bod Carraig and Clárach mountains.

Calman's army could march east and pillage the lands. However, he knew that by the time he reached the strongholds of Clárach or Curraghatoor, the toll demanded by the winter gods would leave him irretrievably weakened. He would be forced to retreat and become the hunted. Thus, he closed his ears to the grumbles of his warriors and chose pragmatism. The strong would survive, even if forced to eat their own.

***

Draighean held Brighid's and Danu's gazes. They did not flinch, and the Sídhe's lips thinned into a smile. *At least they have a fight left in them.* "I am here, yet again, not by choice. You still have a powerful friend in the Aes Sídhe. Still, Mongfhionn has family troubles in Northern Albu and may have no choice but to turn her back on you if you fail again. I can be your ally or your judge and executioner. Choose."

"Will we get our roses and powers back?" It was Brighid who posed the question. Danu shook her head. *This is not the right time, Brighid.*

"That is your first question. Not to ask how to help your people or those who once believed in you. Your selfishness is appalling. Do you want revenge for Báine's death that much?" The brutality of Draighean's riposte shook Brighid. Tears streamed from her eyes as she stood slowly. In obvious pain, she screamed in the Sídhe's face.

"*Bitseach!* You cannot absolve yourself of responsibility. Rather than help us, you declared defeat, removed our powers, and, like a coward, fled to the Halls of the Aes Sídhe. Mongfhionn had many disagreements with our father and mother, but she never deserted them.

"My love is dead. What vengeance will make her rise from the dirt I buried her in or return her to me from Mag Mell? None." Trembling with anger, Brighid pointed to Danu. "My sister has lost her children, who are little more than babies. However, unlike Báine, they are alive. With or without your help, we will find a way to return them to where they belong—in her embrace.

"If all you can do is stand there looking superior and speaking to us as if we're vermin, then, by the Hag, get out of our sight. My sister and I have work to do. *We do not need you.*"

Nuadha's seat crashed to the floor as he jumped up in time to catch Brighid before she collapsed. After Danu and he settled Brighid in her cot, Nuadha turned to Draighean. "My lady, I have no interest in whatever games you play, but this is my home, and you are no longer welcome. Please leave."

"Ouch!" grunted Tisiphone as a red-faced Draighean whirled about, pushed her against the wall, and stormed from the roundhouse. "I do not fully understand your customs and know you are often subject to high passions. However, am I correct in assuming the discussion went poorly?" The laughter that broke out relieved the tense atmosphere.

Danu held a shaking Brighid in her arms. "Thank you. I could not be happier that my son and daughter have an aunt like you. *Táimid ar aon*—we are together."

✳✳✳

Mongfhionn watched Draighean stride across the chamber and smiled. Yet the Sídhe's mien hid the fury smouldering in obsidian eyes. "Congratulations. It seems you achieved our objective of uniting Danu and Brighid. That said, the method lacked subtlety and alienated them. We need both for the war that is to come."

Draighean's mouth parted to protest, but Mongfhionn's dismissive flourish stopped her. "You should have kept your mouth firmly shut and used your ears to hear their concerns and plans. You misjudged Brighid's motivation—it was selfless, not selfish. All she wanted was to rescue Danu's children. Do you consider that bad? You caused her needless pain."

A pale hand gestured to the many groups of Aes Sídhe scattered throughout the Great Hall. "Tell me, Draighean, do you think your sisters are your friends? Do any have the deep love for you that Brighid had for Báine, or Danu and Brighid have for each other, or Danu has for her children?"

Mongfhionn chuckled, and it was not a pleasant sound. "If you believe that, you are delusional, and I will replace you with someone with a brain." Draighean's nascent dissent was quashed, but the tint of humiliation in her cheeks remained.

"There is no compassion or love in the Halls of the Aes Sídhe. It is all politics and power plays. How else are bored demigods to pass the aeons?" Mongfhionn paused, and the fires in her eyes became flickers of sunlight. "Mankind fears us, but they can also love us. Your sisters will never have such feelings for you."

Mongfhionn's gaze became wistful. "Why do you think Medb, others, and I chose a partner from them and had children by them? Why do you think the Goddess defends and is patient with these infuriating men and women? It is because their worship and love sustain her... and us." Mongfhionn stepped forward, reached out, and took Draighean's hand. The black-haired Sídhe was shocked. Typically, the Aes Sídhe did not touch each other.

"Think of how pleasant a warm hand with blood pumping through its veins and arteries would feel. Or a warm body holding you in your cot." Mongfhionn's lips pursed and widened into a broad smile as she saw Neamhain cross the floor and walk towards her. "Look at my daughter, Draighean. Have you anything in your life that comes close to giving you the unconditional love she gives me?

"You have experience and wisdom that spans thousands of their summers. Do not coddle them. Chastise, protect and guide them. If needed, go to war with them." Mongfhionn's lips broke in a broad grin, which made Draighean wary. "Rut them—men or women. Although not as many as Medb. I doubt the Aes Sídhe will ever live her reputation down." Mongfhionn chuckled at her jest. "The experience is not unpleasant."

Draighean stood open-mouthed as Mongfhionn went to meet Neamhain. She stopped, turned, and faced Draighean. "Choose Draighean. Return to Danu and Brighid and mend your fences… or I will replace you."

"Shite!" muttered a confused Draighean. "This will be embarrassing."

* * *

Used to stealth, Tisiphone had little difficulty leaving the roundhouse and farmstead unnoticed in the dead of night. Indeed, her most challenging task was keeping the horses in the barn quiet and assuring them she would return. They had formed an affection for her mare and protested her leaving.

Tisiphone had two tasks to accomplish. The first was to report to Lonán, Aodán, and Barra, although not simultaneously. She would speak with Conall's sons first and then Lonán. Tisiphone breathed out as she rode towards Ráth Na Conall and watched her breath form ice crystals and sparkle in the moonlight.

In Massalia, she had watched jugglers perform for beer, wine, and tips outside the drinking dens. The best at simultaneously keeping many balls or other objects in the air could earn a reasonable living. The others were likely to be found floating in the harbour. She hoped that would not be her fate.

At Ráth Na Conall, Tisiphone's reception was as frigid as the weather. Neither audience was happy with her account, which said there was nothing to report. She omitted that Brighid and Danu were united and that the Sídhe, Draighean, had come… and gone. What would it have benefitted her to provide this? Tisiphone had learnt long ago that there was always a more advantageous time to use information.

Thus, as she rode from the stronghold, Tisiphone turned to pursue a curious observation she had made. A strange smell had tickled her nostrils while she was hidden in the trees watching Brighid and Danu. Having once sampled the scent, it was forever in her senses, and she had smelled it several times since that time.

The fragrance was woodsmoke and not from the roundhouse's firepit. Nuadha's custom was to mix firewood and peat. Tisiphone did not take long to identify that the new bouquet was carried on a westerly wind. Thus, Tisiphone's destination was the Bod Carraig mountains.

***

There was little to do in Ráth Na Conall during winter save eat, drink, exercise, or sleep. Those with a partner or whore rutted. The wolfhounds in the fort competed with the wolves in the forests to howl the loudest. Yet, like the garrison, both slept more than they were awake. Exertion needed food, and food was scarce, at least to the animals.

The plateau of the crag upon which Ráth Na Conall sat was massive and thickly wooded. Thus, clearing several plots of land and building shelters for the increased garrison was not a challenge. There had already been accommodation for two hundred horses when Brighid commanded her riders.

Standing before the firepit roaring in one of the smaller chambers, Lonán clapped his hands and stamped his feet to bring feeling back into his extremities. Aodán, Barra, and Flann did likewise. "What did you make of Tisiphone's report?" Lonán asked.

"She told us nothing, although it was pleasantly served to us," said Aodán. The grunts from the others signalled they agreed.

"I wonder who is paying for her services and what her mission is," said Barra with a smirk. Startled, Lonán's eyes widened, drawing a chuckle from Flann. "Obviously, Lonán thinks she takes his orders. Aodán and I would like to think that our priorities are hers, but I doubt they are." Barra laughed. "Only Flann has no stake in this game."

Aodán scratched at a lump of oatmeal trapped in his beard and joined in the speculation, if only because it patently increased Lonán's unease. "There is, of course, our parents, separate or together. Also, Beacán and Iasg, who adopted Tisiphone after he saved her life."

Barra nodded in agreement and threw more tinder on the fire. "There is also Danu."

"No!" exclaimed Lonán.

"Our sister is undoubtedly angry with us. We know she can be very persuasive and strategic. How valuable would it be to have a resourceful assassin on your side? Who else could get close to us with a dagger?"

"Then there's Brighid," said Aodán.

"Calman Mor killed the bitseach," snapped Lonán.

"That 'bitseach' is our sister and Conall's and Mórrígan's daughter. A fact you should remember," growled Aodán. "She is dead only when I see her corpse."

✳✳✳

Sensing the conversation had moved from light-hearted *craic* and teasing Lonán to imminent violence, Flann coughed. "By way of a digression, what is your intent concerning Niúig? You upgraded the old hillfort and the jetty, and it stands a formidable stronghold with a fleet of ships close by—albeit they have been beached for the winter. It's a prize that someone like Bran of Ráthgeal might like. Only a skeleton garrison defends it."

"Shite!" muttered Aodán.

Lonán grunted. "We'll review Niúig's function after the feast of Imbolg. Who attacks in the winter? Besides, if we lose the ráth, it is insignificant."

Flann's gut and the hairs on his nape told him Lonán's decision was naïve. He remembered the Sídhe, Draighean, and her use of winter as a weapon. He recalled the rígana fought in harsh, wintry conditions. Flann shook his head and shrugged. It was not his problem anymore. He chuckled. *I'm just an advisor and have given my counsel.*

CHAPTER 16

Carn Tigherna

The closer Tisiphone got to the ruins of *Carn Tigherna*, the more pungent the smell of woodsmoke became. The hillfort had been the home of Onchú until Uallachán attacked and destroyed it. Under the orders of the depraved Rí of Caher Conri, the inhabitants of the ráth—warriors, wives, girls, mothers, and babies—had been raped and slaughtered.

Only Onchú's wife and daughters were left alive, although they were violated and taken prisoner. It was Brighid and her riders who rescued them and dispensed justice. However, Tisiphone was unaware of Carn Tigherna's tragic history. All she discerned was the smell of many bonfires and the sight of flames and sparks leaping upwards into the night sky. She heard men and women, even children, behaving like they were at one of the Gaels' seasonal festivals.

Curious, Tisiphone dismounted and tied her mount to a stump where the forest met the treeless ground before the fort. She shivered in the cold air as she stripped and put her garments into a woollen sack. A large clasp drew the edges of the heavy wolf-fur-trimmed cloak tight to her body.

As she approached the hillfort, the carousing, the mouth-watering smell of meat turning on a spit, and the fragrances of beer, wine, and puke brought a smile to Tisiphone's face. As did the unique scent of rutting; for one of her profession, the setting was perfect.

It was past *meán oíche*—midnight. Snow carpeted the dirt, but the roaring fires radiated enough heat to temper the cold, especially inside the broken perimeter walls. As she walked through the shattered gateway of Carn Tigherna, few said anything, but many, men and women alike, licked their lips. Even swathed in a cloak, Tisiphone's body language shouted that she was a woman many would pay gold to rut.

As she hugged the walls of the hillfort, Tisiphone listened carefully, gathering snippets of conversations. She smiled at the frantic rutting of those wanting that short-lived pleasure. For those furthest from the fires, the low temperature limited the time but not their enthusiasm. She learned that the camp's leaders were in the shell of Carn Tigherna's Great Hall, which still had enough unbroken thatch to give a sheltered, dry billet.

The first to approach was unsteady on his feet but became instantly alert when she unclasped her cloak. Dirt-ingrained fingers fondled her breasts. She moved closer to allow her arse to be squeezed and the *pit* between her thighs fingered. Tisiphone moaned, and the sigh was sincere. It had been a long time since her body had been used, and she missed that.

However, this was business, and the closeness allowed her to whisper the price in her client's ear. After having sampled and smelled Tisiphone's body, the transaction was never in doubt. For her part, she was an honest whore and bent over and let him thrust into the hole of his choice. Neglect had tightened her *anas* and pit, but memory and smell stimulated her milk flow in the latter.

She heard the client groan as his thrusting got faster, and the gasp of release as his final rough lunges filled her with seed. Tisiphone smiled as the warm liquid leaked and wet her inner thighs. She straightened only when he withdrew, smiled, kissed his lips, and murmured, "Thanks." A husky purr in his ear was followed by a murmur in hers and a nodded direction.

Tisiphone repeated the process several times before she stood before her target. He was the second-in-command of those gathered in and around Carn Tigherna; the leader had departed earlier to retrieve more of the exiled. The man looked at her and smiled. The women surrounding him, like a blanket, scowled and clung to him. Still, they were no match for Tisiphone's sensuality, which was accentuated by the flickering light of flames and rushlights.

One whore looked ready to challenge Tisiphone, but the blade that appeared in Tisiphone's hand made the *striapach* retreat. The man laughed, and Tisiphone thought it a pleasant laugh. "I was expecting you. My men informed me that you have been progressing up the chain of command." He pointed to a corner where thick hides and several *brait* covered a pile of straw. "It's better than the dirt and probably less of a strain on your back from standing or bending over. The fire will keep us warm."

The tall man, whose hard-muscled body and scars testified to his calling, licked his lips as Tisiphone dropped her fur. He murmured, "Certainly a class well above the other whores in this camp. Shall we talk or rut?" Tisiphone stretched out her hand, stroked his already hard manhood, and stated her price. He roared with honest mirth. "A true businesswoman."

As dawn broke, Tisiphone stirred first and smiled. Someone had put wood on their fire. It crackled happily, throwing out warmth and a pine fragrance. She ran a delicate finger through the dark hairs on his chest and could not resist wandering over his belly to his cock. It stirred, perhaps at the memory of a night of frequent use. *I should have charged him more for an entire night.*

The sudden tensing of Tisiphone's muscles awakened him. "What?" he whispered.

"That's a strange shield," she said, looking at the swooping black raven on a field of red. "Does it have a story?"

Sadness alighted in his brown eyes, and she saw him hesitate as if wondering whether she could be trusted. Sighing, he said, "I was the ceannairí céad of Caher Conrí's shield-wall during Brighid's reign."

"Gossip is that Brighid's shield-warriors escaped to Ráth Na Conall before the final battle between Brighid and Calman Mor."

"Never trust gossip. I have nothing against the new kings, but my warriors did not wish to serve another of Conall's children. When Calman took over Caher Conri, my fighters and more from the headland rátha fled to Bod Carraig. We needed time to rest and consider the future." The captain's eyes narrowed.

"The blades strapped to your thighs, and the long pins in your hair suggest there is more to you than meets the eye. What is a Greek *striapach* doing in Ériu?"

"You and your warriors have nothing to worry about from me," said Tisiphone. "However, if you will trust me, I have a proposition for you." She sniffed the air. "But first, I need a bath… and so do you." She looked hopefully at him. "Is there warm water to bathe in?" His laugh gave Tisiphone her answer.

"I have something better. Do *you* trust me?" Tisiphone nodded warily and was instantly gathered into his arms. He strode towards the northern exit and shouted, "We're going for a bath. Stoke the fires!" Raucous, if good-natured, cheers set Tisiphone's alarm bells ringing, but she was held firm in his grip.

The sound of water splashing over rocks should have been a warning. Yet she was enjoying being in his arms. *What's his name?* Clients rarely gave whores their forenames or family names—or at least the real ones. Her musings ended when he stopped, and she was launched into the air. It was a surprise, and she shrieked, "Bastard!" as she hit the pond's surface and felt the thin ice shatter. She squealed even louder as she sank below the surface of the mountain pool.

It was not long before he was beside her, and she was slapping his face with hands that were rapidly losing feeling. Her frozen nipples scraped against his chest. *Will they snap off?* His laughter infuriated Tisiphone, if only because it was infectious.

"We should get back, or I will lose my manhood and you, your nipples," he said. "This is good for a fast clean up but not soaking." Once again, Tisiphone was swept into his arms and carried at a fast jog to the camp. Rough cloths and a roaring fire soon had her skin tingling and feeling perfect.

"At the least, the little buggers swimming in my pit have been shocked or frozen to death," said Tisiphone. She looked around for her cloak and saw a sack she recognised. Turning to her host, she raised an eyebrow.

He shrugged. "We're not altogether stupid, and you didn't suddenly descend as a gift from the Goddess. My men found your grey where you left the horse. She is a fine mare and has been brushed, fed, and watered. She awaits her mistress in the courtyard."

"Thanks." Tisiphone pursed her lips. "I asked you to trust me." Wariness settled in her host's eyes. "There is a farmstead to the east of here. You could reach it by meán lae if you left at dawn. Come to me there on the next sunset. Come alone or bring a guard. That is your choice." Tisiphone chuckled. "Worst-case scenario, you can rut me again… no charge." Then she paused. "What is your name?"

"I am Olcán Ó Dubhan."

✲✲✲

"I have returned," said Draighean, vainly attempting to reduce the deep flush spreading across her high cheekbones.

"That's somewhat obvious since you're standing before us," said Brighid snarkily. "Did your ma spank your arse and tell you to go play with the nice humans?"

"Brighid!" hissed Danu. "Better her with us than against us." Danu saw the puzzlement on Draighean's face and asked, "What troubles you, Draighean… apart from having to swallow your pride?" It was Brighid's turn to roll her eyes.

"I do not have a ma, so how could she spank my arse?" asked Draighean. Her face was perfectly expressionless.

"Either she has no sense of humour, or we're the butt of hers," said

Brighid, scrutinising Draighean's countenance. She imagined the merest hint of one end of the Sídhe's lips curling upwards before it was brought under control. "Why are you here, Draighean?"

"I am here to provide counsel…" she paused, and this time there was no doubt about the smile, "…and to rebuke when needed." Draighean breathed deeply. "But first, I apologise, Brighid. My words were thoughtless because I did not listen or observe. I caused you pain, and that was wrong of me… very wrong." Silence fell as Draighean spoke. It was uncommon for any Sídhe to admit fault and even rarer when they apologised.

Rós sat closest. Brighid gripped her arm, stood unsteadily, and approached Draighean, halting an arm's length from the Sídhe. The effort made her breathe harshly, and she felt her head begin to spin. "You were a bitseach, but my words could have been chosen better, also. I accept your apology. Thanks."

Brighid rocked to and fro on her feet and smiled thinly. "However, I may need assistance returning to my cot." A hand gripped Brighid's shoulder, and she looked into Draighean's ruby eyes, which was unsettling.

"I can help with that." Brighid felt her chest throb and watched the faded curling symbols on her arms grow darker and more distinct. She wanted to scratch all over her body as a myriad of nerves fired. Shocked, Brighid's hand went to her mouth, and her brat fell to the floor. Blue-black rivers flowed over her body.

"Oh, shite!" said Rós. She looked at Danu, who stood to catch Brighid. Held by Draighean's free hand, she seemed about to climax from ecstasy. She, too, was naked, and, like Brighid, Danu's sigils were in constant motion. Between each of the twins' breasts was a feirdhris. Yet, unlike previously, the flowers were identical, with a pink and white centre and petals with black tips.

"Perhaps you should rest for a while," said Draighean. She nodded to Rós, who instantly grasped the meaning of the gesture and led the sisters to a cot. Then, the Sídhe turned to face Nuadha. "I also owe you an apology for disrespecting your hospitality."

Nuadha smiled, nodded, and looked at Rós. "Perhaps you could kill something for us to eat, although it should be big. I suspect there will be ravenous bellies to fill."

"I can guarantee a suitable target for you," said Draighean to a bemused Rós.

CHAPTER 17

Danu licked greasy fingers, walked to where a deer roasted over a fire and carved several slices of venison. The small group sat outside the roundhouse. Draighean's domain was the winter. Thus, they were pleasantly warm as the sun drifted towards the horizon. The blazing campfire's function was to provide a pleasant backdrop and light.

Blood dripped from the slice of the roasted meat Danu handed Brighid, and she quipped, "Thanks, but this could still be running through the forest."

"Ungrateful bitseach." Danu saw the half-frown on her sister's face. "What's bothering you, Brighid?"

"I'm not sure I want the powers anymore, Danu. I'm grateful for Draighean making me well again and for you finding me…"

"But…"

"Look what we did when we had our powers. It will be impossible for me to pay compensation to those I hurt… there are too many. Will we be any different with them restored? I'm not sure." Brighid breathed deeply. "I think I would like to be normal. Is that wrong?

"Perhaps it would be best for the southern kingdom if we left. Barra and Aodán are good men. They will make good kings, but not if they see us as looking over their shoulders. I will help you retrieve Órlaith and Tanaí, and you can flee to the north." Danu's eyebrow rose at Brighid's choice of words.

"I will join you after I have killed Calman." Brighid smiled grimly. "Perhaps Tisiphone can give me lessons in being an assassin. When Báine is avenged, we can cross the sea to Northern Albu. Our friend Gràinne's a queen in that realm and will give us sanctuary."

Danu was stunned and sat open-mouthed. This was a side of Brighid she had rarely, if ever, seen. Yet it was hard to challenge her sister's train of thought or the appeal of being "normal". She shook her head. "No, Brighid. Whatever we do, we do together."

***

Draighean's cough interrupted the twins' conversation. "I understand, if not completely, your yearning to be ordinary people. The powers that have been entrusted to you are onerous. Perhaps you should look at this gift as a mark of the Goddess's approval and confidence in you. As with your ma and da, you made mistakes and likely always will. Dealing with those trials is part of your growth, and I will be at your side." Draighean paused.

"I will remove your powers if that is what you wish." Danu and Brighid's faces lit up in the light of the fire. "However,…"

"Why is there always a 'however' with a Sídhe?" Danu's pinch to her arse made Brighid cry, "Ouch!"

"You know a war is coming, but you cannot foresee the terrible consequences for Ériu and the people of this island if Messin and the Mhór Midhe are victorious. This is much more than a local fight. You are the only ones who have fought against overwhelming odds and won, and you are the single advantage the people of the South have." Draighean inhaled deeply and exhaled.

"I do not wish to add to your burdens, but as a member of the Aes Sídhe, I must. Without you—both of you—Messin and the Mhór Midhe's philosophy will be victorious and infect all Ériu."

Brighid's shoulders slumped briefly before she straightened up. She looked at Danu. "We can keep our dreams, but apparently, fleeing is not an option."

"Where can we get an army, Brighid, and one that will still fight with us?" asked Danu.

"I may be able to help with that." Startled eyes watched Tisiphone step out of the shadows.

***

"I thought you had deserted us for a higher-paying client," said Danu.

Tisiphone shook her head. "I had to report to Lonán and your brothers." The grumbles of bitseach and traitor were instinctive rather than malicious. Yet Danu and Brighid looked at Tisiphone curiously, if not with enmity.

She shrugged. "If I had not reported, they would have been suspicious and sent patrols to find me. I told them nothing. They were not pleased." Tisiphone looked curiously at Brighid. "You appear much better. Lonán thinks you are dead, killed by Calman. Your brothers are not convinced."

Pointing to a vacant stool, Tisiphone said, "May I?" and sat down. A flash of golden thighs and she pulled a blade from its sheath and carved a large slice of meat. "I'm starving."

"Where have you been, Tisiphone? You took much longer than needed for a journey to Ráth Na Conall and back," asked Danu.

"I had a hunch and investigated it," said Tisiphone. She tapped a pouch, and it clinked. "I made some gold, too."

"We were worried about you, and you were out whoring. The Hag save me from strangling her," said Brighid.

"Not just whoring, although that was pleasurable… as always. I rode to Carn Tigherna."

"The hillfort is deserted and in ruins," said Brighid. "I know because I watched Onchú bury his sons there and helped rescue his wife and daughters."

"True, the fort is in ruins but not deserted. It is a hive of activity." Tisiphone looked at Brighid and said, "It is occupied by some you may know." Tisiphone stared over the fire and shouted, "I think it's safe for you to come closer."

"Shite! Is this a trap, bitseach?"

Tisiphone laughed. "One day, you'll have to trust someone other than your sister, Brighid."

***

Olcán stepped around the fire and bowed to Brighid. "My queen, I am glad to see you alive and in good health."

"*You* were supposed to burn Caher Conri to the ground and then march to Ráth Na Conall. What part of my orders did you not understand?" Olcán's grin was Brighid's answer, and she swore.

"We did the burning but decided that fleeing to Ráth Na Conall would not be in our best interests. So, we joined with others from the headland hillforts and travelled east to Carn Tigherna. There, we were going to plan a way forward. Several nights ago, Tisiphone came into our camp, and now I am here."

Olcán glanced around, and Brighid's and Danu's hands moved towards their swords. Observing their reactions, Olcán laughed and put up his hands. "Can you not hear the growling bellies of my guard? Ten shield-warriors stand twenty paces from the farmstead's gates to ensure this was not a trap *for me*. The smell of roasting meat must be driving them crazy." Everyone laughed, and Danu nodded to Olcán.

Then she turned to Rós and said, "Perhaps you should have hunted two deer." Danu faced Olcán. "I should introduce those whom you may not know. This is Nuadha Ó Dubhghaill, the former resident of Caher Conri and our host. His companion, Rós, is an excellent hunter and archer." Danu smiled and turned to Draighean. "And this is Draighean, a member of the Aes Sídhe."

"The Hag!" gasped Olcán.

"Not at this moment," said Draighean, to loud peals of laughter.

***

The craic around the campfire ebbed and flowed. "How many warriors do you command, Olcán?" asked Danu.

Olcán dipped his head to Brighid. "I have one hundred of my queen's shield-warriors of whom I am their ceannairí céad."

Brighid clapped her hands. "We have a warband, Danu. Our da and ma started with fewer." Her face fell when Olcán coughed. Did he have other plans?

"There are also four hundred warriors from the headland hillforts and a few minor ríthe. Most of the remaining nobles fled to Clárach. A few may have travelled to Ráth Na Conall."

"Five hundred warriors," said Danu. Her rose pounded in her breasts, and she felt Brighid's thud in concert. "I think, Olcán, you are about to receive a significant promotion."

* * *

Between meán oíche and dawn, the conversation around the campfire rose and fell. Brighid watched Draighean and nudged Danu. "Have you ever seen Draighean take note of men in *that* manner?" Danu shook her head.

"I hope you're mistaken. She seems obsessed with Olcán, but his attention has been on one person this night—Tisiphone, and she encourages it."

"Leave this to me." Brighid stood, stretched, and sat down beside Draighean. "You seem to be quite taken by Olcán. What prompts your sudden interest in men, if you don't mind me asking?"

Draighean seemed embarrassed if a Sídhe could have that emotion, and her lips pursed. "Mongfhionn told me I needed a good rutting. Olcán looks like a strong specimen." Brighid choked on her beer, tears streamed down her face, and beer gushed from her nostrils. A startled Danu rose, but a raised hand and a mouthed "I'll tell you later" kept her in her seat.

"I have no objection to you dipping your toes in that river, Draighean. However, Olcán does appear to be smitten with Tisiphone. In the interest of camp harmony, I would counsel you to cast your eyes over his companions. I'm sure one of those would satisfy your immediate need."

"Thanks, Brighid. Your advice is welcome."

***

"We need a base of operations," said Danu. "We cannot impose on Nuadha's hospitality much longer. But where?"

"Niúig," said Brighid. "I hear the garrison is small—about fifty warriors. It sits on the cliff, so its western flank is well protected. It has long sightlines to the north and bogs to the south and east. Our brothers have thoughtfully strengthened the old hillfort and its jetty." Brighid wiped bloody juice from her chin. "Capture the ráth, and we also get a fleet."

Danu did not wish to curb Brighid's rising enthusiasm yet shook her head. "Perhaps our initial ambitions should be more modest. We need warriors, horses, chariots… and weapons and armour. You and I have burned our bridges with Onchú at Curraghatoor and Aodh at Clárach, so we should expect no help from either."

Brighid's eyes glittered. "I could steal horses from Curraghatoor's corrals. They're far enough from the ráth that we would be undetected. They'll never miss one hundred from their herds."

"What about Aoife? We could use her chariots," asked Danu.

"She hates me because of Báine and what I was like." Brighid choked on her words, and tears splashed the snow. "I am not a good person, Danu. I did awful things and let others go unopposed." Brighid fell silent.

***

Danu whispered to Nuadha, "My sister and I are in your debt and will not forget you gave us sanctuary."

He smiled and said, "Time changes us, sometimes for good, sometimes not. Only the Goddess knows which path we will follow." Then Nuadha chuckled. "That said, you owe me several barrels of beer and new furniture. I doubt either will survive this night."

CHAPTER 18

Carn Tigherna

"Why should we trust you with our families… again? You ruled as ty-rants and abandoned your people." Danu and Brighid coloured at Ciar Ó Róich's candour. He was the king of one of the headland forts west of Caher Conri before Calman's invasion. An honourable man, Ciar was highly respected among those gathered in Carn Tigherna and spoke as their leader.

A similar height to the twins' father, Ciar's eyes were also steel-blue and piercing. However, whereas Conall's hair was auburn, Ciar's was blond, long, and braided. Unlike most of the men of the clann, his whis-kers were full but trimmed. Like their da, Ciar projected authority and presence.

He's handsome. Why have I never seen him before? The question vexed Danu, and her irritability with herself surfaced. So far, her choice of men left a lot to be desired. Drawn to Ciar's deep, baritone voice, she listened intently.

Olcán had asked Ciar to call the meeting. While Olcán's warriors had recommitted to Danu and Brighid as their rígana, the rest of those encamped in Carn Tigherna's ruins followed Ciar. Previously crowned by acclaim, this time, Danu and Brighid had to put forward a defence and an argument to persuade others to follow them. Both knew they stood on marshy ground and were anxious.

"I can remove him, quite bloodily and publicly." Draighean's voice startled the twins from their thoughts. "That will demonstrate the wisdom of giving their oath to you. There's always a leader-in-waiting… perhaps Olcán."

Brighid rolled her eyes. "Violence is not the solution to every problem, Draighean." At that, the Sídhe and Danu shook their heads in disbelief. Brighid's sober expression gave no clue as to whether she was serious.

As agreed, Danu stepped forward and climbed onto a large rock. Her voice was clear and strong when she spoke, although that was Draighean's work. She pointed to the ruins. "Carn Tigherna saw the violation and slaughter of innocent men, women, and children. The ground you stand on has been sanctified by the blood spilt on that terrible night.

"On this sunset, in Caher Conri, a brutal man, Calman Mor, reigns. He delights in violence, and his goals are simple: accumulating power, territory, and wealth. Calman will boast of this as he forces you to watch his followers rape and gut your sons and daughters."

Danu paused. "Yet he is not the only or the primary danger. Before the festival of Bealtaine, a Mhór Midhe army of twenty thousand will descend on Southern Ériu. They will rape, pillage, and enslave, for that is their nature. They know nothing else. Is that who you wish to mimic? Are they the kings whom you want to rule over you? Is that the future you wish for your children?

"Yet *you* will not witness your loved ones' suffering or hear their cries on the slave ships. You are warriors and will die bravely in battle and enter the feasting halls of Mag Mell. The southern ríthe will not come to your aid. They are divided and seek refuge in their strongholds. Yet inevitably, they, too, will bow before the Mhór Midhe."

Danu coughed and offered a hand to Brighid, who clambered onto the rock. "My sister and I are imperfect. We have made many mistakes and will make more. We have been punished for our misdeeds." Danu gripped Brighid's hand. "Brighid's love sacrificed her life so that she could live. Does that not count in her favour? I became a whore to secure alliances for my people. The Goddess blessed me with a son and daughter, but they are held hostage in Ráth Na Conall. Their home has become their prison."

Taking a deep breath and releasing it slowly, Danu continued. "Ten summers ago, Brighid and I…" She smiled at Draighean and said, "…and the Lady Sídhe…" Ripples of nervousness flowed through those gathered. Whispered gossip had become a reality. "Together, we fought Uallachán, the kings of the Connachta and an army of twenty thousand. We prevailed. None in this land can claim that achievement. We ask, we beg, for a second chance to serve you."

"Well said, sister. Perhaps you have a career as a *seanchaí*… if we live to see another summer," whispered Brighid.

∗ ∗ ∗

The crowd fell silent as Ciar stepped forward and climbed the rock. Danu and Brighid wrung their hands anxiously. Draighean still held thoughts of murder.

"The *Fénechas*—the Law—does not require us to be perfect. Rather, it asks us to acknowledge our past misdeeds, desire to do better, and recompense those injured." Ciar paused. "I came to this assembly reluctantly. The smell of my hillfort and my people's farms burning still clogs my nostrils.

"Yet the rígana have spoken well and honestly. I am not a *Brehon*, but I judge they have fulfilled the first two requirements of the Law. The third obligation will be paid when they lead us to victory against the Mhór Midhe." Ciar turned to face Danu and Brighid and bowed deeply. Then he turned to face the crowd and shouted, "The rígana!"

"He is quite handsome, sister, and has a pleasant voice," said Brighid.

"I had not noticed," responded Danu.

"Your feirdhris says differently."

Danu coloured deeply. "Help me down from this rock. We have work to do." Brighid's reply was a hand proffered and a mischievous grin.

***

Danu looked around Nuadha's roundhouse. The building was large enough to be a home for several generations of family plus a few animals. Hence, space was not an issue. Yet Danu knew Nuadha and Rós felt uncomfortable. Until recently, the duo had enjoyed quiet, solitary lives that suited them. Nuadha was also troubled by his sudden elevation from pariah to a councillor on the twins' nascent Chomhairle. A relieved Rós had been spared that honour.

The members of the Chomhairle were seated on rickety wooden benches, which creaked with every movement and threatened to collapse under the weight of unfamiliar arses. The rough wooden table they sat around held basic foods and refreshments. Uneven legs made it rock, making the jugs of beer and water spill over their lips.

"I've been on ships in a storm with less motion," muttered Brighid.

"I'm open to a new table if anyone is skilled in carpentry," said Nuadha, causing everyone to laugh.

Draighean shook her head, making her dark tresses rustle like ravens' feathers. It was a group without acrimony. Yet, with such strong personalities, how long would that last? Could they resolve the differences that would inevitably surface?

Olcán sat beside Tisiphone. Both glared at Brighid when she muttered, "If you want to rut, use the other roundhouse… but keep the noise down." She glanced at Rós and smirked. "There are young ones present." It was Rós' turn to scowl, although that was contrary to the increased beat of her heart. Between Olcán and Danu sat Ciar. Draighean, as usual, preferred to stand.

"There are decisions to be made," said Danu. "What is our priority? Horse warriors will give us flexibility, range, and warning of threats. Niúig will give us shelter, a stronghold, and a base of operations."

"The decision might be moot." Since all knew that Brighid fervently desired cavalry, eyebrows were raised. She shrugged, looked at Ciar and Olcán, and asked, "How many of your warriors are good riders?"

Olcán slapped his forehead and shook his head at the question's simplicity. "Mine are all shield-wall veterans, and there are none better. To them, fighting from a horse is a nightmare."

Ciar stroked his beard. Danu noticed it was a habit he had when thinking or calculating. "By my reckoning, fifty among my warriors would be considered decent riders. A similar number have potential if given training." He nodded to Brighid. "I saw how effective your riders were against the Connachta and began to build a modest force."

Brighid's face lit up, but her enthusiasm was tempered when Ciar continued. "However, we are less than halfway through the winter. Much worse weather, storms, and snowfalls are likely before us. Families with young children and those about to cross the veil travel with us. They will need shelter to survive the season's weather."

"The winter is my domain. I have some 'tricks' to soften its impact," said Draighean, adding ominously, "But only for us." Ciar and Olcán looked at each other, beginning to understand the advantage of having a Sídhe on their side.

"Thank you, my lady," said Ciar. "In which case, why can't we do both?" He looked at Brighid. "In this, I bow to your expertise and experience. How many horses do you need? How many warriors? Can you steal them without getting caught or losing warriors? How long would a raid take?"

Inside, Brighid was effervescent and wildly optimistic, yet she spoke in measured tones. "The main herds of Curraghatoor are corralled deep in the woods north of the stronghold. Horses are hardy; the forest shelters them from harsh weather without erecting substantial buildings. They are likely in open corrals, guarded by a handful of riders."

Brighid dipped her head to Danu. "I would prefer not to kill any of Fainche's riders. We may need Curraghatoor's cavalry and shield-warriors in the future." Brighid looked at Ciar. "If you agree, I will take your fifty best riders, and we will 'free' one hundred mounts. Curraghatoor is only a short tramp from here. One sunset should be enough time to accomplish our task."

Ciar nodded and then looked at Danu. "If you agree, Brighid should immediately make for Curraghatoor with my..." He looked at Danu and smiled an apology. "...sorry, *our* warriors. In the meantime, we should organise the remaining shield-warriors and their families and start the trek to Niúig. The forest will allow us to remain undetected until close to the An Bhearú River and Niúig." Ciar shrugged. "After that, the Goddess will favour us or not."

A sudden change in Ciar's mien worried Danu, and she wondered what had prompted his look of distaste. "Unfortunately, there will be those among us who only think of themselves and do not share our goals. Men and women, even those close to us, can hide their true desires and loyalties.

"Some may wish to negotiate terms with the Mhór Midhe or ingratiate themselves with Ráth Na Conall. Thus, eliminating or capturing Brighid and you would be to their advantage. Olcán and I will do all we can, but we cannot fully protect you from danger."

"We have lived a life of peril since we were adolescents," said Danu.

A cleared throat drew everyone's attention to Tisiphone, for she had been quiet during the discussions. A smile as sweet as honey graced her lips, but her words sent shivers along the others' spines. "You may be unable to stop them, but I can... and will."

Tisiphone had made her choice, but her brow furrowed. "However, maintaining my deception with those in Ráth Na Conall may be impossible. Having one who can get inside their defences may be useful—if only to kill. The choice is yours."

Lost in their thoughts, the group fell silent. Ciar looked at Danu and smiled. "Perhaps, rather than bore everyone, you and I should discuss the details of our attack on Niúig separately."

"Now, who needs a roundhouse?" asked Tisiphone. Brighid giggled like an adolescent, and Danu scowled. Yet Brighid's feirdhris knew that Danu's pulse raced and her heart beat faster when she looked at Ciar.

***

Fainche's favourite horse was soon to give birth. Thus, she kissed Onchú and their daughters goodbye and told them she would return before dawn. Onchú offered extra guards because wolves were always prowling for food, and there were always horse thieves. But Fainche shook her head and said, "I will be fine. Who's about on a midwinter's night?"

As Curraghatoor's gates closed behind her, Fainche strode down a path she knew intimately to the forest and her mare. It was a cloudless night, and her torch fluttered in the light breeze. She sensed nervousness in the herd as she passed the corrals on either side of the path to the birthing stables.

"Wolves," she muttered, chastising herself for not taking Onchú's offer. That she had not seen or passed any guards made Fainche frown. "They'd better not be warming their arses near a fire or their cocks in a whore," she growled and vowed to speak with their ceannairí céad on the next sunrise.

A whinny made her smile. Fainche recognised her horse's voice, even from a distance. On a crisp night, sound travelled long distances and was crystal clear. She sighed in relief as the mare's call held no hint of fear or anxiety. Fainche laughed. Of the two, she was likely the most nervous. The foal was a gift for a precious person—the baby she carried. She loved Onchú's four daughters, but this child would be theirs.

A fire slumbered in a stone firepit at the far end of the birthing stable. Fainche immediately walked across the shelter; a few pokes with an iron rod and several logs encouraged dormant embers to flames. Warmth and light banished the cold and darkness. Yet the light also threw a strange shadow. Fainche's hand went to the blade hanging from her belt, but two arms grabbed her from behind and held her while she was disarmed.

"Release her. She's an old friend," said Brighid, emerging from the shadows. "It has been a long time, Fainche. I'm glad to see you looking healthy. If it's worth anything, you may tell Onchú I approve of his choice of partner." She looked at Fainche's belly and smiled wistfully.

"Congratulations on your future arrival. I presume it's Onchú's."

Panic and dread filled Fainche's mind. Her hand went immediately to her stomach, and fear filled her face. "You! You're dead," said Fainche. She feverishly looked for a weapon or a path to escape. "Touch my baby, and all Curraghatoor will hunt you down, and I will personally see you staked."

"The Hag, Fainche. Do you think so little of me? What did I ever do to you?" Brighid appeared genuinely hurt, which surprised Fainche. "Why would I harm your babies—both of them? By the way, you may be in for a long night with the foal. She's not lying perfectly in her mother's womb."

"Why are you here, Brighid? The dead and the banished usually keep low profiles."

Brighid chuckled and moved into the light. Fainche saw the obsidian eyes and the tongues of fire reflected in them. She blinked several times to assure herself that she saw correctly. The curling symbols on Brighid's face were in constant motion in the flames of the fire.

"No," gasped Fainche. "It can't be."

Arms spread wide, Brighid grinned. "Yes, the evil twins are back together… and so is the Sídhe, Draighean." Brighid exhaled. "As much as I would like to stay and talk about old times, I'm on a tight schedule. I am 'borrowing' one hundred horses. Please tell Onchú I'll pay him for the stock later." Brighid turned and began to walk away but stopped after a few paces. "If I were you, I would get much better guards."

"Shite!" swore Fainche. *The bitseach knows I can't leave my horse.*

Outside the stable, a loud laugh rang out. Then, in a more menacing tone, Brighid added, "I saved Onchú's former partner and his daughters from being raped to death. He is in my debt. Please advise him to reconsider the company he's been keeping and whose side he is on."

* * *

Onchú was livid and was barely restrained by Fainche and his daughters from executing the guards. They had been found freezing and tied to one of the corral's fences. Apart from bruises and deep embarrassment, they were unharmed.

"Are you sure it was Brighid? Lonán is certain she's dead. Although, without a body, Aodán and Barra are less convinced."

Fainche's cheeks flushed, but not because of the roaring fire. "Of course, it was Brighid. I'm pregnant, not delusional." The giggling of Onchú's daughters did little to improve Fainche's or their father's temper. Onchú strode back and forward, muttering threats and curses.

"You say Brighid has her powers back? Maybe it was the fluttering light in the stable." Again, Fainche glared at Onchú for what his words implied. "As for the rest, she was probably bluffing."

Fainche shook her head. "I don't think so. What will you do?"

"We should inform Ráth Na Conall," said Onchú. "We're supposed to be allies and of one accord."

"What version will you tell them?" snapped Fainche. "What I saw and heard or the hallucinating, pregnant hand-fast partner version?" The bite in Fainche's voice made Onchú wince.

"For the moment, we will do nothing and say nothing. Hopefully, Brighid stole the horses because she and Danu needed gold to flee from Ériu. They have friends in Northern Albu. Perhaps we'll never see them again." Fainche's raised eyebrow told him she did not believe Onchú's rationale. From the constant hand wringing and tugging of his beard, neither did Onchú.

CHAPTER 19

Niúig

In summer or autumn, the journey from Carn Tigherna to Niúig would be a pleasant sunset march through lush meadows, fields of corn, and woodlands of oak, ash, and alder… pine, too. Under the forest's protective canopy in the winter, the snow was not as deep, and the cold winds were not as biting.

Still, the elderly, the young, and mothers with babies in their bellies could not cover the ground as quickly as warriors. Hence, it was four sunsets before Danu's and Brighid's fledgling army and their families set camp within sight of the ancient bridge that traversed the An Bhearú River.

"Will it hold us?" asked Danu. Her tone suggested she needed convincing. A small group stood on a hill overlooking the river. All clutched heavy cloaks, and their teeth chattered uncontrollably in a brisk wind. Close by, Draighean had foregone her cover and could have been standing on a beach in the Great Sea.

"My scouts report the bridge is old, but the foundation piles appear strong. It should be fine for our purpose," said Brighid. "If not, we will have a long, freezing swim. The river is five hundred paces wide, too deep for walking, and we have no boats." She pointed to the fort. "The challenge is the ringfort's long sightlines. They will see us as soon as we cross the river, and the landscape is largely *droimnín*, providing little cover."

"From what you tell me of their ballistae, that will make us the perfect target," said Ciar. "Does the weapon have weaknesses?"

"A target, bunched together and moving in a straight line, is the worst option. The bolts would plough the warriors into the ground. The elevation of the hillfort is not high, so the machines can be depressed to strike, even close to the hillfort's wall," said Danu.

"That's joyful to hear," said Brighid.

Danu looked strangely at Brighid. The younger twin, although not by much, returned the stare warily. "What?"

"What if the target was moving fast and weaving like a ship tacking in a strong wind? Large ballistae are not easily moved, although there is the possibility that the Roman in command may have faced this tactic."

"Let me consider that, but what would provide a diversion for the shield-warriors? They will be very exposed, and even running, will be much slower than my riders," said Brighid.

"The stronghold is in a bay, is it not?" The question posed by Draighean drew quizzical looks.

"Is there a point to the question, or are you simply admiring the view?"

"Sarcasm can be quite wearing, Brighid. I was hoping you might have a grasp on weather phenomena caused by the cold winter and the sea."

"Please, Draighean, we're freezing," said Danu, pulling her wolf-fur-lined cloak closer.

"You do not need to be cold," said Draighean peevishly before continuing her train of thought. "Fog or, more precisely, a sea mist might be a suitable veil if its appearance is timely."

"Can I kiss her, Danu?" asked Brighid.

The group laughed, apart from the Sídhe, who looked nonplussed. "I am only becoming familiar with men, Brighid. Females, I have not considered... yet." Danu looked at Draighean and wondered if she was serious. The glimmer of a smile gave her the answer.

***

Dawn broke as three walked across the bridge. A short distance away was a snow-covered mound, which the trio climbed. Draighean dropped her cloak; bathed in the rising sun's light, she stood pastel pink. She was, of course, naked, which was a problem for Brighid and Danu. It had been ten summers since they stood similarly on Ráth Na Conall's walls.

"You know what to do."

"It's fine for you. You never need clothes in any weather, but why us, in these conditions? We'll freeze," whined Brighid.

"Which are you questioning? My work, your feirdhriseacha, or your sigils?"

Draighean's rebuke brought colour to Danu's and Brighid's cheeks. Reluctantly, their cloaks joined Draighean's on the snow, and they stood naked on the hill. Immediately, their bodies quivered and shook, and their teeth chattered. "I told you!" was on the tip of Brighid's tongue when the sun's fingers touched her curling symbols, and warmth flowed through them. She looked at Danu and muttered, "How is the bitseach always right?"

"I will lead, and you will follow. When my song changes, do not alter yours. Are you ready?" The twins nodded, and all three lifted their hands to the sun in a clear blue sky.

The *Songs of the Sídhe and the Rígana* began low but soon climbed to unnatural heights. It seemed a pleasant song to those in the forests and fortress of Niúig, warming the hearts, minds, and bodies of all it touched. As the trio's ululations rose, the wolves in the forest joined, and the song became a weapon.

For those in Niúig, it was a hallucination that suddenly changed. Despair and dread flooded the minds of the garrison. Icy fingers wrapped around their hearts and squeezed, but this was not a lover's embrace. On the ramparts, Decimus Augustus swore and shouted for his men to stuff wool in their ears and ready the ballistae. Beside him, a young man pissed his triubhas, but he was the first of many. Only many hours of training and muscle memory prevented the machines' teams from abandoning their posts.

"Prepare for an attack!" bellowed Decimus. He cursed Lonán Ó Neill for his lack of foresight and called on Apollo and Mars for help.

In the skies above, a great eagle soared. "Your effete gods have no power in my lands," mocked the Goddess. To Decimus, her voice sounded like a high-pitched whistle.

The mood of the chanting from the trio on the hill changed, and Decimus heard an authoritative voice in his mind. *Lay down your arms and surrender, Roman.*

He shouted, "No!" although to what creature he did not know. "Load the ballistae!" he roared, waiting for his enemy's next move. "Prepare to fire!"

In the distance, Decimus saw a large warband cross the bridge and ride towards the fort. He laughed. This he could fight. The ballistae's bolts would end their day in a slush of blood and bone. A shout behind him made him turn around, and for a moment, he thought his eyes betrayed him.

A dense white mist formed in the bay and moved steadily and purposefully towards the hillfort. When its tendrils touched the walls of Niúig, frost covered them like moss on a stone. Yet the fog did not stop to envelop the hillfort; instead, the phenomenon continued to move along the coastline until it reached the river crossing.

Another shout, and he faced north again. Joined by one of the three on the hill, the large warband divided into three widely spaced groups of riders. Each group of riders zigzagged towards the ráth. Decimus cursed yet admired the mind behind the tactic. Assured his walls were strong enough to repel mounted besiegers, Decimus smiled at first. Then he frowned. *What am I missing?*

A flicker of movement caught Decimus' eye. He glimpsed another of those on the hill dash into the mist and disappear. "Shite! Shields to the walls."

***

Standing on the walkway of Curraghatoor's wooden stockade, Onchú turned when he heard Fainche's footfall. His expression was grim. "I apologise. I was wrong… very wrong." The constant and unnerving howling of wolves awakened the ráth. Yet above that, the unmistakable voices of Brighid, Danu, and Draighean rang out clear and full of power.

"We have a choice to make, my love…" said Fainche, "…and it is not an easy one, especially for an honourable man. Do we stand with our new allies in Ráth Na Conall or plead for forgiveness from our former rígana?" Onchú's shoulders slumped, and, to Fainche, he suddenly looked every one of his fifty-four summers.

"What honour? I abandoned them. This is my fault."

"How can that be true?"

"I dislike Lonán, but he was right when he accused me of being a poor advisor to Danu and Brighid. Had I stood firm, perhaps this situation may have been avoided. Instead of imminent war, a united people would celebrate ten summers of peace at Bealtaine. The Mhór Midhe would fear us, not see us as divided and easy pickings."

Onchú looked at Fainche and took her hand. "I feel very old, my love. Too old to deserve your affection."

Deep blue eyes flashed. "Do not ever say that again," said Fainche in a tone harsher than she had meant. In a softer voice, she asked, "What does your heart say?"

"My mind says that we're in deep shite, no matter what I decide. Mórrígan, Brighid, Danu—mother and daughters—and even the Sídhe have one thing in common. They are vengeful, pitiless bitseacha." Onchú scratched the whiskers on his chin. His lips pursed. "My heart says I would not have this kingdom were it not for Brighid and Danu, nor would I have my daughters. Brighid did not harm you when she had the opportunity."

As he took Fainche in his arms, the strength in Onchú's arms belied his age. "Our daughters will be starving. They're worse than ravenous wolves after a night's sleep. After we eat, we shall talk more."

"Procrastination?"

"Of course."

＊

"Well, that's a clear message," said Barra.

At sunrise, a rider could break his fast in Ráth Na Conall and, at a canter, arrive in Niúig to have a beer and eat with friends at meán lae. Sound travels much quicker. As with Curraghatoor, the ululations of Brighid, Danu, and Draighean, supported by a chorus of wolves in Na Comaraigh's forests, roused the garrison. Most stood open-mouthed on the stronghold's walls.

However, Barra did not refer to the wailing, which anyone with a brain knew originated in the east and most likely from Niúig. Instead, he pointed to the ring of flowering blackthorn bushes that had sprung up around the hillfort and the heavy snowfall. He looked at a disturbed Aodán.

"Wasn't the Sídhe who advised Brighid and Danu called Draighean—blackthorn? The game has changed, brother, and not in our favour. We are family, but instead of supporting Brighid against Calman and reasoning with Danu, we left one to die and exiled the other. How will we explain that to our ma and da?" Barra ground his teeth. "Now we face a powerful and united trinity."

Aodán shook his head wearily. "As kings, we listened to bad counsel and made poor choices. We must do better." Aodán turned to face a shaken Lonán. "Please explain why we are about to lose a recently up-graded stronghold, its armoury and ballistae… and a fleet of triremes?"

"It is a temporary setback. All campaigns suffer obstacles. This is real life, not a planning meeting." Regaining composure, Lonán said, "They had surprise on their side. When the winter is over, we will take back Niúig."

"And you don't think our sisters have anticipated that?" snapped Aodán. At Lonán's sceptical look, he said, "Yes, 'sisters'. I know Brighid's

128

voice. She is not dead, and she and Danu have recovered their powers."

Barra glared at Lonán. "And, unlike us, they appear quite happy to fight in the winter. How strong are they? Obviously, they are not so foolish as to attack Niúig with a handful of warriors, even with a Sídhe at their side."

Aodán asked, "Where are Tisiphone and her companion? We may need their talents."

"Who knows?" growled Lonán and left the walkway. His injury removed his ability to show his anger, making him furious.

***

"I think we may have achieved one of our parents' goals," said Aodán.

"Yes, but I do not think they meant for us to be killed by them… at least, I hope not," said Barra.

"Double the guard on Órlaith and Tanaí," said Aodán, watching Lonán retreat. "The last thing we need is any harm to come to them."

***

The snowstorm began at dawn and materialised out of nothing. It was now meán lae, and the earthworks were rapidly disappearing. The blizzard that assaulted Caher Conri reduced vision to twenty paces. Deep snowdrifts piled up against any structure and threatened to overflow the walls.

Calman stood on one of the few unbroken stretches of the stone wall and looked towards the defensive berm. He shivered, but not because of the bone-chilling cold. He had heard rumours of a great winter storm that buried the Connachta for several seasons. Previously, he had considered such reports as grossly exaggerated. Now, Calman was not so confident.

"It's a freak weather pattern," he muttered. "It can't last." *But what if it does?*

CHAPTER 20

Niúig

Unlike Brighid's riders, who screamed like the mná sídhe and continually changed direction, Danu's warriors jogged silently towards Niúig. Showing great discipline, they kept to the narrow strip of coastline concealed by Draighean's hovering white mist. The snow on the ground muffled their steps such that the waves lapping the riverbanks and shale beaches made more noise.

Followed by Ciar and Olcán, Danu led the warriors because only she could sense how close they were to the headland fort. The cracks of the ballistae made her wince. She prayed for Brighid's safety and that the Goddess had accepted their early-morning sacrifices. That she felt a warm embrace from the Goddess and not the coldness of recent summers gladdened her.

***

Decimus shouted continuously at his ballistae teams as he strode along the walkway. Paradoxically, in the freezing temperatures, men and women sweated profusely. The bolt-throwers were formidable but not made for striking a widely spaced, rapidly moving target. Thus, the fruits of their labour were miserly, and most riders escaped his missiles.

Soon, they would be close to the walls and beyond the ability of his ballistae to depress further. *What is their plan?* Frustrated at the lack of an answer, he bellowed, "Shields to the northern wall. Prepare to use javelins." Decimus had fifty shield-warriors under his command, and he heaved a sigh of relief at the stamp of feet and the rattle of shields and weapons.

Niúig's ráth was circular and not a massive stronghold like Ráth Na Conall. The original wall had been erected as a double stockade of pine and oak. Twenty summers ago, the fence had been faced with stone, yet that had fallen into disrepair until Lonán supervised its renovation. *Stupid bastard! Why strengthen the fort and then abandon it?* Decimus wondered if the enemy knew the fort's strength. He remonstrated with himself. *Of course, they do. Why else would they attack?*

Regardless of whether the ráth's shape gave him an advantage, Decimus knew he needed many more defenders to fully man the parapet and repel the besiegers. Forming a shield-wall was impossible. He did not have the numbers. The Roman scratched a head of cropped hair that looked like the bristles of a horse brush. He had no idea of the size of the force cloaked by the mist. Did he face tens or hundreds of warriors?

Decimus growled in frustration. He had barely enough cauldrons to feed his garrison, let alone use them to pour oil, water, and embers on any besiegers. He observed a handful of riders separate from the main force and wondered why. He watched them dismount, heard stone strike against stone, and saw wisps of smoke. Soon, sparks became flames, and Decimus' frustration boiled over. He bellowed at the ballistae teams to aim at the fires, yet the riders predicted his actions and spread out.

The hooves of Brighid's riders crunched through the crust of unspoilt ice as they galloped along the foot of Ráth Na Niúig's walls. Decimus roared at his warriors to use their javelins. Yet, with his lack of numbers, hitting a target that moved so quickly was in the hands of Serendipity. Again, he wondered what his foe's strategy was. Why did they risk the riders? The answer came on the heels of his question when he heard the crack of pottery smashing against stone and wood.

The smell of pine and brimstone wafted into frozen nostrils as the vessels broke against the ballistae, the walls, and the northern gates. "The bastards." Helpless, Decimus watched flaming arrows arch in the sky and fall on the hillfort. It was not long before the gates and some ballistae were smouldering. The wood was wet, and thus, dense white smoke drifted along the walls. Bouts of coughing spread as lungs inhaled soot and eyes streamed and stung.

A female warrior alongside Decimus screamed as a pottery jar broke near her, splashing her triubhas. A flaming arrow truck a nearby ballista, and the fire quickly followed the flowing pitch. Decimus lifted her and threw her, shrieking curses, into the courtyard. "Better broken bones than burned," he growled.

"Twenty warriors form a shield-wall at the gates. The rest remain alert," shouted Decimus.

✳✳✳

The pottery shattering against the ráth's walls made Danu smile and whisper, "Nice tactics, Brighid." It was the sign Danu had waited for. She shouted, "*Ionsaí*—attack!" and sprinted for the walls. Behind her, Ciar, Olcán, and over four hundred warriors broke from the mist's cover and charged towards the ramparts. Simultaneously, Brighid's riders leapt from their horses and fought for purchase on the stone rampart. Curses at broken nails and skinned knuckles and knees ascended.

Danu knew Decimus' defenders on Ráth Na Niúig's walls were thinly spread. Yet walls were walls, and even a small force could hold a larger one at bay. An extended siege was out of the question. There were families in the forests to the north shivering in the cold. Risks had to be taken. Danu's strategy relied on stretching Decimus' warriors beyond their breaking point.

The rígana's army split into five bands and attacked the walls at multiple points. On the hill to the north, Draighean intensified her chanting to foment confusion and hopelessness in the defenders' minds. As Danu reached the apex of the defences, she grasped the inner stakes and scrambled over the stockade.

She smiled. The walkway was covered in snow and ice, yet her bare feet felt as if they stood on the warm sands of the Great Sea. Danu howled and was instantly greeted by Brighid's ululations above the gateway. The defenders on the ramparts stared in disbelief and horror at the naked rígana. Each grasped the blackthorn shafts of a pair of double-bladed half axes.

The besieged looked into obsidian eyes gleaming in the morning light and saw the dark, curling sigils flow with power. Niúig's garrison's hesitation was brief but sufficient for the remainder of Danu's shield-warriors and Brighid's riders to surmount the walls.

***

Fifty opposed five hundred as Danu and Brighid faced Decimus. "We do not wish to kill you or slaughter the garrison. However, if you force us, we will. Surrender. You have been outfoxed and are well-outnumbered. The injuries to both sides are mostly bruises and broken bones. What sense is there in brave men and women spilling their blood for a hopeless cause? Live and fight another day, either with us or against us."

Decimus glared at Danu. His pride had suffered most of all, yet that was a poor reason to throw away the lives of those he led. He shrugged with resignation and bowed. "Ráth Na Niúig is yours. Congratulations on your victory." He turned to face his warriors and bellowed, "Lay down your arms. The rígana guarantee the safety of you and your families."

He stared at Danu. "That *is* your promise, isn't it?"

"It is. However, I would caution against the impulse to speak on behalf of me or my sister in the future," replied Danu. Decimus dipped his head and looked at his sword before lifting it. The act was met by several spearheads pricking his back. He chuckled and, in a slow movement, offered the blade hilt first to Danu.

"Keep it. Your head would lie at my feet if I thought you dishonourable."

"I am hurt, sister. He should have surrendered to me since I was the first to enter the fort." Danu rolled her eyes in mock irritation.

"You can accept the surrender of Ráth Na Conall, Brighid. Perhaps that will make us even?"

Brighid laughed aloud. "You know I will keep you to that promise."

"And I will be delighted to honour it. However, our sisterly craic embarrasses Decimus." Danu looked at Decimus and asked, "Are there other ceannairí céad or civic leaders in the fort?"

"No," said Decimus.

"You must be pissed off at being abandoned by Lonán and my brothers." Spying Ciar and Olcán hovering nearby, Danu called out, "Disarm the ráth's garrison and sequester them in a secure chamber. Also, please send a detachment of shield-warriors to ensure the masters of the ships know the fleet is under new management."

Danu turned to Brighid. "Please send a few riders to our camp and give Nuadha the news. Apologise and prevail on him and the people to spend one more night in the woods until we have assessed our capacity and accommodation. I think we will need to build additional living quarters." Danu put a hand on Brighid's shoulder as she turned away. "Your riders did exceptionally well. Did you lose any?"

"We lost three, and a handful are injured but will recover. We should take care of the dead's families," answered Brighid before adding, "We're too small to lose any riders, Danu. We need to train the other fifty that Ciar mentioned." Brighid's eyes glinted. "And we should steal more horses." Danu chuckled and turned to Ciar and Olcán.

"Decimus will give us a tour of the ráth after completing the immediate tasks. Then we shall meet in the Great Hall to eat and plan our next steps."

***

Fainche warmed her hands over the blazing fire as she paced the wooden floorboards of the chamber. Impatient and anxiously twisting her fingers, she awaited Onchú's return from Cnoc Duíginn. In his absence, the news she received from Niúig stunned her. Fainche put another brand on a fire that rapidly consumed all in its path… it was an apt metaphor for the rígana.

The time for equivocation was over as a messenger from Ráth Na Conall waited in another room. She turned as the door opened and ran to hug Onchú. "What news from Sláine and Daráine?"

"They are nervous at the return of the rígana. Sláine had hoped Danu and Brighid would lick their wounds and disappear. I don't think Daráine considered that likely." Onchú tugged on his whiskers. "Oddly, Daráine seemed less troubled by the prospect of the rígana's return. I spoke with Sláine alone before I left, and he indicated that Barra Mac Conall had taken to Daráine. More than that, the admiration was reciprocated."

Onchú lifted a cup of wine from a table, swirled the green liquid, and chuckled. "This is a season of turbulent waters, Fainche. What news have you, apart from the somewhat fractious envoy in the outer chamber?"

"Ráth Na Niúig fell to the twins, apparently without much bloodshed. Brighid and Danu have recruited an army of five hundred, including fifty riders. The Goddess smiles upon them, and the Sídhe, Draighean, is with them. She sent explicit messages to Caher Conrí and Ráth Na Conall."

Fainche allowed herself a thin smile. "The irony is the rígana have a stronghold, ballistae, and a fleet of ships, all courtesy of their brothers, plus whatever weapons and armour were stored in the fort. I would not be surprised if Niúig's garrison changed loyalties. What's next?"

"Danu and Brighid might attack Ráth Na Conall from the sea."

"No. I meant what's next for Curraghatoor, and you know it," said Fainche irritably.

"Well, we should expect to lose more horses. Brighid will not resist another raid."

"So, we increase the guards," said Fainche. Onchú shook his head.

"No, that would be a senseless loss of life. Cut out one hundred horses from the herd. Ensure they are the best stock. Brighid will know if they're not and steal others. Corral them separately to make it obvious."

"Lonán Ó Neill will not be pleased."

"The brothers are the ríthe, not Lonán."

"What will be our position with Danu and Brighid?" asked Fainche.

"Good neighbours," said Onchú. "We will visit Ráth Na Niúig with gifts for their new home. You and I will deliver the horses." Fainche rolled her eyes.

"You play a dangerous game, Onchú. The messenger from Ráth Na Conall?"

Onchú chuckled. "We will engage in diplomacy. He will lie to me, and I will lie to him." The Rí of Curraghatoor frowned. "The wind has changed, Fainche, and we may be swept aside. My concern is how the rígana will greet us. Likely, and with good cause, they think I betrayed them."

"They need us." At Onchú's raised eyebrow, Fainche said, "Curraghatoor has the largest number of riders and horses. Brighid will understand that."

CHAPTER 21

Niúig

The blade caressing her throat was colder than usual, and she sensed several layers of skin part under its keen edge, yet without drawing blood. The message was clear: "Your life is mine to take." Aoife had not seen or heard her assailant. The wind and the gentle lapping of the river made more noise. Yet as she stood motionless, Aoife could feel hot breath on her ear.

"I don't think we have met. I am Tisiphone."

"Lonán's assassin."

The knife pressed harder, and Aoife tried not to flinch. She was unsuccessful, and a thin trail of blood trickled down. "I belong to no one." The voice held an edge sharper than the blade. "My apologies. I had not intended to cut you. It will heal quickly and without scarring." Aoife wondered how a killer could have such a pleasant, seductive tone.

"May I know your name?"

"I am Aoife Ni Cináed."

"Aoife?"

Tisiphone removed the blade from Aoife's throat, grasped her shoulders, and spun her around. They stood face-to-face. Since both were taller than average, their gazes met. Observing an almost imperceptible tensing of Aoife's muscles, Tisiphone shook her head.

"You would be dead before the tips of your fingers touched any of your impressive array of weapons. And that would be a pity." Tisiphone's demeanour looked as if she were trying to solve a puzzle. "Aoife… are you Báine's friend? The one Brighid has never ceased grieving for and likely never will." The look of anger in Aoife's eyes made Tisiphone grip her blade tighter and adjust her stance. *Perhaps I might have to kill her.*

"The bitseach killed Báine. She may not have been the one who wielded the weapon, but she murdered my friend… my sister." The young woman's voice was thick with emotion, and Tisiphone sensed and felt compassion for Aoife's deep pain. She shook her head.

"You left before the battle. Therefore, you cannot know what happened. Can you?"

Aoife's eyes widened but remained filled with promised retribution. Still, Tisiphone also observed something else in her eyes. Guilt. "Before the riders' final charge, Báine knocked Brighid from her horse, bound her, and took her place." Tisiphone looked into Aoife's eyes and saw shock. That this was accompanied by Aoife rubbing the wolf sigil above her eyebrow, Tisiphone thought curious.

"Báine sacrificed herself for Brighid… for *her* love. Will you kill the one your 'sister' gave her life to save? If you truly desire to punish Brighid, let her live. Brighid would welcome your blade because she would join her beloved in your Mag Mell."

"Bitseach!"

"I've been called much worse," said Tisiphone. "Brighid and Danu speak of you as a great warrior. That may be so, but you are a pathetic spy. Go. If you return, enter by the front gate, or I will kill you."

∗∗∗

The meeting in Ráth Na Conall was a sober affair, although Flann seemed to enjoy the discomfort of the fort's hierarchy more than he should. Hands clasped behind her back, Aoife stood ready to address those seated. She had been accepted back into the bosom of the garrison. Although probably because they lacked an experienced chariot commander.

Barra, who was well-skilled in horses and chariots, knew Aoife was, undoubtedly, the best charioteer in the ráth. Lonán looked at her with suspicion and distrust. That said, recently, he viewed most people similarly. Aoife had served Brighid for five summers and, in Lonán's opinion, could never be trusted. Aodán reserved judgement, if not disinterest.

Aoife presented her report. "Brighid and Danu took Ráth Na Niúig largely using tactics of deception and with the support of the Sídhe, Draighean. Hardly any blood was spilt on either side." Aoife cleared her throat. "The rígana's powers have returned; it also appears the Aes Sídhe and the Goddess favour them."

"Stay with the facts," snapped Lonán.

"They are the facts," retorted Aoife. "*You* were not there to hear and feel the songs of the Sídhe and the queens. I was. *You* were not there to see a mist rise from the sea to cloak the rígana's warriors from the defenders. *You* did not see Brighid's riders confuse the ballistae teams with her tactics."

"I apologise for Lonán. He is unaccustomed to defeat," said Aodán. His voice was quiet, but the iron it held was as good as a punch to the gut. Lonán's chair scraped on the floor. "Sit down," snapped Aodán. "You will listen and make constructive comments. You will leave this chamber only when Barra or I permit you. Is that understood?" Aodán smiled at Aoife. "Please continue."

"Including Niúig's garrison…"

This time, it was Barra who turned his anger on Lonán. "We have lost ballistae, weapons, ships, and seasoned warriors. Does your incompetence hold any more surprises for us?" He turned to Aoife. "My apologies; please continue."

"Brighid and Danu have a force of five hundred shield-warriors, plus fifty horse warriors. More riders are being trained." The latter part of her statement seemed to cause Aoife concern, and she hesitated briefly before continuing. "On the morning following the ringfort's capture, triple their number, consisting of families, trades, and artisans, walked from the forest to the fort. I think they are the refugees who fled

Calman. More warriors trickle in each sunset."

"There's not enough space in the ráth to accommodate that number, even with our improvements," said Aodán.

Aoife dipped her head. "Agreed. However, the clamour of hammering and sawing is evidence of a high level of building activity. Mostly, this is south of the stronghold, in the previously abandoned settlement of Niúig." Again, Aoife's words caught in her throat as childhood memories surfaced. She had left Niúig when she was seven summers old.

"We should attack now and slaughter them while they are disorganised. It will serve as a lesson to others of the consequences of rebellion and following banished queens," said Lonán.

"You are a brave man, Lonán," said Barra. "I'm not sure I would be so eager to face down a Sídhe *and* my sisters with restored powers."

Lonán scowled and was about to retort when Aoife interrupted. "How would you propose to attack Ráth Na Niúig? The fort sits on the eastern bank of the An Bhearú River, which is over a thousand paces wide at the stronghold's location. Upstream, the water is five hundred paces from bank to bank before it reaches the old bridge. A score of shield-warriors could hold the bridge against you."

Aoife held Lonán's angry gaze without flinching. "They command your fleet of triremes, which patrol the bay and river. Indeed, they may consider an early attack on Ráth Na Conall from the coast. I would." Aoife's words stunned her audience.

"We have become the besieged," said Barra, slumping back in his seat.

"If Danu asks Ráthgeal for an army, we may become the dead. Or, worse, given a slap on the arse and sent home with our tails between our legs," said Aodán. "I had hoped our sisters' reunion would be less humiliating for us, Barra." He looked at Lonán. "Well, what is your strategy?"

"We have the boy and girl," snarled Lonán.

"How often must I remind you that Órlaith and Tanaí are our blood, not hostages? Make that proposal again, and I'll have your head mounted on a spear and displayed on the walls," barked Aodán. "Do your job. Devise a plan for reconciliation which does not require children to rescue you. *Now*, you may leave us." As Lonán stood, Aoife coughed.

"You have something to add?" queried Aodán, looking intensely at Aoife. His mien spoke of admiration and something else. When Aoife held his gaze, Aodán blushed... and so did Aoife.

"This is becoming interesting," murmured Barra.

Aoife glared at Lonán before speaking. "One more fact, which you might find curious. All the banners and flags of Clann Uí Flaithimh and Conall have been removed. In their place flies a new emblem—*Na Feirdhriseacha*. It seems being banished was of little consequence to the rígana." Aoife smiled and added, "Perhaps they are not so different from Conall and Mórrígan."

"The Hag's tits, Aodán. Our ma and da started with a small band of friends fighting for survival on this hill, and look at them now. Brighid and Danu have many times that and a stronghold."

Another cough and again Aoife became the focus of attention. Aodán chuckled. "You know how to keep your audience in suspense, Aoife. Perhaps politics is your future. Please continue."

Aoife looked at Lonán. "While surveying Ráth Na Niúig, I met a 'friend' of yours..." Aoife rubbed her throat where Tisiphone's blade had cut her. "Yet she was not amused to be known as that and almost severed my neck. Her name is Tisiphone, and, from her accent and skin colour, she is not from Ériu."

"Shite!" gasped Barra and Aodán.

"The traitorous bitseach!" growled Lonán.

"I would not call her that within her hearing range. While I do not know the lady, she gives the impression of not taking insults lightly," said Aoife.

"Thank you, Aoife. If you have no further news, you may go, but I may wish to speak with you again," said Aodán.

"I would have no problem with that," responded Aoife and, with a bow, exited the chamber. In her ears was the sound of Barra chuckling.

"So, who do we think Tisiphone works for?" asked Aodán. "It's certainly no one in this room."

* * *

"If we're not fighting or training, we're having meetings," grumbled Brighid, who considered the latter the worst option. "Why can't you go without me?"

"Because, sister, when we began to do that in Ráth Na Conall, I became overbearing, you became embittered, and we lost our thrones," said Danu. "I need and want you beside me. I am too measured, and you are too impulsive. I need you beside me… as equals.

"We don't have anyone to fight now, and you know you also get bored with constantly training. We must figure out what to do next, and the Chomhairle can help us." A grunt was Brighid's answer as her foot touched the first wooden step of the Great Hall.

Ráth Na Niúig was a compact ringfort less than two hundred paces at its widest point. Its walls could, at a squeeze, fit a shield-wall of four hundred warriors and double that if they formed two ranks. Space was limited. The Great Hall, built of oak and pine, was the largest building and sat at its heart. Yet it only measured fifty paces along each of its sides.

Half of the hall's space was set apart for meeting chambers. The rest was divided between Danu, Brighid, Ciar, Draighean, and Tisiphone for their quarters. Nuadha and Rós chose to live in one of the newly refurbished roundhouses in old Niúig. Olcán purportedly lived with his men in the barracks attached to the Great Hall and the armoury. However, it was common knowledge that he spent much of his time in Tisiphone's bedchamber.

Some trades were considered essential for war: blacksmiths, fletchers, and leatherworkers. Thus, they had workshops within the fort. A few premises concentrated on cooking and preparing food. Still, most of that was in the homes of the old settlement and shared amongst the residents. Many artisans and tradespeople also resided in Niúig.

As Danu reached the top of the flight of steps, she paused, turned around, and smiled. It pleased her to hear the normal sounds and smells, yet it made her heart ache for Órlaith and Tanaí. "We'll get them back," said Brighid. At Danu's startled look, she lifted her hands in mock apology. "Did you forget we can see into each other's minds?"

"We need to reset the boundaries."

"Agreed. I do not need to hear your shameless thoughts when Ciar is within ten paces of you. I never knew you had such a vivid imagination, sister. Where did you learn of such perversions? I suppose it is true that the quiet ones are the worst." Danu stood red-faced and openmouthed as Brighid laughed aloud and entered the Great Hall.

I wish I could help soothe your grief and tears over losing Báine, sister.

***

Tisiphone laid a hand on Brighid's arm as they took their seats and whispered, "I met a friend of yours recently. She is an extraordinary young woman, although a terrible spy." Brighid's green eyes darkened but stopped before being completely black.

"You better not have harmed her, bitseach."

"Such loyalty to one whose eyes only speak of your death by her hands. Yet I wonder if the passion conceals a deeper need. You are the only link to one she loved as much as you." Brighid bowed her head, and tears splashed the table. When she lifted her head, she smiled.

"Thank you. Aoife will always have the first strike."

"She knows that. However, knowing you and having met her, I think that would be the worst of all solutions—for both of you."

"Is something the matter, Brighid?" asked Danu.

"No." Brighid sniffed and wiped her eyes with the back of her hand. "Tisiphone has informed me that an old friend of ours has been observing us from the far bank of the An Bhearú. We can confidently assume Ráth Na Conall is fully informed of our activities." Brighid looked at Tisiphone. "I think it's safe to say you will not be met with open arms by

Lonán or our brothers."

Tisiphone dipped her head. "I have my orders, and they do not change. Neither does it mean my usefulness to you is diminished."

"Will we ever learn of your true client or his instructions?" asked Danu.

"Who said it was a man?" replied Tisiphone and chuckled.

Draighean, who, as usual, preferred to stand, gave a great belly laugh. "I like her. She speaks like one of the Aes Sídhe."

"Back to business," said Danu. She looked at Decimus. "Have you or your men decided to stay or march for Ráth Na Conall and fight us on another sunset? From a practical perspective, we could use the additional space."

Chuckles rippled around the table but ceased when Decimus stood, bowed, and slapped his right hand against his polished bronze breastplate. "I am not a politician, but it strikes me that your mother and father desired to see their daughters reconciled. All other things can be resolved in battle or by negotiation." The Roman paused and smiled. "You have my oath to serve and die for you."

"The men and women who serve under you?" queried Danu.

"Given the demonstration of your unconventional tactics, they arrived at their decision much faster than I." Decimus laughed. "Plus, they are angry that they and their families were abandoned without a thought. They, too, will swear an oath to the rígana."

"That's a relief," said Ciar. "We need to prepare for an attack from Ráth Na Conall. Additionally, we need a battle plan to deal with Calman and an invasion by the Mhór Midhe."

"There will be no attack by your brothers," said Tisiphone. The looks of scepticism around the table required a response, and she added, "By now, Aoife will have reported our situation. That will include our main defence, the An Bhearú River, guarded by our fleet."

Tisiphone paused and looked pensive. "Lonán has not been himself since we landed in Ériu, but I cannot see him being so foolish as to attack us. Anyway, your brothers would not allow it."

"A stalemate then," said Danu. "We do not have the warriors to besiege and take Ráth Na Conall." Danu's voice cracked. "Or to rescue my children." Ciar's hand on Danu's forearm and a softly spoken "We will find a way" confirmed what gossip and rumour posited. "What of Caher Conri and the Mhór Midhe?" asked Danu. "We can't just sit and wait until the Mhór Midhe hammer drops."

"Caher Conri and the Mhór Midhe have their troubles," said Draighean. The enigmatic smile on the Sídhe's lips drew a scowl from Brighid.

"Are you going to inform us lesser beings?" asked Brighid.

"Different, not lesser, Brighid," chastised Draighean. "Caher Conri is buried under snow, the height of two average men, as is Cnoc Uisnigh and much of the domain of the Mhór Midhe. I doubt Messin's army will march before the festival of Bealtaine." She looked at Danu and Brighid. "You have time to negotiate alliances."

"What of Ráthgeal? The Mhór Midhe threaten Bran, even in his mountain stronghold. Can we 'borrow' Bran's warriors to take Ráth Na Conall?" asked Brighid.

Danu shook her head. "I would prefer not to ask. The price would be too high." Brighid felt the pain from Danu's rose and held her twin's hand.

"I am sorry. I will not bring the subject up again." Brighid looked around the table. "Any other suggestions?"

"I could remove Bran. Then, Ráthgeal's army would become ours or, more specifically, Tanaí's, with Danu ruling as his *Leasrí*—regent." The shocked silence was more due to the confident tone of Tisiphone than the proposition.

"She thinks like one of the Aes Sídhe." Draighean smiled at Tisiphone. "Are you sure your ancestors have no Gael blood?"

"She may be deadlier than our uncle, Beacán," whispered Brighid in Danu's ear. "Perhaps we should accept her proposal." Danu shook her head and coughed.

"Thank you, Tisiphone. We will bear that in mind." Still, Danu's eyes said, "We will talk of this later." To Brighid's disappointment, those gathered began discussing plans and inventories.

Shouts from outside and a loud banging on the door interrupted the discourse. Soon, a flush-faced guard entered. "Horses at the gates!"

"Shite! Who's attacking us now?" asked Brighid.

* * *

The biggest shock to Onchú as he crossed the doorway's threshold was seeing Nuadha. Long-buried memories of his torture in Uallachán's camp rose to haunt him. Nuadha was Uallachán's brother and, in Onchú's eyes, equally as guilty. Instinctively, his hand went to his sword.

"That would be a grave error, Onchú," said Danu, and her eyes reinforced her claim.

"You have strange companions, Danu," said Onchú as he placed his hands on the table. However, the glare of hate remained.

Danu dipped her head and pointed to vacant seats and a table with food and refreshments. "Please be seated. Eat and drink. Fainche must be tired from the journey." She looked at Fainche. "Congratulations on your impending arrival. I trust all has gone well so far." Fainche smiled nervously and dipped her head.

"It is good to see you, Onchú," said Danu, turning her attention to the rí. "Did you bring your daughters with you?" Onchú shook his head. "Perhaps next time." Danu looked deep into Onchú's eyes. "As to Nuadha, we banished have to stick together." Onchú winced at the bite in Danu's words.

"Nuadha gave Brighid and me refuge when she was near death. He could have turned us away, but unlike our 'friends', he did not." Onchú squirmed again. "Nuadha has reluctantly emerged from seclusion and, even more hesitantly, has become Niúig's Civic Leader."

Looking to change the subject, Onchú spotted Tisiphone, smiled, and said, "You change allegiances quickly." It was an attempt at humour but failed miserably.

"You also have changed loyalties and likely will again," said Tisiphone, "Why else are you here?" Onchú cringed, Fainche bristled, and Tisiphone fingered her blade.

"We did not come here to be insulted," snapped Fainche, caressing her belly as if sensing the rising peril.

"Then why did you come here? Did I harm you or threaten your life in the stables? No, I wished you and the baby well and meant it." Brighid transferred her stare to Onchú. "As for you. Who saved your daughters from a life of rape and slavery?

"Yet you have done nothing but disparage and insult us since entering this room. If you cannot be civil, go back to Curraghatoor, but leave the horses. It will save me the trouble of stealing them."

An ominous silence descended until Ciar spoke. "Perhaps, since I have only come recently to this group of old and new acquaintances, I can navigate the conversation into less turbulent waters. I am Ciar Ó Róich, formerly a rí of one of the western headland forts and now battle commander of Na Feirdhriseacha's army. Beside me is Olcán Ó Dubhan, previously of Brighid's shield-warriors and senior ceannairí céad. I suspect you know the remainder.

"I have heard of you, Onchú Ó an Cháintigh, and am acquainted with your reputation as a warrior and an honourable man. You take a great risk by sitting here, for Ráth Na Conall watches us." Ciar looked at Danu and then Brighid. "Is it surprising we wish to hear why you are here?"

"My apologies for being an arsehole, especially when not in my home. My only excuse is that I was quite taken aback at the members of this gathering." Onchú looked at Danu and Brighid and smiled. "Yet, perhaps, I should not have been surprised. You were never exactly conventional." He looked at Brighid. "The horses are a gift, so stealing them is unnecessary. Fainche chose them, so you know their quality.

"As to why we are here. Is it not obvious? The land is in turmoil, and an invasion is imminent. I would like to know your intentions."

"That is uncomplicated," said Danu. "We aim to take back Ráth Na Conall by negotiation or war. Then, we will march on, defeat, and destroy Calman. After that, we will repel the Mhór Midhe." Danu smiled at Draighean and laughed. "Our friend from the Aes Sídhe advises us not to worry about the Mhór Midhe until after Bealtaine."

"Do you intend to kill your brothers?" asked Onchú.

Brighid and Danu exclaimed, "The Hag, no! They are our blood. Why would we take their lives? The Goddess would never forgive us."

"Tell him, Danu," said Brighid.

"Tell me what?" asked Onchú.

"My son, Tanaí, and daughter, Órlaith, are held in Ráth Na Conall, whether guest or hostage, it does not matter. I intend to get them back… at any cost."

"The Hag!" gasped Fainche and clutched her belly.

A nudge from Brighid prompted Danu to speak again. "You should also know that Tanaí is Bran Mac Labraid-Loingsech's son and the heir to Ráthgeal's throne."

"Shite! Lonán never informed us of that. And Órlaith?" asked Onchú.

"She's the daughter of Óengus Dubdétach, a rí of the Ulaid and a commander of the Cróeb Ruad," said Danu.

"Do they know of the current state of affairs?" Onchú dreaded the answer.

"Yes. Understandably, I was upset at being banished and separated from my babies. I sent messengers to both. It may not have been my most prudent or rational decision." Onchú sat back in his chair, clasped his hands behind his head, and roared with laughter. "That was not the reaction I was expecting, Onchú," said Danu, looking at Fainche with concern.

"I should have been a better counsellor to both of you and must assume a large portion of responsibility for what has happened. The land's troubles undeniably began when your bond was sundered, but now you are together. Who am I to argue with the Goddess's work? If you will forgive my poor judgement, you have my oath, support, and army." Cheers echoed off the walls.

"What of Cnoc Duíginn, Onchú?" asked Danu. "Will Sláine side with us? His network would be invaluable, and he's the wealthiest of the southern ríthe because of his mines."

"Sláine, like his father, values Cnoc Duíginn's neutrality above all else." Onchú rubbed his beard and smiled at Brighid. "Yet he and Daráine have always had a fondness for Brighid." A frown settled on Onchú's brow. "However, there is a complication."

"What?" asked Brighid.

"There are strong rumours that your brother, Barra, was quite enamoured by Daráine. Also, she was happy to accept his adoration and return it in kind."

Brighid shook her head and looked at Danu. "Nothing is ever straightforward in our family."

CHAPTER 22

Niúig

Danu watched nervously as Brighid exited the ringfort. Since Tisiphone's encounter with Aoife, Brighid performed the same routine each morning after breaking her fast. Danu knew her path because she assigned riders to watch over her sister. She sacrificed and prayed to the Goddess that if Brighid's quest ended in tears, they would be tears of joy.

Draighean stood alongside Danu. "This is dangerous, Danu, not just to Brighid but to repulsing the Mhór Midhe. I need two sisters standing as one. Also, because of the Dog Roses, there is no guarantee that you would survive Brighid's death."

"This is something Brighid needs to do, Draighean. I want my sister to be happy. If death accomplishes that, how can the Goddess blame her?" Danu pulled the heavy fur closer, turned around, and walked across the yard. She had business with the Chomhairle. *Perhaps Brighid's morning rides were how she avoided the meetings.*

***

The sound of the black mare clip-clopping across the wooden bridge soothed Brighid. Yet it was over too quickly, and the hooves were silenced by snow as she walked the horse in a southwesterly direction towards Ráth Na Conall. Brighid's rose pounded in her chest. She sensed Danu's anxiety and whispered, "Thanks for understanding."

Tisiphone had informed Brighid that, despite her warning, Aoife continued her daily reconnoitring of Niúig. Aoife was not stupid, so why did she ignore the threat? Hope rose in Brighid's chest and, with it, her heartbeat and pulse. Was Aoife also looking for a resolution?

"Whatever," she huffed. "I'm tired of not knowing, of hiding. Better my bleeding head lying on the snow than regrets of never taking a chance." Yet, was this more evidence of her impulsive, selfish nature? If dead, she would be in Mag Mell and reunited with Báine. Would Danu survive? What would be Aoife's fate? "The Hag's bony arse! I was never meant to do all this thinking. That's Danu's strength, not mine."

Brighid's horse whickered and dropped its head. The sharp tug of the reins pulled Brighid from her musings. She looked up and smiled. "She's as reliable as the sunrise." Brighid breathed deeply and resolved to confront Aoife. They had watched each other on previous sunrises before turning about and returning to their forts. It was a strange yet comforting ritual but was ultimately frustrating for both parties.

* * *

"Shite!" muttered Aoife as she watched Brighid approach. Their theatre brought a strange contentment to her, but she sensed something was different this morning. What had changed? Why was Brighid closing on her and not turning around? That was the safe choice. Why alter it? Aoife continually weighed Tisiphone's words and wondered if they were true. Was Brighid as unhappy as she?

Aoife missed what she had been and the joyful vibrancy of her childhood. As a child, she had been fearless. She smiled, recalling her defiance of the slavers and killing the wolf, Silverback. Her blue eyes no longer sparkled as they once did. She could feel it. Aoife snorted. She had heard people remark on it when they thought she was beyond hearing them.

Lost in her thoughts, Aoife started when her horse pulled up. She was less than twenty paces from Brighid. "Bitseach!" Aoife swore as she watched Brighid dismount and hang her weapon belt over the horse's back. *Being unarmed will not save you.* Her wolf sigil throbbed, and she noted how Brighid smoothed the mare's mane and velvet shoulders and whispered in its ear. The mount shook its head as if in disagreement. *Is she saying "Goodbye"?*

A fresh overnight snowfall added depth, and Brighid's leg muscles felt it. She trudged through the knee-deep snow towards Aoife and stopped midway. Aoife dismounted, and Brighid heard the whisper of a longsword drawn from a wool-lined scabbard. She looked to the sky and smiled. There were much worse ways to die. She fell to her knees and felt the cold seep through her triubhas. Then Brighid pushed the long auburn braid aside, bared her neck, and bowed.

***

"Bitseach!" shrieked Aoife. "You can't put this on me."

"Be merciful. End it, please. Free us both. The burden of losing you and Báine is too great for me to bear."

The only sounds were the tinkling of reins and boots crunching through the crust of snow as Aoife moved closer. It seemed an interminable time, although likely only moments had passed. Brighid trembled and wished it was over. She heard snow trampled underfoot and felt Aoife's arms around her. Tears soaked her hair.

"How could I take the life of one she loved and gave her life for? I miss her so much, Brighid. I should have stayed to fight alongside her. The dreams told me I could save her, but I was afraid." Guilt racked Aoife, and she sobbed sorely.

"*No!* Báine never wished that, and neither did I. Your visions are mischievous or misinterpreted," said Brighid, holding Aoife's head with hands numb with cold. As they rose, Aoife gazed at Brighid's face and saw the dark curling designs and emerald eyes that now sparkled. Brighid held Aoife's eyes, and for an instant, a wolf grinned back. *Shite! I've stared too long at the snow.*

"The Hag, Brighid, what do I do now?"

"You have a brother and family in Ráth Na Conall. You will always be welcome in Niúig, but that is your choice, and I will never pressure you to join us. Do what you think is best for you and your family." As Aoife watched Brighid mount her mare, wave, and ride for the bridge, she turned to find big brown eyes looking at her.

"Don't you say a thing. Not one snort."

****

It was between meán oíche and dawn. Danu lay naked and breathless. The covers of the cot were strewn over the floor. She relished the warmth of the roaring fire and the body lying beside her. Danu's head rested on Ciar's chest, and her long tresses were plastered to it. The passion of their first rutting raised a pink flush over her body and a sheen of sweat on his.

The pleasant throbbing in her pit testified to how much she enjoyed Ciar's attentions. That he was a thoughtful lover instantly changed her miserable track record with men. Danu opened her mouth and moistened her lips. She wanted to taste and revive his manhood again.

Instead, she looked into his eyes and said, "I hope Brighid isn't listening."

"What? How could she? She's at the far end of the hallway," said Ciar.

"We can read each other's thoughts and 'talk' without words. It's one of the benefits of our powers." Realising how strange this must sound, she added, somewhat defensively, "We have guidelines, and she promised not to pry."

"And you believe her?" Ciar laughed at Danu's innocent faith in her sister.

Danu giggled like an adolescent girl and nodded. "Yes. She thinks I'm perverted with everything I think of when we're close." Danu pursed her lips. "You realise that everyone thinks we've been rutting since we first met, too!"

"Now that is intriguing. What sort of things do you think about? Openness is always good in a relationship." Danu's answer was a playful slap on Ciar's face.

"I wouldn't want to corrupt you."

"Feel free to sully my virtuous heart." As Danu leaned over, her breast caressed Ciar's arm. She opened her mouth to whisper something extremely lewd, but, at that moment, a fist banged on the chamber's door. Shouts of "Warriors, riders, and chariots approaching!" filled the air.

"Shite! What arsehole attacks at this time of the night?" complained Danu. Then she rolled her eyes. *I would.* She stepped into boots and pulled a heavy fur-trimmed cloak around her. As she walked into the hallway, she was met by Brighid, who winked mischievously at Ciar and her.

"Your rutting's quite boring! Try doing some of that stuff you always think about. It'll be more entertaining for me… and Ciar."

"Bitseach!"

***

On the northern wall, warriors and leaders assembled. Decimus shouted, "Stand ready!" to the ballistae teams and ordered the braziers and torches to be lit. Olcán and Tisiphone looked unamused at having been disturbed, as did Draighean and the brawny young man beside her.

"It is strange," said Decimus, "for attackers, they don't appear to be in any hurry." He looked at Danu and Brighid. "Are you expecting guests?" Both shook their heads, although Brighid had a hopeful sparkle in her eyes.

From the shadows came a shout. "The Hag's arse! Point those ballistae somewhere else. We've had enough jeopardy for one sunset, and there better be something to eat and drink. We're starving."

Brighid looked at Danu, beamed, and shouted, "Open the gates. They're friends."

***

Aoife and Cass were overwhelmed and a mite embarrassed at the reception from Niúig's garrison. It contrasted starkly against Ráth Na Conall's welcome and Lonán's sour face. That said, they experienced anxiety when invited to the meán lae meeting of the Chomhairle. Apprehension transformed into shock when they saw Nuadha. Aoife gripped Cass' arm with enough force to make him wince.

"What's that *tuilí*—bastard—doing here?" Intended to be a whisper, Aoife had not considered the intimate size of the chamber.

"As I recall, Onchú had the same reaction," said Nuadha. The smile showed he was amused rather than insulted.

"Nuadha is a friend and gave shelter to Brighid and me when all others deserted us," said Danu disapprovingly.

"My apologies, my queen," said Aoife. She bowed to Nuadha. "And to you, also. I meant no offence. Since Lonán and the queens' brothers assumed command of Ráth Na Conall, strangers have not been welcome. Even loyal warriors, such as my brother, are looked on with suspicion. According to Lonán, we are tainted by having served the rígana."

Aoife paused for a few moments and nervously tugged her braid. "Still, I believe your brothers do not share Lonán's contempt, and in the end, it worked in Niúig's favour." Aoife looked at her brother and smiled. "I thought it would be myself and a few chariots who would leave Ráth Na Conall, which was risky enough. Instead, I found Cass at my side and most of the garrison that served under Danu."

"How many followed you and Cass?" asked Danu in a voice that wavered between hope and disappointment. The question was irrelevant as most in the room knew the answer. Its purpose was to allow Danu to calm her roiling emotions and stem the cascade of tears that threatened to be released. *I was an awful queen to them.*

Brighid put her hand on Danu's. "We both were, sister."

Danu signalled Ciar. "This is Ciar Ó Róich, our battle commander. Perhaps, Ciar, you would bring Aoife and Cass up to date. After that, we must design a plan to recover Ráth Na Conall quickly. The winter moves on, the festival of Imbolg draws near, and we need to prepare for war with the Mhór Midhe."

***

"Clearly, they were more loyal to two disgraced and banished queens than to you," snapped Flann.

The ordinarily restrained veteran finally exploded following Lonán's rants, accusations of collusion, and threats of reprisals. However, given that the offenders had fled the fort, the object of Lonán's retaliation remained unclear. Perhaps that was why Cináed had been asked to the meeting. Was Lonán considering punishing the civilians? Flann looked at Aodán and Barra, who looked far from amused.

"Whom did my father name as your replacement, Lonán? I know there must be one… in case of injury or other circumstance." The question from Aodán startled Lonán, and his jaw dropped. The implication was clear. "I do not doubt you were a veteran warrior who served my father well. However, you seem out of your depth in our present situation.

"We have been outwitted and outfought by my sisters. They started alone and separated. Now, the exiles from the western promontory forts, a substantial section of this ráth, and Tisiphone are with them. They have a stronghold and a fleet. Furthermore, we have received confirmation that Onchú has given his oath to Brighid and Danu. Who's next? Aodh in Clárach, Sláine in Cnoc Duíginn, and Bran in Ráthgeal?"

Aodán turned to Barra and exchanged glances. "Barra and I have decided that you should step down as our primary counsellor. Flann will take your place. In deference to your service, you may attend meetings and suggest courses of action.

"However, any more missteps and we will revisit our decision. Barra has sent several riders to Cnoc Duíginn, proposing we join Sláine and Daráine for Imbolg. We have suggested they also invite Danu and Brighid. It is time to negotiate an agreement with our sisters."

"They will not attend, for they will perceive it as a trap," snarled Lonán.

"They will attend because we will bring Órlaith and Tanaí with us. What mother would forego the chance to see her children?"

***

The Chomhairle, plus Aoife and Cass, met in one of the Great Hall's smaller chambers to discuss the messenger from Cnoc Duíginn. "It's a trap," said Brighid. All but Danu nodded in agreement. Brighid saw the anguish in her twin's face and the constant wringing of her fingers. She felt the beat of Danu's feirdhris and her sister's pain.

Brighid knew that, like their father, Danu would put the people and the clann before herself. However, Brighid would not allow that, and so she stood. "We are going to Cnoc Duíginn, and I will brook no arguments to the contrary. My sister will celebrate Imbolg with her children. Anyone who objects should leave the room." No chair moved, and Brighid smiled. "Thank you."

Then Brighid's jaw set, and her eyes darkened. "Of course, this is a trap, although I highly doubt Sláine is involved. Thus, we should discuss how to avoid the snare. Even better, can we take advantage of it?" A hand gripped Brighid's as the room emptied, and she gazed into Danu's eyes.

"I will never forget this, sister, and will always be in your debt."

CHAPTER 23

Spring—Festival of Imbolg—Cnoc Duíginn

Aodh scowled at Onchú and Fainche. If anything, his demeanour worsened when his gaze turned to Sláine and Daráine. "Why have I been invited to this house of intrigue?" That Daráine tittered at Aodh's description of Cnoc Duíginn and followed it with a less than genuine "Sorry" did not help.

"Cnoc Duíginn is neutral territory, which you well know," said Onchú. His patient tone did not reflect his inner irritation. "The current occupiers of Ráth Na Conall and Ráth Na Niúig will be vital in the upcoming war with the Mhór Midhe." He clasped battle-scarred hands tightly and rested them on the table. "Would you rather we took to the battlefield? Only Messin Corb and Calman Mor would benefit from that."

Stubborn and unwilling to concede, Aodh pointed to Sláine. "*He* has always favoured Brighid. That is hardly impartial."

"Sláine is a rí like you and me, and Daráine, a rígan. *They* should and will be treated with respect." Onchú was gratified to see Aodh's cheeks flush red. "Sláine and Daráine helped Brighid escape from Uallachán's and Cairbre's grasp. In turn, Brighid saved their lives. Of course, they have an affection for each other. As I have for my adopted daughters who saved my life."

Onchú held Aodh's gaze. "Moreover, are you seriously contending that Clárach has never had intrigues? I recall two, both of which ended in the executions of your brothers." A chair scraped on the stone floor as Aodh started to rise. The shield-man's hand on Aodh's shoulder curtailed his obvious intent.

"It does no harm to hear what Onchú and the others have to say," whispered the warrior. As with his father, the hefty warrior had known Aodh since childhood. Few believed he was just the rí's protector. Indeed, there were strong rumours that he was Aodh's chosen heir. The man chuckled. "Think of how much you'll save by spending Imbolg here than heating and feeding guests in Clárach's Great Hall."

"What is being proposed?" asked a chastened Aodh.

* * *

Brighid and Danu laid their armour aside and Draighean her black cloak, which was the closest to a shield she wore. Like Tisiphone, they wore diaphanous white gowns fashioned in the style of Greek chitons. The dresses touched the floor, concealing their bare feet. The hems and necklines of each dress were scalloped and embroidered in different colours: gold and red for Brighid, silver and blue for Danu, and crimson for Draighean.

"I feel quite undressed," whispered Tisiphone as the party was announced, and they crossed the Great Hall's entrance. At Brighid's raised eyebrow, she laughed. "Perhaps I could prevail on Draighean to gift me a small selection of your curling symbols, which, due to our dress material, are very plainly…" Tisiphone laughed, "…and quite deliberately, I think, on show."

Draighean chuckled. "That can be arranged—even for a Greek."

A protesting Aoife followed the quartet. She had never worn a formal dress, let alone one which revealed every curve. Still, defiantly prominent dusky-pink nipples suggested she did not find the ensemble totally abhorrent. Cass, Ciar, and Olcán formed the rearguard as the party from Niúig walked up the hall's central aisle towards the high table.

The women's hair was braided and piled on their heads. It made them look elegant and taller and increased the aura of power radiated.

Sláine had decreed no weapons, but the group sidestepped his wishes. The hairstyles were a practical way to conceal long, thin daggers disguised as hairpins. In a similar vein, their thick gold wristbands hid small, poison-coated blades.

"You must be aware that under Tisiphone's influence, it is probable that each of the women is better armed than the men present," whispered Barra in Aodán's ear. His brother said nothing, and curiosity made Barra track Aodán's gaze. He chuckled. "As I recall, brother, you dared to point out my preoccupation with Daráine." Aodán looked suitably embarrassed. Barra winked. "Don't worry. I prevailed upon Daráine to seat Aoife beside you. Enjoy my Imbolg gift."

✳✳✳

Only the presence of Órlaith and Tanaí thawed the frosty demeanours of those present. Spying Danu, they screamed, "Ma!" and, like slippery eels, escaped their nurses and eluded the grasping hands of Aodán, Barra, and Lonán. Flann stood aside and grinned. Danu went down on one knee and held her arms open.

Only Ciar's steadying hand prevented Danu from falling over under the impact of the young missiles as they launched themselves towards her. Tears streamed down Danu's face as she hugged Órlaith and Tanaí. "I have missed you so much," sobbed Danu.

The initial onslaught over, Órlaith stepped back. She looked curiously at her ma and then Brighid. For a moment, Tanaí also looked confused. Danu wondered if she had done something wrong. Then she smiled and called Brighid closer. "This is my sister, Brighid. She is your aunt. We look alike because we are twins, but you can tell us apart by the colour of our highlights."

Brighid had never met her nephew and niece, as they were born after she left Ráth Na Conall. She looked nonplussed and uncertain about the proper protocol for the situation. Following Danu's lead, she dropped to one knee and opened her arms. Órlaith looked at Brighid curiously and curtsied very formally.

Then, with a nod of approval to Tanaí, both leapt into their new aunt's arms. Soon, tears flowed from Brighid and ended only when Órlaith looked at her and pointed to the feirdhris. "Will I get a rose like ma and you when I'm older?" Blinking tears away, Brighid pointed to Draighean. "Ours are a gift from the Lady Sídhe. You will have to ask her. She is called Draighean."

At the Sídhe's fearsome demeanour, Órlaith shook her head and stepped backwards, but Brighid held her hand. "She looks fierce but has been a faithful friend to your ma and me and, if you allow, will be one to Tanaí and you." Draighean laughed and stood alongside Órlaith.

"Perhaps you deserve a reward for your bravery, although maybe not a feirdhris… yet."

Órlaith said, "Ouch!" and pouted briefly when the Sídhe touched her shoulder. She glared accusingly at Draighean and scratched the offending area. Her eyes, as green as Danu's, widened as she saw the blue and silver design, which glittered as she moved. She stared at Draighean, bowed, and smiled. "Thank you, but how did you know I like winter and snowflakes?"

"I know many things, Órlaith, and one day you will, too."

Across the hall, Aodán tapped Barra's shoulder and pointed to the happy group. "Bringing the children, although well-intentioned, may not have been one of my best tactical suggestions. If negotiations fail, the consequences of attempting to cleave Danu from Órlaith and Tanaí will be bloody."

Barra nodded. "Yes, and with Draighean blessing Órlaith, it would surely be us who would die in Cnoc Duíginn." Barra rubbed his chin. "Still, why would we separate our sister from her children? Would Mórrígan or Mòrag have tolerated anyone tearing us from their breasts?" Barra held Aodán's gaze and then looked at the happy group.

"We have repeatedly told Lonán the children are not pieces on a fidchell board. Are we not just as guilty? Can you envisage our father, Conall, being so foolish? I cannot. As ríthe, we should apologise to

Danu and let them be. As brothers, we should ask Órlaith and Tanaí's forgiveness and beg them to accept us as uncles."

A few paces away, Lonán's expression became darker.

***

As Sláine's guests ate and drank, the conversation around the table was replete with the inconsequential. When Aodán and Barra could be prised from Daráine's and Aoife's sides, they recalled happier times in Lugudunon with Danu and Brighid.

Everyone regaled Órlaith and Tanaí with embarrassing tales of their mother, aunt, and grandparents. A promise was reluctantly made that they would journey to Gaul to meet Conall and Mórrígan. Still, Danu and Brighid looked at each other and wondered how welcome they would be.

On the periphery of Danu's family, Ciar joined Aodh, Fainche, Onchú, and Sláine. That conversation, once past inquiries of Fainche's health, turned to Aodh's crankiness at having once more been forced into making unpalatable choices by a member of Conall's family. That Danu and Brighid had executed his younger brother, Glaisne, albeit with Aodh's consent, did not help.

Like a *lincse*, Tisiphone prowled the Great Hall, assessing threats. This translated into whom she might have to kill before the gathering ended. She smiled at Órlaith and Tanaí and remembered her mission and the wisdom of it. As she swept the chamber, Tisiphone caught the eyes of Lonán and briefly felt sorrow for his loneliness. His demeanour was that of an outcast—lonely, resentful… and murderous.

"This is not good," muttered Tisiphone. A brief clench of her arse cheeks confirmed the comforting presence of the hidden dagger.

***

"You are responsible for this mess," said Aodh.

Ambushed by Danu and Brighid, Aodh responded with his usual candour. Brighid bridled at his words, but Danu remained fond of the cantankerous, aged Rí of Clárach. She smiled pleasantly and placed her hand on Aodh's. *Danu's much better at politics than I am. I would have introduced him to a blade.*

"You know that is not true, Aodh," said Danu. "Neither you nor Onchú can wash your hands of complicity. Where were you when Brighid and I needed sound counsel or a kick up the arse? I looked upon you as a father and, had things gone differently with Glaisne, would have called you that unreservedly." Danu felt Aodh flinch and try to withdraw his hand, but she gripped it with the strength of a wolfhound's jaws.

"Brighid and I are stronger than we once were, Aodh. Yes, we made mistakes. The biggest was the schism that tore us apart. Apart, we are terrible queens. Our people suffered, and we deeply regret that and will make restitution when and where possible." Danu's grip tightened on Aodh's hand, making the king wince at its strength.

"However, together, we defeated the Connachta armies and brought prosperity. That will never be possible if the Mhór Midhe win. Whom will you ally with? The Mhór Midhe or us? That is the choice you must make. Like other times, Clárach cannot sit this one out." When Danu released Aodh's hand, he turned abruptly and walked to where his shield-man stood.

"You spoke well, sister," said Brighid, quickly hugging Danu. "It is in the Goddess's hands now."

"I can remove Aodh and his shield-man and make both look like natural causes," said Draighean. "Or Tisiphone can do what she enjoys, that is, apart from whoring." She chuckled. "That one should have been borne a Sídhe. If I could choose a sister, it would be her." The Sídhe sighed and picked up the thread of her previous conversation. "Strategically, Clárach would be without a king, without heirs, and easy to conquer." Draighean's matter-of-fact tone sent chills up both sisters' spines.

"No, we will leave it to Aodh's conscience and the Goddess," said Danu. Brighid nodded in agreement.

✳✳✳

"You shall surrender yourselves and will be returned to Lugudunon for judgement and sentencing," Lonán spoke, interrupting Aodán, who had started to rise. "That is your father and mother's command. To do otherwise is treason and subject to immediate execution."

"Thus speaks the voice of reason," said Danu. It raised a smile from the others and a glower from Lonán. "You were a brave warrior, Lonán. I respect your long service to my parents and Clann Ui Flaithimh. I am sorry for the injury you received, yet how are you different from hundreds of other brave warriors who have fought for the tribe? You have become a blunt weapon, dulled by battle and of no more use than a club."

Danu paused, and her eyes narrowed. "Also, your memory fails you. Perhaps age has corrupted your thinking? You and my brothers pronounced judgement and banished Brighid and me. We were cut off from Clann Ui Flaithimh and made outcasts. According to the Fénechas, we are no longer subject to the tribe's laws or will."

Danu's eyes darkened until they were almost black. "You had your chance to execute me and failed. Now, hold your tongue, *servant*. Stand aside, and let kings and queens talk."

Lonán's hand went to his scabbard. Danu's voice was cold as ice. "Again, your memory fails you. You would be dead if your weapon were not set aside for this gathering. You don't know the power Brighid and I can call upon." Danu stared at Lonán. Her eyes were obsidian and glittered, and the curling sigils were in constant motion.

"Now, *sit down!*" The force of Danu's voice compelled Lonán to obey.

***

When Danu turned to face the table, her eyes had regained their natural colour, and the designs slumbered. Smiling, she said, "I apologise for the unfortunate start to our discussions. Perhaps, if you allow, I will start by laying our terms on the table."

Before Danu could speak, Aodán and Barra rose. A furious Aodán pointed to Lonán. "This man speaks neither for Barra nor me nor our mother and father, whose intentions he misinterprets. Any authority he held has been revoked and transferred to Flann. He has no rank at this meeting and attends only by our charity and unwillingness to embarrass him publicly."

Aodán took a sip of wine and dipped his head to Sláine. "On behalf of my brother and me, I apologise for Lonán's intemperance. If he speaks again, and with your permission, our men will escort him to your dungeon." Sláine nodded.

"Our brothers have spines, Danu," whispered Brighid.

After a short break, the discussion continued as Danu rose. She smiled without malice and addressed her brothers. "Brighid and I deeply regret placing you in an untenable position. Yet your choice is simple. Join the other ríthe to help us fight the Mhór Midhe under Brighid's and my command. The alternative is to take those who wish to go with you and leave.

"I assume quinqueremes are wintering in Northern Aremorio and will return in the spring." A slight dip of Aodán's head gave Danu her answer. "Your probable intention was to secure Brighid and me and return to Massalia and Lugudunon. Unfortunately, we will not be accompanying you."

Danu looked at Aoife and Daráine, whose cheeks instantly flushed and smiled. "Yet I think there are other complicating factors."

Aodán rose and smiled disarmingly at his sisters. "Like Lonán, you make assumptions without fully understanding our orders. But for the sake of argument, what if we refuse to give up Ráth Na Conall?"

"Then, after we have celebrated Imbolg, we will fight. Brighid and I must settle this dispute to focus on Calman and to prepare for the Mhór Midhe."

"You do not have the numbers to besiege and take Ráth Na Conall," said Aodán. "You built a solid fortress, sister."

"My throat is dry, Brighid. Perhaps you would outline how our brothers cannot win." Brighid rose and smiled as pleasantly as Danu.

"We already outnumber Ráth Na Conall's garrison. More disaffected warriors and their families flock to the Na Feirdhriseacha banner daily. Indeed, we have trouble building sufficient accommodations at Niúig." Brighid looked at Onchú and dipped her head. "Curraghatoor is with us, which means your riders are at a significant disadvantage."

"Shite!" exclaimed Barra. "We have ballistae."

"So do we, and remember, bolt-throwers, large and small, are mobile. Lonán's tactics have placed you in a weak position on the fidchell board. In addition, courtesy of Lonán, we have a fleet of triremes to defend against an assault on Ráth Na Niúig."

Aodán and Barra glared at Lonán. He scowled back and said, "They still don't have the numbers to take Ráth Na Conall and know it. She's trying to intimidate you into surrendering, and it looks like she's succeeding." Contempt flowed from Lonán's lips.

"They also have Clárach," interjected Aodh. He looked at Aodán and Barra. "I am sorry, I like you, and Brighid and Danu are bitseacha, but they are battle-proven."

"Cnoc Duíginn also supports the rígana," said Sláine.

"You still don't have the numbers for a siege," growled Lonán.

"We have the Lady Sídhe," said Danu, rising from her seat. "She has Calman Mor in Caher Conri and Messin Corb in Cnoc Uisnigh buried under their worst snowfalls in generations." Danu turned to Draighean. "However, I'm sure she could expend some of her talents on making Ráth Na Conall little more than a block of ice." The Sídhe dipped her head.

Danu smiled, which made her brothers very nervous. "Also, did you not agree that Bran Mac Labraid-Loingsech could return for *my* son after Imbolg? I wonder how many thousands of his warriors will accompany him. As for Órlaith's father, Draighean informs me that Óengus Dubdétach and a thousand Cróeb Ruad warriors are two cycles of the moon from us.

"Make up your mind. Join us or return to Ráth Na Conall and prepare for battle." Danu looked at Brighid and then at Aodán and Barra. "My sister and I would prefer you fight alongside us as ríthe, but we will not shrink from war."

Barra stood, looked at Draighean, and held her gaze without shrinking. That made the Sídhe wary. "Will Calman break out of his frozen stronghold before the main Mhór Midhe army attacks?" Reluctantly, Draighean nodded. "Then the same would apply to Ráth Na Conall. Yes?" Again, she nodded.

"Our garrison is one thousand veteran shield-warriors strong." Barra scratched his chin deliberately as if calculating and looked at Aodán. "How many Clann Ui Flaithimh warriors winter in Aremorio, brother? The five quinqueremes indeed winter in the port." Barra smiled. "Yet there are also three thousand more shield- and mounted warriors. Pytheas' trading ships regularly travel along the rivers from Lugudunon to Aremorio. They can carry warriors as well as goods."

"You're bluffing, brother," said Danu.

"Quite possibly. However, much as I am loathe to agree with Lonán, even with your allies, you do not have the overwhelming numbers to take Ráth Na Conall. Also, you have no guarantee that Ráthgeal will fight with you. Thus, the crucial question for you is how many hundreds of warriors will you and your allies lose in besieging Ráth Na Conall? Enough to tip the balance in the war with the Mhór Midhe?"

"Shite, Danu. I thought you were good at playing fidchell," murmured Brighid.

"What is your point, brother?" asked Danu, barely able to stop grinding her teeth.

"We are ríthe, like the others seated at this table. Please give us the respect of the office you give them. We have much to learn, but we are not the eejits you so readily look down on and insult." Danu's face flared red, although this time with embarrassment. "More than this, treat us as the brothers you have known since our birth."

Barra paused. "Otherwise, prepare for battle. We will work with you and the ríthe. We will not surrender to you."

Aodh turned to Onchú and chuckled. "I am enjoying this visit much more. Is it not a pity that you and I did not have the balls to speak this directly to Danu and Brighid?" Onchú nodded.

✳✳✳

Lonán's face looked like thunder as he surveyed the gathering. The slapping of backs and embraces of those who may not have been enemies but had vastly different perspectives made the veteran cringe. Defeating the enemy utterly had been his guiding principle, not politics and compromise. *Do I know any of these people?*

"This is not a defeat, Lonán. Conall and Mórrígan will be pleased with the outcome. Lessons have been learned, and the family is united." The voice startled Lonán, and he looked at Tisiphone. It was a look that caused Tisiphone to frown. Instead, she kept on smiling.

"Whore," spat Lonán. His demeanour was that of a disgruntled man who had seen his plans shatter and was not cunning enough to disguise his anger.

"Shite!" muttered Tisiphone. Then she said, "Beware, Lonán Ó Neill. I have my orders, and they are to end *anyone* who harms any member of this family. You are no match for me. Stand down or die."

✳✳✳

"We don't want to leave you, Ma," wailed Órlaith.

It was meán lae immediately after Imbolg. The kings and queens gathered with their guards at the gates of Cnoc Duíginn to say their final goodbyes. All but Sláine and Daráine stood beside their mounts. The horses, sensing a long ride, stamped the ground impatiently. Daráine grasped Barra's hand with a strength that made him wince and only reluctantly released him. Aoife looked at Aodán with an expression that said she wished Ráth Na Conall was her destination.

Órlaith's words and tears threatened to break the dam that Danu had carefully constructed. Instead of a flood, only trickles ran down her cheeks. "Tanaí and you will be safe with my brothers. Everyone is on the same side now, and I promise to join you in three sunsets." Danu smiled, kissed Órlaith on her forehead, and did the same with Tanaí.

New to the role of an aunt, Brighid was still determining the proper protocol and rocked from foot to foot. Finally, she muttered, "The Hag!" She started when Ciar whispered in her ear.

"A simple hug will say everything."

Inhaling, she walked to where Danu and the children stood. Kneeling before them, she took Órlaith in her arms first. She whispered, "As you grow older, you will find that rígana often have disagreeable duties. Be brave, and we will see you very soon." To Tanaí, Brighid said, "Protect your sister," and hugged him. His smile told Brighid she had done well.

"Thank you, sister," said Danu.

CHAPTER 24

Bod Carraig

At a fast canter, a rider departing Cnoc Duíginn at dawn would arrive in Ráth Na Conall in time to eat the meán lae meal without breaking a sweat. However, it was winter, snow lay knee-deep on the ground, and there were forests and a mountain valley to negotiate.

Therefore, when Lonán proposed that Órlaith and Tanaí would find the journey less tiring if the party camped overnight, Aodán and Barra were surprised but heaved a sigh of relief. Lonán's concern for the children's wellbeing was a positive sign. Perhaps he had accepted the new strategy and alliances. Undeniably, having an amenable and experienced warrior on their side for the upcoming battles with the Mhór Midhe would be an advantage.

The party camped on the forested northern bank of the *Abhainn Na Siúire River*, midway between the two rátha. Aodán, Barra, and the children slept by a roaring campfire and dreamt of happier days. The ríthe's naivety was cruelly exposed when they awoke to a dawn shattered by the cries of Órlaith and Tanaí and sword blades at their throats.

"*Tuilá!*" roared Aodán. "You'll go to the Otherworld for this." He and Barra reached for their weapons, but they had been taken. Mocking laughter greeted them, and the sight of blood-soaked snow marked where their guards' bodies lay. They had been stabbed and their throats cut by men they thought were comrades.

"Bind them to trees. Cut them, but not fatally. The Goddess will decide whether the cold or the wolves finish them off," shouted Lonán.

Barra took after his adopted father, Torcán. Hence, he was a brawler, and those instincts kicked in. With a roar, he charged the two warriors who approached. He felt a satisfying pleasure at the sound of bones breaking as his fists connected with cheekbones, jaws, and noses. He bit and spat pieces of ears through blood-stained teeth. Grunts and curses drew more warriors into the fight. He was finally subdued by a sword pommel to his temple.

"What, no resistance from you?" sneered Lonán. "Does your brother do all your fighting?"

"A hundred against one is poor odds. Fight me, man-to-man, and we'll see which of us is the better warrior." Aodán spat in disgust. "But you won't because you're a coward who kidnaps babies. My revenge will be to watch my sisters strip the skin from your body and the ravens feast on your eyeballs… while you're still alive, traitor," snarled Aodán.

"You are the traitor, not me. I follow Conall's and Mórrígan's orders."

"I know my mother and father better than you. Your interpretation of their orders would never be true. You are sick like a rabid wolf, and your life is forfeit. Consider yourself fortunate that Mórrígan is far away, for you know her retribution would show no mercy," said Aodán. Lonán's sword's hilt delivered him into oblivion.

✶✶✶

It was not long before the brothers regained clarity. They struggled against their bindings, but it was useless. Only Órlaith and Tanaí sobbing disturbed a forest that had fallen unnaturally quiet, with no wind, bird or animal noises. Órlaith looked at Tanaí, wiped the tears from her eyes, and said, "Don't worry, our ma will find us."

Those around the children mocked her words but stopped abruptly when Órlaith ceased sobbing. Feeling the sigil on her shoulder throb, Órlaith looked at the sky and opened her mouth. Like a wolf pup calling to its mother, Órlaith howled. At first, the *Song of Órlaith* was weak, fractured, and felt strange to her, but soon it rang out clearly.

"Shut her up. Gag the bitseach if you must," bellowed Lonán.

Yet as he spoke, the wolves in the forests and mountains amplified Órlaith's refrain. Lonán smirked when the yowling fell silent, but his joy was short-lived. In the east, a howl of anger and promised retribution rose into the morning sky. *Danu's Song* was joined immediately and strengthened by Brighid's.

Draighean's Song, more potent than Brighid's and Danu's, tore the veils protecting the kidnappers' minds to shreds. In their heads, they saw terrible visions of the Hag. They heard the apparition hiss, "You have taken my wards. You will die on this dirt and in this time, but my vengeance will follow you into the Otherworld."

Órlaith smiled and looked at Lonán. With a child's simple faith, she said, "Our ma is coming." None in the camp challenged her.

✳✳✳

Brighid's and Danu's calm, cold demeanours caused consternation among their friends. Where were the fiery emotions and promises of revenge? Only obsidian eyes and roiling sigils gave a clue to their turmoil. Danu smoothed her horse's velvet black shoulders before turning to address the group of travellers.

"We will be in Ráth Na Niúig before meán lae. Lonán and whoever travels with him journey westwards. Likely, his destination is Caher Conri and sanctuary with Calman. I doubt Calman will refuse a gift that, at worst, could be used to negotiate terms. My children will be safe with Calman for a time. However, his nature dictates that Lonán will die once Órlaith and Tanaí are handed over."

Danu's eyes glittered. "I will not allow either to happen. My children will be returned, and Lonán will suffer long and die badly while I watch."

Turning to Aoife, Danu said, "I know Órlaith is unharmed, but I have no knowledge of Aodán or Barra. Take the warriors accompanying us and ride east along the Abhainn Na Siúire. I cannot guide you much more than that. When you find my brothers, go to Cnoc Duíginn.

Inform Sláine and Daráine what has happened and ask them to send messengers to Onchú and Aodh."

"Why not Ráth Na Conall? It's closer," asked Aoife.

Danu shook her head. "Those who remain in Ráth Na Conall are unaware of our reconciliation. If my brothers are badly injured, you could find yourself in the dungeons at best but more likely executed as a traitor." Danu took Aoife's hand. "No. We will accomplish what is needed with Na Feirdhriseacha's forces."

To Ciar, Danu said, "In these conditions, it will take Lonán ten sunsets to travel to Caher Conri. Ships will travel much faster. When we arrive in Niúig, take Olcán and Cass and board enough triremes to transport two hundred shield-warriors and twenty wolfhounds."

Danu sighed resignedly. "Apologise to Decimus for weakening the garrison, but I think he will understand. I assume you know the bay on the southern coast of Caher Conri's headland." Ciar nodded. "Good. Disembark there. Set up camp in the forest east of the promontory. At all costs, Lonán must not reach Caher Conri."

Next, Danu turned to Brighid. "When we arrive at Niúig, go to the riders' quarters and choose your best warriors. You and I will ride for Caher Conri and kill anyone who tries to stop us."

Tisiphone stepped forward. "And me?"

Danu smiled. "I think I understand your mission better. It is to shield, not to assassinate, isn't it?" Tisiphone dipped her head. "I will not stand in your way. Take what supplies and weapons you need from our stock. We can replenish them from Niúig's stores." Danu held Tisiphone's hands and her gaze. "Protect my children. Kill without mercy."

As Tisiphone walked to her mount, Draighean appeared at her side and put a hand on Tisiphone's slender left upper arm. The assassin flinched, although not at the touch. "It is neither a rose nor a snowflake, but you will understand its meaning. Among other things, it will allow you to sense Órlaith's presence."

Draighean looked at the heavy wolf-fur cloak Tisiphone pulled over her shoulders. "I doubt you'll need that now." Tisiphone dipped her head. She glanced at her shoulder before mounting the grey and smiled at Draighean. Her design was a sprig of blackthorn with a five-petaled white flower and a circle of thorns.

"I will remain in Niúig," said Draighean to Danu. "I could bring a westerly wind, but it would slow both your and Lonán's journey and make navigation challenging for the triremes. However, I will make the land south of the Bod Carraig mountains firmer for horses." Draighean's face took on an ominous expression. "I will also make their dreams so terrible that they will welcome the bean-sídhe." As Danu turned, Draighean's hand stopped her.

"Your brother's words were prescient. I sense Calman's warriors are digging themselves out of their hibernation. Be wary."

* * *

Sunset and sunrise passed, and the growling and barking came closer. In the watery meán lae sun, Aodán and Barra saw dark shapes moving through the trees. "Any suggestions?" asked Barra and once more tried to loosen his bindings. But his feet and hands were numb, and his ties were bloody. Like previous attempts, he failed.

"Stop your teeth chattering. Every beast in the forest can hear that noise. Perhaps you should offer the wolves a few toes as a gesture of good faith. Yours are bigger and uglier than mine."

Barra grimaced through a badly bruised jaw and loose teeth. "You're the one with brains, and that's all you can suggest." Yet Barra's humour disguised his rising alarm. Aodán's voice was slurred, and he coughed raggedly. "Stay awake, brother. We can't allow our minds to fail us, and I want to spit in the eye of the wolf who thinks he can eat me."

Aodán's head snapped back, and he looked at Barra through red-rimmed eyes. "I shouldn't have trusted that tuilí. It's my fault we're in this mess. I put my nephew and niece in peril." His body shuddered, and once more, his chest convulsed in a bout of coughing. As Aodán opened his mouth to speak, he spluttered, and it seemed to Barra that tiredness threatened to overwhelm him.

"The Hag's tits, Aodán. Snap out of it. This was not your fault, and you're not leaving me to sort this mess out alone."

Barra trembled and felt his head as heavy as a pail of milk. His chin touched his chest, and he shouted, "No!" Then he summoned his remaining strength and bellowed, "Lift your head and talk to me!" Yet his voice trailed off at the sight of the grey wolf that padded into the camp, followed by five others. Barra growled at the beasts. In reply, the pack snarled, spread out, and padded closer.

* * *

Was it the wind, or did I hear a voice? Aoife's eyes burned as she scoured the white vista along the northern bank of the Abhainn Na Siúire. Panic rose in her breast and increased when she heard wolves howl. She pointed in a northwest direction and shouted, "They must be over there! Spread out and ride hard, or the wolves will feast on kings."

The scene before Aoife brought memories flooding into her head. The small wolf's head tattoo above her eyebrow throbbed. *Why is it doing that?* As a child of seven summers, she had taken up a spear and faced down the huge wolf, Silverback, that threatened her mother. Afterwards, Aoife prevailed upon her Ma to permit the design as a reward.

Now she saw a beast's jaws, a forearm's breadth from Aodán's face. Its breath formed a white mist that drifted over his head. In anticipation of its next meal, drool flowed from the wolf's cavernous mouth, which opened to show its large fangs.

"No!" roared Aoife.

Longsword in hand, Aoife charged the alpha wolf. Was it the surprise at being confronted that stalled the beast's bite? Or the sting of her blade's point as it travelled down its wedge-shaped head and sliced the predator's black nose? That would become the subject of campfire debates.

Aoife knew her initial slash caused only minor damage, no more than a cut from a blade of grass. She stepped a pace closer and, with feet set wide apart, steadied her stance. Gripping the sword in two hands, she readied to strike again. The wolf's lips drew back in a nightmarish smile of long incisors. Aoife muttered, "Shite!"

Yet Aoife could not see that when her wolf sigil throbbed, it became visible to the beast. The beacon reminded the predator of a communal memory of the small two-legs who faced and killed Silverback. With a dip of its head, the predator growled and barked before turning and disappearing into the forest, followed by the pack.

"The Hag's arse," muttered Aoife in relief.

When she looked at Aodán and Barra, panic filled Aoife's eyes. They looked like wax statues. *Are they still alive?* Selfishly, she prayed to the Goddess for Aodán's life. In the fading light, she blushed as she sensed the Goddess's disapproval and mumbled, "Sorry." Perhaps as a lesson, it was Barra who spoke first.

"It's cold in Mag Mell?" he slurred before his chin fell to his chest.

"*Build a bonfire. Now!*" roared Aoife. "They'll never make it to Cnoc Duíginn unless we get heat into their bodies."

✳✳✳

"*Rut the Hag!*" Ciar's exclamation was in sympathy with the reactions of the two hundred warriors who leapt from the salt and frost-encrusted triremes' decks into the bay's freezing waters. Instantly, they felt their balls and nipples turn to ice. Yet the shock was fleeting, and the fighters soon sweated with the exertion of tramping through knee-deep snow. Their goal was the treeline, two sunsets' march to the northwest.

Ciar gazed in astonishment at the towering peaks of snow and ice that formed the start of the headland and continued as far as the eye could see. Mountains had always guarded Caher Conri, yet their height appeared to have doubled. He pointed to the west. "Caher Conri must be buried under this. I pray to the Goddess it becomes Calman's tomb." Open-mouthed at the demonstration of the Sídhe's power, Cass and Olcán could only nod.

"Remind me never to get on the wrong side of Draighean," said Olcán, laughing nervously.

***

In his fortress of ice and snow, Calman swore at everyone he could think to blame except the Goddess. However, if she chose to see into his heart, she would find herself at the head of the list. He and his one-hundred-strong bodyguard built their winter quarters within the ruins of Caher Conri. The broken walls added strength and resisted the unceasing falls of snow and freezing rain. Thus, the makeshift wooden shelters they erected stood firm.

The same could not be said for the many barracks hastily constructed between the ráth and berm. The shelters would have been perfectly adequate against the wind, rain, and a typical winter's snowfall. Calman growled, "This is not normal." His belly rumbled in sympathy. Their food stocks had diminished alarmingly.

Calman's army had become cave dwellers. Yet his bones told him the season had become spring. The time was a guess since Calman had not witnessed sunrise for three cycles of the moon. The packed snow had softened, allowing the separate barracks to dig tunnels, sometimes using their bare hands. Very few had brought shovels, crowbars, or pick-axes. Only the furthest quarters were not connected; likely, they were frozen tombs.

The rí cursed as he began to understand the impact of the unrelenting storms. Three barracks had collapsed under the weight of the snow. "Eejits!" rasped Calman. Did they not know how to build a substantial shelter? Near starving, several quarters had turned on the weak and eaten them. The strong would not sacrifice themselves for their comrades. Weapons were drawn, and bloody fighting broke out. Soon, there was too much flesh to consume. Many fell to disease and the cold.

"One thousand warriors dead or waiting for the bean-sídhe," Calman said to his shield-man, "and it's not over." The Mhór Midhe leader tugged on a scruffy beard. His agitation was evident, yet none remarked on it. Calman was cruel and did not take criticism kindly. He stared at his protector. "We must break out of this tomb or starve." His face was grim when he added, "The Hag, but we may still starve if we can't find food. Organise work teams."

✳✳✳

In Cnoc Uisnigh, Messin Corb railed at the purple-grey skies that continued to dump snow on his domain. Yet, in recent days, he detected a reduction in the size and density of the snowfalls. He wondered about Calman. Was the tuilí still alive? Cnoc Uisnigh sat on a high hill above the white blanket shrouding his kingdom. He doubted Calman would have the same fortune.

Messin prayed to the Goddess that spring would come soon and the snow would melt. Yet he also knew the thaw would bring widespread flooding. He huffed. After generations of the Mhór Midhe praying that the deep freeze would pass, they might get their supplications answered. Overflowing rivers and the resurrection of the deep bogs of the Midhe might be the immediate future.

Could he hold the alliance he had built before the snowfalls? *I must. How else will I be remembered?* Stabbing pains in his belly bent Messin double. Since the winter storms, the agonies had increased in frequency and duration. Messin knew his time was close, and the bean-sídhe drew nearer.

CHAPTER 25

Cnoc Duíginn

The blood drained from Daráine's usually pallid face until it was as white as the powdered snow blanketing the hillfort. She fought against fainting as four burly warriors carried Barra and Aodán through Cnoc Duíginn's gates and into the Great Hall. The ríthe looked like corpses on the makeshift litters. Only by focusing on immediate needs and practicalities did Daráine stay strong and upright.

With a fortitude that masked her roiling emotions, Daráine strode ahead of the litters, shouting orders to servants. "I want rooms for Aoife and the kings and roaring fires, food and refreshments in each one." She looked at a shocked Aoife, who gripped Aodán's hand and bellowed again, "Warm quarters, hot food and beer for the guards accompanying her. They are exhausted."

Sláine looked at Daráine and understood her anguish. He nodded and spoke to his shield-man without knowing the trouble they faced. "I want guards posted at the ríthe's doors immediately. Double the sentries on the ramparts and gates." Turning to Aoife, he said, "You have likely saved the kings' lives. When Aodán and Barra are comfortable, Daráine, you and I will talk."

***

After what seemed like an age but probably was only a short time, Daráine and Sláine listened to Aoife's story of kidnapped children, kings left as food for the wolves, and Lonán's treachery. Daráine held Aoife's hand as she choked on her words. She put an arm around the young woman's slender shoulders as the dam Aoife had built crumbled, and tears burst through.

Daráine had never witnessed her brother so full of wrath. Sláine had a sharp mind and a talent for assessing people's character, but he was also gentle and introspective. She knew he was very loving and overly protective of her.

And so, both women were shocked, not at Sláine's outrage but at his reaction as he tossed his chair aside and paced the stone floor of the small chamber. He prowled the room, his face puce with anger, swearing bloody revenge. Still, Sláine's outrage was understandable; Daráine's had yet to take form.

"*The tuil!* How could I have misjudged his nature so badly? It's my fault. I should have discerned his looks and mannerisms." He stopped and faced Daráine. It looked as if, in an instant, Sláine had aged ten summers. Finally, he slumped, head in his hands, and wept. "Those poor children. I delivered them into the hands of a madman."

"Brother, the blame cannot and will not be laid at your feet for this," said Daráine.

"Daráine is correct," said Aoife. "Your concern speaks well of you, sir, but Lonán fooled everyone, not just you. Yet I believe that you have described him perfectly. He is not in his right mind, and only the Goddess knows what changed or ails him."

***

Keeping to the shadows, bare feet tiptoed along a hallway illuminated by flickering rushlights. "Cnoc Duíginn has many hidden passageways. I can show you a more discreet path to Aodán's chamber." Aoife almost jumped out of her skin and pulled the dagger from the sheath strapped to her thigh.

Daráine giggled at Aoife's reaction. It was her only relief on a dark night. She stepped from an alcove that Aoife knew was not there a few moments ago, looked at the knife, and chuckled. "You have no enemies in Cnoc Duíginn, Aoife. Indeed, I would like us to become good friends. We are of a similar age and share a lot in common." Daráine dipped her head in the direction of Aodán's room.

"I'm not sure a lowborn chariot warrior has much in common with a queen," responded Aoife. She tried desperately to devise a plausible explanation for her presence outside Aodán's bedchamber. "I simply wished to ascertain whether Aodán needed anything before I, too, retired to my cot."

Daráine shook her head. "If we are to be friends, we should be honest. That's what confidantes do." It seemed to Aoife that Daráine's lip trembled, perhaps at the prospect of being spurned. *She must be very lonely.* "I saw devotion in your eyes and how you gripped Aodán's hand as he was carried into Cnoc Duíginn. That went well beyond simple duty."

Aoife looked at her toes, which she thought were quite ugly. A moment later, she looked up, and tears flowed down her cheeks. "I thought he was dead, and I had lost him. I have already lost one who was closer than a sister to me. Another would be too much to bear." Daráine's heart went out to one in so much pain. She stepped forward and embraced Aoife until her sobbing subsided.

"Friends?" asked Daráine.

"Yes, friends," snuffled Aoife.

"Good. My home has many secrets. Let me show you how your room connects to Aodán's."

✳✳✳

As the concealed door closed behind Daráine, Aoife stepped closer to Aodán's cot. She watched him toss and turn in the bed. Was he reliving recent events, or did other issues trouble him? Aoife took a deep breath, whispered, "Shite!" and let her *léine* fall to the floor.

Aodán's body felt like a block of ice as she snuggled up and held him in her arms. "I'm here," she whispered. After a while, she smiled, for it seemed as if Aodán was less troubled. His murmured, "Aoife," brought tears and smiles. She hugged him closer and kissed his ear. "I am here and always will be, my love."

***

Between meán oíche and dawn, Daráine heard Barra swear and growl, "I need to piss."

"Do not even think about pissing in the bed." Daráine's scolding voice made Barra chuckle. "There is a pot at the foot of the cot. If you miss or knock it over, you will clean up the mess."

By the light of the fire, Daráine watched Barra slowly stand. She saw his face grimace in pain at the required effort and observed how his legs were unsteady. She wiped tears from her eyes but smiled as she heard pee striking the sides of the pottery vessel.

"You piss like a horse, Barra. I hope the pan is big enough!"

Daráine welcomed Barra's laugh. Yet it quickly became too much for him, and he coughed raggedly as he stumbled back to the cot. He stopped, examined his feet and hands, and then his manhood.

"Are you missing anything?"

"Just making sure. We were in the cold for a long time."

"You are fine. I've already given you a complete examination."

A glance downward and an impish look settled on Barra's face. "But is everything in working order? That is the critical question. One look at your tits and my friend is usually rock hard." Panic resonated in Barra's tone. "Look at it, now… cold, shrivelled and lifeless."

"It just needs a little encouragement. Come closer." Daráine smiled, opened her mouth, and sucked on a finger. The inference was blatant.

Barra stooped and turned to fall back into the cot but stopped suddenly, exclaiming, "The Hag, I'm a selfish tuilí!"

"What?"

"I should check on Aodán. He was in much worse shape than me."

"I wouldn't advise that… unless you wish him or Aoife never to speak to you again." Barra's laughter was genuine relief, and, this time, it did not result in paroxysms of coughing.

"I'm glad. That pair are far too intense. Having a sense of duty is good, but there must be a limit. Those two deserve some fun." Barra slipped under the pelts and turned to Daráine. "Now, where were we?" He moaned as the coverings moved, and a warm, wet mouth enveloped his cock. Then he heaved a sigh of relief as he felt his manhood grow stiff.

"See, I told you. Everything is in perfect working order. This time, I'll do all the work. Still, there's a limit to how many sunsets you can avoid your responsibilities to satisfy me."

Barra grinned as he felt Daráine straddle him and her pit swallow his manhood. "Seems like you missed me." Daráine's slap echoed off the chamber's walls.

CHAPTER 26

Sliab Crocta Cliac Mountains

The foothills of the *Sliab Crocta Cliac Mountains*, which ran parallel to the Bod Carraig range, were swathed in dense pines. Tisiphone was bemused as she rode through the trees. Everything around her said the weather was bitterly cold, yet she wore only a Spartan peplos and felt pleasantly warm.

She selected the garment over a chiton for its shorter length and long side slits. Tisiphone smiled. Among whores, the dress's common name was *phainomērídes* or "thigh-showers". It was a logical choice for her because it allowed faster access to the weapons strapped to her thighs.

She whispered, "Thanks," to Draighean and nearly fell off her rose grey mare when the Sídhe responded, *"You are welcome,"* as clearly as if she was beside her. Tisiphone shook her head. *Will I ever understand these people?* In her land, the priesthood and the nobility used the gods to subject citizens to their will and, hence, to garner more power and wealth.

She huffed. The only good thing about her gods was the numerous festivals and obligatory drunken orgies to celebrate them. For a whore, they were an exhausting time but always great for business. It seemed the Goddess of the Gaels took her role much more seriously.

The assassin sniffed the air and smiled, although not in a pleasant way… her face bore an assassin's mask. Faint scents of woodsmoke and body odour tickled her nose. Those she tracked remained far away, but the distance to being within a knife strike steadily diminished.

Tisiphone had developed a fondness for Órlaith and Tanaí, if at a distance. Like Draighean, she considered them wards, so she wanted to rush ahead. Yet she knew death lay on that path, so she settled her breathing and thanked her horse. The snort from the mount made her smile. This time pleasantly.

"Stay safe, Órlaith," whispered Tisiphone into the wind. The pleasant throbbing in her shoulder reassured Tisiphone that Danu's daughter was well. *Will I ever have children? Would I be a good mother? Would Olcán make a good father?* "What in the name of Apollo am I thinking? I'm a whore and an assassin. How could I be a mother?" she shouted into the wind.

I think you'd be a good ma.

This time, Tisiphone fell from her horse. Fortunately, she landed in a deep drift of snow. The voice and the giggle that followed it were from Órlaith.

***

Órlaith smiled and hugged Tanaí. "Be brave, brother. Our ma and her friends are coming for us." She reached out and ladled hot stew into Tanaí's cup. "Eat. We must keep our strength up and be ready to move quickly." Tanaí smiled and nodded. Órlaith was his sister. Why would he not believe her? She had always looked after him. In his childish heart, Tanaí promised the Goddess that he would protect Órlaith when he was older and bigger.

"What are you smiling at?" Lonán scowled at Órlaith from his perch across the fire. Órlaith bit her tongue to stop the smart-arse reply forming on her lips.

"Oh, this stew is hot and tasty. Perfect for this cold weather," said Órlaith, smiling again. In her heart, the child knew Lonán did not believe her. She also realised that Lonán's eyes held the look of madness. Órlaith's sharp ears picked up rumbles of discontent among the warriors when she and Tanaí walked around the camp. Many wondered how Lonán had beguiled them. Remorse made them overly friendly with Órlaith and Tanaí as if preparing a future defence. *Gold is why you are here, and that is a poor excuse.*

Her musings were cut short as a warrior charged into the camp, stopping at Lonán. She breathed harshly and, had she been a horse, would likely have been slaughtered and used for food. Lonán looked up from his meal and stared at her. There was no recollection of who she was in his eyes, which was unsurprising. Lonán did not know who most of his band were. They were tools, and he saw no use in becoming friendly with them.

"Well!" he snapped.

"We are cut off from the headland and Caher Conri," said the woman. "The ráth is buried under a mountain of snow. We will have to wait until the spring thaws before reaching its outer berm." The warrior paused. "Also, campfires stretch along the approach to the headland. The warriors carry Na Feirdhriseacha shields. Over two hundred and possibly four hundred shield-warriors block our path to Caher Conri."

"Lies," growled Lonán. "How could they have got there so quickly?"

"They likely arrived three or four sunsets ago on the ships we left behind at Niúig." Lonán stood, and the look in his eyes made the woman reach for her sword. She was too late.

"Lies!" shouted Lonán, thrusting his sword into the warrior's belly. A massive hand grasped her shoulder, pulling her further along the blade until she reached the hilt. Blood spewed from her mouth, and in a final act of defiance, she spat in Lonán's face. When the sword was withdrawn, the corpse slumped to the ground.

"Does anyone else wish to tell me lies?" bellowed Lonán before sitting on his tree stump.

***

Two riders rode into the camp as the warband broke its fast. The band had a handful of horses from the ríthe's capture. As the riders dismounted, the tension was palpable. Hence, wisely, both took time to feed, water their mounts, and talk to comrades before approaching Lonán.

The corpse of the slain scout remained on the frozen dirt, explaining the anxiety of those who watched. Sensibly, the pair plotted an escape path, gripped their reins tighter, and kept their mounts close. "One hundred riders approach from the east along the southern foothills of Bod Carraig. They bear the colours of the queens."

Forewarned, the two did not wait for Lonán's response. Instead, they remounted their horses, turned, and cantered to a distant part of the camp. Lonán sat silent, staring into the flames. He ignored the uneasy whisperings of the band. They overheard the messengers' reports and knew they were trapped. The gold they were promised was little more than a fantasy.

***

It took a cycle of the moon, but a small band of Calman's warriors finally carved a narrow, two-man-wide path through the snow. Panting and exhausted, they broke through the last few paces. In the moonlight, they stood at the neck of the headland.

Their first instinct was to celebrate, but the smell of woodsmoke and the chain of campfires curtailed any delight. "Shite!" muttered the leader of the group. Then, he made a surprisingly good decision. "Close the end of the path with snow," he ordered. "We can't allow whoever this is to see or track it back to Caher Conri. Then we will return to Calman and report."

***

As sunset fell, a naked figure wove a jagged path dipping in and out of and around the camp's perimeter. Like a spirit, she made no noise and left only faint impressions in the thin covering of snow in the forest.

At times, Tisiphone was close enough to slit the throats of the guards posted but resisted the temptation. Instead, she listened to their grumbles and their fear of Lonán. According to their discussions, many were contrite about their part in Órlaith and Tanaí's abduction. They also knew they were being hunted.

Hidden from Lonán's warband in a hollow, Tisiphone pondered her dilemma. Should she attempt to rescue Órlaith and Tanaí or foment terror within Lonán's camp? Both choices would inevitably invite discovery, but which was the safest for the children? They were under guard at the centre of the encampment as Tisiphone had expected.

She could ride her mare and its companion into the centre of the camp at a gallop and grab the children. However, that course had too many steps and the certainty of discovery. Órlaith was clever, but would she be strong enough to hold Tanaí on the horse's back while trying to escape? Tisiphone shook her head. *Too risky.*

The assassin had no doubt she could indiscriminately kill the camp sentries and many within the camp. But what would be the point? The odds were against her. Even if she targeted and killed Lonán, how would that help the children? She would have the remaining warriors to deal with. Tisiphone growled in frustration. She looked into the night sky and opened her lips to pray, but to whom—Apollo or the Goddess? "Shite!" she muttered. *Why did everything have to be complicated?*

Silver-white in the moonlight, the owl's black, unblinking eyes watched Tisiphone's every move. Sharp ears heard her every word from its perch in the ancient oak. The Goddess preferred her eagle persona, but that bird's eyes were useless at night. Still, the deity had a limited time. The Hag and those who ruled the Otherworld did not like others using a form they claimed.

"A distraction. I need a diversion," said Tisiphone. As the assassin's lips formed the words of a prayer, the owl screeched several times. She stood and turned in time to see the bird launch into the air and disappear. Tisiphone shook her head and whispered, "Thank you, Goddess."

✳✳✳

Olcán heard the owl's screech and tapped Ciar's shoulder. "Someone is suggesting we send the signal." Ciar chuckled and nodded to Cass. A formidable shield-warrior, Cass also had a rivalry with his sister about who was the better archer. He picked up his bow, nocked an arrow to the bowstring, dipped its pitch-soaked head into a fire, and quickly shot it into the air. He repeated the process several times, and then the trio waited.

East of Lonán's camp, Danu smiled and nodded to Brighid as they spied the three flaming arrows arching high into the meán oíche sky. "We are missing one," said Brighid. "I hope she is safe. I have grown to like her."

Tisiphone's expertise was with close-quarter weapons, yet she was not unskilled with a bow. She smiled as she pulled the notched stave from its sheath and strung the bow. Moments later, she sent three flaming arrows high into the air.

Danu smiled at Brighid. "Everyone is in place. Now, it's time to drive them mad." In Ráth Na Niúig, Draighean stood naked on the ramparts and lifted her hands. The song that flowed from her lips rose high in the starry sky and descended on Lonán's camp. Soon, Draighean was joined by Brighid and Danu.

In Lonán's encampment, Órlaith opened her mouth and began to sing. Brighid, Danu, and Draighean smiled and strengthened their voices and Órlaith's. The surprise came from the north when a fourth voice full of anger and promised retribution rose. Four watched on the walls of Cnoc Duíginn astounded and perturbed at *Aoife's Song*.

At the wolf howl from the north, Brighid turned to Danu. "You will recall I said we might have a rival queen in Aoife to contend with. She was only seven summers then. She's much older now."

"As I remember, my answer was, 'Would that be bad?' My answer has not changed, and I can think of no one better to protect our brother," said Danu. "It is time to join our eager friend's chorus." To those in the camp, the howling voices of Aoife, Brighid, Danu, and Draighean seemed clearer, and the flaming arrows in the east and west noticeably brighter.

Chaos reigned in Lonán's camp as minds were filled with terror and nightmarish visions. "Shut that child up," roared Lonán, but none dared to approach Órlaith. It was a good decision, for the Goddess awaited an excuse to bring her peculiar brand of horror. Harming Órlaith would have given that to her.

"Form a shield-wall around the children!" roared Lonán. He pointed to a group of warriors. "You will guard the girl and boy. Fail me, and you will die… very painfully."

"As if we're not going to die horribly, anyway," muttered a female warrior. No one disagreed with her.

＊＊＊

Tisiphone's darker skin and the ash and dirt stripes she layered over it made her practically invisible. Still, she cursed as, cat-like, she moved closer to the circle of shields. She knew a well-formed shield-wall was almost impossible to breach without superior numbers or mounted warriors. *How can I get to the children?*

In Tisiphone's mind, she told Órlaith to be ready to move quickly and prayed the girl heard her. The assassin would have smiled had she seen Órlaith whisper in Tanaí's ear and watched her arrange and draw the edges of his heavy, fur-lined cloak together.

The comely killer looked upwards and muttered, "A little help would be welcome now." A lone cloud moved across the moon, and the landscape fell into darkness. "Better than nothing," muttered Tisiphone.

She wondered whether protocol decreed that she needed a sacrifice to bring her supplication to the Goddess's attention. In her head, she heard the Goddess chuckle. Tisiphone's ears detected a low growling at the camp's western edge. Soon, it became a loud howling and barking. *Wolfhounds!* Tisiphone whispered, "Thank you," and moved purposely and silently forward.

＊＊＊

The unearthly howling from the witches tormented Lonán's warband. The more rational argued that it could be endured since it did not cause physical injury. The wolfhounds' baying, hot breath, and slavering mouths shredded their argument.

The first hound hurled its hard-muscled body against a shield and followed through with a snapping jaw that ripped flesh from the warrior's face. She fell screaming to the frozen ground. Silence, if not death, came when her throat was torn out.

A breach was made, and the thuds of hounds against other shields widened the impact. One weakness of a shield-wall is that once ruptured, the formation can fall apart quickly. The already fragile warriors' discipline crumbled on a moonless night, and their faith in Lonán dwindled rapidly. A torrent of wiry-haired beasts, each the size of a man, bounded through the gaps. Soon, the pack were biting and snapping at any spot of exposed flesh.

Sensing the presence of Órlaith and Tanaí, four wolfhounds separated from the pack and padded towards the children. Growling and with muzzles already bloody, the dogs sounded and looked fearsome. Tanaí's eyes were wide with fear. "Should we run, Órlaith?"

Órlaith shook her head. "We could never outrun them, Tanaí. However, I believe they won't harm us." Órlaith offered a prayer to the Goddess and, in what she hoped was a reassuring tone, said, "We will wait until Tisiphone comes for us."

***

Tisiphone moved resolutely through the chaos of screaming warriors and snarling hounds. On Draighean's advice, she had changed her primary weapons to well-balanced but heavier knives with forward-curving blades. She slashed left and right as she moved through the mayhem. Warm blood splashed her body, and, like the wolfhounds, Tisiphone became a gore-soaked nightmare.

Two wolfhounds challenged her, causing Tisiphone to pause her path to the children. The dogs bared their teeth and snarled at her. She felt the sigil on her arm throb and growled back. She saw disappointment in the hound's eyes before they moved on to another target. Moments later, Tisiphone spotted Órlaith and Tanaí and smiled at their four-legged guards as she padded towards them.

Órlaith's startled look and shake of her head should have been a warning. Relief at finding Danu's children uncharacteristically overwhelmed Tisiphone's professional detachment. Thus, the shield bash to her spine surprised her and made her grimace. Had she not already been moving, Lonán's follow-up staff across the back of her thighs might have ended her mission.

"Whore!" bellowed Lonán.

"Bastard!" screamed Tisiphone. Blinking furiously to refocus her vision, she rolled forward and then to the side before crouching. Rebalancing the knives in her hands, Tisiphone took comfort in their weight. Still crouching, she circled her quarry mesmerisingly.

"Run, oath-breaker. I hear Brighid's and Danu's riders' horns and the battle cries of shield-warriors closing on you."

"The children are my way from this, bitseach," snarled Lonán and stepped towards Órlaith. Yet the limping Lonán could not ignore the four wolfhounds who rose from the snow-sprinkled forest floor and took positions between him and his prize. Brought up sharply, he swore.

"Retreat. There is no path to Órlaith and Tanaí, only death by the hounds' jaws or my knives." Tisiphone refused to let Lonán's gaze stray as she closed on him. "The dogs might show you mercy, but I will not. I am the children's protector, as I am the brothers and sisters. Conall and Mórrígan wanted unity and reconciliation, not death."

Tisiphone sensed the wolfhound attack had lessened in its intensity as more fell to spear and sword slashes. Long before Danu and Ciar entered the camp, Lonán's warriors would reorganise, and she would be trapped. Thus, Tisiphone circled and launched herself at Lonán's back. His *scíath*, this time to her side, made her cry out.

"Broken ribs," she muttered. Rolling away, she renewed her attack. Tisiphone felt her knives strip wood and leather from Lonán's shield. However, she needed to find flesh. Lonán grunted as a blade carved a deep gash in his forearm. A backhanded scíath bash flung Tisiphone close to the hounds. She yelped as she landed hard on the frozen dirt.

"*Fight clever*," said the voice in her head.

Tisiphone looked into the hound's eyes. "Some help would be appreciated," she slurred through split and swollen lips. "Attack!" shouted

Tisiphone and again leapt at Lonán. She prayed the children's protectors would sense what she wanted them to do. They did not.

However, when Órlaith shouted, "*Ionsaí!*" the wolfhounds leapt forward.

"I should have known," snorted Tisiphone through blood-plugged nostrils. She heard the hounds' whimpers as Lonán's massive fists punched them to the ground, and a booted foot kicked them. Enraged, they attacked again and sank teeth into muscled thighs. Triubhas were a poor defence against canine teeth. Lonán's staff lashed at the hounds. A wolfhound's skull was crushed; it yelped and died.

Tisiphone cursed the hound's sacrifice, yet the diversion allowed her to move behind Lonán. She crouched low and gripped her knives. Boiled leather armour reinforced by iron scales protected the burly warrior's back but not his thighs. Two deep slashes across the backs of Lonán's legs brought him to his knees. "I offered you a path to safety, and you refused it. Now you will face Danu," hissed Tisiphone.

"Bitseach!" bellowed Lonán at the pain.

"The wounds are deep enough to let you crawl, but you will never walk again," snarled Tisiphone, gripping Lonán's hair and yanking his head up. She heard the horns and horses of Danu's riders and the bellows of Ciar and Olcán's warriors and smiled. "Vengeance is here." With a vicious slash, the pommel of Tisiphone's knife met Lonán's temple.

✳ ✳ ✳

In Cnoc Duíginn, there was considerable consternation at Aoife's behaviour and the unsettling writhing beneath her skin. Indeed, after Aoife's performance on the stronghold's walls, she had turned about and walked, trance-like, to her chamber. There, she lay down and resumed her sleep.

The following dawn, as she broke her fast, Aoife steadfastly repudiated the descriptions of her performance. Indeed, she became angry at what she perceived as a prank taken too far. Thus, Aoife stormed from the room, leaving Aodán, Barra, Daráine, and Sláine perplexed and at a loss as to the remedy.

Aoife lay on her cot sobbing. Yet that was not unusual, for, despite her reconciliation with Brighid, each day, she continued to grieve sorely for Báine. *Why are they doing this to me? I thought I could trust Aodán… and Daráine.*

"*I remember a child of seven summers who enjoyed life so much she asked me to end hers rather than let her grow old.*" Startled, Aoife sat bolt upright and stared in the voice's direction. "*I recall the same child confronting the slavers who had put her family in chains. Before me, I also see the child who killed the wolf, Silverback, to save her mother.*"

The voice from the chamber's deep shadows was melodic, yet Aoife thought there was a hint of sadness and perhaps disappointment. There was no mistaking who spoke. "Shite!"

The Goddess laughed. She remembered the child who frequently used the word and her raucous laugh. Where had she gone? "*On that day at the beach, I planted a seed in you, Aoife. I have stayed the hand of the bean-sídhe and watched and waited to see what shoots would sprout. Silverback saw inside you and was happy to die by your hand. Why are you afraid to look inside to accept who and what you are?*

"*Do you think that wolf's head painted above your eye was chosen by chance? Do you think your performance on Cnoc Duíginn's walls was an accident? It was not, although it was long overdue.*"

"I miss her." Aoife choked on her words.

"*Ah, the crux of the matter and the wall that imprisons you.*" The tone was one of disapproval. "*Of course you do, child, and up to a point, you should. Yet you have travelled well beyond grief… as has Brighid.*" The Goddess smiled as Aoife bristled at her words.

"*The seed in you can grow as strong as an oak staff or become twisted and gnarled and only good for birds to build nests and shite on. If you keep bitterness, regret, and a thirst for revenge in your heart, your path will be the latter.*" The Goddess seemed to pause, perhaps to choose her words carefully.

"But…"

"Do not interrupt me, child. This is a time to listen and decide." Aoife flinched, for the Goddess's tone had sharpened. *"You could not have prevented Báine's death. One wolf cannot prevail against one thousand warriors. Whatever visions you imagined did not come from me."*

In a more compassionate tone, the Goddess said, *"How do you think Báine feels when I permit her to look down on you from Mag Mell? When she hears you claim the guilt for her death? Does she smile or weep?"*

Aoife's eyes widened and then teared up. The voice softened, if briefly. *"Always treasure her memory and the love she had for you and Brighid, but do not build your future on it."* The Goddess's inflexion became firm. *"I need a wolf. Aodán will need one at his side. Is that you, or do I need another?*

"You are no longer a child, Aoife, but tell me you wish to be with Báine, and this time, I will grant your desire and find another for Aodán. Choose."

Aoife felt her skin writhe, and panic welled up in her breast. "I won't grow fur… or a tail, will I?" The Goddess's laughter at one who had become a child again seemed to shake the bedchamber's walls, and Aoife expected guards to storm into the room.

"No, although you should not give me such tantalising ideas. Become the child you once were, Aoife. I must go, and you should apologise to your friends. They love you and meant well. Help Brighid. Like you, she needs to grieve less and live more."

✷✷✷

Aoife was nervous and took a deep breath before she re-entered the chamber. The faces of her friends broke into broad smiles as she walked towards the table where they consumed their morning meal. As she got closer, their expressions became quizzical. *What has the Goddess done to me?*

"Sit beside me… please," said Aodán, pointing to the empty seat.

Smiling, Aoife gripped the chair's back but paused before she pulled it from under the table to sit. "I have an apology to make. It has been explained that my 'performance' at meán oíche was real, and you were being good friends. Thank you." Aoife sat down and reached for the bowl of oatmeal.

Barra had many admirable qualities, but subtlety could never be described as one. "I love the silver braid. It goes well with your raven-black hair. The black nails are an attractive touch, too. Are they natural or painted?"

Shocked, Aoife examined her fingers and muttered, "The bitseach." In her head, she heard the Goddess's laugh. Aoife smiled mischievously, looked at the food, and then at Daráine. "I was hoping for some red meat, preferably bloody. Perhaps you would inform the kitchen of my preference for future meals."

Daráine nodded warily at her friend. Aoife's raucous belly laugh instantly released the tense atmosphere. However, their relief was tempered by the noticeably longer canine teeth revealed when she opened her mouth. Barra looked at Aodán and smirked. "Do you wonder who explained our reactions to Aoife?" Then he chuckled and said, "I suspect you are in for more surprises this night."

Turning to Aoife, Barra said, "Take it easy on my brother. He remains more fragile than me."

✳✳✳

At meán lae, a hundred warriors emerged from the snowbound entrance of the path cut in the snow into the light of a weak sun. "The Hag's tits!" exclaimed Calman. "What happened here?" Those around him shook their heads and looked anxious. Mounted on spears were one hundred warriors' heads. The ravens had already feasted on the eyes, and only empty black sockets stared at Calman.

As the band walked through Lonán's camp, a warrior brought a shield with a dog rose painted on its face to Calman. He was puzzled by the unknown design and then smiled. "The rígana are settling accounts," he said, laughing aloud. "That is good for us. Let them waste their strength on killing each other."

He looked around the campsite. The headless corpses scattered across the camp had been stripped of anything of value. Calman bellowed, "Carry the dogs back to Caher Conri. The meat will make good stews." Then he turned to his shield-man and said, "I don't care how you achieve it, but I want whatever is left of my army dug out of this snow. We only have a short time to take advantage of our enemies' disarray."

* * *

Flann found himself commander of Ráth Na Conall's garrison by default. Standing on the walkway, he looked north and ruminated over recent events. Where were Aodán, Barra, and Lonán? Had they been drawn into a trap in Cnoc Duíginn and killed? Where had one hundred of the fort's shield-warriors gone? Had they deserted like Cass and Aoife?

Of more concern and the subject of constant gossip in the ráth, what did the howling in the forests signify? Was it a premonition of a wolf attack like the one ten summers past? He hoped not. Flann had faith in the queens and was reluctant to concede to the most popular rumour that the rígana had regained their powers and had vengeance on their minds.

He turned to face Cináed, whose temper had lost heat since Cass and Aoife reconciled. Albeit, he was troubled at which side they had chosen. "I suppose all we can do is wait," said Flann. Cináed dipped his head.

* * *

Danu and Brighid stood before Lonán in the deepest cell in Cnoc Duíginn's dungeons. His wounds had been stitched and bound, and the bleeding staunched, but for Lonán, it was no consolation. Looking into the shimmering black eyes of the rígana, he saw no mercy. Whatever remained of his future would be full of pain and eventual death.

"I did my duty," he rasped.

"Are you telling me that our parents commanded you to kidnap my daughter and son—their grandchildren? Tisiphone disputes that assertion. Or to leave their sons to freeze to death or be eaten by wolves? Is that your claim? Frankly, it is incredible, and we do not believe you," said Danu. Her voice was colder than the winds that swirled around the stronghold.

"Then kill me, bitseach. I did what I had to do. My conscience is clear."

"You're a sick man, Lonán. You will have your desire… but my sister will decide when and how," said Brighid.

***

Flann stood on the northern wall of Ráth Na Conall. Beside him were Aodh and Onchú, and neither looked happy. *Rut the Hag's arse, what is happening and why will no one tell me?* Finally, at the end of his patience, he opened his mouth to demand an explanation. He was stopped by Onchú, who pointed to a large warband midway between the Abhainn Na Siúire and the hillfort.

"Shite! It's an attack." Yet Flann was puzzled at the infuriating calmness of Aodh and Onchú. His eyesight was poor beyond two hundred paces. Hence, Flann could only see blurred, shimmering figures even when the warband reached Ráth Na Conall's foothills. Thus, he did what seemed reasonable and shouted, "Assemble the shield-walls on the ramparts. Arm the ballistae."

"That may be precipitous, Flann. I would advise you to stand down the garrison, especially the ballistae," said Aodh. "Although as an honour guard, they may be appreciated."

"*Póg mo thoin*—kiss my arse! What the Hag is going on? Whose side are you on?" Onchú whispered in Aodh's ear, and the king laughed. "I apologise, Flann. I did not know your eyesight was so poor. I suggest you trust us until those approaching come within the range of your vision."

"The Goddess preserve me," gasped Flann as the figures on the four leading horses sharpened into two kings and two queens. Each carried their tribe's banners, and behind them marched warriors who mostly wore Na Feirdhriseacha on their shields.

"Open the gates!" bellowed Barra. "Your queens have returned." Those on the ramparts and the civilians who joined them stared, dumbfounded at the sight of Brighid and Danu. A hand touched Barra's arm, and he looked into Danu's eyes.

"That is not quite accurate, brother. May I speak?" Barra's eyes widened, and he nodded. "My brothers, the Ríthe of Ráth Na Conall, have returned to their stronghold. My sister, Brighid and I, the Rígana of Ráth Na Niúig and Na Feirdhriseacha, are pleased to visit with our brothers." Aodán smiled and dipped his head in appreciation.

Danu signalled for an open wagon to come forward. At the gasps from the crowd when they saw the bound figure of Lonán, she said, "We have a judgement to pronounce on the traitor Lonán Ó Neill, who kidnapped my children and left your kings to the mercy of the wolves." Cries of *"Tuile!"* ascended and were swiftly followed by suggestions on how he should die slowly and painfully.

As Flann watched the procession enter through the eastern gateway, he turned to Aodh and Onchú. "Is there any reason you could not have explained who approached?"

Onchú laughed and slapped Flann's back. "It was much more fun this way." He added more soberly, "We were not altogether sure who had survived."

CHAPTER 27

Ráth Na Conall & Caher Conri

Those gathered had just broken their fast. Yet Ráth Na Conall's Great Hall was packed to its rafters. Anyone who could not find room to stand climbed the vertical oak beams and, legs swinging, perched precariously on the cross-timbers. Crowds thronged the stronghold's courtyard, ramparts, and walkways, hoping to hear glimpses of the proceedings.

Barra dipped his head to Daráine's ear. "Where on earth did they come from? I feel like a stranger in my domain."

The long, solid oak table, which usually sat on a raised plinth at the room's far wall, was positioned at the Hall's centre. Seated on chairs and benches around it were the ríthe of Ráth Na Conall, Clárach, Cnoc Duíginn, and Curraghatoor, and the queens of Ráth Na Niúig, Cnoc Duíginn, and Curraghatoor. Their advisors, shield-men, battle commanders, and one assassin sat beside or stood behind them.

The civic leaders of Ráth Na Conall and Niúig were seated uncomfortably together. The entry of Nuadha caused ripples of anger but also grudging respect that he had thrived as an outcast. Aoife, Cass, and Ceara, Cináed's hand-fast partner, strong-armed a protesting Cináed into sitting beside Nuadha.

That Nuadha was the Civic Leader of Niúig, a position Cináed once held, rubbed salt into old wounds. To Cináed, Nuadha's reputation could never be expunged. Ironically, Nuadha would be the first to agree with Cináed.

Draighean stood and peered around the chamber. Her eyes settled on a group of Druids. She smiled at them, and they glowered at her. It is paradoxical how those of a spiritual persuasion are often at war with each other. "Do you have a leader?" asked the Sídhe. "Let him stand and be recognised."

"Shite!" said Barra. "Is she deliberately picking a fight?" A tall, lean man stood and pushed his hood back, revealing a full head of slate-grey hair. "Where do they get these Druids? They all look the same, especially the sallow skin tone. Must be all the years spent training in caves." Barra's comments drew a mix of rebuke and choked laughter.

"I am the leader of this grove and those in Southern Ériu. My name is Iarlugh Ceann-Laith."

"You are conversant with the Fénechas?" The look on Iarlugh's face flitted between incredulity and scorn at the question.

"Of course."

Draighean pointed to an empty seat at the table. "Then why have you not taken your seat at the table? Our business is the judgement of Lonán Ó Neill." As the Sídhe spoke, the doors to the Great Hall swung open, and Lonán was dragged in between two burly warriors.

"I will not be a party to a decision you and those at the table have already taken. I am a Brehon and interpret the Law to determine a just opinion." Iarlugh held Draighean's gaze without flinching. "I am no man, woman, or creature's mouthpiece."

"An honest Druid will be a new experience for me, and I have been called worse things than 'creature'."

✳✳✳

In Caher Conri, Calman Mor was more frustrated than angry. The warmer winds of spring challenged the grip of winter snowfalls. That said, mud, slush, and water ponds, some of which deserved to be called little lakes, replaced the pristine white landscape. Clothes, boots, and bróga rotted, as did toes and fingers. The stench of decay was inescapable.

The headcount of his force was worse than Calman feared.

According to his chieftains, of the three thousand men and women who marched from Cnoc Uisnigh in the autumn, only half had survived the winter. Furthermore, five hundred might never survive the illnesses and infections ravaging the camp. The most common sound in the encampment was ragged coughing.

"Do you have any choice other than to return to Cnoc Uisnigh and ask Messin for more warriors?"

Calman's instinct was to kill the man like he had the other king. He stayed his dagger because this rí's warriors were better prepared for the snow and now outnumbered Calman's. Thus, the balance of power in Caher Conri was not in Calman's favour.

The king continued. "We have barely enough to hold Caher Conri's crumbling walls. Our one piece of fortune is that the beasts of the forests in their dens and burrows are emerging from hibernation, and the rivers are thawing. That will provide fish and meat for hungry bellies and make our fighters less likely to rebel."

The idea of having to report to Messin that he had been outwitted, his force reduced to a third of its size, and he had accomplished nothing made Calman grind his teeth. *Do I have a choice?* His scouts reported that the southern ríthe and peoples once again had united under the banners of Conall's sons and daughters.

He preferred to dismiss reports that said the rígana had regained their mystical powers, and a Sídhe rode with them. However, given his army was buried in an ice tomb during the winter and Brighid lived challenged his beliefs. Calman growled, and the rival rí fingered the grip of his sword. *The man is not stupid.*

Calman shook his head, signalling there was no threat from him. The hand still hovered near the sword's hilt. "You are right. I shall travel to Cnoc Uisnigh for an audience with Messin. Use the remaining warriors as you see fit and cause as much chaos as possible. I would not advise direct attacks since you will probably be heavily outnumbered. Assume the bitseacha and their pet Sídhe know your numbers."

***

The following dawn, a small group marched through the forested land bordering the northern coast of the headland. The ground among the trees was firm, but that would change when they emerged onto more open land. They had no horses… all had been eaten.

His imminent humiliation rankled Calman. Still, the journey gave him time to consider possible alternatives. *Perhaps Messin is dead.* Calman was observant and knew that the king was gravely ill. He smiled. If Messin died, no one would challenge him for the throne of the Mhór Midhe. Furthermore, he could become Rí Ruirech with minimal violence. Of course, he would execute some chieftains and minor ríthe as examples, but everyone would expect that.

Calman frowned. His plans might crumble like dry dirt if his failure in Caher Conri was exposed. Calman looked at his ten guards. *They must die.* Another thought slipped into Calman's head, and he smiled.

***

Teachta, the young messenger and Tisiphone's former companion had a mind for detail, the oratory of a seanchaí, and the passion of one who thought Lonán was the most despicable person under the skies. Amplified by Draighean so that all within and without Ráth Na Conall could hear, a litany of Lonán's crimes flowed from the young man's mouth. Cries of tuilí and calls for a painful death increased with each word Teachta spoke.

"He reminds me of Tadhg Ó Cuileannáin, Danu," said Brighid. "Yet will he finish before the people storm the Great Hall, drag Lonán into the square, and tear him limb from limb?"

Danu shook her head. "You and I will decide Lonán's fate." In the skies, a great eagle screeched, and Danu smiled. "With the Goddess's approval."

"How do you think the Druid will decide? He might be sympathetic to Lonán because he is old and doubly crippled after Tisiphone's work."

"His face gives little away, but his questioning is perceptive," said

Danu. "It will be embarrassing if Iarlugh allows mitigating circumstances to dictate his sentence. However, one way or another, *we* will ensure Lonán gets what he deserves."

"Does anyone speak on Lonán Ó Neill's behalf?" Iarlugh looked around the room but to no avail. Finally, he gazed hopefully at Nuadha. Perhaps one who had suffered as an outcast would have empathy. Two circumstances forestalled Nuadha's intervention. He considered Lonán's behaviour as contemptible as his brother, Uallachán's, and the dark looks from Brighid, Danu, and the Sídhe were frightening. He shook his head.

Iarlugh shrugged. He had hoped for better but expected nothing less. The crimes were heinous. "I find it sad that a man who faithfully served his king with distinction should in his later years go against his oath and have no arbiter to speak on his behalf.

"What was Lonán Ó Neill's frame of mind when he misinterpreted his orders from Conall and Mórrígan? Was it a wilful act? Other witnesses had no difficulty with Conall and Mórrígan's instructions, which seemed quite straightforward. That said, they were presented from two perspectives and in separate meetings, which was unhelpful."

Iarlugh stood. "In my judgement, and according to the Law, Lonán's corruption of his orders was deliberate. He is a bitter man, disappointed with his diminished authority and infirmity. Thus, I find Lonán Ó Neill guilty. Furthermore, I can assign no eiric that would satisfy the Law or those who were victims of his actions, especially those against innocent children.

"I declare Lonán Ó Neill an outcast from Clann Ui Flaithimh and Na Feirdhriseacha. He sought to sever the thread between the life and death of innocents and kings. Therefore, his life is forfeit." Iarlugh looked at Brighid and Danu. "I suspect the rígana have a suitable punishment in mind. He is yours to execute according to your consciences and the Goddess's will."

Danu and Brighid stood and faced Lonán. "You wished to kill my children and my brothers. My sister and I could never cause you the pain you deserve." A glimmer of hope appeared in Lonán's eyes. It was extinguished when Danu pointed to Draighean and Tisiphone. "However, they can and will."

The screams of Lonán O Neill rang out from sunrise until long into the night when the wolves took his body and the bean-sídhe his spirit. In the Otherworld, his torment was eternal.

∗∗∗

After meán lae, the Great Hall was cleared except for those who needed to design a strategy to repel the imminent invasion of the Mhór Midhe. Sláine stood to speak first. "My informants tell me several things. Firstly, Calman travels with a small guard to Cnoc Uisnigh and an audience with Messin. For obvious reasons, it will be a humiliating meeting for Calman.

"The second report is unwelcome. Messin has exceeded his expectations for his invasion army. He has twenty thousand warriors promised and will likely be closer to thirty thousand when he marches at Bealtaine."

Sláine paused and looked at Danu. "Finally, and I am not sure if you will consider this good or bad news. Órlaith's father, Óengus Dubdétach, is ten sunsets' march from Ráth Na Conall or Niúig. It seems the plunder has been good, and he and his men are in good spirits!"

"We could do with his warriors if not his presence," said Ciar, looking at Danu. Her cheeks flushed pink.

"Despite his reputation, Óengus is not unreasonable and chaffs at the lack of opportunity beyond the Black Pig's Dyke. Among the Ulaid, he is one rí among many. Given how quickly he marched south, he evidently cares for Órlaith, but maybe he also sees an opportunity." Danu looked at Sláine. "I am curious, Sláine. Do you know if Óengus journeys with only his warriors or do his people accompany him?"

"My scouts say those travelling number around four thousand." Sláine slapped his head and smiled. "They must have families with them." Danu inclined her head and looked around the table.

"We still have much land in the south where a rí could carve out a kingdom." She looked at Aodh and Onchú. "Perhaps to anticipate what Óengus might be thinking, you could select a few possible parcels of land."

"Northerners are nothing but trouble," grumbled Aodh. "The warriors would be welcome, though." The cantankerous king looked at Danu with a father's concern. "You're frowning, Danu. Why? This could work out well for you." He glanced at Ciar. "Apart from a few wrinkles to flatten." Brighid giggled, and this time, Ciar and Danu coloured. With a cough and a deep breath to settle her thoughts, Danu returned to business.

"The frown concerns Tanaí's father, Bran Mac Labraid-Loingsech. Tanaí is his sole heir, although that could change. He's a king who likes to rut virgins before the hand-fasting ceremony. However, Bran has a kingdom, a mountain stronghold, and does not lack gold or cattle. He can field five thousand warriors commanded by that tuilí Gobán." Danu looked at Draighean. "Given how his father died, he has no love for the Aes Sídhe."

"Like his father before him, I can remove him." Draighean smiled and dipped her head at Tisiphone. "Or we could let Tisiphone have the honours this time."

Danu shook her head. "I would prefer not to tell Tanaí I had a hand in his father's death. Bran and Óengus are immediate complications. However, since Calman has journeyed to Cnoc Uisnigh, perhaps we should remove those who remain at Caher Conri." Aoife and Brighid practically leapt out of their chairs at the thought of avenging Báine's death.

"Perhaps we should take a break to eat, drink, and piss," said Danu. "I would like to speak with Brighid and Aoife… alone."

∗∗∗

In a small chamber off the Great Hall, Danu turned to Brighid. "I would like you to suggest that Aodán and Barra lead the attack on what remains of the force at Caher Conri."

Brighid's face flushed red. Was the bitseach falling back into old habits? "You can't ask us to do that, Danu," said Brighid. "Why would you even suggest it? You know what they did to Báine."

Aoife's turmoil was evident in the darkening of her eyes, the writhing shapes under her skin, and the lengthening of her nails into black claws. Having never witnessed Aoife's changes, Danu was shaken. Brighid remembered the wolf images she had dismissed as illusions caused by snow blindness. "The Hag. I should have known," she murmured. Instantly, she felt guilty.

Danu recovered first. "Please calm down, Aoife… and Brighid. It seems I didn't express myself clearly." She looked beseechingly at Brighid and inclined her head towards Aoife.

Brighid immediately put her arms around Aoife and murmured soothing words in her ear. That Danu was genuinely flustered at their reactions lowered the heat. Also, Brighid's feirdhris did not seem upset, which tempered her demeanour. "Start again, Danu. Take a deep breath and slowly explain what you meant."

"With our and Draighean's powers, we could easily disregard Aodán and Barra and bully them into doing everything we want. However, that would be unfair, unwise and unsisterly. It is an attitude that divided us and the kingdom. They are kings as much as Aodh, Onchú, and Sláine; they just don't have as much experience. They need to have real roles and tasks to accomplish, and they need that before Bealtaine." Danu inhaled deeply.

"I propose letting Aodán and Barra lead the attack on the force that remains at Caher Conri. However, it makes sense if Aoife and you accompany them because you know the terrain better than anyone." Danu stopped talking and looked hopefully at Brighid and Aoife. She sighed in relief at the smiles on their faces.

Brighid turned to Aoife. "Much as I hate to admit it, she was always better at fidchell than me. Let's return to the meeting. If you agree, I'll magnanimously cede to my brothers." Aoife dipped her head. Danu and

Brighid were delighted that Aoife's lapis-blue eyes had returned.

"I have one thing to suggest, Danu." An eyebrow was lifted, and Brighid chuckled. "If we can't agree with Ráthgeal, Niúig will be attacked first and long before the Mhór Midhe invade. We should agree on the division and location of warriors and their families."

Danu inhaled and took a sip of water, relishing the coldness in her throat. "You underestimate your talent for strategy, Brighid. Let's return to the meeting." As Aoife turned and walked to the door, Danu put a hand on Brighid's arm. "You go ahead, Aoife. I have sisterly stuff to share with Brighid."

***

As the chamber's door closed, Brighid said, "What's going on, Danu? What 'sisterly' stuff?"

"You saw Aoife's reaction? The eyes, the hair, the claws, and what was going on with her skin? I thought she was about to go full wolf on us. What is she? We're out of our depth, Brighid. Let's talk with Draighean. Maybe she can counsel us on how to help Aoife." Danu's dog rose thumped in her chest, and she bit her lip.

"You've been a slut, sister, but motherhood has had a beneficial impact on you. Of course, you're right. I've been stuck in my misery and haven't looked out for Aoife… or you. We'll talk to Draighean after this meeting."

As the duo entered the Great Hall, Draighean looked up and smiled. Brighid whispered in Danu's ear, "The bitseach knows what we've been discussing." Then she laughed. "What's the point in whispering when she reads our thoughts? Although, given the deviant thoughts you have when you're around Ciar, she's probably getting some good relationship tips."

"Bitseach! You promised to stay out of my head."

Are these the sisterly things you spoke of? Aoife's innocent question made Danu's and Brighid's mouths gape. "Shite, Danu. She can read our thoughts, too."

Across the Hall, the raucous belly laughs of Aoife and Draighean echoed off the walls, drawing puzzled looks from those seated around the table.

CHAPTER 28

Caher Conri & Ráth Na Niúig

In the Bod Carraig foothills, Ruairidh Mac Carmag, the leader of the Cinn Péinteáilte contingent, jogged through a ribbon of pine and oak trees and felt his spirit refreshed. At last, he and his Forest People warriors were far away from the suffocating closeness of Ráth Na Conall. Soon, they would leave the mountains behind and enter the lush meadows and ancient woods which bordered Caher Conri's promontory.

Barra's and Brighid's riders and Aoife's chariots were ahead of Ruairidh. As usual, Aoife's carbaid gave the mounted warriors a wide berth. As they bounced over small droimnín that looked like ripples in a green sea, none wanted their comrades' or, worse, the horses' blood on the vehicles' long, spinning knives.

Brighid shared tales of Clann Ui Flaithimh's most famous chariot warrior, Gràinne Ni Fearghal, in light-hearted conversations over several evening campfires. On the next sunrise, after breaking her fast, Aoife rode at the apex of the chevron of five chariots.

Her face was flushed, although not because of the wind. Brighid's tales of Gràinne fighting naked no longer seemed outlandish, and she could barely restrain the howl that fought to escape her lips.

What or who am I?

✳✳✳

Life is replete with coincidences, whether by design or because a mischievous Serendipity had too much time on her hands. Concurrently with the Ráth Na Conall force travelling west, Dubhgall Mac Rónain led his Mhór Midhe warriors out of the ruins of Caher Conri. Once past the narrow headland, to the east was a range of hills; to his left and right were broad swathes of meadowland and forest.

Dubhgall paused to consider his options. After being cooped up for a season in a snowbound Caher Conri, his warriors were impatient to pillage and plunder. That was understandable. However, haste often leads to rash decisions and an early death. Dubhgall and his chieftains knew little about the land east of Caher Conri. Were the farms and settlements like those on the promontory and others within a half-day's canter? Burned and razed to the ground.

As he sat around the meán lae campfire, Dubhgall sought advice from the chieftains but received little that made sense. He had no idea how far they would have to march to find opportunities to satiate the warriors' desires, whether carnal or avaricious. Several groups of scouts had not returned, and that was troubling. Where were the southern hillforts? What size of garrisons defended them? Should he divide his force? Dubhgall quickly dismissed the latter option. He had barely one thousand warriors in good health.

He stood, exasperated at his chieftains. "The Hag's tits. You're useless. You would plunge headfirst into a lake, not knowing its depth. Only a meeting with the bean-sídhe might open your eyes."

In response, the chieftains growled and muttered impotent curses. Yet none would challenge Dubhgall. His reputation as a warrior was well-deserved. The only difference between him and Calman was that Calman would have killed them already. With a shrug of muscular shoulders, Dubhgall said, "At sunrise, we will take the hill route."

Groans accompanied Dubhgall's choice. "You need the exercise after doing nothing during the winter. When we reach the eastern end of the mountains, one hundred will form the vanguard and walk in a skirmish line." Dubhgall paused to take a few gulps of spring water.

"Everything in our path dies."

***

The size and make-up of Aodán's and Barra's forces were difficult decisions to make, but Barra successfully argued for mobility. Hence, Aodán requested one hundred riders from Curraghatoor, in addition to Brighid's one hundred and the original two hundred who had travelled with them from Gaul.

Aoife had made it clear that she was going with or without permission. Her desire for vengeance made Aodán and Brighid uneasy, but who could refuse her? Certainly not Brighid. As for foot warriors, including Ruairidh's contingent made sense as, apart from being fierce fighters, they could run as fast as the horses and still fight better than most warriors.

The challenge was Aodán's shield-warriors. Representations from both strongholds' ceannairí céad pleaded for their inclusion. Still, how would they keep up with the highly mobile force? The stalemate was broken when Aodán proposed that he and Olcán would lead two hundred shields to Caher Conri. Given their strong protestations over being left out, the foot warriors could hardly object when he announced they would travel by sea.

***

"Are we expecting company?" asked Decimus, pointing to the north.

"He made better time than I expected," said Danu. Alongside her on the ramparts, Ciar grunted something uncomplimentary while Draighean laughed. Having watched Olcán board a trireme, Tisiphone fretted, struggling with thoughts she had never dealt with previously. *Why am I getting close to this man? It's not who I am.*

As the warriors came closer, their hazy outlines sharpened. It was hard not to admire the body's discipline. Apart from the children who played games and harvested berries on the edges of the column, the families accompanying the Ulaid army were as well organised as the fighters.

Óengus Dubdétach strode ahead of his people with his shield-woman alongside him. He could have ridden a horse, and no one would have objected. The rí, however, thought that inappropriate. If those who fought with him walked, then so should he.

Danu smiled. The Cróeb Ruad wore sleeveless shirts, and some wore no tunics. "They are proud of that tattoo…" she said, "…and rightly so." She turned to Ciar. "We should greet them rather than confront them from our walls. A guard of one hundred would be appropriate."

Turning to Decimus, Danu said, "Take command and make the ballistae ready… just in case this goes awry." Finally, she faced Tisiphone. "Ready Órlaith, but do not let her out of your sight."

∗∗∗

Óengus turned to his shield-woman. "It's a good sign that Danu comes to greet us. I will meet her… alone. If things go badly, slaughter the tuilí… inside and outside the ráth."

The warrior smiled and dipped her head.

∗∗∗

"Things must be changing in the north, Óengus," said Danu, inclining her head toward his tall shield-woman.

He laughed. "It worked out well with my cousins, Aoibheann and Bláithín, so I expanded the experiment. Truthfully, Móirne's not the strongest warrior in my army, but she is the best." He chuckled again. "She's not just for decoration, even though she is quite attractive." Óengus examined Danu closely. It had been over three summers since he had last seen the mother of his daughter, and the difference was striking.

"I don't think you are the woman I once knew, Danu." He looked over Danu's shoulder to a disconcerted Ciar and laughed. "And it appears I have a rival?"

Danu flushed, smiled, and said, "If agreeable, we can continue our discussions in Ráth Na Niúig. I think a personal guard of ten, your shield-woman, and a handful of chieftains, with their shield-men, would

213

be appropriate. A few servants if you wish. However, as you can see, the fort is not huge, and accommodation is limited. Therefore, I suggest your people and warriors stay in the settlement of Niúig and its allied barracks. Depending on our dialogue, we may need to build better accommodation."

Óengus dipped his head to his shield-woman, who took a position at his side. About to walk past Danu, he was stopped by a hand on his arm. "Someone wants to meet you." Two horses cantered from the ráth. As they got closer, the smaller pony stopped, and Órlaith dismounted. There was a moment when father and daughter looked at each other uncertainly.

"Da!" shouted Órlaith and ran to Óengus.

"My banphrionsa," said a happy father, hugging Órlaith with muscular arms.

∗∗∗

"At least, this time, it's not freezing and snowing," said Aodán as the two triremes glided into the bay south of Caher Conri. Cedar and oak hulls crunched onto the sand and gravel beach.

Olcán laughed. "Obviously, you never grew up in Ériu. The water will turn your balls blue, regardless of the season. What's the plan?"

"You know the landscape better than I do. Brighid mentioned a trail or valley formed in the rock that leads directly to Caher Conri's southern wall. I doubt they'll expect an attack from the sea," said Aodán.

"Is an assault wise? We don't know Calman's strength and only have two hundred shield-warriors. Perhaps we should head northeast and meet up with Barra's force."

Aodán's chin set in a remarkable semblance of his father. He was wise enough to know this command was how he and Barra would be measured. *The Hag if I will disappoint my sisters… or Aodh and Onchú.* However, any retort was cut off when a northerly breeze picked up the stench of decay and infection and threw it at their noses.

"That's unnatural," said Olcán, his eyes watering at the assault on his senses. He pointed to a wake of buzzards high in the spring sky. "And that is not good news for someone."

"We may be in more danger from whatever created the smell," said Aodán, grimacing. "We will climb the southern wall. In a worst-case scenario, we will retreat to the ships and regroup."

***

The walls of Caher Conri were cracked, scorched black, and missing large chunks of rock. Hence, they were no challenge, even to the heavily armoured warriors. Indeed, the thickening melange of awful smells may have been the fort's best defence.

Aodán and Olcán gasped at the horrors before them as they surmounted the ramparts. The inner courtyard of Caher Conri was strewn with emaciated bodies and corpses. The stench of piss, shite, corruption, and infection hovered over the fort like an early-morning mist. "Take every precaution. Do not touch anything!" bellowed Aodán. "If any remain alive, put them out of their misery, but use your spears."

"We should have brought some of Iarlugh's druids with us. This belongs in his realm," said Olcán. "It's also a lesson on why we shouldn't piss off the Sídhe."

Aodán's warriors carefully picked their way around the muddy yard and the sodden outer defences between the walls and the defensive berm. Few of the Mhór Midhe had the strength to stand, let alone resist. Seeing limbs and cadavers with gnaw and bite marks made Aodán's stomach churn.

"Bind your hands and cover your mouths and faces," shouted Aodán. "Behead only those you sent across the veil and avoid splashing blood on your skin. The rest is not our responsibility. Build bonfires in the outer yard and burn everything until only ash and scorched dirt remain."

The flames from the fires rose high into a starless, meán oíche sky as Aodán addressed his warriors. "Strip and throw everything you're wearing onto the fires. We'll wash in the sea and change armour and clothing on the ships." There were no objections to a cold bath for once, only relief at being away from a cursed Caher Conri.

"Bring plenty of torches," shouted one wag. "We don't want to miss our female comrades' fine arses and tits."

"At least we've got something to be proud of… unlike your cocks," retorted one woman.

"I'm so hurt," replied the man to screams of laughter.

"Remind me to promote him," said Aodán. In answer to Olcán's quizzical look, he added, "He just took everyone's mind off the horrors we witnessed."

***

From the vantage point of a hilltop, Dubhgall watched the red sky over Caher Conri, scowled and swore. "We will need a new base of operations," he said to his chieftains. "And a way to avoid the jaws of a trap. If the bastards are behind us, there's likely more before us."

***

Outside the small chamber, a cluster of the nervous and the curious gathered. In the former category were Ciar and Móirne, Óengus' shield-woman. Ciar paced the hallway in evident turmoil over a meeting over which he had no control and no way to argue his case.

"It seems we have a common interest in what will arise from Danu and Óengus' deliberations," said Móirne. Ciar gazed into Móirne's green eyes and saw something more than a shield's loyalty. He smiled weakly and nodded.

"It would seem so."

***

Inside the room, the conversation between former lovers who, in Órlaith, had a bond only death would sever danced a reel around the core issue. "In three sunsets, the ríthe of Clárach, Cnoc Duíginn, and Curraghatoor will share a feast with us. I hope you will attend," said Danu.

"Until then, feel free to wander around the fort and the settlement. Take a ship and explore if you wish." Danu chuckled and then, in a more thoughtful tone, added, "Órlaith will want to accompany you. However, she will be attended by Tisiphone."

Óengus dipped his head. "Thanks. That is acceptable. A Greek protector is unusual, but she is not all she seems to be. Is she? Does Órlaith have servants or more 'traditional' guards? I'm fine with them accompanying us, too." He took a sip of water from a pottery cup. "You have not mentioned Ráth Na Conall, my intended destination until my scouts alerted me otherwise."

"There were issues which needed to be resolved and have been to everyone's satisfaction. We are of one accord now. My brothers, Aodán and Barra, are the Ríthe of Ráth Na Conall. Brighid's and my home is Ráth Na Niúig." At Óengus' raised eyebrow, Danu laughed. "I take it I was not overly complimentary about my sister when we previously met."

Óengus shook his head. "The words 'bitseach' and 'striapach' were the least offensive words you commonly used."

"It took losing someone precious to bring us to our knees and senses." Danu's eyes misted over. "Brighid's loss was much greater than mine, for Órlaith and Tanaí are alive."

"I am sorry to hear that. Will Aodán and Barra join us for the feast?"

"No, they and Brighid travel to Caher Conri to confront the advance warriors of the Mhór Midhe."

"You appear to do a lot of fighting. The Connachta ten summers past, and now the Mhór Midhe. However, that may explain why we made excellent time during the latter part of our march. Messin Corb's chieftains did not appear to want a major confrontation." Óengus laughed. "Even when we provoked them."

"Does the fighting bother you?" asked Danu.

"Not at all. It was getting boring and civilised in the North. Plus, there were too many intrigues." Óengus' face held a look of distaste. "I loathe politics."

"I could make the case that the South would be good for you and your people… for cattle, farming, fighting, and wealth." Danu smiled provocatively, but Óengus' eyes narrowed, which unsettled her. He inhaled deeply, then exhaled and halted the dance.

"Look, Danu. I know you, and I rutted. Likely, it was more pleasurable for me than you. Yet apart from Órlaith, whom I love more than I ever would have thought, we have no relationship." Danu looked curiously at Óengus, whose cheeks had coloured. "Besides, there are *complications*."

Danu laughed aloud, relieved that one issue had been resolved. "I think we should invite those who stand outside into our meeting. There will be two very relieved persons who cross the doorway."

"You won't mention any of the last stuff to Móirne, will you?"

His answer was Danu's peal of laughter. "If you think Móirne does not know your desires, there is no hope for you, Óengus."

Ciar and Móirne looked at each other outside the room and wondered what the laughter signified.

✳✳✳

Barra pointed to the red glow in the night sky. "My brother has claimed first blood." Aoife, Brighid, and Ruairidh nodded between chewing on the greasy haunches of roasted rabbits. He looked at Brighid and Aoife. "Which path would you take? After the winter, they will be looking for supplies and plunder, so I assume they will be heading in an easterly direction… towards us."

"West of Caher Conri, there are broad tracts of grassland and forests on either side of the mountains. Although, they're more like huge hills than highlands. Midway through the range is a valley that veers southeast into the large plain where we're camping. The dale is about six thousand paces wide, perfect for horses. If we let them get past that, the distances are about four or five times bigger, and they will be much harder to trap."

"That settles it. We split up. Brighid and I will each take half the riders, and Aoife will have her chariots. Brighid will ride towards the middle of the valley. I will stay on her left, and Aoife will take up a position on her right."

Barra glanced at Aoife and rubbed his chin. "My concern is that Aoife only has five chariots, each with one warrior." He chuckled. "Aodán will not be happy if I put you in undue peril." Aoife blushed and bit down on a gamey thigh.

To Ruairidh, Barra said, "Place your warriors in the forests on the northern side of the mountains. We will drive the Mhór Midhe towards you. If Aoife is in a precarious situation, her carbaid can seek refuge in the forests."

CHAPTER 29

Ráth Na Niúig

No Gael can resist the opportunity to feast and drink. Thus, as the sun set, Óengus and Danu hosted the royalty of Clárach, Cnoc Duíginn, and Curraghatoor. Fainche sat beside Onchú, surrounded by their daughters and a new baby girl firmly latched to her breast. For his part, Onchú suffered an unremitting wave of jesting about being well-outnumbered and how their dowries would impoverish him. Beside Sláine sat a glum-faced Daráine, who discovered Barra would not be at the feast.

It is one of the most pleasant events I have hosted in ten summers. Danu breathed deeply and exhaled. There appeared good reason to believe Óengus would seriously consider remaining in Southern Ériu. He and the other kings, even the ordinarily cantankerous Aodh, had quickly bonded and were regaling each other about battles and comparing scars. They resembled fisherman boasting about who caught the biggest fish.

Midway between sunset and meán oíche, a breathless Cass shoved revellers aside and charged down the centre aisle of the Great Hall. Reaching the high table, he settled his breathing before saying, "An army. An army is at the northern gate. Decimus has prepared the ballistae and is waiting for orders. The shield-wall has formed on the ramparts."

Óengus dipped his head to Móirne's ear. Brushing aside her red braids, he whispered, "Slip out. Go to our camp and ready our warriors."

***

Sitting on a reddish-brown bay, Bran, Rí of Ráthgeal, cut an impressive figure even in the flickering light of torches and braziers. A head taller than most, his body was solid, if slightly overweight. Long black hair hung in braids over his shoulders, and a full beard and whiskers touched his chest.

With arms spread, Bran called out, "I have come to visit my son, Tanaí, and enjoy your hospitality." Then he indicated the army behind him. "Open your gates, or my comrades will remove them."

"You may enter with your shield-man and a guard of ten—no more. As for your threats…" Danu dipped her head to Decimus and a volley of flaming bolts shot from the ballistae. Frissons of fear rippled through the Ráthgeal ranks. "This time, the missiles are celebratory… in your honour. Next time, I will demonstrate how we destroyed the Connachta."

The convivial atmosphere in the Great Hall chilled the moment Bran took his place at the high table. Kings and queens eyed the guest from Ráthgeal suspiciously. "I do not see Gobán. It is rare for you to be without him at your side," said Danu.

"His belly aches. He sends his apologies," said Bran with a dismissive wave. Yet Danu's feirdhris throbbed, and her curling sigils flowed like black rivers. She stared at Bran and was gratified at his startled look, for she knew her eyes were black as night. Like Óengus, he had never seen Danu in her full glory.

"That is a pity. I was hoping to renew our acquaintance." Danu beckoned to Draighean. "This is my friend, Draighean, of the Aes Sídhe." Bran's Adam's apple bobbled and down, and his pallor became sickly green. "She knew your father before his sudden death and is *very* familiar with Ráthgeal."

Bran felt uncomfortable and decided a jest might break the room's ominous atmosphere. A leer formed on his lips as he looked at Óengus and nodded in Danu's direction. "It seems we have something in common after sampling the same fruit. We should compare notes." Bran laughed loudly at his vulgarity.

"Arsehole!" said Óengus in a broad Northern accent.

* * *

"Do you not find it curious that Bran has not once inquired about Tanaí since entering the hall and being seated?" asked Ciar.

"Shite!" replied Danu, but her intention to confront Bran shattered when Órlaith ran into the Great Hall, screeching, "Tanaí is gone! Tanaí is gone!"

Several things happened almost simultaneously. With a speed that astonished everyone, Tisiphone was behind Bran and grabbed his braids. His head was yanked backwards, exposing his throat, and a blade slid across it. A thin stream of blood dripped down his neck, staining his shirt.

"Move, and the next cut will sever your arteries, and you will slowly bleed to death," hissed Tisiphone.

The substitute shield-man and Bran's ten-man guard correctly thought their king was in danger. Thus, they did what they were paid for and unsheathed swords. The shield-man died quickly as Ciar's sword swung and cleaved his head; the personal guard died from blades and spears before they moved more than a few paces towards Bran.

"What have you done with Tanaí? Where is Gobán? I doubt he is as ill as you claim. What was the plan?" Bran's blustering disappeared, and he trembled as he looked into Danu's obsidian eyes and watched the symbols on her skin writhe. At that moment, Bran knew that he had severely misjudged the mother of his son and heir.

"I don't know… this was not my instruction." Sweat rolled down Bran's waxen face.

"He is lying," said Draighean. "Leave him to me. I will break his mind and get the information. He will be a slobbering idiot afterwards, but that is on him." If Danu's mien made Bran sweat, Draighean's fierce look and cold words made him piss his triubhas.

"Gobán and the army will follow the An Bhearú to the bridge, traverse the valley that divides the mountains, and then veer east until they reach Ráthgeal. They will not harm Tanaí. He is my heir." Foolishly thinking he held the advantage, Bran regained some composure and smiled slyly. "Tanaí is guarded by Ráthgeal. Cede your position, Danu. Accept reality."

Draighean turned to Órlaith's servants and guards. "Take the child to her room and guard her with your life. She should not see this." As Órlaith was led sobbing from the Great Hall, Draighean turned to Bran. "You should have learned the lesson of your father's death."

To Tisiphone, she said, "Finish him."

"No!" squealed Bran as Tisiphone's blade bit into his flesh and was drawn agonisingly slowly across his throat. Grasping frantically at his throat, Bran, Rí of Ráthgeal, failed to stem the red liquid spurting from his arteries. He died painfully, drowning in his blood.

"Remove his head. It will prove that Tanaí is, by the Law, the new Rí of Ráthgeal," said Draighean.

CHAPTER 30

Bod Carraig & Ráthgeal Mountains

On the walls of Ráth Na Niúig, Danu turned to Draighean and Tisiphone. "I will ride with my cavalry; Ciar and Cass will follow with the shield-warriors." She peered into Draighean's smouldering ruby eyes. "Do what you do best."

Danu gazed at Tisiphone's face and could not prevent a shiver traversing her spine. The visage was a mask, which gave nothing away, but there was death in the dark brown eyes. Danu said, "I am sorry to call on you so soon after you rescued my children from Lonán. Please find and protect Tanaí."

"The riders of Curraghatoor will follow you," said Fainche. Danu started as the Rígan of Curraghatoor stepped from the shadows. She was dressed for battle and handed a protesting daughter to Onchú. "I have only one hundred with me. I wish we had brought more."

"Thank you." Danu choked on her words. She and Brighid had recently and foolishly numbered Fainche and Onchú among their enemies. Dressed only in her curling designs, Danu descended the walkway and strode to the open gateway where her horse and riders awaited. She was brought up abruptly. Before the gateway stood Óengus and Móirne. Behind them were the Cróeb Ruad warriors.

"Only a coward takes a child from its mother," said Óengus. "My warriors are ready to fight alongside Na Feirdhriseacha… if you accept our help." Óengus chuckled and, in a voice loud enough for Danu's shield-warriors to hear, said, "Besides, we can run faster and longer than your fighters!" From Danu's fighters came shouts of "*Póg mo thoin!*" along with other less polite suggestions.

"Thank you, Óengus," said Danu.

"I like your 'armour'. Perhaps you can encourage Móirne to do likewise." A growl gave Móirne's answer. In response, Danu bared her teeth. In the moon's light, Óengus was uncertain whether it was a grin or a predator about to kill its prey. She mounted her mare, settled her arse on the silver-fringed, blue diallait, and lifted her arms to the meán oíche sky.

In the moonlight's silver beams, Danu's designs flowed outward from her dog rose like black rivers. She opened her mouth and howled, sending a cry for vengeance into the air. On the ramparts, Órlaith added her song. Shortly after, two harmonising refrains rose from the west. They were followed by a chorus of howling from the forests' wolf packs.

"This is a strange family, Óengus. What have we got ourselves into?" asked Móirne.

"The Connachta were practically unbeatable until Ailill passed beyond the veil and Medb, who was of the Aes Sídhe, returned to the Mounds. Perhaps this is the time of Na Feirdhriseacha."

Óengus turned to face his warriors and bellowed, "*Ní ghéillfear, nó cúlú*—no retreat, no surrender! Kill the Ráthgeal bastards!" The combined force instantly took up his cry. Amplified and flung at Gobán's army by Draighean, the sound slammed into the Ráthgeal warriors like a massive wave against a cliff.

***

Almost at the ancient bridge and with the *An Charraig Dhubh* mountains in sight, Gobán's force staggered to a halt. The *Song of Draighean* brought turmoil and visions of their dead king to their minds. Sheets of lightning made the army starkly visible.

"Shite!" muttered Gobán, flicking a late-spring snowflake from his shoulder.

Perched on the shoulders of a burly warrior who strode alongside

Gobán, Tanaí said four words. "My ma is coming."

***

"No!" gasped Brighid as the songs of Danu and Órlaith were joined by Draighean's *Song of Dread*. The pain in Brighid's chest mirrored Danu's loss, bringing her to her knees. When she arose, Brighid's eyes gleamed obsidian. What began as a low rumble quickly ascended to a howl, of which any wolf would be proud. Aoife joined her, surprising everyone around the campfire, although not Barra and Brighid.

"What has disturbed you?" asked Barra when Brighid's and Aoife's songs fell silent.

"We need to finish this mission quickly. Bran has abducted Tanaí," said Brighid. "Our blades may be needed elsewhere. If only to prevent a greater slaughter."

"It's meán oíche," said Barra. "Therefore, we have a choice. We can mount up now and ride to the valley you spoke of or wait and gallop at dawn. You know the terrain, so I'm happy to leave the decision to you."

Truthfully, Brighid was torn between wanting to mount up and ride immediately and the unfamiliar voice within her that urged caution. She sighed. *This will be a long night for me.* "We should wait until dawn. Even at a canter, we risk our horses in the darkness. In the better light, we can gallop and still be at the end of the valley before the Mhór Midhe arrives."

***

After the awfulness of Caher Conri, Aodán's warriors camped on the beach along with the ship's crews. They heard the howling in the east and the response by Brighid and Aoife, which was much closer. Aodán's anguish was apparent to Olcán.

"Something is wrong, but I do not have my sisters' gifts to determine the cause." He turned to the senior helmsman. "Which would be quicker to intercept Barra? Sail south and then east or march north and east?"

"I wish I could say sailing would be quicker, but our path would be

226

to sail south until beyond the headlands and then turn east where the land broadens. You would likely still have a two or three-sunset march after disembarking. However, you will cut the time by half if you leave from this camp at a jog, although you are still looking at least one sunset."

"The Hag preserve me," said Aodán. "I wish I had a feirdhris like Danu or Brighid… or even Órlaith's snowflake."

"Or Tisiphone's blackthorn blossom," said Olcán. "I see a pattern of discrimination against men. *You* should speak with Draighean." At Aodán's raised eyebrow, he laughed. "Or maybe not. What's our plan?"

Aodán stood and stretched. "Rouse the camp. We march immediately."

***

"The *cailleachan*'s—witches'—winds and snowfall prevent us from using the mountain passes to cross as planned. Instead, they force us to take a path along the southern slopes of An Charraig Dhubh." Gobán's shield-man looked perturbed, as did the handful of chieftains who broke their fast around campfires. Gobán wanted the army to keep moving, but the leaders refused. They did not want to add a rebellion to their rising troubles.

"We did not mind fighting Danu if she refused Bran access to Tanaí. However, no one said anything about kidnapping a child and one who may already be our king if the Sídhe's visions are true. He's Bran's only known male heir. No matter how this ends, the High Council and the people will look dimly at his mistreatment." The chieftain held Gobán's eyes without flinching. "Your folly will tear the clann apart and weaken us before our enemies."

"As for Bran, was his execution part of your plan? What are *your* ambitions?" Gobán scowled at the accusation and opened his mouth to bite back. However, the most senior of the chieftains had not finished and continued to speak, albeit with one hand on his axe and a guard of trusted warriors behind him.

"We know the Mhór Midhe are gathering. Perhaps they will consider

Ráthgeal an easier nut to crack than the rígana and her brothers. With Bran gone, there is no kinship with Messin Corb to keep us safe. Worse, until Tanaí comes of age, Danu has every right under the Law to govern in his place, and she will have no love for us."

Gobán tugged and twisted his whiskers. Truthfully, after a life of faithful service and sound counsel, he had advised Bran poorly. He saw Clann Ui Flaithimh in disarray and the rígana banished. Thus, he expected Ráthgeal's warriors to cower whoever occupied the forts into acquiescing to Bran's demands.

Furthermore, he had imagined himself as the new Rí of Ráth Na Niúig after negotiating access to Tanaí. *How was I so mistaken?* Unwilling to accept full responsibility for his rash choices, Gobán cursed his informants and the political whispering of several members of Ráthgeal's High Council. *Tuilithe!*

Discovering a reinvigorated Danu and the Sídhe presiding over a feast with the kings of the south was a shock to Bran and him. Óengus' thousand Ulaid warriors was a significant, if lesser, blow. More in hope than substance, Gobán assured an uneasy Bran that Óengus would not take sides. *Blunder piled upon blunder.*

Usually a pragmatic man and careful strategist, Tanaí's abduction was opportunistic and out of character. Bran knew Gobán's illness was feigned. At the worst, Gobán thought he could carry the boy to Ráthgeal. There, from a position of strength, he would negotiate Tanaí's custody and Bran's release. A successful battle commander, Gobán made the fundamental mistake of underestimating Danu's wrath and ignoring Serendipity's penchant for mischief.

Now, he faced a rebellion from his chieftains, whose priority was saving their skins. A sizeable army closed on his force, yet where were Danu and her riders, and what was her plan? Gobán growled at the rising dissent. *Old women!*

"Do not insult me," snarled Gobán. "You knew that Bran and I did not bring two thousand Ráthgeal warriors to Ráth Na Niúig for a *céili.*

We will put politics and recriminations aside until we return to Ráthgeal. What we face is a simple battle between matched forces. I have been Ráthgeal's battle commander for fifteen summers and have never lost a fight. I do not intend to lose this one."

***

The grey was lathered with sweat, and its breathing was laboured. Tisiphone smoothed its velvet shoulders, and a tear rolled down her cheek. She whispered, "Sorry," for she had driven the mare almost to death to catch up to Gobán's warriors. With a slap of its dock, she said, "Go home," and prayed it would return to Niúig safely. Then she swung up onto the spare.

Flurries of snow swirled around Tisiphone as she walked the mount closer to the jagged lines of Ráthgeal's army. Together with the gloom of dawn, it proved an excellent camouflage and favoured her plan. Wisely, Gobán's army kept to the forested foothills of An Charraig Dhubh rather than risking being caught in the open meadowland. Still, by meán lae, the enemy would reach the break in the An Charraig Dhubh range and would have little choice other than to emerge into the open land. That did not suit Tisiphone's strategy.

Reasonably, Tisiphone visualised Tanaí kept under guard at the centre of the army. She was wrong and cursed the time wasted. The boy was at the front and kept close to Gobán. She observed Tanaí surrounded by and passed from shoulder-to-shoulder by burly men. *This will get bloody. I need a diversion and to make my move before they emerge from the forest.*

***

The main body of Gobán's force kept to a reasonably tight formation as it traversed the forest. The same could not be said for the third that formed its trailing rearguard. Made up of the least fit and older warriors, they constantly bemoaned the debacle… the weather… and not being paid. Echoes of the Sídhe's song lived in their head, making them anxious.

Thus, the news that two large forces were within sight and jogging…

not walking towards them, increased their unease. Only the harsh shouts and threats of the ceannairí céad kept them going. Typically, the chieftains were at the front with Gobán. The rank and file had no doubts they would be sacrificed without remorse to save their chieftains' skins.

The foot warriors trembled at the war cries of the Cróeb Ruad and Na Feirdhriseacha and the first cries of pain. They looked to their leaders and asked, "Do we stand or flee?" but received no answer.

"The rear is under attack," said the young messenger after controlling his breathing. "There are reports of a thousand warriors at our rear. Our fighters need orders. Otherwise, they will scatter."

Gobán's shield-man snapped, "Tell them to turn and fight. They'll be reinforced soon."

The envoy's expression said, "I don't believe you," and he was correct. The shield-man had no intention of alerting Gobán because it would achieve nothing. Gobán and the chieftains would not turn and fight. Their goal was to enter the stronghold of Ráthgeal with Tanaí and as much of their force intact as possible. Once there, the pendulum would swing back in their favour.

The timing was Serendipity's whimsy, although she had the nodding consent of the Goddess. As the messenger delivered his report, Óengus' warriors struck the body of the Ráthgeal army with the force of a battering ram. The messenger sneered at Gobán's shield-man. "It seems the chieftains, and you will have to fight after all," he said before turning and striding to join his comrades.

At the edge of the forest, Tisiphone was about to move closer to Tanaí. She heard Danu's wolf call and smiled. *I have my diversion.*

✳✳✳

In the west, Aoife's screaming and yowling rang across the valley. She knew it was unnecessarily dramatic, but she had spotted the Mhór Midhe, and Aoife wanted to ensure they heard and saw her.

The spoked wheels of the chariots bounced over terrain drying out from the winter's snowfalls. Spinning knives glinted in the meán lae sun.

Pointing her longsword towards the column of warriors, Aoife bellowed, "*Ionsaí!*" Pulled by a team of four horses, her carbad leapt forward, followed by the other chariots.

"Rut the Hag!" swore Dubhgall as the Mhór Midhe warband emerged from the forested foothills and onto the valley floor. Typically, they would have been welcomed by placid cattle grazing contentedly on the meadowland. His warriors were tired after the winter's horrors and the long tramp from Caher Conri. Hence, he hoped to let them rest, hunt for food, and strengthen their minds and bodies. Reenergised, they would resume their aggression.

The last thing Dubhgall wanted, or was prepared for, was to fight real warriors, not farmers. Yet before him, speeding across the plain, were five war chariots. *At least it's only five.* Instantly, he cursed the thought and scanned the landscape. *There must be more.* Where was the enemy's main force? How close were those who burned Caher Conri? "Keep a tight formation and form a spear hedge. We've dealt with carbaid before." The words were spoken confidently by a leader respected by his warriors.

Aoife's chariot swerved as if to speed along the front row of his defences, throwing mud and clods of grass at his spearmen. The tactic surprised Dubhgall. Moreso, when each chariot did the same. *Why? What is the point?* His question was answered within the same breath when he heard warriors curse and others shriek as javelins were thrown, striking shields and flesh.

Dubhgall watched helplessly as Aoife's chariots repeated the tactic repeatedly while keeping at least ten paces from his spears. Once the vehicles exhausted their supply of javelins, they switched to heavy, lead-weighted darts. A few of the more dexterous took up bows. In the time it took him to count to one hundred, Dubhgall had lost that number of foot warriors, dead or injured. He bellowed, "Close shields! Hold the formation!" as a score of fighters stepped forward to confront the carbaid.

The Mhór Midhe king heaved a sigh of relief when the barrage stopped. Yet his jaw dropped as Aoife's chariot attacked again, and his admiration for the driver's skill grew. The carbad sped along the front rank, but this time close enough for the spinning scythes to gouge, break shields, and shatter spears. Aoife howled like a wolf as, with perfect balance, she swung her longsword left and right. Those close enough to see the warrior's black eyes, roiling sigils, and talons recoiled. *What apparition were they fighting?*

Often, it only takes a trivial movement or diversion to disrupt a battle plan. Aoife's chariot stopped twenty paces from Dubhgall's spearmen. He watched the naked female warrior nimbly jump onto the cret's rails. The message sent by her thrusting pelvis needed no interpretation.

When Aoife turned and taunted Dubhgall's force with the gyrations of her pleasantly rounded white arse, his angry and humiliated warband ignored the shouts of "Stand firm!" and charged towards the chariot. As Aoife's feet touched the floor of the cret, her driver had turned the vehicle around and sped towards the forest.

* * *

The clash of steel and shrieks of pain rose to a crescendo as Gobán's rear and middle ranks were attacked. He swore and bellowed orders to fight but did not break the march to Ráthgeal and safety. Still, if the vaunted reputation of the Cróeb Ruad warriors was anything other than myth or clever disinformation, Gobán knew he was in peril.

He railed at his chieftains, whose warriors, like their leaders, fought as if in two minds. "Get your men and women under control," he shouted. "If only to preserve your worthless lives." Hidden by the trees at the forest edge, Gobán squinted across the snow-dusted plain dividing the mountain range and swore again. On the wind, or was it in his head, he heard a cackle that bore a strong semblance to what he imagined was the Hag's voice.

* * *

The voice above the storm was unnaturally clear in the swirling snow and winds, even to those in Gobán's disintegrating rear. "Surrender, Gobán. Hand over my son and *your* king."

Danu and Fainche's riders walked their mounts forward until they were barely a hundred paces from the treeline. In Danu's right hand, she gripped Bran's bloody head by its long black braids. As she opened her mouth to speak again, the storm around her subsided, and a sheepish sun threw off its blanket of clouds. The eerie silence that descended was broken only by the sound of horses snorting.

Lifting Bran's head high, Danu swung it like a sling several times and hurled it towards the forest. A strong gust of wind caught the skull and urged it closer to the Ráthgeal ranks. It rolled until finally stopping at a shocked Gobán's feet.

"Here is your king. Release my son, or as the Goddess is my witness, I will slaughter all of you."

* * *

The battle edged relentlessly towards the veteran warriors who formed the bulwark surrounding Gobán and the chieftains. In need of guidance and explicit orders, the fighters found confusion, acrimony, and threats.

Tisiphone smiled, patted her mare's shoulders, and mounted. She was tempted to try one of the howling incantations of the Sídhe or the rígana but shook her head. The closer she got to Tanaí without discovery, the higher the probability of success. Tisiphone's speed built, and soon, the canter became a gallop. Momentum knocked surprised warriors aside as if they weighed less than a feather.

Fifty paces from Tanaí, several of his guards spotted her and shouted for others to block her path. Tisiphone thanked Brighid for the lessons in managing a horse using only short phrases and her knees. She pulled her curved knives free. Blood spurted from slashed faces as she urged her mare forward, negotiating trees and the warriors surrounding Tanaí.

She looked up and saw Tanaí's eyes widen. Tisiphone thanked the

Goddess for the child's calm temperament, for he gave nothing away, and his husky mule had his back to her. In return, the Goddess refreshed the horse's strength, and it surged forward. Tisiphone winced as a spear raked along her thigh, her knife swung, and the top of a red-haired skull flew into the air.

Counting the slashes to her legs and torso was impossible, but Tisiphone knew by the burning muscles in her arms that she had replied to every cut. She grew lightheaded from the blood loss but growled, "No." She had a mission and a promise she would not break. The blackthorn on her shoulder throbbed, and Tisiphone smiled.

"I will confuse them," said the voice in her head.

"Thanks, my friend," replied Tisiphone.

It was perfect coordination. Perhaps her best. Tisiphone's knife swung as she bent over the horse's shoulder, gripping its flanks with her knees. With one hand, she lifted Tanaí from his guard's back and with the other, Tisiphone slashed the back of the warrior's neck. Arterial blood splashed her mount, and in reply, the horse crushed the sentinel's spine as he stumbled and fell under its hooves.

"Hold me tight, Tanaí. We're not out of this yet."

Tisiphone was thankful that the horse seemed to know his path. Her head swam from the unceasing blood loss as more blades cut her legs and spears raked her back.

Gobán screamed in rage as mare and rider, slick with blood, galloped past him and crossed the treeline. Had he lost his fidchell piece? With ears plugged with blood, Tisiphone heard a muffled bellow of, "*Stop the bitseach!*" and the garbled shouts of warriors racing to intercept her.

She felt her horse falter and prayed, "No. Please, just a few more steps." Tisiphone sensed the ground tremble and heard horns blare out, but she was fast losing consciousness. The blood-sodden diallait slipped, and she gripped Tanaí tighter. "You'll be safe, I promise."

As the pair tumbled from the horse, Tanaí whispered, "I know."

***

"She didn't exactly stick with the plan," said Barra. Brighid grinned hugely and wished Báine could see Aoife's bravery. Perhaps the Goddess would allow her to watch from Mag Mell.

Brighid pointed to the carbaid. "She achieved what we wanted, and her chariots can go much faster. She is holding them back to encourage the Mhór Midhe to chase her. However, Aoife will cross the forest line well before that occurs." Brighid looked at Barra. "How should we adapt to the new 'plan'?"

From the rise at the entrance to the valley, Barra pointed to Dubhgall. The Mhór Midhe king shouted and railed at his warriors. "That is one very unhappy leader. Look how spread out his force has become. We can rely on Ruairidh to attack when they enter the tree line. If you attack the rearguard, I'll hit them in the middle."

Brighid nodded, turned, and walked down the gentle incline to where her riders waited out of sight of the Mhór Midhe. She unfastened her armour, dropped her mail shirt to the grass, and swept onto her mare's back. With a howl, Brighid led her riders first at a canter and then at a gallop towards the enemy. Her brother shivered. His last images of Brighid were of obsidian eyes, dark swirling sigils, and a bare white arse.

Be safe, sister.

Thanks, brother.

"Shite!" muttered Barra. Were his thoughts no longer his own? He laughed out loud at the insanity of the situation. Still, perhaps he understood his father's relationship with the fearsome Mórrígan a little better. Barra mounted his horse, shouted, "*Ionsai!*" and led his riders towards the body of the Mhór Midhe.

***

Dubhgall's dilemma was clear and unpalatable. He heard the blast of hunting horns and saw two bodies of riders gallop towards his force. One would attack his rear, the other his middle. "The young bitseach led us into a trap," he muttered. A wry smile perched on his lips at Aoife's tactics. *She's clever. I wish she were on my side.*

Should he stand and fight or continue the dash to the forest? The latter seemed the only way to keep the momentum going and regain control of his warriors. *Yet what awaits us in the woods?* Still, that could be moot. It was a long jog to the treeline, and even fit men could not out-run horses. Instead, Dubhgall bellowed, "Ignore the riders. Kill the hors-es." It was a good strategy for one who had never fought against cavalry.

Brighid's riders, their black-tipped white foxtails swinging from their helmets like demented foxes, slammed into the rear of the Mhór Midhe. Dubhgall's warriors felt as if an avalanche of huge boulders had hit them. Those not bounced aside fell victim to the volleys of javelins and darts each horse carried. Bony hooves felt like iron as the mounts lashed out; yellowed teeth tore flesh.

Already in a loose formation, the rear of Dubhgall's force crumpled under the impact and shattered. Many tried to flee and escape the riders' long blades, long-handled axes, and maces. Backs were cut to the bone, and skulls were cleaved and crushed. The howling nightmare which led the riders only increased the terror.

Finally, the rump of Dubhgall's warriors dropped scíatha and spears and ran. They heard Brighid shout, "Attack the main body!" and the hope of escape rose in their chests. The expectation shattered when Aoife's chevron of chariots re-emerged from the forest and, banners cracking like whips, sped towards them. Steadily, the carbaid gained on the disorganised rabble. Yet the fitter retained hope of sanctuary in the forest on the valley's southern edge.

Their optimism was cruelly dashed when Aodán's and Olcán's shield-warriors emerged from the treeline. Many of Dubhgall's deserters fell to their knees, pleading for mercy. There was no compassion in the eyes of Aodán's fighters, and the Goddess had turned her back on the Mhór Midhe.

✳✳✳

An Charraig Dhubh forest resounded with the shrieks and death cries of men and women and the clash of blades. A constant flow of messengers told Gobán and his chieftains that their rear was destroyed. Assaulted on two sides by Óengus' and Ciar's warriors, the torso of Ráthgeal's body was caught in a vice's jaws whose teeth bit deeper and deeper. Standing forward on the treeline, Gobán fumed as he watched Tanaí and the assassin carried by Danu's riders from the battlefield.

"Surrender!" roared Danu. "My patience has limits. Your army is defeated, and your warriors will die because of your vanity. Act like the commander you once were. Yield and save further death and injury. Do not force me to enter the forest; I will leave no one alive."

"Negotiate terms, Gobán," said the senior chieftain. "Our strength is reduced by half, and they have yet to send their riders into battle."

"She's bluffing. We can…" The blade at Gobán's throat stopped his assertion. His shield-man bellowed, "Treachery!" and moved to defend his commander. Spears were thrust into his chest and back from all sides, ending his foolish loyalty to Gobán. A chieftain's sword removed his head.

"You have options, Gobán, but only because you have served Ráthgeal well," said the senior chieftain. His sword point pricked the soft flesh under Gobán's chin. "Die now, negotiate terms of surrender, or challenge the rígan. Those are your choices." In response, Gobán shrugged off his guards, strode to the tree line, and entered the plain.

* * *

"Face me in battle, Danu Ni Conall, Rígan of Ráth Na Niúig. The winner will choose the levy to be paid." Gobán walked forward another twenty paces and repeated his challenge.

"He is desperate, Danu, and likely, there are spears at his back for this debacle. Yet tradition dictates you must accept the challenge," said Fainche. The two tall mares the rígana sat on bumped against each other, impatient to join the battle.

Danu nodded. "It is a custom made by eejits." She flashed teeth at

Fainche, and the Rígan of Curraghatoor's blue eyes instantly narrowed.

"This is not the moment to break the ritual, Danu."

"If you think the remaining chieftains will surrender when I kill Gobán, I have underestimated your intelligence." Danu's obsidian eyes glittered, and she chuckled. "Nothing in the lore says I have to dismount, does it?"

Fainche sighed. "I suppose not. The Goddess go with you."

"When I kill Gobán, attack." Fainche dipped her head.

Gobán watched Danu walk her horse forward and smiled. *How can she defeat me?* Did he know that ten summers before, the Connachta's Rí Ruirech had similar thoughts before Danu castrated him and removed his head? When the horse began to canter, a frown settled on Gobán's face. When the canter changed to a gallop, he swore, swung his shield around and hefted his axe. "The bitseach!"

The pounding hooves seemed like thunder in his ears as the image of Danu grew larger. Gobán stared in disbelief. *She must dismount.* To Gobán, it was as if time slowed to allow him to ponder past misdeeds. He watched as Danu smoothly wrested a javelin from the sheath strapped to her horse's shoulders, raised the weapon, and hurled it towards him. For a moment, Gobán admired the skill of his enemy. *My shield is strong.*

His confidence ended when the momentum of the throwing spear split the wooden scíath, and the iron spike thudded into his chest. Gobán staggered backwards under the force of the throw. He looked up in time to see Danu's black eyes grip his own and the mace descend. In the moment before his head was reduced to pulp, Gobán heard Fainche shout, "*Ionsat*!"

✳✳✳

The Ráthgeal chieftains and warriors scattered, left rudderless at Gobán's demise, seeking to save themselves. One hundred and fifty horses charged into their midst. Javelins and darts were thrown, and axes, maces, and swords were hefted. Like a knife parting summer butter, there was little resistance as the riders carved a trail of blood and gore until finally linking up with Óengus' and Ciar's forces.

Broken in spirit and body, the Ráthgeal army threw down weapons, fell to their knees, and pleaded for mercy. As Danu walked her mare along the long line of prisoners, few would meet her black gaze or look at the gore-soaked body of horse and rider. "Are there leaders among your number?" she called out. "Let the chieftains and ceannairí céad step forward."

When no one moved, Danu turned to her commanders. "They committed treason. Cut out one in five and stake them." Unrest rippled through the defeated as a handful of chieftains stepped forward. Shouted curses were followed by the thud of fists as the ceannairí céad were expelled from the rank and file. Some remained surly, but most trembled and locked their gaze on the dirt.

Danu inspected the chieftains. "Your honour in standing forward is laudable. Still, you followed poor leaders in Bran and Gobán." Then Danu hissed, and all flinched. "Worse, you kidnapped *my* son. That I will not forgive." The rígan dipped her head to her ceannairí céad and said, "Stake them."

When Danu turned her gaze on the remainder of Ráthgeal's captains, she said, "You are veterans of many battles, but like your chieftains, you failed your men and my son, your king. He would not be well-served by men of such poor judgement." Danu looked at Óengus and Ciar. "Gut them. The Goddess will decide how long they will suffer." Cries of anguish became shrieks of pain as blades opened bellies.

"As for the rest of this pathetic army, I will give you a chance of redemption. When I call on you, you will come. If you do not, I will raze Ráthgeal to the ground and kill every man, woman, and child." Danu turned to Ciar. He was glad her eyes had softened and returned to their natural green. "Send these warriors back to Ráthgeal, but strip them first. We may as well make some profit from this tragedy."

* * *

Ruairidh was irked as he watched the battle, and so were his Cinn Péinteáilte warriors. He sympathised with the beleaguered Dubhgall, who stood at the centre of his diminishing force, bellowing commands to stabilise the Mhór Midhe formation. The king had decided that not knowing who or what was in the forest, his safest tactic was to stay out of the trees.

Hence Ruairidh's disappointment. It was his first real battle since arriving in Ériu, and it looked like it would pass him by. He looked to his second-in-command, a stocky, average-sized female who looked as hard as granite. "What do you think?"

The young woman grinned and inclined her head towards the battle.

"I agree. Why should Barra and Brighid have all the fun?" Ruairidh paused before adding, "Tell our people to stay well away from those bloody scythes on Aoife's chariots."

Barra swung his mace at another Mhór Midhe warrior with the same result as his previous efforts. The man's head disappeared in a pink-grey spray of pulped brain. At a roar from the forest, he lifted his head to see Ruairidh's band charge with their traditional clubs lifted high. That said, Ruairidh preferred to wield two hammers that the brawniest blacksmiths would have trouble raising.

Dubhgall had no doubt he would die. The contingent of painted warriors who charged from the forest and the shield-wall marching steadily towards the mêlée added two additional fronts that his shrinking group had to contest. The howling apparition's chariots ran down the few who broke away.

Therefore, Dubhgall decided that he would choose how his life would end. Roaring curses, he looked for the giant with a mane of red hair and bushy whiskers. Ruairidh was happy as he swung his twin hammers in a wide circle. He felt the iron heads tremble as they connected with flesh. No matter where the weapons struck, the momentum guaranteed that the trauma inflicted would be crippling or fatal.

A shout and a nod from his second-in-command drew Ruairidh's attention to the approaching Mhór Midhe leader. Finesse with weapons is a narcissism best left to the training circle or to impress young virgins into spreading their thighs. In a skirmish, it could prove deadly. Ruairidh moved like a bear, and those can be surprisingly nimble, whereas Dubhgall's stride had the grace of a wolf.

"Shite!" grunted Dubhgall as he parried Ruairidh's hammers with his spear after the initial onslaught and felt his bones judder. The wind rushed past his ear as one hammer scraped his cheek. He could hardly believe how quickly, independently, and precisely, the other club swung. This time, he growled and winced as the weapon's head glanced off his side.

"If yer intention is to wear me out, I should warn you I haven't broken a sweat yet," said Ruairidh as the combatants circled each other.

"I intend to kill you," replied Dubhgall with a grin. He watched Ruairidh swing the hammers in hypnotic circles, hoping to discern a pattern that would give him just one edge, one chance. It seemed like ages, but it was likely moments before he spotted the weakness. Dubhgall struck, and he felt the spear's leaf-shaped tip tremble as it opened up Ruairidh's flesh.

His path to victory was short-lived as he felt a hammer slam into his back and heard the dull crack of his spine as it snapped. As he stumbled to his knees, Dubhgall felt a creeping numbness radiate from his injury. "You tuilí, you changed the rhythm," gasped Dubhgall.

Ruairidh wiped the blood from the wound on his side. "I had to. Ye'r too good for me to take chances. Ye'r better than most I've fought, but they weren't good enough either." The hammer descended, crushing Dubhgall's skull, and he entered Mag Mell.

Aodán, Barra, and Brighid stood on the crest of the rise and watched the few hundred Mhór Midhe survivors rounded up and executed. The three were anxious to return to the rátha, which meant the Mhór Midhe were killed quickly. Now, they watched the riders and shield-warriors behead the corpses and strip the bodies of anything of value.

Aoife's chariots circled the battlefield just in case anyone had eluded them. Brighid knew Aoife was worried about what had transpired at Ráth Na Niúig. As for Ruairidh, he and his warriors had already departed and were marching back to Ráth Na Conall.

On the next sunrise, Aodán, Olcán, and their contingent would jog south to the coast and board the triremes. That way, the mobile forces would likely arrive at their destinations approximately at the same time as the foot warriors.

CHAPTER 31

Ráth Na Niúig & Cnoc Uisnigh

Standing in the hallway outside the bedchamber, the sisters listened to the sounds of grief and mourning. "Was the slaughter necessary, Danu?" asked Brighid. Her voice was sad, not angry. "It was like something I would have done, not you. And for what gain?" Brighid inhaled deeply. She felt the dog roses pulse, but not in harmony.

"It was for Tanaí, for my son," snapped Danu. "Would you have let him die?"

Brighid restrained her emotions, which was a victory, and spoke in a measured tenor. "Tisiphone rescued Tanaí... one horse, one warrior. You and Fainche had one hundred and fifty riders. A targeted strike with Tisiphone at its apex would have retrieved Tanaí."

Danu's tormented eyes glared at Brighid. "You don't understand," she hissed.

"I know you killed hundreds of *Tanaí's* subjects, injured hundreds more, and executed capable leaders. Bran paid with his life; Gobán died in the duel. Both deserved their fate. How do you justify the others? How will humiliating Ráthgeal encourage it to fight with us against the Mhór Midhe? More likely, they will want revenge. I would, and so would you."

Brighid sighed as if not wanting to continue. "They were Tanaí's subjects. Even if Gobán carried him to Ráthgeal, an army of Brehons and Druids would have upheld your right to be his Regent. No one could have stopped you from entering Ráthgeal… peaceably. The throne was yours. Who knows who will reign in Ráthgeal now?"

Danu crumpled to the hallway's floor. The shout of *"Bitseach!"* escaped her lips as a faint whisper and was followed by a cascade of tears. Brighid sat beside her sister and held Danu as her body was racked with sobbing. "I couldn't bear to lose one of my babies again. All I could think about was getting him back. I gave no thought to the cost. Am I evil, Brighid? Am I mad? Have I learned nothing?"

"No, sister, you are neither evil nor mad, although we once deserved that mantle. We knew we would make mistakes. The difference is that we will face the consequences together." Brighid inclined her head towards the chamber's door. "Our friend is dying in that room. She gave no thought to giving up her life for Tanaí. We cannot allow that, but what can we do?"

✳✳✳

The atmosphere around Tisiphone's cot was funereal. She had not moved in three sunsets. Only the almost imperceptible movement of her breasts and an occasional sigh supported the hope that she lived. Her body was a mass of angry bruises and thick scabs. Blood and water wept from numerous cuts.

On the orders of the Druid leader, Iarlugh, she was naked and lay not on a bed of straw but on soft wolf furs, which were changed and burned daily. His reasoning was sound. Tisiphone's back had as many, if not more, lacerations as her front. Thus, she needed to be turned regularly. It was a task that made those watching wince as if experiencing Tisiphone's pain.

Olcán was distraught and had not left her side since returning to Niúig. Occasionally, he looked into Danu's eyes with a gaze that asked, "How many times does she have to save your children? Help her." For their part, Danu and Brighid looked to Draighean, but she looked as helpless and stricken as they did.

"Please do something… anything. I was near death from an axe blow in the forests of Gaul, and the Sídhe, Mongfhionn, healed me. The bean-sídhe stood at Brighid's side on Bod Carraig, but you held her back. Can you not help Tisiphone?" Danu choked on her words, and her tears joined Brighid's on the stone floor.

As a member of the Aes Sídhe, she was supposed to be impervious to human trials, to maintain a porcelain façade of arrogance and dispassionate neutrality. Draighean failed miserably on both counts. Unlike Danu and Brighid, Tisiphone was not her responsibility. Yet she was the first human Draighean genuinely bonded with and perhaps loved. She was her sole friend.

"I have visited the Halls of the Aes Sídhe and begged for help. Mongfhionn told me the remedy was within us, but I am not and never have been a healer. Iarlugh has more knowledge in that area than I do." Danu and Brighid hugged the Sídhe. A sure sign of her distress, Draighean did not object and said, "Only the Goddess can help."

∗ ∗ ∗

"You appear to make a habit of near-death experiences." Tisiphone's eyes opened wide, which she knew was impossible given the gunk that glued her eyelids together. *"You present me with a great problem, Tisiphone. You are not a Gael and thus cannot enter Mag Mell. Yet, undoubtedly, you deserve the honour. Given your past and those idiot Greek gods your people worship, you would likely end up in Tartarus if left to their judgement."*

Tisiphone flinched, and the Goddess shook her head. *"I will not allow that. You have served me and my wards too well for that."*

"I could live, Goddess." The voice was small but filled with hope.

The Goddess chuckled. *"Yes, you could, but that would need a miracle. What vessel can I work through? Like Mongfhionn and even Medb, Draighean is a better Sídhe now that humans have touched and moved her. Yet that does not help you. She only knows rudimentary healing skills; your body is far beyond her talents. People forget the Aes Sídhe are not omniscient, and I need a channel to work through."*

Tisiphone envisaged the frown on the Goddess's face and tittered. "Sorry, I never considered a god having human emotions." The room fell silent. "I am always curious about plants. You never know when they can be used to kill, disarm… or heal."

"Is this going somewhere? I like you, but I do have other responsibilities." Frustrated at her helplessness, the Goddess's tone was waspish.

"The healers in the fort told me that a common name for the feirdhris is 'witches' briar'."

The Goddess roared with laughter. *"Clever girl. It would be a great shame to lose you to Tartarus. Please try to delay your next 'near-death' experience until I can find a loophole to allow you into Mag Mell. Sleep well, my servant."* The Goddess's hand waved over Tisiphone, and she fell into a deeper sleep. Around the cot rose wails, and tears cascaded down cheeks. All thought Tisiphone had been taken from them.

Cracked lips opened to whisper, "Witches' briar."

"Shite!" muttered Draighean and turned to Danu and Brighid. "Her life is in your hands."

Several sunsets later, Tisiphone's eyes fluttered open. She felt claustrophobic and trapped and began to panic. Yet she was also pleasantly warm. She sneezed as a tress of auburn hair tickled her nose. The bodies on either side of her stirred. "I haven't taken part in an orgy in a while," she croaked. On either side, Danu and Brighid clung to Tisiphone as if her life depended on it, which it did. All were naked.

"I like your hands on my arse and tits." Tisiphone giggled. "But your breath is disgusting."

"Bitseach!" The twins rose slowly from the cot with mock anger. Drained by the previous sunset's ministrations, their knees buckled. Olcán and Ciar caught and carried them to two seats.

A haggard Draighean and relieved Iarlugh hovered over Tisiphone. Olcán's hand gripped hers, and she smiled at how comfortable it felt. "Thank the Goddess. Someone washed the grime from my eyes, and I can see," she whispered. Everyone laughed with relief, and instantly, the atmosphere in the room changed. This time, the tears were of celebration.

"You may wish that were not true when you see what they have done to you," said a severe-looking but thankful Draighean. "However, I am absolved of the blame since I can lay the fault at yours and *their* feet." The glint in the Sídhe's eyes made Tisiphone wary.

***

Moments later, the chamber door opened, and a servant passed Órlaith and Tanaí to Danu. Standing at the foot of the cot, a solemn Órlaith said, "My brother and I cannot thank you enough, Aunt Tisiphone, for protecting us." The child's composure broke, and she ran to the head of the cot, knelt, and threw her arms around Tisiphone. Tears soaked Tisiphone's hair. "Tell me if I'm hurting you," said Órlaith.

Tisiphone shook her head and whispered, "You can never hurt me."

Tanaí walked forward. He had a puzzled look on his face, pointed to Tisiphone's breasts, and said, "Wow!" Tisiphone's face flushed a deep red, as did others in the room. The men nodded in approval.

"I'm sorry, Tanaí, I should have covered myself," said Tisiphone.

Tanaí shook his head. "You're being silly, Aunt Tisiphone." He smiled and pointed again. "Look at the pretty flowers." It was as if a curtain fell from each person's eyes. They looked anew at the vines of feirdhris and blackthorn flowers carpeting Tisiphone's body.

"I think that together, we did an amazing job, Danu, but did we have to make her more beautiful?" asked Brighid.

As for Tisiphone, she cried and kept repeating, "They called me Aunt." She had a family.

***

"Search him for weapons," ordered Messin Corb as Calman entered the chamber. Located off Cnoc Uisnigh's Great Hall, the small room was typically used for pre-meeting negotiations. Calman smiled confidently as he entered the room. Apart from the Rí Ruirech, only Messin's shield-man and a guard of ten occupied the space.

"Not a friendly greeting, my king." Calman bowed, yet the act spoke of arrogance, not supplication.

"One who lost Caher Conri, three thousand warriors, and two ríthe…" Messin smiled, and Calman did not like the look in the Rí Ruirech's yellow eyes. "…and oh yes, I forgot, who killed his guard to prevent me from knowing the facts should not be so confident of life."

Messin rasped, "You deserve no welcome other than a blade to open your belly. Did you think I was stupid enough to let you go adventuring without ensuring I had eyes on you?"

Calman's eyes narrowed, and he looked around for an escape route. Messin's laugh echoed off the stone walls. "There is no fleeing this room, Calman. Save by the bean-sídhe. What was your plan? A dagger to my heart as I slept. You always had little imagination. I am truly disappointed in you."

"Why am I still alive?"

"I will choose the time of my death… and yours, too," said Messin. "Unfortunately, I need a battle commander, and you remain my best option." Calman breathed easier, and his mind considered his alternatives. Again, Messin's cold laughter echoed off the walls, and Calman shivered.

How did I underestimate him so badly?

"You have no subtlety. A blind man could read your intentions. You will accept the role of battle commander under *my* terms. Otherwise, you will die here and now, and the wolves will feed on you." Messin paused, and Calman thought he looked like a buzzard examining a corpse.

CHAPTER 32

Ráth Na Niúig

Rós was unhappy. Her fingers twisted in sympathetic anxiety as she rocked from one foot to the other. She stood in Ráth Na Niúig's court-yard, observing those called to the meeting enter the Great Hall. Among them were kings, queens, civic leaders, battle and garrison commanders, shield-men and women, and the senior helmsman of the fleet. There was even a Sídhe and an assassin.

"Why the Hag do they want me?" she muttered.

When Nuadha conveyed the rígana's request for her presence, she screamed, "No!" After accusing him of betraying her, she stormed from their Niúig roundhouse and had not been seen for three sunsets. It was their first argument in over ten summers. Now, Rós felt ashamed as she recalled the hurt in Nuadha's eyes. A tear rolled down her cheek as he walked past her on his way to the meeting. He smiled at her, but she could not meet his eyes.

"Shite! Why can't they leave me alone?" Rós' exasperation escaped her lips with venom and was much louder than she had intended.

"Because you have a unique talent we need." Brighid's voice came out of nowhere, and Rós almost jumped out of her skin. "Whether ci-vilian or warrior, no one can or will escape the battles that will soon be upon us… including you."

"Do you have to sneak up on people?" snapped Rós, whirling around to face Brighid. The shift in Rós' demeanour from the typically gentle young woman with a smile for everyone to the combative crea-ture who confronted her made Brighid take a step backwards.

Caught off-guard, Brighid could do little but gaze awkwardly into the most beautiful pair of grey eyes she had ever seen. *Why have I never noticed them before?* Instantly, Brighid felt guilty at her betrayal of Báine, and her cheeks flushed. The conflicting emotions made her feirdhris pound in her chest.

Rós, clearing her throat, jerked Brighid back to the bubbling con-frontation. *Get a hold of yourself, Brighid.* Still, she was gratified at the pink highlights in Rós' high cheekbones. *Is she also embarrassed? Why?*

"I promise the reason we asked you to the assembly is nothing bad. No one will force you to do anything that makes you uncomfortable. Also, you know most of those attending and some quite well, including me and Danu. We have not suddenly changed, and we consider you our friend." Brighid inhaled deeply, took a step closer and held Rós' hand. "If it helps to ease your worries, sit beside me."

Rós nodded. Another tear rolled down her cheek, and she sobbed. "I've hurt Nuadha. Even if he forgives me, how can I forgive myself?"

"Nuadha will forgive you. Of that, I have no doubt. As for forgiv-ing yourself, I can offer no advice, for I have found that to be the hardest of all battles."

✻✻✻

Danu's gaze and eyebrow lifted as Brighid and Rós entered the cham-ber. She observed that they held hands and that Rós sat beside Brighid. Alerted to the shift in Brighid's aura, Danu's feirdhris throbbed content-edly. Hope bubbled up. *Is Brighid moving on from her grieving for Báine?*

At the thought, Danu immediately looked at Aoife, who entered the room with Aodán. She sighed, relieved when Aoife prevailed on Aodán to take the vacant seats beside Rós. *Thank you, Aoife.*

Once all were seated, Danu rose. "I would like to welcome Rós to our gathering. I know this is not what she would have chosen for herself. Hence, her presence is doubly appreciated." Danu glanced at Brighid and chuckled. "That said, she has an ally in Brighid, who considers our meetings overlong and a waste of time." Brighid nodded enthusiastically in agreement as everyone laughed.

"We have lots to discuss, but I will begin by addressing why Rós is with us." Danu looked at Rós and smiled. "That way, you can avoid the rest of our discussions if you wish…" Danu's eyes caught Brighid's. "…however, sister, I am afraid you are here to the end." More laughter rippled around the table.

"We have weaknesses to address before the Mhór Midhe invasion. I think Rós can help us with one. Undoubtedly, she is the best natural archer of our tribes." Shouts of "Yes!" blended with the rap of pottery cups and jugs on the table. "Brighid and I 'cheat' with our powers. Yet, even with that advantage, I would not wager against Rós in a contest between us."

Danu turned to an embarrassed and open-mouthed Rós. "We need a band of archers, probably about two hundred. I would like you to train them. Ciar, Olcán, and Aodán, along with their ceannairí céad, have agreed to suggest suitable candidates. You can add your selection if you wish and will make the final decision." Danu paused to take a sip of water.

"Sadly, you have only two cycles of the moon to train the archers. I hope that is enough." After a short pause, Danu said, "We would also like you to lead this group. However, we will understand if you think it is one step too far."

As Danu resumed her seat, Rós gripped the oak table and stood. Her face flushed, and she looked anxiously around the table. Her gaze fell on Nuadha. "Please forgive me for being hurtful. You never deserved it." A broad smile and a dipped head from Nuadha gave his response. Next, Rós looked at Danu. "It seems a long time since we first met in Nuadha's farmstead. I should have known better than to question your intentions."

Rós smiled and nodded. "I will train Na Feirdhriseacha's archers."

Cheers resounded around the Great Hall. "As for leading the band, perhaps we should set that decision aside for the moment." She smiled at Brighid and Danu. "I may be a good archer but a terrible leader."

***

The meeting resumed after a short break at meán lae. Danu was delighted to see Rós return, and so was Brighid. It was Decimus who opened the discussion. "Our ballistae are an advantage over the Mhór Midhe, but we need more and not just the large ones that sit on Ráth Na Conall's and Ráth Na Niúig's walls. The smaller ones are more mobile."

"Our fleet of triremes is an advantage, but we need to determine how to use the asset effectively," said Danu. Decimus looked at the senior helmsman. "Can ballistae be mounted on your triremes? I envisage them as floating ramparts." The grizzled seaman scratched the almost white bristles of his short beard.

"I have heard that some of the Great Sea nations, including Dionysius, are testing ship-mounted ballistae and other weapons, such as stone and Greek fire throwers. Even on the open seas." The helmsman paused, and his blue eyes twinkled. "The triremes' upper decks are essentially flat. The An Bhearú River is deep and wide to the old bridge, and the currents and tides are manageable." He looked at Decimus. "We should run a few trials to determine the flaws in your proposal." Decimus nodded.

A cough directed the eyes of those seated to Aoife. "We need more chariots. The terrain north of Niúig is ideal for carbaid, but we only have ten vehicles between the two forts. Calman Mor didn't bring war chariots on his incursion. Does this mean the Mhór Midhe do not use them in battle? In which case, that would be in our favour." Aoife looked at Sláine and smiled. Her question did not need words.

Sláine dipped his head and said, "I shall find out."

Danu looked around the table, content with the tone of the discussion. "Barra, Brighid, and Fainche should decide how best to use our riders." Danu looked at Onchú and said, "I assume we have no issues about horses if we need more."

Onchú inclined his head, yet there was a troubled look on his face, and Danu watched as Fainche put a hand on his arm and whispered in his ear. Quizzical looks from Brighid and Danu prompted Fainche to explain. "Unsurprisingly, our daughters are excellent riders and well-trained in using weapons.

"Three have requested positions in the battle. On merit alone, it will be hard to refuse them. Yet, as you are aware, not so long ago, Onchú lost much at Carn Tigherna." Fainche smiled weakly. "Only Úna does not wish to join her sisters. Her talents lie in healing… and other things."

Draighean's laugh echoed off the room's walls. "I have heard gossip of these 'other things' and look forward to meeting Úna. In the meantime, I am sure Iarlugh will be delighted to have her help in the healing tents and rooms."

Onchú groaned, "No," at the thought of Draighean's potential influence on Úna. Seeking to divert the conversation, he looked at Danu and said, "Because of Tanaí, you are Regent of Ráthgeal. On whose side will Ráthgeal fight if called? Ours or Messin's. They could add a substantial number of shield-warriors to our army."

"Their recent defeat at my hand, unsurprisingly, has made Ráthgeal wary of supporting us. I sent Teachta to request their leaders' attendance at this meeting. As you can see, they have chosen to sulk rather than participate," said Danu.

"If they choose not to come to Tanaí's aid or, worse, take the Mhór Midhe's side, I will see Ráthgeal reduced to ashes and its people scattered across Ériu or sold." Those gathered shivered at the cold certainty of Danu's words and her glittering black eyes.

✳✳✳

"I hate to pour cold water on such an amicable gathering," said Aodh.

"No, you aren't!" Danu's retort was instantaneous but delivered with a flash of teeth and eyes, which had regained some semblance of normality.

Aodh dipped his head and laughed. "Tactics and strategies are all very well, but ignoring Ráthgeal, we have three thousand shields. Possibly, with the levy of my, Onchú's and Sláine's nobles, that may increase to five thousand."

He looked at Onchú, who nodded in agreement. "Yet we face twenty thousand or more of the Mhór Midhe, plus the inevitable glory seekers and mercenaries. Those are not great odds." As Brighid and Danu rose to defend their position, Aodh's raised hand stopped their words.

"Please, do not remind me that you faced a similar army of the Connachta and won. I was there, but we're older now… especially me. Have you considered the ramifications for the people of the battle and its aftermath? Should we lose, all those around this table will likely be in Mag Mell, but our people, and quite possibly our sons and daughters, will be violated and sold for gold or slaughtered."

"What are you suggesting, Aodh?" asked Brighid. "That we should surrender? Even if we do, the people will still be despoiled, sold, and killed."

Aodh shook his head. "Even at my age, I will fight alongside my warriors and friends. Yet perhaps it would be useful to impress on Messin Corb that it will not be an easy campaign for him. Meet with him and acquaint him with the realities. What is there to lose? Apart from anything else, the Goddess will be pleased we have done everything to avoid war."

"The delegation would be walking into a trap, Aodh," said Onchú.

The old king's eyes twinkled, and he looked at Draighean and Tisiphone. "Do we not have those among us who can snare the hunter or reduce the number of kings we face? At worst, we can gain more time to prepare and strengthen our defences."

The meeting was almost at a close when Aodán's chair scraped over the floor as he stood. "We assume that Messin will concentrate his attack on Ráth Na Niúig. Why? Are there no paths to the southern kingdoms through Caher Conri, Cnoc Duíginn, and Curraghatoor? Should we discuss contingencies?"

"A good observation that should have been addressed at the start of this meeting." The speaker was Sláine. His criticism drew hard stares from Brighid and Danu, yet he did not hesitate to give his opinion. "That said, and as Aodh has pointed out, we have limited numbers of warriors. Hence, focusing on where best to defend or attack makes sense.

"The path to Niúig is the shortest and most direct for the Mhór Midhe. If Messin chose Caher Conri or Cnoc Duíginn, it would add a half-cycle of the moon to his march. Hence, we would have time to redeploy our forces." Sláine looked at Onchú. "In the case of Curraghatoor, the delay would be less, and Onchú would have to stall the attack until our assets were repositioned. Messin Corb will know this."

Onchú smiled and nodded his agreement with Sláine's summary. Addressing Aodán again, Sláine said, "I agree that this should have been discussed earlier, but I doubt that Danu has got the strategy wrong."

Aodán looked at Danu, whose lips held the last moments of a frown, smiled, and said, "What else are brothers for, if not to keep their sisters on their toes?" Relieved ripples of laughter circulated the Hall. Then Cináed stood.

"Oh, shite!" muttered Aoife.

Her da smiled. "My sons and daughters chastised me. Ceara admonished me for my churlish behaviour. I apologise to all in this room, specifically Nuadha… and Danu. Neither deserved my misdirected anger." Cináed inhaled deeply. "However, I must correct a misconception." The room instantly tensed again.

"You do not have five thousand warriors. By my reckoning, we have double and perhaps three times that number." Incredulous gasps circulated the Great Hall. Cináed smiled and said, "Will the people of the Mhór Midhe freely fight alongside their warriors? I doubt it. Yet our people fought alongside Danu and Brighid against the Connachta." Cináed looked at the ríthe and rígana.

"What makes you assume we will not fight at your side this time? As before, we can hold spears and dig ditches."

✳✳✳

Teachta observed the almost imperceptible shake of Tisiphone's head when Aodán and Danu asked him to take the request and terms for a meeting to the Mhór Midhe. Yet how could he refuse to play such a pivotal role? It might result in both armies retreating to their homelands and embracing peace.

He would be forever remembered in tribal lore. Furthermore, he was an envoy and a good one at that, not a warrior. This was his profession; this was how he fought.

The tall messenger nudged his horse to keep it moving towards Cnoc Uisnigh's gates. Rider and mount passed the countless rows of tents that, like tiny waves, rippled out from the Mhór Midhe's stronghold. He muttered, "Shite!" at the size of the enemy force. *How can I count so many shelters?* As Teachta dismounted, he was surrounded by a handful of hard-faced warriors who rubbed calloused knuckles or fingered blades in anticipation.

He gulped as he strode, still guarded, down the central aisle of Cnoc Uisnigh's Great Hall. However, Teachta exhibited no anxiety and resisted sideways glances to identify potential escape routes. He ignored the cold stares of his enemy, who parted to allow him passage while muttering threats of torture and a painful journey to Mag Mell.

At the centre of the high table sat Messin; seated on his right was Calman. Teachta could not decide which disturbed him more. Messin's predatory gaze or Calman's cold, dark eyes. The latter seemed devoid of humanity. Surrounding both men were the chieftains and high nobles of the Mhór Midhe. *And a right pack of cruel tuilithe, they look.*

"If you have come to deliver the surrender of Conall's sons and daughters, the people, and the lands of Clann Uí Flaithimh in Ériu, then you are welcome. If not, we will have fun watching you die slowly and painfully before we accomplish the same outcome by war," said Messin.

The Rí Ruirech's voice was strong, yet Teachta noted the brief notes of fragility and pain and how Messin looked at his distended belly as if it were an enemy. He observed the eyes of Messin's nobles and shivered. It was as if they were looking at a cadaver. *The Hag! He's dying.*

Teachta surveyed those seated at the high table more closely, and in their gaze, he saw men who would commit any atrocity to advance their ambitions and increase their wealth. Yet in Calman's mien, he saw fury, frustrated ambition, and a promise of death. *Why does Messin keep a viper beside him? A serpent's nature never changes.*

He inhaled and exhaled several times to steady his breathing. "The sons and daughters of Conall and Mórrígan wish to meet to discuss peace. They suggest the northern end of the valley that divides An Charraig Dhubh and borders the Mhór Midhe's lands.

"They hope both parties can negotiate a path forward that does not include war or increase the suffering of both peoples. The meeting will be held according to the rules of the Fénechas. If the Brehons judge either side breaks the Law, that party will cede defeat." A ripple of laughter filtered along the table. It fell silent when Teachta added, "The Druidic Council of Ériu and the Brehons will ensure compliance."

At the harsh stares and shaking heads, Teachta raised his hands and pleaded, "What does it cost to have one meeting?"

"There is always a cost, envoy, and often it is paid by an innocent," replied Messin. "We will meet with the ríthe and rígana." At Messin's nod, Teachta was seized by his brawny guards.

"I am an envoy, protected by the Law and the traditions of hospitality," shouted Teachta as he struggled to escape the grip of his guards.

"How many of your profession live more than a few summers? That is the true measure of the Law and tradition." Messin looked at Teachta and then the king's shield-man. "I will not kill you, but for it to have any meaning, payment must be made for your request. He needs his tongue to speak our response, but he only needs one eye to find his way back to Ráth Na Niúig."

Teachta screamed at the hiss of released liquid and the excruciating pain of an eye ruptured by the glowing orange-yellow blade laid across it. Yet it did not stop Teachta's lips from forming a satisfied, if grim, smile. He had achieved his mission. As he was bundled onto his bay mare's back and tied fast, Teachta slumped over its shoulders. He heard the slap on the horse's rump before blackness overtook him.

***

Aodh winced at the sight of Teachta's disfigured face and the accusing look in Tisiphone's eyes. Her gaze promised retribution on those whose words had resulted in the envoy's pain. *Will my life end with an assassin's blade?*

The room's mood simmered between wrath and anticipation. Teachta had not moved in three sunsets. That said, the rise and fall of his chest confirmed he was alive and not in mortal danger. Also, an examination of his body showed he had not suffered further torture or violation. Thus, Iarlugh concluded that the young man needed time to rest and recover from the trauma.

Draighean, perhaps experimenting with humour, asserted that the scar and the future wearing of an eye patch would give the effete young man the ruggedness of a warrior. It would open many young girls' legs, and thus, the injury was not all bad news.

True or not, the comment drew raised eyebrows and murmurs of "Inappropriate" from those gathered in the bedchamber. Balance was partially restored when Draighean confirmed she could help with the blistered facial scaring. Recovering Teachta's eye was, however, beyond her healing powers.

***

"Messin Corb is mine to deal with," hissed Tisiphone. There was no hint that she would be open to negotiation, and no one around Teachta's cot challenged her. Instead, any argument Tisiphone had was with herself.

First, there was Danu and Brighid, Olcán, Órlaith and Tanaí, and now Teachta. *How can I be an assassin when I feel for people?*

"Perhaps that is what makes you a good assassin. Speak with Beacán and Iasg when next in Gaul. They may have the answers you seek." Tisiphone started at Draighean's intervention but was stopped from delivering an angry retort by Teachta's voice and his trembling hand on hers.

"Messin is dying… slowly and painfully. You would show him compassion by killing him." Teachta smiled at Tisiphone and then looked at Danu. "He accepted your offer to meet." Having drained the limits of his strength, Teachta fell back into a restful and well-deserved sleep.

Brighid looked grimly at Danu. "If what Teachta says is correct, it is reasonable to assume Calman will command the Mhór Midhe horde."

Danu nodded. "It is also likely that Messin's death will be Calman's first victory. We should plan for this."

CHAPTER 33

An Charraig Dhubh

From their vantage point, Ráthgeal was far to the east. To the northwest was Cnoc Uisnigh. In the pass dividing An Charraig Dhubh, one hundred Na Feirdhriseacha shield-warriors and the same number of Clann Ui Flaithimh scíatha marched behind Aodán and Danu. Few of the warriors were happy, and all were unanimous—their numbers were too few to protect their king and queen.

"The Hag, Danu, how did you convince me this was a good idea? Better still, how did Aodh persuade you?"

Danu looked at Aodán and shook her head. "You'll probably make a great king, especially if you lay the ground for a catastrophe *before* the battle begins." Insulted and embarrassed at Danu's chastising tone, Aodán reddened and his jaw set. The smirk on his sister's face lowered the temperature. "It is a sister's duty to tease, but you must learn to be a better fidchell player, or others will relieve you of your gold… or your life."

Aodán growled, "Bitseach." He inclined his head to the north, where a similar-sized warband approached. "It's a trap." Danu nodded in agreement. "Yet how will Messin Corb break the truce agreement and not bring the wrath of the Brehons and the Druidic Council down on his head?"

"With enough gold, Brehons, Druids, and even oracles can be bought," said Danu. A grunt behind the duo reflected Iarlugh's displeasure at the rígan's judgement, yet the Druid saw no point in disputing the remarks. "I, too, am curious how Messin and Calman will circumvent the Law." Danu sighed and looked at the sky. "We have the Goddess and Draighean on our side."

"Great, we'll all have a céili in Mag Mell to celebrate crossing the veil."

Danu shook her head. "Beware, brother. Neither the Goddess nor the Aes Sídhe is known for their sense of humour, even less one as dry as yours. How does Aoife cope with such pessimism? She has always been an example of vitality and optimism."

Aodán laughed loudly and winked. "I have other talents, sister." He smirked like an adolescent before adding, "Barra's not the only one well-endowed in one particular area." Danu rolled her eyes, and her belly laugh echoed across the valley.

"Be thankful Aoife's out of earshot, or her black talons might carve tracks in your soft flesh." Danu frowned momentarily and muttered, "None of us is sure about the limits to her nascent powers. She might know what we say and think." Danu looked at the horizon and the tints of red and orange spreading across the sky. "Sunset approaches. The meeting is arranged for between sunrise and meán lae. We should make camp in the forest."

Aodán nodded. "Should we take precautions?"

"Of course. I have no doubt Messin plans a surprise, and there's no sense in handing him or Calman our heads on a platter."

"He's expecting two kings and two queens. He won't be happy at being deceived," said Aodán.

"Who cares?" snorted Danu. "Do you expect the conversation to last more than a few acrimonious sentences?"

∗∗∗

The small group dismounted fifty paces from Messin's pavilion and handed their reins to several shield-warriors. Aodán and Danu strode ahead of Ciar, Draighean, Iarlugh, Onchú, and Tisiphone. All were in full battle armour, although for Danu and Tisiphone, that meant gossamer-thin chitons that rose and fell with the light morning breeze. The Sídhe grasped her blackthorn staff and wore a black cloak. *Did she have any other?*

Messin's shield-man met them and indicated the tent. "The Rí Ruirech and Calman await inside. Please leave your weapons on the table before you enter." The broad-shouldered warrior's demeanour spoke of a man expecting to be obeyed. Hence, his scowl when Danu shook her head, smiled, and pointed to a nearby mound.

"The Goddess has blessed us with a pleasant morning. It would be churlish to show her disdain. We will meet under the skies." She looked at Tisiphone. "Besides, you can never tell where an assassin might be concealed under shelter." Danu indicated the table.

"Place the table on that knoll. Bring seats for us and as many as you need for the Rí Ruirech's party."

The shield-man bristled at Danu's orders, turned about, and stomped into the tent. A belly laugh rose from the pavilion, followed by Messin's command. "Do what the bitseach asks. When they are seated, send someone to tell us." A short time later, Messin, Calman, and several chieftains sat at the table facing Aodán and Danu.

"I see you play fidchell," said Messin.

Danu nodded. "It is a favourite of my family, and we are quite expert at the game. Do we need introductions, or should we skip the pleasantries of protocol?"

"I don't think we'll be here long enough to become better acquainted. Do you?" replied Messin.

"You don't look well, Messin. Indeed, my envoy, the one you treated so poorly, informed us that you looked ready to cross the veil. I recommend Southern Gaul. The climate will be much better for your health. There is only death for you here." Danu's pointed look at Draighean and Tisiphone drew wary looks from Messin and Calman.

Next, Danu turned her gaze on Calman. "You look in much better health than the three thousand you abandoned in Caher Conri. My sister, Brighid, asked me to convey her wishes to you. She hopes to meet you… soon. She says she has unfinished business to conclude." The smile on Danu's face was glacial.

Recognising the conversation was spiralling beyond his control, Messin seized on Danu's words. "Where is your sister? And your other brother? The agreement was that all four were to attend this summit."

"My sister hates meetings." Danu smiled innocently and looked at Aodán. "Have you seen our brother?" Aodán fought to restrain a huge grin and managed to limit his facial contortions to the appearance of dimples. He shook his head. Danu sighed as if exasperated. "He's likely at Cnoc Duíginn. He's quite besotted with Daráine Ni Sláine."

"You do not appear to be taking a meeting that *you* proposed seriously," rasped Calman.

"The dog has a voice," responded Danu. That she spoke to Messin and ignored Calman had the Mhór Midhe king reaching for his sword. A sharp word from Messin saw a red-faced Calman retreat.

Messin glanced around. Danu was much too confident. Then he chuckled. "You will not tempt me to break the Law that easily. Perhaps we could discuss the reason we are all here… your surrender. You are vastly outnumbered."

"I recall Maine Athramail, Rí Ruirech of the Connachta, telling me the same thing. He died by my hand, and his army was vanquished and sent back to Chrúachain with their tails between their legs," said Danu.

"I am not Maine," snapped Messin.

"True. Maine dared to challenge me. I doubt one who stands in the shadow of a bean-sídhe can do the same. My envoy said it would be merciful to kill you, but I am in no mood to be compassionate. I will let the Goddess…" Danu looked at Tisiphone. "…or *her* hand deal with you."

"You are here to surrender and will not provoke me to foolishness. My offer is this. Take your families and as many as your fleet can carry. Go back to Gaul, where you belong. Perhaps your da will give you a kingdom to rule." Messin paused and glared at Aodán and Danu. "Southern Ériu will be mine by surrender or by blood. Choose which."

Danu pursed her lips. "There must be some misunderstanding. We did not ask Teachta to talk about surrender, but rather about a path to peace." The glare from Danu's eyes startled Messin. Yet the response on his lips was curtailed when Danu said, "But perhaps he was screaming in agony at the time."

Those around the table rose, and hands went to swords. Bloodshed seemed imminent until a howl arose from the forest to the southeast. A second howl from the southwest quickly followed it. Both made Danu smile. She paused as if listening to a message delivered and spun around to face Messin and Calman. Both started at the change in her.

Danu's green eyes were obsidian and gleamed. Her sigils flowed constantly, drawing power from the sun's rays shining through the gossamer chiton. She smiled coldly. "You may have been under the delusion that my sister's and my powers were gone. Not so." She looked at Draighean, who had shed her cloak and stood a terrifying figure in pastel pink.

"Apart from putting a face to my enemies, my only curiosity for this meeting was how *you* would circumvent the Law and tradition. Brighid is in the forest to our east and has just answered that question.

A glance at Iarlugh showed his fury at Messin's breaking of the Law, which he held sacred. "The people and tribes of Ériu hallow the Law. You will have some explaining to do to the Druidic Council and the Brehons," said Iarlugh. "Yet I suspect the rígana intend to chastise you before the armies of Ériu are assembled to lay waste the land of the Mhór Midhe."

"We must take our leave of you. I must deal with some errant subjects of my son, Tanaí. They are not well led and have been deceived by those at this table," said Danu, her lips thinning into a chilling smile. "Oathbreakers need a lesson in loyalty."

The thunder of five hundred horses and ten chariot teams caused Messin's eyes to widen. He and Calman reached for their weapons. Danu shook her head. "Put your blades away if you wish to live to see the sunset. The Sídhe is impatient with me for constraining her desire for blood sacrifices."

There was no charity in Danu's demeanour when she said, "Unlike you, my brothers, sister, and I had no intention of breaking the Law. However, know this: no quarter will be given when we next meet."

* * *

"The Hag's arse! We should have killed them while we had the chance," said Calman as he and Messin watched Aodán and Danu gallop east.

"You are deluded if you think that with only two hundred warriors, we could overcome Danu, the Sídhe, and the one whose body was clothed in flowers. Clearly, you failed to kill Brighid. As for the fourth witch, who is she?"

"They can field no more than five thousand. That will not change. How many is the Mhór Midhe army?" asked Calman.

"There are twenty thousand camped around Cnoc Uisnigh. My gut says that is not enough. Levy more from the farms and villages. Arm any who are thirteen summers and over. Male and female, I don't care. We will sacrifice them to exhaust our enemies." Messin paused to consider another idea. "Send messengers to mercenaries and outlaws and advise them of an opportunity. We'll flood the southern ríthe's and rígana's domains with them.

"The Mhór Midhe army will march two sunsets after the festival of Bealtaine. Numerous objections and appeals will stall any action by the Druidic Council until the invasion. When we have defeated the southern ríthe and rígana, the Council will have no party to defend."

CHAPTER 34

The Forests of An Charraig Dhubh

"Our scouts inform me there are about two thousand Ráthgeal warriors in the forest. Óengus and Ciar have moved into place on the southern flank, Ruairidh is gnawing at their ankles on their west side, and we are here," said Aodán.

Aodán looked at Barra, who was highly animated about the upcoming battle. Curiously, Brighid seemed less enthused about the potential clash. He glanced at Aoife, who had become much more comfortable fighting naked in her chariot. That said, nudity was mainly a non-issue in Gaelic society, except for formal occasions. The Cinn Péinteáilte preferred to fight undressed… unless it was deep winter. A grin appeared on Aodán's lips but was summarily curtailed and replaced with a frown.

"Why the sour face, brother?" asked Danu.

"Aoife avoids talking about the changes she is experiencing. I thought we were close enough to share." Uncomfortable about the direction of the exchange, Aodán quickly changed the subject of the conversation. "Good men and women will die here… on both sides."

"Ráthgeal deserves to be punished, and will be, for disrespecting Tanaí," snapped Danu, turning obsidian eyes on Aodán.

I thought this was about disrespecting the Law, not Tanaí. Did our talk during Tisiphone's fight for life mean nothing to you? Brighid's voice shook Danu. *You are my sister, and I will fight alongside you, but this will be a dark and bloody day.*

Aodán shuddered at Danu's coldness. *Is she my sister?* Then he shrugged. *Is there any difference between Danu or Brighid and our ma?*

For her part, Danu saw a glint of steel in Aodán's blue eyes and watched his jaw stiffen. She heard Aodán's thought and pursed her lip. *He's so much like our da.* "Out with it, Aodán. What is bothering you? Brighid and I gave up being tyrants and have no intention of embracing that philosophy again. Speak your mind… please." Danu smiled, and Aodán saw a green hue return to her eyes. "And yes, I *am* your sister."

"Boundaries," growled Aodán, but he was happy to see the hint of pink on his sister's cheeks. "The Ráthgeal warriors are no different from ours but are badly led. They will fight bravely, die for those leaders, and take many of our shields with them." Aodán paused, and Danu's eyes asked, "What?"

"The Mhór Midhe vastly outnumbers us. Can we afford to lose more to injury and death? Surely, war and blood spilt should be our last strategy, not our first."

Again, Danu's cheeks reddened, and she felt the fine hairs on her nape stiffen. *I did not engineer the imminent confrontation with my subjects; Messin did.* Yet one phrase began to circle endlessly in her mind… *my subjects.* Shite! Danu's shoulders slumped, and deep green eyes looked helplessly at Aodán.

"I just want you to consider *all* options, Danu," said Aodán. Then he smiled. "Barra, Brighid, you and I will fight as a united family. However, we should pray that the Goddess permits us to end the battle quickly."

∗∗∗

"Where are the warriors Messin promised?" The Ráthgeal Leader posed the question to his shield-man. The burly warrior was also the second-in-command of the army now gathered in the forests of An Charraig Dhubh. Two thousand fighters massed in the trees, ready to avenge the slaughter of Bran, Gobán and their chieftains by Danu.

Messin had assured the Leader that Danu, snared between the Mhór Midhe and those from Ráthgeal, would be crushed. The first sign they had been duped was the howling from the rígana and the Sídhe. It was followed by news of Messin and Calman's retreat to Cnoc Uisnigh. No Mhór Midhe warriors took their place.

The Leader's shield-man was a veteran of many battles. Thus, his reputation gave him greater freedom to express his opinion. "Did you expect Messin to keep his word? I didn't and said as much in planning this campaign. If I recall correctly, I was shouted down for being disloyal and a traitor." The tall warrior swept an arm in a circular motion.

"Our men and women have been sacrificed. I have reports of a small force of Cinn Péinteáilte biting our eastern flank like a cloud of horseflies. Likely, they are placed to intercept a retreat to Ráthgeal. A large division of horses and war chariots await to our west. Based on the organisation of the army that defeated Gobán, I suspect a sizeable army of shield-warriors is moving toward our southern flank."

"Chariots are useless in the woods," said the Leader.

The shield-man nodded. "I agree." The Leader heaved a sigh of relief. It was short-lived. "However, horses are not. If I were their battle commander, I would use them to drive us out of the forest and onto the plain and the blades of the chariots."

"I need solutions, not *I told you so*," rasped the Leader.

"The advantage is with our Regent, Danu, and whoever is with her, including her sister, her brothers, a Sídhe, and one other. We may be similar in number but are outmatched in power." The Leader winced at being reminded of Danu's status. In Tanaí's absence, she was Ráthgeal's rígan. The Goddess did not approve of queen-slayers, and neither would the people.

"I need counsel. Based on your experience, what is our path out of this?"

The shield-man looked his commander in the eye. "That depends on how you wish to be remembered. As the leader who saved his warriors from certain defeat and bloody slaughter. Or the one who threw his men and women into a meat grinder."

The Leader frowned. "Either way, I am not getting out of this alive.

Am I?"

The shield-man shook his head. "No, and that is a great pity. Danu and Brighid would have been rígana well worth fighting under and for."

"Choose an envoy to go to Danu. Make it a good choice because many lives depend on his words."

***

Word filtered through Danu's ranks of a Ráthgeal envoy who wished for an audience. Riders were dispatched to ask Ciar, Óengus, and Ruairidh to stay their warriors and join the other battle leaders. They arrived in time to see the messenger jog back into the forest.

At Óengus' raised eyebrow, Danu said, "The Ráthgeal chieftains have requested a meeting. We have agreed for them to come to us at meán lae after the next sunrise." She smiled at Aodán. "The Goddess favours you."

***

As the sun rose to its apex, ten faced ten across a makeshift table of tree trunks and stumps. The Ráthgeal Leader bowed to Danu and said, "My queen."

"It's a pity you did not grasp that before kneeling to Messin Corb." The Leader winced at Danu's sharp tone. "How many more of your chieftains and ríthe do I need to kill to get that into your skulls?" The Leader regarded three pairs of black eyes and a ruby-red pair and shuddered. Danu smiled. "I apologise. Diplomacy is not my strongest skill. Therefore, my brother Aodán, Rí of Ráth Na Conall, will speak for us."

"What is your petition?" asked Aodán.

The Leader stood and bowed. "Messin Corb misled us. However, the blame is mine. I should have spurned his call to oppose you." He looked at Danu and bowed again. "Your son, Tanaí, is our rí, and none in Ráthgeal disputes his claim to the throne."

The Leader took a deep breath and nodded to those seated with him. Few looked happy. "You are Ráthgeal's Leasrí and Queen until Tanaí is of an age to rule. Our behaviour was treasonous. We led the people of Ráthgeal as poorly as Gobán and the chieftains who died with him."

Returning his gaze to Aodán, the Leader smiled wanly. "The men you see before you are resigned, some reluctantly, to death by your hand. However, I have two requests. One is known and agreed upon by all seated. The other is a personal petition." The Leader inhaled deeply before continuing. "The warriors in the forest are brave. Their only fault is loyalty. I ask that you spare their lives."

The Leader turned to his shield-man. "At some personal cost, this man is the only one who spoke against siding with Messin. He is loyal and respected by Ráthgeal's warriors. I ask that you spare his life."

Aodán rose as the noble sat. "As you say, your lives are forfeit. However, because you have averted a meaningless slaughter on both sides, I promise your deaths will be quick." Aodán paused and looked at the Leader's shield-man. "How many ceannairí céad are within your ranks?"

"A score at the most," replied the shield-man.

"They will be executed, too. Is that a problem?"

"It is a problem with a solution… *if* you promise to spare the lives of the shields. I am happy to die if that makes your decision easier."

"I like this man, Aodán," murmured Brighid.

"How many warriors does Ráthgeal have?" asked Aodán.

"Three thousand, counting those in the forest and the ráth."

"Will they fight under your command and against the Mhór Midhe?"

"I believe they will," answered the shield-man.

Aodán looked at his companions and saw each dip their head. That said, Ruairidh's nod was reluctant, given he was about to miss yet another battle. Beside him, Brighid chuckled and whispered, "With the numbers the Mhór Midhe will assemble, you'll have enough fighting to do."

After a quick conversation with his brother and sisters, Aodán stood again. "We agree to your terms, providing the ceannairí céad are executed with the chieftains. The chieftains may also choose how they die." Aodán looked at the shield-man, and his eyes narrowed.

"*You* will present Ráthgeal's army, less a small garrison to guard the stronghold, on the plain before Ráth Na Niúig a half-cycle of the moon before Bealtaine. If you do not, then after we have defeated the Mhór Midhe, my brother, sisters and I will raze Ráthgeal to the ground and sell your people into slavery. Am I clear?" The shield-man bowed.

"Aodán reminds me of our da, Danu," said Brighid, grinning.

"I agree, sister."

CHAPTER 35

"You have news." The messenger who stood before Onchú dipped his head.

"Five thousand approach Curraghatoor from the north. There are two thousand Mhór Midhe raiders, and the rest are outlaws and mercenaries. Curraghatoor has perhaps three sunsets to get the people, horses, and cattle to safety."

Onchú tugged on his whiskers. "Thank you. Get some food and drink." As the messenger turned on her heels, Onchú added, "Do not tell the rígan."

***

Aoife raised her head from the warmth of Aodán's chest and looked him in the eye. "What am I, Aodán?"

"Hopefully, my queen."

In the light thrown by the roaring wood and peat fire, Aoife saw Aodán's cheeks blush. It was the first time he had voiced that for which Aoife prayed nightly to the Goddess. Yet that was not what she had asked, and Aodán knew it.

"Have you spoken with my sisters or Draighean?"

Aoife shook her head. "Everybody's busy preparing for the invasion. I haven't had a chance." Aoife's voice trailed off, mirroring the weakness of her explanation.

"That sounds like procrastination, Aoife. I know my sisters better than Draighean, but I think all would be disappointed to hear you say that." Aoife's brow furrowed, and her lips pouted at Aodán's gentle chiding. He watched her skin move as if in turmoil, and her eyes darken. Momentarily, he wondered if he should be afraid but shook his head. *Never.*

"I'm not an expert in such things, which, given my ma and sisters' 'talents', is an indictment of me."

Aodán steeled himself to ignore the writhing beneath Aoife's skin and to resist flinching at all costs. He slipped his arm under Aoife's shoulders. "Perhaps the simplest explanation is that you have not come to terms with the Goddess's gift. I do not believe she would give you something evil or harmful."

He chuckled. "If the Goddess didn't favour you, you would be dead, not honoured." Aodán paused and said, "Seriously, perhaps you have not fully accepted or explored your new abilities. Thus, your body is reflecting the conflict in your mind?"

"I don't want to lose control," whispered Aoife as she buried her head in Aodán's chest.

"Perhaps you need to lose control to gain it."

"Since when did you become a philosopher?" Realising how sharp her words sounded and feeling Aodán recoil, Aoife blushed and said, "I'm sorry."

"Do you think Danu and Brighid are not in control of themselves?" Aodán snorted. "I think often they are too much in control. Like tightly coiled ballistae skeins, the tension needs to be released occasionally. I'm glad Danu has Ciar because that helps, and you have me." Aodán frowned. "Brighid is the one I worry about. I wish she could find someone."

But I change, Aodán, or would if I allowed it. I don't want to hurt the ones I love. Aoife enjoyed the sensation of Aodán's chest rising and falling. She felt him inhale deeply and waited for him to speak. "This conversation has turned a full circle. You must meet with Draighean and my sisters to allay your doubts and fears."

Aodán playfully rubbed Aoife's soft, dusky-pink nipple with his thumb and felt it stiffen. *That's a good sign.* "Perhaps I can divert your thoughts to those of a more physical nature."

"Rutting is not the answer to everything, Aodán."

The huskiness of Aoife's voice betrayed her, and she rolled on top of Aodán. She felt his manhood open her pit and whined like a wolf at the growing pleasure inside her.

✳✳✳

It was a half-cycle of the moon until the festival of Bealtaine. In the fields north of Niúig, Brighid watched Rós drill her recruits and smiled. She admired the younger woman's natural aptitude for organisation and training. While Rós was quick to praise, she did not flinch from admonishing her students when needed. Indeed, she had bluntly told a score of warriors to stay in the shield-wall as they had no talent for archery.

Brighid had much in common with her ma, Mórrígan, whose band of riders were expert with bows as well as swords and axes. Thus, she had pleaded with Rós to train an additional one hundred of her band. She would have preferred two hundred but considered that might overburden Rós. As she observed Rós, Brighid knew she had underestimated the young woman's talent.

Later, as the sun hovered on the horizon, Brighid nervously approached Rós' and Nuadha's roundhouse. She knew Rós was alone because she had watched and waited until Nuadha departed the roundhouse to meet with Cináed. The two men were to discuss allocating work teams for the defensive ditches.

Brighid was gripped by uncertainty as she stepped across the open entrance. She would have turned and fled had Rós not called out from the shadows. "Come in, Brighid. Sunset is almost upon us, and I've started to light torches." In the gloom, Brighid imagined Rós was smiling. The darkness was dispelled as Rós lit more rushlights, and Brighid saw she was right. "Are you cold? I can light the fire, too."

Brighid shook her head and, in a voice that was much too throaty, said, "No, thanks, I'm fine." A moment of awkward silence descended until Brighid held out her hands and blurted, "Danu and I are delighted you've decided to lead the archers. However, you'll need armour. Perhaps you will accept these as a gift. I hope I judged your size correctly."

In Brighid's trembling hands, she carried a boiled-leather cuirass. It was stained blue and had matching leather archer's gauntlets. Slung over her arms were an iron and bronze helmet with blue and white horsehair plumes trailing from an acorn-shaped nub and a broad belt with a gold and silver buckle.

"The cuirass has iron scales sandwiched between the layers. I didn't think you'd want chainmail. I prefer it, but it tends to be heavy and takes a while to get used to." Brighid paused, adding, "But I can get the blacksmith to make you a mail shirt if it's your preference."

Rós danced with joy as she held the cuirass, which surprised and delighted Brighid. Rós grinned. "No one has ever given me presents… well, not since my family crossed the veil." Rós' voice cracked as memories she had long tried to bury surfaced. "Nuadha sensed this, and so we sidestepped the issue." The tear that rolled down Rós' cheek had a mate that ran down Brighid's.

"I'm so sorry, Rós. Forgive me. I didn't know."

"No, Brighid. I should cherish the memories of my family, but I also must move on. I've grieved for over ten summers, which is too long. I'm learning to do that with Nuadha's help… and yours." A second awkward silence fell, but this time, Rós broke it.

"I want to try it on." Brighid stood open-mouthed as Rós' léine dropped to the dirt floor. She stood naked, holding the cuirass in her hands. "You have a good eye, Brighid. The size and shape seem a perfect fit. Have you been watching me?" Rós giggled, and Brighid blushed. "Will you help me try it on? I've never worn armour before."

Brighid felt the heat rise in her cheeks as she stepped behind Rós.

She admired the soft curves and cleft of her *tóin*—arse. She barely resisted the temptation to cup Rós' rounded *tóineanna*. Cursing the clumsiness of her fingers, she fumbled with the bronze buckles. *The Hag, they've never troubled me before.*

Exasperated, Brighid turned Rós to face her. She admired the upward curves of Rós' breasts before murmuring, "You're beautiful."

The cuirass fell to the dirt floor as Rós said, "And you're over-dressed."

***

In a bedchamber in Ráth Na Niúig, Danu smiled at her pleasantly throbbing feirdhris and rolled on top of Ciar. "Brighid is happy."

Ciar laughed and whispered, "Boundaries."

***

Onchú stood alone on the northern walkway of Curraghatoor and listened. The sounds of horses snorting and blowing came from the corrals in the forests to the north. He turned to watch wagons loaded in the courtyard with his accumulated wealth… gold, silver, and jewels. Riders had been sent to warn nearby forts, settlements, and farmsteads. Others were assigned to the herds of horses, which were the source of Curraghatoor's prosperity.

"When were you going to tell me?" Lost in his thoughts, Onchú started and turned to see an angry Fainche.

"At the family meal this evening," said Onchú.

"Why did you assume I would agree? Do you truly know me?" Fainche shook her head. "I am your hand-fast partner in bad times and good, and I will stay and fight for my partner, family, and home. If the Goddess wills it, I will die at the side of the man I love."

Onchú grasped Fainche's shoulders, and she flinched at the strength of his fingers. She would have bruises. He looked into her eyes and saw defiance and love; she looked into his eyes and saw steel. He would not retreat. She crumpled and fell against his chest. Tears soaked his tunic. "You cannot ask me to go, to leave you. Come with me… and our daughters," pleaded Fainche.

"Sláine was right. Curraghatoor needs to slow the tuilithe down. Two hundred of my best warriors will stand with me. Our walls are strong, and we'll make the bastards bleed." Fainche opened her lips, but a calloused finger halted her words.

"I cannot fight in two minds, Fainche. I must know that you, my daughters, and my people are safe. As their queen, you must lead them and Curraghatoor's riders to safety in Ráth Na Conall. It is closer than Niúig." Onchú felt his tunic sodden with Fainche's sobs.

"You have given me the ten best summers of my life, Fainche. I want more, but the Goddess has a plan for me… and you." Onchú cupped Fainche's chin and kissed her full lips softly. Then he looked into deep blue eyes and said, "Please don't fight me on this."

With a chuckle, Onchú added, "I'm not suicidal, Fainche. The Goddess preserved me from death at Uallachán's hands. Perhaps she will favour me with another miracle." In a more sober tone, Onchú said, "It will be the rígana and ríthe's instinct to rescue Curraghatoor. You must convince them not to. They need all the warriors and riders for the main battle with Messin, which I still believe will occur at Niúig."

Fainche nodded her assent. However, her mind feverishly considered how Onchú's words could be reasonably misconstrued.

✻✻✻

At meán lae, the first sign that the ríthe and rígana's planning and strategising may have been in vain was the stampede of horses that emerged from the forest and churned the waters of the Abhainn Na Siúire into froth. Fifty riders herded them. The remaining Curraghatoor horse warriors and the levy of foot warriors from Onchú's nobles guarded the people, their cattle, and whatever possessions they could quickly toss into the string of wagons.

"The Hag, Aodán. What is going on?" asked Barra.

"Whatever it is, it is not good. Those are Curraghatoor's herds. Who else in Southern Ériu breeds horses of such quality and number?"

Aodán rubbed his chin. "Send a rider to Ráth Na Niúig, requesting their presence. We may need to alert Aodh and Sláine, too." As Barra descended the walkway, Aodán turned and bellowed, "Shield-wall to the ramparts! Ballistae teams, prepare your machines! Now!" He smiled as he heard Barra shouting for his riders to stand ready.

CHAPTER 36

Ráth Na Conall & Curraghatoor

Danu and Brighid galloped through the eastern gates of Ráth Na Conall as the sun sank below the horizon. Aoife, who had swapped her chariot for a horse, Ciar, Draighean, and Tisiphone accompanied them. Brighid sniffed the air, and her nose wrinkled. "I smell horse shite… lots of it. What is going on?"

"I don't know, Brighid, but I sense it is not good," answered Danu.

In the chamber of the Great Hall, Fainche gripped the oak table for strength. Her knuckles were white, and her eyes were puffy and raw from crying. Yet Fainche's well of tears had dried up. Now, her visage was angry, ferocious, and vengeful. Behind Fainche, her daughters sobbed uncontrollably. Yet, like Fainche, their faces were also consumed by promised retribution.

Úna had not ceased chanting since she departed Curraghatoor. Her voice was low, urgent… and chilling. That she gripped a blackthorn staff drew concerned glances from those gathered, although not from Draighean. The Sídhe smiled and marvelled at how one so young had such a deep knowledge of ancient curses. *One to watch.*

"We must organise a rescue. Onchú cannot be left to fight alone," said Barra, to nods from Aodán and Brighid. Danu remained quiet as if knowing this was not their choice to make.

"No." Fainche's voice was low but firm. The sobbing from her daughters grew louder. "Onchú commanded there should be no rescue by the forces of Clann Ui Flaithimh or Na Feirdhriseacha. I, and you, will not dishonour his wishes. He and his *caomhnóirí* will defend Curraghatoor and slow the Mhór Midhe rabble. He believes the attack is a feint and the main battle will still be at Niúig."

"I will go. I am not of your tribes," said Tisiphone.

"That is an issue we will remedy when you return," said Danu.

"It is too dangerous for the lady to travel without an escort," said Ruairidh to a raised eyebrow from Tisiphone. "My warriors will be honoured to serve as her caomhnóirí. Since we are Cinn Péinteáilte, I don't see that breaking Onchú's wishes. The forests around Curraghatoor will suit us. We will leave as soon as the lady is ready."

"Thank you," said Fainche. Tears from a replenished reservoir splashed the oak table.

"I, too, will travel with Tisiphone and her 'guard'," said Draighean, "and I am definitely not of your tribes."

Aodán looked at Barra and inclined his head. The younger brother said, "My riders will take a position on the southern bank of the Abhainn Na Siúire. None of the Mhór Midhe will pass us."

"My riders will join you," said Brighid.

"As will those from Curraghatoor," said Fainche.

"And my chariots," said Aoife.

✳✳✳

"May we talk, my lady?" Aoife twisted her fingers and looked apprehensively at Draighean.

"There were more opportune times before this, Aoife." Draighean's disapproving tone caused Aoife to redden. The Sídhe sighed and, in a softer voice, said, "However, I understand the Goddess's benevolence has caused more challenges than resolutions. What bothers you the most?"

"I don't want to stop being me or to lose control. Aodán thinks I have not come to terms with my gift, and that is the root of the movement beneath my skin. I'm afraid of what I might become, my lady."

Tears welled up in Aoife's eyes, but she fought them back.

"Aodán is more astute than I have credited him. The Goddess does not give gifts to make men and women worse, Aoife. Humans have more than enough capacity to do that themselves. The Goddess's blessing is to make you better. Not to supplant what you are with a new 'persona' or form. You will always be Aoife. However, it will not work as planned if you continue to fight against it.

"Indeed, it might harm you. Two personalities in one body are a recipe for disaster. The Aes Sídhe are fully aware of that struggle. Our battle with the Hag is eternal."

Draighean breathed deeply. "I have no insights or revelations for you." Aoife's eyes held disappointment, and her lip trembled. "However, apart from other talents, I suspect the Goddess has given you the ability to transform into a wolf."

The Sídhe shook her head at Aoife's startled look. "Come, come, Aoife. I cannot believe that you haven't considered this. In your dreams after the death of Silverback, did you run and fight as a wolf? Your wolf design throbs in times of danger, doesn't it?"

Aoife nodded. "Yes, but they were dreams... nightmares." Panic rose in her eyes.

"Gods, the Aes Sídhe, and some true witches can take the form of an animal or bird. The Goddess favours an eagle; Danu met mine, a wolf, in the Bod Carraig forest when she sought Brighid."

"Yes, but you and they are different. I'm human."

Draighean pursed her lips as if considering whether to divulge a secret. "You are not the only human with this gift. Have you heard of Gràinne Ni Fearghal?"

Aoife eyes widened, and she nodded. "The queen who's a chariot warrior. Can she change?"

"Yes, but not in quite the same way. I was thinking more of her daughter, Brianag. She's about your age and could transform into a wolf since she was fifteen summers old."

"Can I meet her? Maybe when all this is over."

"Perhaps. However, I am trying to say that our animal enhances us, whether human or deity. It does not replace or supplant us. Even in wolf form, *you* will be in control and fully aware of what is happening around you."

Draighean lifted Aoife's chin and smiled. "I hope this is helpful. Brighid and Danu have found I am not so fearsome as to be unapproachable or never challenged. I am here to help." The Sídhe's lips curled into a smile. "However, I will chastise you if you act foolishly or wrongly."

As a happier Aoife walked away, Draighean pondered if her example of Brianag was the best she could cite. That young woman's powers continued to challenge and cause anxiety among the Aes Sídhe.

＊＊

Surrounded by dense pine, oak, and alder forests, Curraghatoor sat atop a steep hilltop protected by two rings of earthworks and ditches. Hence, by any measurement, it was a tough nut to crack. The Mhór Midhe rí, whom Messin chose to lead the raid, was confident his two thousand warriors had numerical superiority over the ráth's garrison.

He also had three thousand arseholes, outcasts, and bandits who meant nothing to him. Without the slightest guilt, he would sacrifice all of them to wear down Curraghatoor's defenders without risking his men. In this, he considered himself no different than Messin or Calman. Even the vaunted rígana could never wipe their hands clean of the innocent blood they had spilt.

The crack of the ten ballistae on Curraghatoor's battlements, followed by the whoosh of displaced air and flaming bolts, disabused him of his assumptions. Indeed, those who surmounted Curraghatoor's first defensive earthworks suffered less than those who remained in the forest.

Fiery bolts slammed into the trees. Great pines burst into flames, engulfing his warriors. The scent of pine mingled with burning flesh as human torches ran screaming from the treeline into the open killing grounds. More volleys skewered them.

"The Hag's arse!" cursed the Mhór Midhe king. Then he bellowed, "Run towards the defences!" He knew his force would only be safe when they reached Curraghatoor's walls.

***

The two were twins, brother and sister. They were only sixteen summers old and yet were veteran raiders and thieves. At seven summers, they were cast out by a mother who spread her legs for food. As a result, the woman was exhausted and had more children than she could rut men to feed.

Their father was one of the nameless. If he knew of them, he did not care because he had paid their Ma's price—a loaf of bread. In his defence, he had kept his side of the bargain. Many did not.

Thus, the opportunity to pillage and plunder Curraghatoor as part of the Mhór Midhe horde was too good to pass up. Victory was assured because they had overwhelming numbers. With their share of the plunder, they would cast aside a life of thieving for a small farmstead. Both shared the dream and together, they ran screaming towards Curraghatoor with the horde.

Still, the boy had a native cunning and knew death awaited those at the front of the mob. Thus, he held his sister back. They jogged at the centre of the chaos, using those around them as a shield. The adolescents had no knowledge of bolt-throwing machines until those who ran beside them lost heads and limbs to the leaf-shaped iron heads. Others were pinned like chickens on a spit by arms-length spikes.

He gripped his sister's arm but almost lost his hold because of the gore that slathered them. She winced as his grip tightened and made to protest, but that was curtailed when she swallowed a mouthful of arterial blood from another victim.

Her face, a mask of crimson, broke when she opened her eyes. They sat blue circles on a white background on a field of red. She wanted to throw up. That her tunic stank of vomit proved she did. Yet, her brother did not allow her to slow down or stop.

"We must reach the walls, sister, or we will die."

***

Onchú looked along the walkway and cursed the dwindling supply of bolts and sling slugs. "Use the bolts first," he shouted, "and then the slings. Save the javelins for when they reach the foot of the stockade. Bring up the cauldrons and set them on the braziers."

The Rí of Curraghatoor mused that the ballistae had spilt much blood, likely making the enemy fearful of advancing. Yet the numbers removed from the battlefield had not decreased significantly. He growled in frustration. The horde was undisciplined, and had he retained his riders, they would have carved great bloody swathes through the Mhór Midhe. *Hindsight is always infallible.*

He prayed to the Goddess that Fainche and his daughters arrived safely in Ráth Na Conall. He also hoped that level heads had discounted any attempt to rescue him and his warriors. Once more, he looked across a battlefield splashed with blood and limbs. The stakes populating Curraghatoor's two rings of ditches further reduced the attackers' numbers, as did the burning straw soaked in pitch.

Yet Onchú knew the trenches would eventually be overcome, if only by bodies. He turned to his shield-man. "We have time. Put in place what we have discussed. I want Curraghatoor to be nothing more than ash should we be overwhelmed."

***

Covered in blood and soot from the burning ditches, the twins lay choking and gasping for breath on the upward slope of the final trench. They thanked the Goddess that they still lived. Behind them, the cries of those with stakes erupting from their shattered bodies increased. The carnage stank of blood, piss, and shite.

Before them, at the end of a long, gentle incline, towered the double stockade of Curraghatoor. At three spears high, it seemed impossible to climb. She made to clamber over the ditch's lip, but his strong hand on her slender shoulder stopped the move.

They heard more screams and sniffed even fouler smells, and she trembled. The torrents of boiling oil, pitch, and water did not kill, at least not instantly. Instead, they maimed and disfigured, creating monstrous likenesses of what were once men and women. The unrelenting volleys of javelins and slings were a mercy compared to the horror spewed from the smoke-blackened cauldrons and braziers.

By the boy's estimate, at least a third of the Mhór Midhe horde were dead or injured and unable to fight. Naïvely, he prayed the king who led them would sound the retreat. Surely, the cost was too great. Yet all he heard was the sound of the war horns and shouts of chieftains urging, compelling them forward. At that moment, the young man finally acknowledged that he and his sister were disposable.

"I think we will die today, brother," said the girl.

He smiled and tenderly wiped the gore from her eyes and lips. His sister's long blonde hair braids were matted and stained red with blood. "Maybe, but we will never be separated."

✳✳✳

In a clearing south of Curraghatoor, Draighean held her hands up. Her song rose to ask the Goddess for mercy for Onchú and the hillfort's garrison. However, the other side to the refrain was the dissonance, which confused the minds of the Mhór Midhe and increased their fear. Unsympathetic shouts of "No one said this would be easy" came from the Mhór Midhe chieftains.

Onchú smiled and dipped his head. *Great timing… as usual.* The great oak gates of Curraghatoor opened, and the last one hundred of the hillfort's defenders strode forward. The iron rims of scíatha clashed as the shield-wall, twenty warriors wide and five rows deep, blocked the gateway. Each had four javelins, three to throw and one for stabbing.

The resounding ring of metal on metal caused the Mhór Midhe attack to pause. Howls of derision and laughter rose at the puny force. It was quickly replaced by cursing and swearing as ribbons of dense black smoke curled upward above Curraghatoor's stockade. On the walkways, in the buildings, and the courtyard, braziers had been overturned. The pitch and oil-soaked timbers were an invitation the flames would not refuse.

The Mhór Midhe shrieked, angry and frustrated, as fires devoured their promised plunder. They charged, and three hundred died when they came within the range of the javelins. The berm of the dead and injured began to rise. Lubricated by blood, the meat grinder of the shield-wall set about its grim work.

The young man stared wildly at the fort. His dreams of a better life dissipated in the smoke of a burning Curraghatoor. He looked with crazed eyes at his sister, and she flinched. She put a hand on his arm, but he swatted it away. "Stay here. *Do not move from the ditch*. I will find our future."

As she watched him clamber over the ditch's edge and run towards the shield-wall, the girl wept and mouthed, "You are my love and my future."

Onchú breathed harshly and brought his sword down on another skull. It shattered, splattering brain matter over him and his shield. His muscles ached, his hands were stiff from congealed blood, and his joints complained that he was no longer young. Blood streamed from innumerable cuts, and he felt his life seep away. His warriors were in no better shape, and he winced at their laboured breathing and the grunts as more blades cut them.

Who will remember us? Then he smiled—Fainche, his daughters, and his friends. Onchú roared, "We are not alone! We will be remembered. We will be avenged." The warriors shouted, "*Tá*—Yes!" Renewed, the meat grinder recommenced its bloody carnage, and the berm of bodies rose higher.

There was no strategy behind his actions. Armed with a spear, he ran towards the obdurate wall of shields. His rage blinded him yet gave him the strength to surmount the berm of bodies. Bare feet sank to his ankles in the slush of dirt and blood. He fought to release them from the mud that entrapped them. Suddenly, the ground released him, and he lunged forward.

The unexpectedness of his release combined with its momentum. He thrust forward with his spear, heard it scrape along the scíath before him, and felt it twist. The explosive grunt was from the warrior to the left of the shield, who felt the spearhead penetrate under his arm. The young man did not know he had injured the king because an axe cleaved his head.

On the edge of the ditch, a young woman wept.

In a bedchamber in Ráth Na Conall, Fainche clutched her breasts and felt her heart break.

***

Twenty remained, and they carried Onchú's body to the centre of the courtyard and the heart of the inferno that was Curraghatoor. No Mhór Midhe could follow, for unnatural flames guarded the gateway. Skin blistered and burning hair smelled of brimstone, yet none of the shield-wall flinched, stopped or stumbled.

With a final salute, they laid Onchú's body reverently on the scorched dirt and formed a guard around him. They did not suffer long after they paid their respects. The Goddess took away their pain, and the mná-sídhe guided them to the feasting halls of Mag Mell.

***

Tisiphone lay prone on the grassy slopes before a burning Curraghatoor. The stench of smoke and burning flesh clogged her nostrils. Fury and vengeance filled her mind. She wanted to sneeze but had long since disciplined her body to obey her. She felt the heat of the fierce fire and knew it was unnatural. No one would despoil the bodies. *Thank you, Goddess.*

As a homage, she would walk the ashes later… just in case. Now, she lay in a patch of flowers, patiently waiting. A few stepped on her, but she did not cry out, curse, or kill. Most saw the lifelike thorns and avoided the spot. Thanks to Danu and Brighid, she had never had better camouflage.

Tisiphone frowned. She sensed the anger, wrath… and helplessness of the Sídhe. "There was nothing you could do," she whispered. To anyone close, it was no more than a summer breeze.

"*I know, yet it does not help,*" came the reply on another breeze. "*The 'heroes' approach, Tisiphone.*"

"I hear them, Draighean. They boast of a great victory yet have little blood on their clothes. Their stains are from walking through the fields of their dead. The true leaders died on Onchú's shield-wall." *I will change that.*

"*Ruairidh waits in the forest,*" murmured Draighean.

"Good."

✳✳✳

There were five, and as they came upon the patch of flowers and thorns, they divided to go around it. Thus, they surrounded the apparition that rose in their midst. Several hesitated, and Tisiphone's curved blades slashed their throats. They fell to their knees with hands grasping at the garish red mouths that grinned and spouted blood.

The others unsheathed swords and circled the apparition. One stabbed at her and laughed triumphantly as the blade slid along Tisiphone's side. She mouthed, "Ouch!" and then grinned unnervingly. Where there should have been an ugly gash, there was not a scratch. *Thank you, Draighean.*

"*Be aware. Blackthorn can be cut down, and even with the healing power of the dog roses, you are not immortal,*" chastised Draighean.

Tisiphone pushed aside the chieftain's shield and moved inside his thrust. Open-mouthed, he stared down at the blade that punched a hole in his belly. His eyes opened wide at the awful pain of a slash that opened his stomach with no more effort than a hot knife piercing winter butter. The final upward rip released his guts, and blood seeped from his lips.

To the remaining rí and his chieftain, it seemed time had paused and then suddenly restarted, but this time with their three comrades bleeding out on the grass. "There's only one of her and two of us. She can't kill us both," said the king.

Tisiphone laughed unpleasantly. "There were five of you several breaths ago." She crouched and balanced her knives, switching grips in hypnotic movements that flowed seamlessly like a river. The chieftain growled and hoped his eyes deceived him. The designs appeared to change to reflect the assassin's stances.

"We will attack simultaneously and from opposite sides. One of us will get a mortal strike," said the rí.

His friend nodded and moved towards Tisiphone. The rustle of grass and snap of twigs distracted him, and he turned to see the king flee from the combat into the forest. The laugh of Tisiphone mocked him. When he returned to the fight, she was in his face. The pain of the twin stabs to his chest shocked his body. The blades at his neck crossed and uncrossed, and his head dropped to the dirt.

The king imagined he was safe in the forest. Other warbands were moving towards Ráth Na Conall. He would join and lead them. He thought he saw a tree move and dismissed it as fantasy. The granite-hard arm that crushed his larynx disabused him of such solace and left him gasping for breath on the forest floor. Ruairidh laughed as Tisiphone jogged into the clearing.

"Are you looking for this one?" he asked.

She smiled. "Thank you for saving me an extended chase, although his end was inevitable." Tisiphone moved as close as a breath to the rí who pissed his triubhas. With a quick flick of her blade, his trousers fell to the forest floor. He stood naked, held between two Forest People warriors. He would have dropped to his knees and begged for mercy had they allowed, but they did not.

The knives were a blur in his eyes as Tisiphone carved deep, bloody gashes in his chest. He felt excruciating pain and the sticky wetness of his thighs. "You would have been an unworthy father," hissed Tisiphone. The last vision he saw was the points of two blades entering his eyes. He screamed, and blackness took him and did not release him.

"I'm glad you're on our side," said Ruairidh. Then he turned and snapped orders to his warriors. To Tisiphone, he dipped his head and said, "We have more blood to spill." She watched his back until the forest swallowed him.

＊＊＊

The young girl walked through the slop and gore of the battle. Swarmed by clouds of blackflies attracted to the dead and decaying corpses, she kept her mouth closed firmly shut. She heard men celebrating the "victory", yet it did not seem like a triumph. Two hundred had slaughtered two thousand, and there was no treasure… just ashes.

Unsurprisingly, thwarted goals and avarice overwhelmed sound decision-making. Shouts of "To Ráth Na Conall" increased. The warriors coalesced into warbands and moved southward. She did not think it was a good idea. If a small garrison could slaughter so many, what could the might of Ráth Na Conall do? The horde was leaderless. Rumours circulated about an assassin who killed the leaders who did not die at the shield-wall. She spat. *They were cowards.*

She tried to find her brother, but that proved impossible. He was buried under hundreds of corpses. She choked on her sorrow, and tears streaked the blood and grime of her cheeks. It was hard to accept that her brother was a corpse. *Why did you do it? Why did you leave me alone?*

It was not planned, but she found herself in what had been Curraghatoor's courtyard. Like a cloud, she had drifted in its direction. The girl's feet were soon black from the ash. She shuddered because she knew it was human. The ash felt warm on her bare feet, and she shivered. *It's as warm as a living body.* More tears tracked her cheeks. *They had families, too.* Her toe touched something hard at the courtyard's centre, and she knelt to uncover the object.

Her heart beat faster as she stood and held up the ring. It had the most enormous emerald she had ever seen. She wiped the ash from it with the remains of her tunic, and it sparkled in the sunlight. She had found her treasure, but the cost was not worth it. She had no one to share it with.

The blade on her throat made the girl freeze. In her ear, she heard Tisiphone's terrible voice. "The ring is not yours. It belongs to the Rígan of Curraghatoor and her daughters. Hand it over, or your life ends now."

She turned slowly, unafraid of the blade or the pressure of its edge on her slender neck. Emerald eyes matching the colour of the ring's jewel held pitiless brown eyes. *It's such a pity. She has beautiful designs on her body.* The young woman lifted the ring and held it out. "What worth is it to me? My brother and lover is dead. Will the jewel bring him back?"

The swiftness of her movement took Tisiphone by surprise. The sudden twist of the swan-like neck and the tremble of the blade as it bit deep into soft flesh. Tisiphone could have eased the pressure on the knife and might have saved the young girl's life. Instead, she held her hand steady. Lips mouthed, "Thank you," before the light fled emerald eyes. Another corpse fell to the ash.

A tear rolled down Tisiphone's cheek. *I would have liked to have known her.*

* * *

The roar of the Cinn Péinteáilte as they dropped from the trees was deafening and followed by the dull cracking of skulls and ribcages as hundreds of clubs sought revenge for Onchú. In an accent incomprehensible to the Mhór Midhe warbands, Ruairidh shouted commands to kill and herd the horde towards the Abhainn Na Siúire.

Thus, the many warbands, not knowing how many attacked them, fled south towards Ráth Na Conall. However, this time, it was not to plunder and despoil but to escape the painted monsters who crushed skulls. When they ran from the forest, the momentum kept the chaotic horde charging. When they reached the banks of the river, they thanked the Goddess for the water.

The loud snorting and the stamp of bony hooves took their terror to new heights. This season, the Abhainn Na Siúire was no more than a stream bubbling over pebbles. To a horse or chariot, it was not a barrier. The cries for revenge from Fainche and her daughters were followed by Brighid's and Aoife's songs. In Ráth Na Conall, Danu and Órlaith joined the chorus. Úna's incantations became darker and darker.

It could never be described as a battle. Several thousand Mhór Midhe against a thousand horses, chariots, and the Cinn Péinteáilte would never be enough. As the slaughter began, the Abhainn Na Siúire turned red, and the stream's level rose.

Several sunsets later, the conspiracies of ravens and packs of wolves were still feeding on the flesh of the Mhór Midhe.

✳✳✳

The bedchamber door opened, and Tisiphone entered. She could think of no worse task that she had ever undertaken. Yet it had to be done. On a carved chair, Fainche rocked her baby, Onchú's daughter, in her arms. Tisiphone found it impossible not to think about how Onchú would never see his daughter grow into a young woman.

She walked to the seat and knelt before Fainche. Then she laid the ring and seal of Curraghatoor on Fainche's lap. "Sorry is not enough, but it is all I can say."

"Thank you. It is enough."

CHAPTER 37

Bealtaine

In Cnoc Uisnigh, there was considerable debate about whether the rígana had deliberately allowed the sole survivor of the raid on Curraghatoor to escape the massacre of the Mhór Midhe. The man was a fool because a wise man would have put as much distance as possible between himself and Messin or Calman.

His participation in the discussion was brief, ending when his throat was cut for being a coward. Still, the man's graphic description of the slaughter of five thousand Mhór Midhe warriors and the rabble of mercenaries and outcasts who accompanied them caused anxiety among the Mhór Midhe hierarchy.

"Of course, he was allowed to escape, and he has served the witches' purpose well," snarled Messin. "Useless bastards!" he spat as he watched the chieftains and ríthe exit the chamber. Only he and Calman remained.

"It was a simple raid. Five thousand against several hundred. It should have been easy. Instead, we lost one-fifth of our army and sowed doubt in the minds of the chieftains and kings," said Calman. "What will happen when we fight the massed armies of Ráth Na Conall, Ráth Na Niúig, Ráthgeal, Clárach, and Cnoc Duíginn?" he asked.

"Do I see fear in your eyes, Calman?"

Calman shook his head. "No, it is respect. Something that, even now, you fail to give the rígana and their allies. *You* gave them a victory, and the chieftains and ríthe of the Mhór Midhe know it. It is not our tradition to reward failure."

Messin held Calman's gaze, but the Mhór Midhe battle commander did not flinch or break the stare. "We have far superior numbers," said Messin. "If the reports are true, they are gathering farmers to fight. Devise a plan. Surely, you can win against peasants."

"Are we not using children to fight on our side? Who will be the better warrior? A child of thirteen summers or a farmer's son or daughter?"

Calman turned on his heels and walked from the chamber. He felt the heat of Messin's anger and smiled. Patience had paid off, and the Rí Ruirech of the Mhór Midhe had publicly shown his weaknesses. Who did the tribe's nobles want to lead them? A dying old man whose judgement was suspect or him.

***

"We cannot hope to fight Messin's army face-to-face and win. They still have over twenty thousand warriors. We must first reduce their advantage," said Decimus. His statement was blunt and not well received. The mood in the Great Hall became even frostier when he added. "We can field perhaps seven thousand shields. If we were defending, this would be more than adequate... *but we're not.*"

"There are the riders, chariots, archers, and the triremes," said Brighid. Her chin jutted out, and her feirdhris pounded in her chest. It was matched by Danu's, although hers was measured anger. Aoife's skin no longer looked as if snakes had slithered underneath it. Instead, more defined patterns were taking their place, although none could determine what they represented. However, they throbbed in sympathy with Brighid and Danu's unhappiness. *Had Decimus dismissed the value of the mobile contingents?*

"Contrary to what you may think, I am not disparaging either our mobile forces or the archers." The tension in the room became less ominous.

Danu looked at Decimus, and her eyebrow lifted. "But..."

Decimus dipped his head in acknowledgement. "But they must be the first to meet the Mhór Midhe. Only the riders, chariots, archers, and mobile ballistae can attack Messin's horde, inflict significant damage, and hope to survive. They are the only ones who can cause chaos and damage and lead the enemy onto our shield-wall."

Brighid looked at Rós. The bean-sídhe who stood behind her smiled. "No! There must be another way." She looked at Danu. *I can't lose her, sister.*

Danu put her hand on Brighid's. "You would not hesitate to give your life for her. She has the right to do the same for you."

***

It was his idea. Hence, Decimus was not surprised when his presence was required in a smaller chamber off Ráth Na Niúig's Great Hall. Danu deferred to Aodán, who pointed to the seat on the opposite side of the table. In turn, Aodán ceded to Barra.

It made sense; Barra, by a small margin over Brighid, was the better tactician for mounted manoeuvres. That said, both would have gladly stepped down for Fainche, but she and her daughters still mourned Onchú's death.

"We have accepted your premise if brutally stated, that the mobile and ranged forces should be the point of our spear. Our only revision is that you will lead this phase of our strategy. Ruairidh will accompany you as protection for the archers and ballistae teams. As you declared, death is inevitable in war, but we are at a numerical disadvantage. We cannot throw lives away senselessly," said Barra.

Decimus smiled wryly at Barra's emphasis. This time, Aodán shook his head. "This is not penance or punishment, Decimus. That would be foolish. My brother and sisters believe you are the best to command the force, as do I." Aodán inhaled deeply. "Our scouts have informed us that the Mhór Midhe are a half-cycle of the moon's march from the northwestern end of the valley that divides An Charraig Dhubh."

"The archers..." Brighid choked on her words before recovering,

"…and the other contingents requested are gathering as we speak and can depart for the valley at meán lae if you wish. However, I suggest that, before leaving, you and the leaders of your command should meet with Cináed and Nuadha to familiarise yourselves with the various obstacles the people… and Draighean have devised."

* * *

As Decimus exited the room, a small but strong hand grasped his forearm. "I will accompany you," said Tisiphone. "You never know when an assassin will be useful."

"As will I," said the shadow that broke from the hallway's wall. Draighean chuckled. "You never know when a Sídhe will come in useful."

As the force set out and jogged or cantered towards An Charraig Dhubh, people thronged the parapets of Ráth Na Niúig. The thunder of hundreds of *bodhráin* rose, accompanied by the roar of the throng. It was matched by the banging of spears on shields from the assembled shield-walls who formed an honour guard.

"How many will we see again?" asked Ciar.

"All of them," replied Danu. "Here or in Mag Mell."

* * *

"It's a trap," said Calman as he examined the mouth of the valley.

Arrayed behind him were over twenty thousand Mhór Midhe fighters. They stood loosely in rows of seven or eight hundred, awaiting the order to march into the vale. At the front of the column were the "disposables"—the young, the elderly, the drunk, the avaricious, and, as always, the glory seekers. For many, the only thing they had in common was pissing their triubhas.

"Of course it is," said Messin. "That's why we have the front ranks full of the unimportant and outcasts. They will exhaust whatever snares the witches have devised."

Calman shook his head and wondered why he had ever considered Messin wise. "I am informed that the Greeks never use slaves in

296

warships because they are unreliable and, in the heat of battle, are just as likely to turn on and kill their masters as to fight." Calman pointed to the vanguard. "At best, they will run at the first sign of trouble. At worst, they will turn on us with the weapons we gave them, and we will still have to face and overcome the traps."

Messin grunted and was about to rebuke Calman when a shriek came from the black-cloaked figure astride one of An Charraig Dhubh's peaks. It was followed by howling from the forests on either side of the valley and more from the mother and daughter who stood on Ráth Na Niúig's walls.

Tisiphone smiled. *I want a howl like that.*

Be careful what you wish for.

As Calman predicted, the front ranks, their minds in turmoil, panicked and fled to the edges of the forests lining the valley.

***

"Battle has commenced," said Calman, turning to Messin, but the Rí Ruirech of the Mhór Midhe writhed on the ground. Messin did not know what agony was greater. The awful cackling in his head, the visions of the Hag, or the pains in his belly that felt like red-hot blades stabbing him repeatedly.

"Help me," gasped Messin. He breathed harshly, his face flushed red, and the veins in his eyes burst as he fought to regain control of his body. Around the king, a protective ring of warriors kept the curious away.

"Of course, my king." Calman knelt beside Messin and put one hand around the king's shoulders to support him. Yet, as he was raised into a sitting position, Messin felt the point of a blade prick his belly. "Is it the Goddess or the Sídhe whom I should thank for the timely intervention and diversion?"

"You've signed your death warrant, Calman. My men will execute you."

"These…" Calman dipped his head to the circle of guards. "…are *my* men. Your nobles deserted you after the debacle at Curraghatoor. They saw no future with a king whose mind was failing and who lived under a death sentence from the Goddess."

Calman chuckled. "Besides, the Mhór Midhe have no other battle commander who can win this war but me. You said it yourself." Feeling an inordinate sense of satisfaction, Calman plunged the dagger into Messin's belly and twisted it.

"*Tuil!*" gasped Messin. He felt his guts spill onto the grass together with the canker, which was the actual cause of his demise.

"Inform the ríthe and chieftains that the Rí Ruirech had an unfortunate accident and has sadly died. Also, I am taking full command of the Mhór Midhe." Calman paused and smiled. "If any object, kill them."

* * *

"Now that is strange," said Decimus. Barra, Brighid, and Fainche dipped their heads in agreement. They had observed the chaos and heard the screams of pain as the Mhór Midhe vanguard reacted to the *Song of Draighean*, with many falling into nearby pits and snares.

Barra growled, "*Tuilithe!* Children. They send children to fight us."

"Their blades will kill you as much as those of veteran warriors. I was fourteen when I completed my first contract." Tisiphone's cold words sent shivers along spines.

"They appear to be withdrawing," said Brighid.

* * *

Calman brought the ríthe and chieftains of the Mhór Midhe together in his pavilion. Unsurprisingly, there were fewer than expected due to the meán oíche visits from Calman's loyal bodyguards.

That said, Calman was smart. He knew, of those who had sworn an oath to serve him as Rí Ruirech of the Mhór Midhe, at least a third would happily put a blade in his back. Indeed, if he did not have a successful war, Calman knew that, like Messin's, his life was forfeit. It was the tribe's way.

However, Calman had an unshakeable confidence in his ability as a battle commander, and few contested his belief or talent. "Avoid the patches of blackthorn, not because of the thorns but because they will hide pits and traps." Raised eyebrows greeted his assertion. He laughed and said, "There are those of the Connachta who wish to see the rígana humbled. It was a camouflage often used by the queens in their war with the Connachta.

"The valley is narrow, and the rígana are fond of their ranged weapons. We should not give them a target. Keep away from the tree lines." Ripples of agreement greeted this tactic. That said, Calman could not care less about their understanding. He just needed their warriors. "We will keep the 'disposables' in the vanguard. What other use are they?" This time, laughter followed his command.

"We can do little against the Sídhe's incantations, save keep strong minds and threaten our weaker warriors with death if they falter. The same applies to the queens." Calman paused, and his brow furrowed. "Going by their howling, they appear to have added to their number." He inhaled before speaking again. "The survivor of the massacre at Curraghatoor spoke of an assassin who killed the ríthe. Keep your guards close."

***

"Here they come," said Decimus. "Everyone to their positions."

The Roman watched the column of Mhór Midhe contract and smiled as they avoided the broad swathes of blackthorn and moved closer to the western side of the valley. *Danu is a clever tactician.* He shivered as the *Songs of Aoife, Brighid, Danu, Draighean,* and *Órlaith* filled the air. Soon, they were joined by the wolves in the forest and the wolfhounds who accompanied the mobile contingents.

He whispered, "Thank you," in response to the westerly wind, which raised the fine hairs on his nape as it rose from a zephyr to a steady breeze. The reply of *You are welcome* sent shivers along his spine.

Decimus smiled, although with no great sense of satisfaction, at the shrill cries of pain and the dull crack of broken shin bones and ankles that resounded across the valley. The forearm-deep holes dug by hundreds, maybe thousands, of children were also populated with short, shite-smeared stakes.

＊＊＊

Calman's sigh of relief at the sounds of pain hid his concerns. His army was midway into the valley and had met no resistance… save the ankle-breaking snares and some ditches they were meant to find.

Where are the ditches filled with stakes? Where are the ranged weapons? Will they only fight on the plain before Ráth Na Niúig? The latter had a logic to it, given their horse warriors and chariots. The promontory fort of Niúig would be a strong defence in a siege. Once again, he grimaced at the constant shrieking and awful visions in his head, set his jaw, and took another step.

＊＊＊

When the Mhór Midhe vanguard passed the valley's midpoint, Decimus shouted, "Now!" He was disturbed, if grateful, to find his voice magnified by Draighean. His longest-ranged weapon was his simplest—the sling. Everyone knew how to use a sling since childhood, and most carried three or four coiled around their waists. Almost one thousand warriors stepped beyond the treeline.

The whirring sound of long braided flax and wool cords rose steadily until released with a sharp "snap". Soon, the mid-section of the Mhór Midhe reeled under unrelenting volleys of stones and lead slugs. Flesh was bruised and broken. Skulls were cracked, and warriors fell, clutching faces streaming with blood. "Shields!" shouted the chieftains. Yet not all carried scíatha or helmets. Many were too poor to afford shields; armour was a luxury only the nobility could afford.

Frustration and anger prompted a section to break from the Mhór Midhe column and rush the tree line. In response, the slingers switched effortlessly to throw underhand and picked them off. The rain of stones and slugs continued until the barrels and pouches were empty.

＊＊＊

In the silence that followed, the slingers disappeared into the forest. *"Tuilithe!"* roared Calman as he surveyed the broken bodies of the unconscious and the dead scattered on the valley floor and heard the moans and cries of the injured. The enemy had not touched his vanguard. *They attacked my veterans.*

The looks from his chieftains said, "You should have known." Calman wondered what was next but did not have long to wait for an answer. The smell of woodsmoke carried on the wind tickled his nose.

"Shite! Keep your shields up!" he bellowed.

The crack and sigh of released skeins were followed by the whoosh of one hundred ballistae bolts. Decimus wished he had one hundred more. Yet he also said a prayer of thanks to the civilians who had carried the field ballistae to the forest and stockpiled the bolts. Each weapon had one hundred missiles. Given added impetus by the westerly wind, volley after volley carved a deep trench of blood and gore into the heart of the Mhór Midhe army.

Unlike the slings, the ballistae's bolts cleaved limbs and heads and pinned comrades in deathly embraces. A pink mist of carnage rose above the Mhór Midhe. On the valley's slopes, the mná-sídhe shrieked and swept down to harvest the spirits of the newly dead. Men and women raised scíatha for protection but found they were useless against the brutal force of the missiles.

The smell of woodsmoke became more substantial, and Calman swore and cursed the Goddess. It was a mistake that she would not forget. Behind the rearguard, his supply and weapons wagons were in flames. Fanned by the wind, the fires quickly spread. Cattle caught in the barrage of iron died and were consumed by the infernos.

In the forest, Decimus prayed to Apollo and the Goddess for the safety of the volunteer teams who manned the ballistae. Most had assumed they would not return from the mission.

"What next?" railed Calman. He wished he had not asked when he spied smoky trails smudging the clear blue sky. Rós' archers shot arrows, bound with pitch-soaked rags, and lit by small fires. Each missile flew up, reached the apex of its arc, and dropped. Men and women became human torches as clothes and hair were set alight. The death toll was not significant, but the terror was.

Infuriated, Mhór Midhe warbands broke ranks and charged the western foothills. Rós' archers reached into their second and final quiver of thirty arrows. Calmly, they targeted those who entered their killing field. "Target the chieftains!" shouted Rós. Behind the bowmen and women, Ruairidh's Cinn Péinteáilte moved closer.

"How many more do you want to lose?" bellowed Calman to his ríthe and chieftains. "Get your warriors back into the formation." Yet battle rage and bloodlust are often more powerful motivators. Many chose to enter the forest to pursue the archers and ballistae teams. Instead, they met the iron and wood clubs of the Cinn Péinteáilte.

***

Calman looked upwards, hoping to see a purple-grey expanse and the dark clouds of thunder forming on the horizon. He was disappointed. The sky was that of a perfect summer, blue and cloudless. He whirled around, taking in the chaos and snapping orders to the ríthe and chieftains. His flow of commands and venom was interrupted by the sound of hunting horns.

"Rut the Hag!" he gasped. Yet how much of a surprise was it? He bellowed, "Close lines. Spears to the front. If you break ranks, *I* will kill you."

Few of the Mhór Midhe had faced mounted warriors. Thus, the thunder of thousands of bony hooves on ground hardened by the spring winds and a lack of rain was inconceivable. The blaring horns and raucous battle cries accompanying it increased their alarm. Furthermore, the sight of the leader's long, ash-grey hair braids swinging and the wrath evident in her and her daughters' demeanour prompted hundreds of prayers to the Goddess. They were ignored.

Calman's curiosity was piqued as the riders galloped towards the strip of flowering draighean that edged the western tree line. He examined the ribbon of the thorny shrub more closely and saw it was wide enough for three chariots with battle knives attached.

The realisation of his error dawned on Calman and made him swear. The blackthorn hid no traps. It was misdirection and gave the riders a free path along his flank. In his head, Calman heard the Sídhe laugh. "*Bitseacha! Striapacha!*" he bellowed. "Spear the horses!" As an afterthought, he added, "They will not dismount!"

* * *

Fainche's primary concern was avoiding the spinning scythes of Aoife's chariots. Each was nine hands long. Thus, she had devised a risky strategy. Now, she prayed to the Goddess that it would work. Once again, the Mhór Midhe vanguard was ignored to concentrate the riders' limited inventory of javelins and darts on Calman's experienced warriors. As the cavalry galloped along the Mhór Midhe's left flank, they flayed the enemy with a hailstorm of iron.

Wails of agony rose from the Mhór Midhe's flank. Yet only from the injured, for the mná sídhe had taken the spirits of the dead to Mag Mell or the Otherworld. Calman's fighters cursed an enemy that steadfastly refused to engage. Those who broke ranks to challenge the riders were bundled aside by the massive horses or met a bloody end as hooves crushed bones and maces turned their heads to a pulp.

Fainche, her long-handled axe unsheathed and bloody, looked ahead. The riders needed an exit, a weak spot in the Mhór Midhe ranks, before the horses became exhausted and were easily brought down. To slow down would be suicide. Near the entrance to the valley, Fainche heard a different horn followed by a wolf howling. She smiled. *Thanks, Aoife.*

* * *

The Mhór Midhe's fear level ascended to new heights as Aoife's ten battle chariots entered the fray. Propelled by four hardy horses instead of the usual team of two, the carbaid drove along the enemy's left flank at breakneck speeds. More javelins and heavy darts flayed the Mhór Midhe. Aoife savoured the shrieking and screaming as the cries rose ever higher.

Yet the enemy's fear had not peaked. Calman and his seasoned warriors knew what to expect. They grasped spears and watched the chariots wheel around for a second run. The carbaid closed on the flank until the spinning bronze scythes scraped and broke the wooden scíatha. Men screamed as arms that gripped shields were cleaved. The foolish who closed on the chariots were later found in bloody pieces.

"One more time!" Calman heard the naked, gore-splattered apparition in the leading chariot scream. As Aoife's vehicle's blades carved a bloody path at knee level, her longsword slashed and cleaved heads. She heard a crash behind her and prayed that those in the chariot passed beyond the veil quickly. Ahead, she watched Fainche turn into the body of the Mhór Midhe and called for more speed.

She heard Calman and his chieftains castigate their warriors, roaring, "Have you forgotten how to fight chariots!" It was followed by the rattle of thrown spears bouncing off the creta. The curses of drivers and warriors at new scars increased. Aoife grimaced at the crash of another carbad. It was followed by screams from the Mhór Midhe, who were crushed by the vehicle or whose heads were cleaved by the blades that had snapped and spun directionless missiles through the air.

Aoife bellowed, "Disengage!" and prayed that Fainche's strategy worked.

✳✳✳

The wedge's tip that forced a break in the Mhór Midhe comprised Fainche, her daughters, Barra, and Brighid. Behind her, Fainche grinned at Brighid's unnerving howling. Instinctively, she knew the rígan's eyes were a nightmarish black, and her curling designs flowed unceasingly over her naked body. She heard Barra roar as he bludgeoned the enemy with a mace that dripped blood and had ribbons of flesh hanging from its flanged head.

Fainche worried less about her daughters alongside her, but her brow furrowed when she thought of Úna, whom she envisaged standing, arms spread on Ráth Na Niúig's walkway. *"I am with you and my sisters, ma."* Úna's pledge and other incantations that stiffened the hairs on Fainche's nape repeated itself. Men and women stared in horror at the quartet and fell away. *What did they see?*

In disbelief, Calman rubbed his eyes and snarled, *"Cailleach*—witch." For once, he was right.

Standing on the mountain, Draighean admired the dark, swirling mist that surrounded Fainche and her daughters. Yet the Sídhe was troubled. She had not felt a witch as powerful as Úna in many centuries and knew her sisters of the Aes Sídhe would not be happy. *There are boundaries for a reason, humans!* Still, Draighean would not be outdone by a witch. She lifted her blackthorn staff and uttered a howl that burst eardrums.

Bloody and tired, the riders cut a path through the Mhór Midhe. Finally, they burst through Calman's right flank and galloped into the forest. Those who followed found that Ruairidh and his Cinn Péinteáilte had not left the trees.

The Mhór Midhe war horns reverberated, ordering a retreat.

* * *

In the deep darkness between meán oíche and dawn, the camp whores had been rutted, and the remaining stocks of beer drunk. Hence, most finally succumbed to sleep. As Tisiphone moved through the camp, she left no more trace than a shadow. She felt an undeniable nervousness among the Mhór Midhe and intended to raise their level of terror.

She thanked the Goddess that men were so predictable and that Olcán was the exception to her observation. Watching a beautiful, naked woman walking towards them evoked thoughts of lust long before fear and danger. They saw Tisiphone's breasts and pit before her knives… and they died.

Tisiphone smiled as she padded towards another chieftain's tent. Yet she also frowned at the innocent blood she had let flow into the earth. The remorse was a new and unwelcome intrusion. *I had no choice. They chose their sleeping partner imprudently.*

The sky took on hues of grey and purple rather than black. As she chose another target, Tisiphone knew dawn was close and, with it, her discovery. She heard shouts across the camp as shield-men entered their chieftains' pavilions, only to find death. She looked at Calman's shelter. *Just one more.* Then she remembered Draighean's words. *You are not immortal.*

Tisiphone shrugged. Calman was Brighid's to deal with. "He's yours, Brighid," she murmured, walking through the dawn gloom and into the forest.

"*Thank you,*" came Brighid's reply.

Tisiphone smiled and sighed as she found where her mare was tethered. *Such strange people.* Then she chuckled at how quickly she had accepted the absurdity.

CHAPTER 38

Ráth Na Niúig

"What more can we do?" Danu directed the question at Ciar but received a round of *"Kill the tuilithe!"* from her Chomhairle. All, except Cináed and Nuadha, were assembled on the walls of Ráth Na Niúig. The civilian leaders reluctantly agreed to accompany those who could not fight—mothers, young children, the sick and the elderly—to safety in the bogs south of the hillfort. *Calman will need another army to pry our people from the marshes.*

Further along the walkway, Draighean held a heated discussion with Úna, ending in the Sídhe asserting, "We will discuss this after the battle." The dark demeanours of the duo made Fainche's brow knit. *What was in Úna's future?*

No matter how often Brighid assured Aoife she had no guilt to bear over Báine's death, her shame at not standing with her lingered. In a corner, although there were few of those in a ringfort, Aodán held Aoife's hand and assured her that all would be well. She had almost lost him. How would she react if it happened again? *Why does he avoid clarifying his role in the battle?* "Shite!" she muttered, barely restraining stamping her feet. In the sky, a great eagle cried as the Goddess chuckled at the re-emergence of the child.

Tisiphone, bearing the cuts and bruises from her visit to Calman's camp, looked at Olcán and felt helpless. *This is his battleground, not an assassin's. Why do I want the things a killer cannot have? That is for "normal" people. A* cough from Olcán reminded Tisiphone that he stood at her side.

His lips touched her ear, and he whispered, "We're on the edge of a great battle, and all I can think about is rutting you."

Tisiphone choked on a breath and spluttered, causing looks of concern from those around her. She reddened and glowered at the unrestrained guffaw from Draighean. Then she smiled and murmured, "If Barra and Daráine can sneak away and spend some time together, I believe we can, too."

Brighid paced the walkway in a permanent state of agitation and fear. Still, the anxiety was not for herself or the battle. *How can I protect Rós?* There were no great forests where Rós and her archers could take cover or get respite from the confrontation. The land before Niúig was a verdant plain with rippling droimnín and a smattering of small mounds. Much of it was planted with corn or grassland used to graze cattle.

In Brighid's future, there was a confrontation with Calman Mor. She had promised to avenge Báine, but would she let her down? Brighid shook her head. *No, I will die first.* Then her thoughts returned to Rós, and she bit her lip until it bled. *Yet I want to live for her.* She sensed movement at her side and looked into Rós' eyes.

"You will do what you must and will not consider me. That is the path to certain death. I refuse to be responsible for you going to Mag Mell before me." Rós spoke quietly and with a strength Brighid had not witnessed before.

Brighid smiled and dipped her head. Then she turned to Danu. "Sister, it is time to end this."

Danu nodded and lifted her hands to the sky. Along the walkway, obsidian eyes glittered and looked into the souls of the Mhór Midhe as Aoife, Brighid, Danu, Draighean, and Órlaith sang.

In a bedchamber in Niúig's Great Hall, the heat of Tisiphone and Olcán's passion rose but not quite to a climax. On the ramparts, the songs paused as if waiting for a missing harmony. Tisiphone's growing compulsion to join the quintet became impossible to resist. She growled,

"The *bitseach*!" and clambered off Olcán.

"I will make this up to you later. I promise." She ran out of the room to the sound of Olcán laughing.

***

The assassin bitseach culled his group of leaders and chieftains with an unerring sense of who was important. *Did the Goddess guide her blade?* Calman Mor growled at his weakness. Why look for excuses? The arse-holes ignored his warnings and paid the price.

Now he ground his teeth at the wave of fear and misery that gripped the minds of the weak—and there were many of them among the Mhór Midhe's army. The rígana's tactic of targeting his experienced warriors in the An Charraig Dhubh valley was predictable. Yet why had he not seen it? *Are they playing with my mind?*

Calman saw eyes that measured his worth… or lack thereof in his nobles' countenances. The dearth of leaders blunted his usual recourse of making an example of the doubters. Calman growled at his vulnera-bility and made promises he had no intention of keeping. He swore. Was this Messin's revenge? Had he become what he hated—a politician?

"Will they ever fight us eye-to-eye?" asked the rí whom Calman had promoted to second-in-command. Calman answered by pointing to the three columns of massed shields arrayed before Ráth Na Niúig. Riders and chariots guarded their flanks.

"Oh, they will fight us, and it will be bloody. However, the critical question is, how many of us will remain when we stand a sword's length from them?" Calman sighed at the rí's perplexed look. "We started with almost thirty thousand warriors. We lost five thousand at Curraghatoor due to Messin's foolishness. Another three thousand died in the valley of An Charraig Dhubh. A similar number were injured and will play little part in the battle."

"We still outnumber them more than two-to-one."

"Do we?" Calman pointed to the Mhór Midhe vanguard assem-bled at the valley's southern end. "They are children, the elderly, and the foolhardy, holding spears in trembling hands."

"We can use them."

"Yes, we can and will."

"Will they attack us?"

The new Rí Ruirech of the Mhór Midhe shook his head. "Would you? I wouldn't. Why should they? They know we are raiders who attack quickly, kill, loot, and retreat. It will take us until meán lae to close on them. We will be tired, and they will be fresh.

"The foot warriors will invite us onto their shield-wall. The horses and chariots will attack our flanks and rear. Their archers will focus on our chieftains and ríthe. The machines on Niúig's ramparts will pierce us when we are within one thousand paces." Calman stabbed a finger at the An Bhearú River. "The triremes bother me. What is their purpose?"

"We need an incentive to draw them out," said the young rí.

Calman tugged on his whiskers, thought momentarily, and then smiled. "Assemble two groups of five hundred warriors—the best ones."

***

Aillean was fourteen summers old and scared beyond comprehension. The village she lived in was comprised of farmers and farm labourers. Her chore was to milk the cows. When Messin's thugs visited the settlement looking for recruits, her mother thought she was safe. After all, she was a girl, and they were looking for boys. At the first screams of her daughter's friends, Aillean's ma realised her mistake, but it was too late.

Most of her friends were dead, brutalised unceasingly by their fellow warriors until their hearts broke or they were caught in the enemy's snares. Aillean survived the battles and the repeated rapes. There were few women in the Mhór Midhe army. They were scarred by their treatment and had become more vicious than the men. The young ones accepted the violations as part of survival or became whores for a crust of bread.

She stared at the brute who commanded the warband she was

assigned to. He smiled lasciviously at her. It was a toothless look that promised more pain and abuse. Truthfully, she had nothing left to defile apart from her mind, and she swore he would never take that. In her short time in the army, Aillean learned to survive, fight, and kill. Her hands were calloused and no longer soft and smooth from spilt milk and pulling cow teats.

Aillean stared at her violator, refusing to give him another victory by averting her brown eyes. In her mind, she imagined a knife in her hand and his head grasped and pulled back to expose his neck. She felt the blade bite into his flesh as she drew it satisfyingly slowly across his throat. She heard him gurgle as he drowned in his blood and its warm, red stickiness as it flowed over her hand.

As the brute watched her, his eyes narrowed, and his hand drifted towards his dagger, and so did hers. Each knew the other's thoughts. Each knew this time was different. Never again would he rut her in the darkness of his tent and feel safe to fall asleep.

The blare of the war horns and shouts of *"Ionsai!"* startled her. Bodies around her jostled and pushed. She felt the momentum grow until she was jogging. Aillean glanced to her left and caught his gaze. "Another time," she mouthed. She glanced to her right as they passed the old bridge.

***

At meán lae, Ráth Na Niúig was no longer a mirage shimmering in the distance. The warriors arrayed before the hillfort no longer seemed like children's toys. With each step that closed the distance, the stone walls became more formidable. Stony faces sharpened into miens that promised pain and death. The swooping ravens on Clann Ui Flaithimh's shields matched the black cloud that soared high above the battlefield.

Calman glanced to each side with rising anxiety. Surrounded by his caomhnóirí, a bodyguard of five hundred of his best warriors, he strode at the front of the army. In this, he had no choice. Traditionally, in crucial battles, ríthe marched in the vanguard. To do otherwise would imply cowardice; no Mhór Midhe king could survive that accusation.

The disposables, those whose lives would be thrown away without a thought, drifted backwards. No cajoling or prodding with spears would make them move at a better pace. Most were civilians conscripted by force, not warriors. They were not accustomed to long marches at a high tempo. Thus, they fell back, exhausted as the Mhór Midhe passed the midpoint between An Charraig Dhubh and Ráth Na Niúig.

The immutability of his enemy concerned Calman. The stone of the ringfort showed more signs of moving than the warriors. Furthermore, the silence was oppressive. The sinister songs of the witches had ceased, as had the thumping of the bodhráin. Even the flags and banners hung limp and silent. *"Bitseacha! Cailleachan!"* he spat. Where was their fire? Their passion.

The water lapping against the first trireme drew Calman's attention to the ships anchored nose-to-arse in the An Bhearú. *What is their purpose?* He had many questions and no answers. One thousand paces later, the vanguard passed the final trireme.

Calman wondered about the rumble of curses and complaints of patches of boggy ground. The scent of pine tickled his nostrils. The flaming arrow that rose high in the air raised the fine hairs on his neck.

***

On the walls of Ráth Na Niúig, Decimus sent the arrow into the powder-blue firmament and watched its smoky trail smudge the sky. Then he bellowed, "Ballistae teams stand ready!" Further along the ramparts, Draighean dropped her cloak. Instantly, her skin glowed pink in the sun as she raised her arms and began her ululations.

Around the walkway, young boys and girls took up knuckle bones and pounded hundreds of bodhráin. The wind that hitherto was absent rose, and the banners and flags of the rígana and ríthe flapped and cracked like whips.

"Ionsaí!" shouted Calman. *"Keep together!"* The command was echoed by his ríthe, chieftains, and warband leaders. It was a terrible mistake.

The coverings of the newly installed ballistae, two on each trireme, were pulled away, and the machines revealed. The sharp slap of bolts in the curved sliders was followed by the sighs of released skeins and the whoosh of displaced air. The gentle rocking of even well-anchored vessels made accuracy a gift from Serendipity. However, the target was impossible to miss, and the screaming began.

On the eastern flank, hidden by a low ridge of waist-high grass and dirt, Rós stood and shouted, "Now!" The first handful of volleys from two hundred bows were held over small fires before being sent aloft. As they fell among the Mhór Midhe, Rós heard shrieks of pain from those struck. Yet they were not her target. Only when she smelled the scent of pine and brimstone did Rós smile.

Shallow channels had been dug into the soft dirt, filled with straw, pitch, and oil, and covered with grass. The drains were not deep enough to raise suspicion or cause harm. That was not their purpose. As the materials burst into flames and spread among the Mhór Midhe, any unity Calman's army may have had fractured. Soon, blood from the carnage of the ballistae bolts and many volleys of Rós' archers joined the flaming, smoky rivulets of pitch.

***

"Get that bitseach!" screamed Calman.

Five hundred warriors broke from the column and charged toward Rós' position. "At least one tactic may be successful," he muttered. Then he bellowed to his ríthe and chieftains, "Get your fighters under control. We can weather this storm if we keep moving forward." At that moment, Calman heard the blare of hunting horns. "*Rut the Hag!*"

Almost one thousand riders took to the field as the ballistae on the triremes fell silent. Fainche and her daughters led half along the Mhór Midhe's right flank, while Barra and Brighid led the remainder to attack the left side. Aoife, under orders to remain out of the battle until the riders retired, stood in her chariot and fumed.

Calman seethed in helpless wrath. He knew these tactics. The riders would flay his flanks with their missiles until their inventory was exhausted. He doubted they would engage unless the Mhór Midhe gave them the opportunity. "When will the chariots attack, and from where?" His answer was a howl from the forests on the western side of the An Bhearú, where Aoife's twenty chariots had been sequestered. Shortly after, iron-rimmed wheels made the ancient bridge tremble.

The bridge was well behind his rear, which troubled Calman, yet it was not his only challenge. The two armies advanced to within a spear's throw when a bellow of "*Ionsai!*" came from the triremes. Hatch covers swung open, and wooden boards slapped against the eastern riverbank. The pounding of feet followed.

Led by Aodán, two hundred warriors from each of the five vessels raced to attack the midpoint of the Mhór Midhe. Since the ships were anchored, they needed only a handful of the usual crew numbers. Thus, they were essentially empty. Calman's ríthe and chieftains swore and looked accusingly at him.

Three volleys of javelins, three thousand spears, were launched at the Mhór Midhe's vanguard. Amid the bloody chaos, the rígana's shield-wall advanced. Simultaneously, one hundred wolfhounds charged through channels in the shield-wall.

On Calman's left and right, the wings of the Na Feirdhriseacha's formation closed to trap and drive the Mhór Midhe onto the shield-wall. Calman had barely enough time to bellow, "*Get the king!*" to his five hundred veterans before a javelin tore a strip of flesh from his shoulder.

Along the front rank, Calman heard the grunts of men and women facing death at the jaws of the hounds. He smelt the pungent fragrances of piss, shite, and stale sweat and found comfort in them. At last, this was an environment he understood. He did not have to think about strategies and tactics. He could do what he knew best. Kill.

***

Danu was uncomfortable in the shield-wall. She could not recall ever fighting in the clann's famed wall, only directing its use. Yet it was not her nature to stand on Ráth Na Niúig's ramparts and watch. The fort's defence was in Decimus' excellent hands. Much as Danu loathed to admit it, she would have been a distraction at best and a hindrance at worst.

Thus, she stood and fought alongside Ciar in the shield-wall. It was a difficult and emotional trial for both. The discipline of the formation was its strength. Danu ground her teeth at the lack of individualism permitted. Each warrior had two tasks. To protect their neighbour and to kill. To fail in either was to put your comrade in danger. *Perhaps I needed to learn this lesson.*

A grunt and a gasp at Danu's side made her glance at Ciar. Blood trickled down his face from a spear slash. "*No!*" screamed Danu. "That is *my* face to cherish or slap."

It was unclear whether Danu's shout and declaration startled the attacker into uncertainty or the realisation she faced the naked rígan of Na Feirdhriseacha. Yet it was enough to let Danu's javelin punch through the woman's nose. A twist of Danu's wrist made a mess of her opponent's brain while easing the weapon's withdrawal.

Danu grimaced at the gush of warm blood that splashed her face, shield, and hand. *When did I become so sensitive?* Beside her, Ciar guffawed. "Every warrior in the Mhór Midhe knows the rígan fights at the centre of the shield-wall. That should make our life easier."

"Sarcasm?"

"Never." Then Ciar bellowed, "Forward for the rígana!"

***

Chariots create and operate in chaos. Thus, the tail of the Mhór Midhe was the perfect environment for Aoife's group. With curved scythes spinning on axle hubs, they swept in and out of the fragmented rear. It could not be considered a rearguard. They sought to protect only themselves… and who would blame them?

The carbaid did not kill many, although they excelled in administering bloody trauma, cleaved limbs, and crippling injuries. Their purpose was to cause terror, which they accomplished on a scale far beyond the other components of the army.

Like cattle drovers, they separated the Mhór Midhe into small groups, culling them for execution. Soon, the gaily coloured creta and trailing banners were plastered in gore. The polished bronze scythes, now a bloody red, no longer glinted in the sun.

Aoife surveyed the battle with a predator's eye and a certain level of satisfaction at the body parts littering the grass. She savoured the shrieks and moans of those with missing arms and legs. Yet, simultaneously, she wished them a speedy path to Mag Mell and a friend with a sharp blade. It was not their fault that they were poorly led.

Her eye fell on a bubble of Mhór Midhe warriors moving against the flow of the army. Were they cowards hoping to escape the battle-field? She shook her head. No, their movement appeared to have a purpose. Hence, she followed the direction of their intent.

"The *tuili*!" she shouted, startling her driver. Aoife understood why Aodán had been reluctant to divulge his part in the battle. She vowed to take him, Barra, and the rígana to task when the war ended. Under her skin, Aoife felt her body roil, and her wolf sigil throbbed. She knew what she had to do, just as she knew, albeit erroneously, that she should have stayed at Báine's side. She howled. "I will not let Aodán die."

As her carbaid circled, continuing their trail of violence, Aoife's eyes, now as black as night, focused on Aodán. Those around her saw a shimmering dark mist surround her. Aodán's position became more perilous as Calman's veterans engaged his caomhnóirí, hoping to cleave him from his warriors. Concurrently, the mist enveloping Aoife rapidly solidified.

The blackness touched Aoife's skin, and her body trembled. The chariot driver felt the cret lurch. When he turned to ask what Aoife intended, she was gone. Only wisps of short black hair lay where she had stood. The driver shivered. Aoife's hair was black as a raven's wings… and long.

✳✳✳

The wolf was huge and black as night. Its head was large, with a white blaze stretching from its muzzle to its forehead. Its long claws were also black. Indeed, apart from the white stripe, the only break in its darkness was its white teeth, and no one wanted to see or be close to those fangs. As the animal bounded forward, those who did not run were bowled aside or slashed with long claws.

Aoife or the wolf? Did it make a difference? She heard Aodán's men shout, "Shield the king!" The scents of battle, blood, shite, and piss filled her nostrils, and she sneezed. She sensed her mouth drool at the abundance of the prey. *Focus!*

She saw the burly warrior who led the attack on Aodán stab and slash with a spear and axe. Some of his men fell as he cleared a path to the king. He knew his Rí Ruirech would forever be in his debt, and as he stood before Aodán, he opened his mouth wide in a toothless grin.

No one knew what terror went through the warrior's mind, but his last vision was of glittering obsidian eyes and a mouthful of fangs. His throat was torn out, depriving him of speech. He did not have long to ponder the blood spurting from torn arteries as the second bite ripped his head from his neck. She would have ripped open his abdomen… instinct said the meat would be good. However, others still threatened her mate and that she would never allow.

Aodán and his warriors stood in shock at Aoife's intervention and the numerous bodies strewn around her. It looked like the work of a pack of wolves, not just one. A shout of "Attack!" from Aodán snapped them back, and discipline was established. He glanced around, but Aoife had gone.

This will be an interesting conversation in our cot.

* * *

Whether from loyalty or curiosity, the chariot driver held his position. He smiled as he heard the vehicle lurch and prayed "Thanks" to the Goddess.

"Some warning would have been nice," he said.

"It was my first time," growled Aoife as she fought with and then spat out a piece of gristle. She congratulated herself for not puking, given the origin of the meat.

"Well, brushing up fur is not part of my duties. That's on you."

"*Tuili*!" Both roared with laughter and sped off.

CHAPTER 39

Calman's flow of messengers reported one sobering observation as the battlefield descended into a slush of blood and dirt. The Mhór Midhe had lost their advantage of numbers. Furthermore, they could not match the mix of tactics, archers, ballistae, ships, cavalry, and chariots used by the rígana and ríthe. The shield-wall relished whatever Calman threw at it. He put reports of a giant wolf rescuing Aodán down to chieftains, not wanting to admit their failures.

The Battle Commander of the Mhór Midhe knew the battle was moving beyond his control. He had just one piece on the fidchell board left to move. Thus, before the ragged and bloodied mass of what remained of the Mhór Midhe, Calman dragged a naked, bruised Rós.

She screamed a litany of curses as she was thrown onto grass wet from the carnage. When she attempted to rise, he kicked her hard in the belly. She fell back onto the mound and puked. She cried out, and cheers rose from the Mhór Midhe. They had had little to celebrate thus far.

"I challenge the rígana!" bellowed Calman. "Fight me. According to our tradition, the victor will take all." More raucous cheers came from the ranks of the Mhór Midhe. Hope had not been fully extinguished in their breasts. "Hesitate, and you will see how long this one survives the attentions of my men... *all* of them." More cheers ascended, accompanied by a display of cocks and shouted crude promises.

In contrast, the armies of the rígana and ríthe were silent, but their eyes promised retribution. Calman gazed around anxiously. Had his information been wrong? Had he chosen the wrong bargaining piece? From the cavalry of the queens came a long howl. Sorrowful initially, at its peak, it changed to a call for vengeance. Calman grinned as Brighid walked her mare forward. *I was right.*

Danu stepped in front of Brighid's horse. "Do not stop me, sister," said Brighid. Yet her feirdhris told her the words were unnecessary.

"I have no intention of stopping you," said Danu. "However, I have one piece of advice. On this one occasion, be the cold-hearted bitseach I was once. Fire will get you killed."

Brighid smiled, dismounted, and pondered her choice of weapons. She selected a pair of blackthorn-shafted maces. Danu raised an eyebrow. "Not your axes?" Brighid shook her head.

"He does not deserve a clean blade. Blunt-force trauma will be much more satisfying."

Danu watched Brighid's eyes become obsidian. Energised by the sun, the curling designs swathing her body flowed like dark rivers. As she watched her sister walk towards Calman, Danu prayed to the Goddess and promised bloody revenge if Brighid was killed.

✳✳✳

"You should have taken what remains of your pathetic, defeated army and retreated, Calman Mor," said Brighid.

"You have not heard my terms, bitseach," said Calman to loud cheering from the Mhór Midhe.

"There are no terms. Your 'traditions' mean nothing to me." Brighid looked at Rós. In a voice that froze the blood of all who could hear, she said, "Kill her, and everyone dies. Kill me, and everyone dies." Brighid's arm rose, and with her mace, she marked the army of the Mhór Midhe. "I see only the dead. *Sin é mo gheallúint*—that is *my* promise."

The shouting of the Mhór Midhe receded to anxious murmuring. The clash of sciatha presaged the enemy's shield-wall closing ranks and was followed by the stamp of feet as they moved to close the gap between the armies. Tack jingled like wind chimes as riders and chariots drew nearer. The cry of skeins tightening on the triremes and Ráth N Niúig's walls broke the eerie silence that fell over the battlefield. Behind Calman, the Mhór Midhe shuffled backwards.

"Do you have no honour, striapach?"

Brighid laughed, which was the most terrible sound Calman had ever heard. "I have honour, Calman Mor, but only for the honourable, and that does not include you."

This time, Calman laughed. "Tell that to the babies and pregnant mothers killed in the settlement my men passed on the journey to Caher Conri. Tell that to the one who took your place. She knew your shame. You have no honour, Brighid Ni Conall, Rígan of Na Feirdhriseacha."

Do not heed him, Brighid. Báine loved you; that is the only reason she took your place. Kill the bastard.

Thank you, Aoife.

"I have changed, Calman. You cannot." Brighid flexed her wrists and gripped the reassuring blackthorn shafts. "Are you going to fight or talk? It will give me no satisfaction to signal my sister to put an arrow in your chest. Yet continue to bore me, and I will."

In the sky, an eagle screeched her agreement.

Calman surged forward, swinging his axe. Brighid felt, more than heard, the rush of the blade and watched with curiosity as its keen edge grazed her shoulder. Both armies fell silent. Then the Mhór Midhe burst into cheers. Calman smiled and moved closer to press his advantage. Yet he stopped as he examined Brighid's shoulder blade. It was unblemished.

"Cailleach!" he gasped, and the Mhór Midhe were suddenly silent.

"No, another deserves that honorific," said Brighid. "Just because I do not wear armour does not mean I am unprotected." With a howl, Brighid leapt towards Calman. Twin maces battered Calman's scíath until the ground was littered with curling strips of wood and hide from its flanged iron head. Breathing harshly, Calman retreated until the spears of the Mhór Midhe pricked his back.

Brighid stepped back a few paces and beckoned her enemy forward. Conquering his rage, Calman refused the invitation and began to circle Brighid. "Even the Aes Sídhe are not immune to iron, bitseach, and you are not one of them."

"Your reputation is either undeserved or exaggerated, Calman Mor. Did you bore your rivals to death? Perhaps I should remind you of what awaits if you fatigue me?"

The red and white feathers of the black shaft that thudded into the earth at Calman's foot fluttered in a momentary breeze. To Calman, it seemed to taunt him… just like Brighid. "My sister is an excellent archer. She could place three arrows in your heart, and you would die before your body rested on the ground."

Desperation crept into Calman's eyes. Still, he was not a coward, and he charged forward. Shield and axe worked together to force Brighid back. The knowing smile on Brighid's lips infuriated Calman. *The bitseach is playing with me.* He roared, rolled to the side, and swung the axe where he expected her to be when he rose from his crouch.

"That was more entertaining," mocked Brighid. The grin on her face made the blood vessels on Calman's neck pulsate as if ready to burst.

Pride, sister. Beware. Remember for whom you are fighting.

Thank you, Danu.

Brighid faced Calman. "You killed my love, tuilí. It is your turn to die."

"Is that what this is all about? All this blood for one striapach."

The crack resounded across the plain as Brighid brought her mace down on Calman's scíath. He quickly tossed the broken shield aside and stretched to grasp the axe thrown to him. The pain was excruciating as Brighid's mace shattered his wrist, and he watched the axe tumble to the ground.

Calman grimaced but gripped his remaining weapon firmly. He watched as she circled him, mesmerised by Brighid's sigils and glittering obsidian eyes. He shook his head and muttered, "Bitseach!" When she darted forward, Calman swung his axe.

Brighid felt the blade cut the air over her head. She heard Danu shriek, "No!" as a long auburn braid fell to the grass and the sound of the shield-wall stamp forward. Still, Brighid had not stopped moving. She relished the roar of pain as her mace connected with and destroyed Calman's left knee. Ripples of anxiety radiated through the Mhór Midhe.

She knew he would never use the leg again. Her lip curled, and in his head, he heard her say, "*A dead man does not need legs.*" As Calman tried to restore his balance using his axe as a crutch, Brighid struck again. The elbow was crushed this time, and the axe tumbled to the dirt. She relished his pain.

"You left her to die, naked… and alone," snarled Brighid.

"Only because you deserted her, bitseach. *You* should have died, not her."

Brighid's howl of sorrow and vengeance made the armies cringe, and their ears bleed. "I know that, tuilí, but I loved her, and *you* took her from me." The mace swung, and Calman bellowed as his remaining elbow and then his knee was smashed. His arms hung limp and useless at his sides as he stumbled to his knees.

"Finish me, bitseach!" he snarled. Although, this time, there was an undertone of pleading in Calman's voice.

"*Why should I? Why should I?*" screeched Brighid. "Live the rest of your life like this, and remember why."

"No, please no," begged Calman as Brighid turned her back on him.

Finish him, Brighid. You are not cruel like him. Be the one I loved, and now she does.

Brighid recognised Báine's voice, and the blood drained from her face. She swayed momentarily, uncertain whether the blackness would take her. Finally, her jaw set, she gripped her weapons and stood before Calman. "Be thankful she asked me to be merciful." The mace in Brighid's left hand broke Calman's jaw before the one in her right hand crushed his skull, splattering brains on the field.

On the mound, Brighid held Rós in her arms. Both were oblivious to the din of the Mhór Midhe's chaotic retreat and the pounding feet and hooves of the armies that pursued them.

***

Pursued by warriors intent on avenging Curraghatoor's sacrifice, what remained of the Mhór Midhe army retreated in total disarray and panic. As they entered the valley of An Charraig Dhubh, many forgot about the deep ditches and snares. Their lives ended on fire-hardened stakes, and their bodies became food for the predators who emerged from the forests that evening.

Aillean, having more presence of mind than many veterans, knew there was no future for her among the Mhór Midhe. Thus, she gathered many young people like her and persuaded them to strike out for the bridge over the An Bhearú River. She heaved a long sigh of relief as she watched the band step onto the bridge and run across it.

Her toes had barely touched the ancient wood when she heard a bellow of rage. She knew instinctively who it was, gripped her dagger, and turned to face the brute who had repeatedly raped and beaten her. She shrugged with resignation and stepped towards the monster. The look on the man's face spoke of cruelty and eventual death. *At least the others will get away.*

Aillean whispered a prayer to the Goddess. However, the petition was not for herself but for those who had crossed the bridge. In the sky, an eagle screeched. Intent on each other, the antagonists were unaware of the chariot that approached. Indeed, only the brute's scream jolted Aillean from her focus. She stood gaping at a monster who looked much shorter than she recalled. His legs had been cleaved at the knee.

"I sense you have unfinished business with this man. The Goddess says this is not your day to die. You are welcome in my kingdom, and I wish you and your friends a long and peaceful life." Aoife smiled. "Visit me in Ráth Na Conall when things have settled down." She tapped her driver's shoulder, and the carbad sped away in pursuit of the Mhór Midhe.

"Thank you!" shouted Aillean, although Aoife was beyond hearing her. A moan caught Aillean's attention, and her gaze turned to the crippled bully whose white bone stumps pumped blood into the earth. *I will have a peaceful life. Yet I have one more thing to finish.*

Moments later, Aillean tossed her bloody blade into the An Bhearú and crossed the bridge to join her friends.

CHAPTER 40

Autumn—Ráth Na Niúig

It was a warm autumnal day. Danu looked at the soft curve of Brighid's belly and arched an eyebrow. Brighid sighed. "Unlike yours, mine was a mistake. Everyone was celebrating. I was lonely, maudlin over Báine, and Rós was hunting." Brighid looked into Danu's eyes and shrugged. "Yes, I was also falling down drunk." She sat down on a tree stump and gazed unhappily across the fields to Niúig.

"It seems we share something else, apart from our feirdhriseacha, Danu." Brighid chuckled at Danu's puzzled look and inclined her head to her sister's growing stomach. "We are both very fertile." She sighed. "At least you have a hand-fast partner. I'm just a slut."

"A child is never a mistake, Brighid, and you know it. You had enough time to do something about it… as did I," said Danu. A slight turn of Brighid's head and a wistful smile stopped Danu's sermonising. Curious, she tracked Brighid's gaze and nodded in understanding.

"If she loves you, she will not reject you for one misstep, Brighid."

Brighid's face flushed a deep red. Yet she smiled broadly as the figure walking towards them looked up and waved. The smile on Rós' face matched the delight on Brighid's.

***

Outside the roundhouse, Brighid stood in the dirt, looking shame-faced at her toes. She had finally summoned the courage to explain the growing curve of her belly to Rós. The initial omens were mixed, although Rós looked disappointed, not angry. Brighid opened her mouth to speak; she would grovel if needed.

A finger placed on her lips stopped her. "Stop me if I am wrong. After a drunken night out with the lads, you rutted at least one, although, from the gossip, it was likely a handful or more." Brighid cringed. "After all, who would forego the opportunity to rut the famous rígan and battle hero?" Brighid blushed furiously and fought back the tears. Rós' words hurt like a dagger to her chest. Yet she had no defence.

Rós pointed to Brighid's belly. "And this is the result." Brighid nodded, and this time, her eyes leaked. "Tell me. Have I got this right? I had no part or say in the process, yet you want me to be a parent." Brighid nodded again, and more tears flowed down her cheeks.

"That seems like a good trade to me."

It took Brighid several moments to process Rós' words. When her lover's fingers lifted her chin, she gazed into a face beaming with delight. "But…" Brighid gulped. "No more rutting strange men."

Brighid dipped her head and said, "I promise."

Rós laughed. "At least, not unless I'm with you."

✳✳✳

A few sunsets later, Danu and Brighid stood on the headland overlooking the An Bhearú estuary. In the field behind them, the screams and laughter of Órlaith and Tanaí vied with the cries of seagulls.

"What do we do now, Danu?" asked Brighid. "Aodán and Aoife rule in Ráth Na Conall, and we are the guests of Barra and Daráine, who are Rí and Rígan of Ráth Na Niúig. You have your children and Ciar. I have Rós and a future wee'un. Yet we have no home or kingdom to rule. What will we do? Rule Ráthgeal? Invade the Mhór Midhe, who are in chaos?

Danu shook her head. "I've had my fill of battles. Óengus and Móirne will rule at Ráthgeal and deservedly so, after helping us against the Mhór Midhe." The elder twin sighed. "The feirdhriseacha will always bind us together and guide us, Brighid. However, you are correct. We are homeless, although not outcasts, this time."

A long pause preceded Danu's next words. "Perhaps we should go home… to Lugudunon. Fainche and her daughters might come with us. They want nothing to do with Curraghatoor. Maybe Íar can be convinced to return to his home."

Brighid's eyes widened. "What sort of reception will we find in Lugudunon? We disappointed a lot of people, especially our ma and da."

"Everybody makes mistakes. Some worse than others." Danu looked at her children. "Órlaith and Tanaí will make stupid judgements, as will yours. We will be angry and disappointed at them… but only for a while. We would never make them outcasts. I must believe our ma and da are the same." She looked at Ciar, who strode towards them. A hint of fear made her lip tremble. "My worry is, will Ciar travel with me?"

"Of course, he will, you eejit," said Brighid. "The man would follow you to the Otherworld. Also, I doubt we will be travelling alone. The Na Feirdhriseacha will want to be where their rígana are." A curious look appeared in Danu's eyes, and Brighid's rose throbbed oddly.

"What are you thinking, sister?"

"We don't have to remain in Lugudunon or even Gaul. Our tribe's seanchaithe tell stories of how our ancestors came from Iberia. I wonder what that land looks like?" Danu shivered in a chill autumn wind and smiled. "The weather will be much warmer than here."

On the walls of Ráth Na Niúig, Draighean laughed and turned to Tisiphone. "Olcán and you should pack your belongings. We are moving."

CHAPTER 41

"You know *they* are on the other side of this impressive mist," said Mórrígan.

Conall nodded. He patted the black stallion's shoulders and asked, "Do we have a plan?"

"I think we are beyond smacking their bottoms, but we can look sternly at them," said Mórrígan. Behind the sarcasm, Conall knew what maddened Mórrígan.

"How could I have known? I thought the mission would give Lonán a purpose."

"It did, but not the one you envisaged." Obsidian eyes glared at her hand-fast partner. "You put our sons, daughters, and grandchildren at risk, Conall. No one doubts that you are a great king and warrior. However, this was not the first time your misplaced compassion jeopardised our family, friends, and people. I will tolerate it no more."

"The plan?" It was an attempt at a diversion and worked as Mórrígan's eyes regained their green colour.

"There is no plan. Our daughters are together; they have learned from hard lessons and are better rígana. Our sons are kings and have earned, not inherited, their thrones." Mórrígan chuckled. "One even has a wolf as his queen. I look forward to meeting her."

"So, we let them make the first move."

Mórrígan dipped her head. Beside them, the Sídhe, Mongfhionn, laughed.

***

"I'm not sure about this, Danu. Between the dawn gloom and the river smoke, we could still slip away." Brighid twisted her fingers in mounting anxiety. Danu smiled and put a reassuring arm around her sister's shoulders.

"You told me our ma appeared to you in a vision." Brighid shivered at the memory. "She has powers we cannot comprehend. Do you think she does not know we are here?"

"Shite! Do we cross the bridge?"

"Not without permission. The last army to cross this bridge laid *Dún-An-Rí* to waste." Danu looked at Draighean and Tisiphone. "Let us announce our presence, as agreed."

Tisiphone smiled. "A chance to practise my new gift." Then she laughed and ruffled Órlaith's hair. "Órlaith has agreed to be my tutor."

Hands raised, five opened their mouths, and *The Song of the Daughters' Return* rose into the sky. It was a poignant chant, a plea for forgiveness and a new beginning. The refrain gained power as the sun rose above the horizon, and shafts of sunlight energised the flowing sigils on naked bodies.

As the chorus swelled, the people of the Na Feirdhriseacha wept and sent prayers to the Goddess. In the sky, a great eagle soared and shrieked her approval. A subtle change in Draighean's song carpeted both sides of the river in blackthorn and dog roses. The flowers' scents joined with the song.

As the song ascended, the river mist dissipated. A gasp arose from those gathered. "I told you she knew," said Danu. On the opposite end of the ancient wooden bridge, three horses, two black and one golden-yellow, stood. On their backs, the riders sat armed as if for war. In Mongfhionn and Mórrígan's case, that meant they were as naked as the rígana. None said a word, nor did the thousand shield-wall warriors arrayed behind them.

Danu's dog rose pounded in her chest and was echoed by Brighid's. *This could go terribly wrong. Have I misjudged and placed my people in peril?* She swivelled on her diallait, saw the Na Feirdhriseacha, and contemplated ordering a retreat.

Brighid's hand on her arm stopped her. "I would not agree to that, Danu, and I am the rash one. We will face whatever happens together. Take a deep breath and walk forward." About to pick up the reins, the sound of hooves clip-clopping on the bridge stopped them and broke the silence that had descended.

***

A bay pony walked to the middle of the bridge and stopped. The small, auburn-haired rider coughed and called out, "I am Órlaith Ni Óengus, Banphrionsa of the Na Feirdhriseacha and daughter of Danu Ni Conall, Rígan of the Na Feirdhriseacha." She coughed again and smiled at Draighean's unspoken encouragement.

Órlaith lifted a slender arm and pointed toward Dún-An-Rí. "I am told that my grandpa and grandma live there. I have never seen them, but my brother Tanaí and I would like permission to visit with them, as would my baby sister Brónach and cousin, Iobhar." Órlaith giggled. "They are too young to ask."

Conall and Mórrígan removed ornate helmets, shook long braided hair free, and dismounted. They walked to where a still mounted Órlaith waited. Conall reached up and said, "Please let me help you down." The wary look on Órlaith's face fled when he added, "I am your grandpa, and this is your grandma. Our grandchildren will never need to ask permission to visit."

Conall looked at Mórrígan and then across the bridge. "And neither will my sons and daughters." Danu and Brighid, babies in their arms and followed by their hand-fast partners, took nervous steps onto the bridge. The comforting throb of their dog roses did little to diminish their nerves. As Brighid came face-to-face with Mórrígan, she held out the baby.

"His name is Iobhar, after your father and my grandfather. Danu's daughter, Brónach, is named after our da's mother. We hope you do not mind."

Mórrígan was speechless as she took the baby in her arms. "It is challenging for me to reprove you while holding this beautiful child." Tears filled the fearsome queen's eyes. "No, I do not mind that you called him Iobhar, and neither will Conall disapprove of your sister's choice. It is a fitting way to remember our parents."

Squeals of happiness made Mórrígan and Brighid turn to see Conall celebrating with Órlaith and Tanaí. As Brighid made to join the growing celebration, Mórrígan hesitated. "What is wrong, Ma?" asked Brighid.

"I am the Dark Huntress. My children have grown up. I don't know how to be a grandma." Mórrígan's tone pleaded for help.

"I didn't know how to be an aunt, but there are two things I have learned. They don't care what we are or were, and if you make the first move, they will do the rest."

***

Órlaith stared at Mórrígan, and the honest scrutiny of a child perturbed the queen. "Is there something the matter, Órlaith?" The queen's voice trembled, hoping not to be disappointed.

A shake of Órlaith's head reduced Mórrígan's anxiety. "No, Grandma. It's just that you look much younger than I expected. You *are* old, aren't you?" In a moment of inspiration, Órlaith asked, "Are you a Sídhe?" The child's eyes lit up at the endless possibilities.

Draighean's hearing could pick up a feather hitting the ground. Hence, it was unsurprising that she heard Órlaith's observation. She studied Mórrígan's face and gasped, "No! It cannot be *you*."

Dark eyes burned into Draighean's. *If I am who you suspect, then you also know the precariousness of your continued existence. I am happy with my family. Leave me be. We will both be happier, and you will be healthier for your choice, Draighean.*

The End

BACKGROUND

Cold climate and bogs

The Iron Age Cold Epoch was a period of unusually cold climate in the North Atlantic region, lasting from about 900 B.C. to 300 B.C. An especially cold wave occurred in 450 B.C. during ancient Greece's expansion.

From lakes to bogs: raised bogs are found almost exclusively in central Ireland (the home of the Mhór Midhe in this tale). When the land surface was "new"—about 10,000 years ago, the glacial rubble left behind created a chaotic terrain of hummocks and poor drainage. The depressions filled with water, creating thousands of tiny lakes.

It was these tiny lakes that, over the ten intervening millennia, became the raised bogs. By 500 B.C., the lakes were filled in, becoming a raised bog. For a period around this time, the climate was colder and drier, and the bogs were much firmer than today.

***

Chariots and fierce warriors

Was the Celt's fierce reputation deserved? Aristotle thought so and wrote, "*We have no word for a man that is excessively fearless … as they say of the Celts.*" Both the Romans and Greeks documented the Celtic battle frenzy. Although not as technologically advanced in martial matters as the Greeks or Romans, the Celts nonetheless ably used the weapons of the day, including chariots. A Roman coin from 110 B.C. dramatically depicts the naked Gallic warrior-king Bituitus of the Averni casting spears from his chariot.

While chariots disappeared in mainland Europe, they certainly remained in Britain and Ireland into the Caesarian era. They are mentioned in the writings of Caesar and Tacitus and the old Irish epic the *Táin Bó Cuailnge (The Cattle Raid of Cooley)*.

The chariot was built for speed. It was of light construction, composed of a roughly three feet square wooden platform resting upon an axle. The platform was enclosed on two sides only, often by a pair of curved loops of bent wood or a single semicircle of wickerwork; the front open to allow handling of the horses, the rear to allow easy dismount.

A single ridgepole joined the platform to its twin mounts, terminating in a yoke that lay upon the shoulders of two ponies. The two spoked wheels, about two-and-a-half to three feet in diameter, were bound in iron. The swift movement and flexibility of this chariot style and its driver's skill are repeatedly encountered in the documentary evidence.

The Celtic war chariot was pulled by two horses but not the large mount of the medieval knight. Instead, in the British Isles, it is believed to have been a breed much smaller and heartier than the modern thoroughbred, related perhaps to the Highland pony of Scotland. In my tales, they are drawn by teams of two or four short-legged, shaggy horses. These horses were first encountered in *Conall II: The Raven's Flight* and were known for their endurance and sure-footedness.

The Celtic chariot served two purposes in battle: conveying elite warriors from one point on a battlefield to another and serving as a fighting platform to engage the enemy. Caesar wrote that Celts in chariots began "*by driving all over the field hurling javelins, and generally, the terror inspired by the horses and the noise of the wheels is sufficient to throw their opponents' ranks into disorder.*"

The Táin Bó Cuailnge, though prone to poetic exaggeration, depicts in its many tales a range of missile weapons carried in the chariot, including small and long spears, darts, and light javelins. In the epic, the Ulster champion Cúchulainn often uses a sling from his chariot to deadly effect.

The Persians reportedly used metal scythes on chariot axles as an added means of attack. They were three-foot (one metre) extensions of the axle and curved. However, no archaeological evidence exists that slashing wheels were ever used by either the Celtic peoples.

That said, the oral and literary traditions in the Táin Bó Cuailnge suggest what the physical records do not. The text mentions a *"sickle chariot"* in which *"every inch … bristled. Every angle corner, front and rear, was a tearing place."* It *"bristled with points of iron and narrow blades, with hooks and hard prongs and heroic frontal spikes, with ripping instruments and tearing nails on its straps and loops and cords."*

The war chariots used in *The Dog Roses: Resolution* use long, metal scythes and teams of four horses to maintain momentum. That said, I am intrigued by the concept of a "sickle chariot", and it will likely appear in a future novel!

(*Chariots and fierce warriors* include excerpts from *The War Chariots of the Celtic Elite* by Andrew M. Scott, *Warfare History Network*.)

GLOSSARY

Words & Phrases

An Chaithne (Strawberry Tree)

An Fiagaí Dorcha (The Dark Huntress)

Anas (Anus)

Banphrionsa (Princess)

Bean-sídhe/mná sídhe (Harbinger of Death)

Bitseach/bitseacha (Bitch/es)

Brat/brait (Blanket/cloak)

Bróga (Shoes)

Cailleach/cailleachan (Witch/es)

Caomhnóirí (Personal guard)

Carbad/carbaid (Chariot/s)

Ceannairí céad (Leader of One Hundred)

Céili (Dance)

Chomhairle (Council)

Craic (Chat/fun)

Cret/creta (Chariot basket/s)

Cróeb Ruad (Red Branch, elite Ulaid warriors)

Diallait (Thick horse blanket)

Droimnín (Small, elongated hills)

Eiric (Compensation)

Feirdhris/feirdhriseacha (Dog rose/s)

Fénechas (Brehon Laws)

Fidchell (Board game)

Geis (Curse/Promise)

Ionsaí (Forward/charge)

Leasrí (Regent)

Léine (Tunic/shirt/dress)

Lincse (Lynx)

Meán lae (Midday)

Meán oíche (Midnight)

Ní ghéillfear, nó cúlú (No retreat, no surrender)

Óenach (Tribal meeting)

Pit (Vagina)

Póg mo thoin (Kiss my arse)

Ráth/rátha (Fort/s)

Rí/ríthe (King/s)

Rí Ruirech (King over Kings)

Rígan/rígana (Queen/s)

Scíath/scíatha (Shield/s)

Seanchaí/seanchaithe (Storyteller/s)

Sídhe (Demigoddess)

Sin é mo gheallúint (That is my promise)

Sleánna (Spears)

Striapach/striapacha (Whore/s)

Tá (Yes)

Táimid ar aon (We are together)

Tóin/tóineanna (Arse/buttocks)

Triubhas (Trousers)

Tuilí/tuilithe (Bastard/s)

Festivals

Bealtaine (Summer)

Imbolg (Spring)

Samhain (Winter)

Tribes

Aes Sídhe (Race of Demigods)

Arverni (Tribe in Gaul)

Cinn Péinteáilte (The Painted Ones, early Picts)

Clann Ui Flaithimh (Conall Mac Gabhann's tribe)

Connachta (Northwest Ireland tribe)

Magh-Breàgh (Mhór Midhe clan)

Mhór Midhe (Mid-eastern Ireland tribe)

Na Feirdhriseacha (Brighid & Danu's Tribe0

Ulaid (Northern Tribe)

Non-Gaelic Words & Phrases

Phainomērídes (Thigh-showers, Greek)

DRAMATIS PERSONÆ

IRISH

Ailill Mac Máta

Aillean

Aoibheann Ni Neill

Aodán Mac Conall

Aodh Mac Aodh

Aoife Ni Cináed

Báine

Barra Mac Conall

Beacán Ó Cathasaigh

Bláithín Ni Neill

Bran Mac Labraid-Loingsech

Brighid Ni Conall

Brónach Ni Ciar

Calman Mor

Cairbre Mac Ailill

Cass Mac Cináed

Ceara

Cet Mac Ailill

Cináed

Ciar Ó Róich

Conall Mac Gabhann

Conchobhar Ó Deargáin

Cúan Ó Neill

Cúscraid Mac Conchobar

Danu Ni Conall
Daráine Ni Sláine
Draighean
Dubhgall Mac Rónain
Eithne
Fainche
Flann
Glaisne Mac Aodh
Gobán Ó Cuilinn
Íar Mac Dedad
Iarlugh Ceann-Laith
Iobhar Mak Brighid
Lonán Ó Neill
Maine Athramail
Neamhain Ni Fearghal
Medb
Messin Corb
Móirne
Mongfhionn
Mórrígan Ni Cathasaigh
Nuadha Ó Dubhghaill
Óengus Dubdétach
Olcán Ó Dubhan
Onchú Ó an Cháintigh
Órlaith Ni Óengus
Rós
Sláine Mac Sláine
Tadhg Ó Cuileannáin
Tanaí Mac Bran Loingsech
Teachta
Torcán Ó Dubhghaill
Uallachán Ó Dubhghaill
Úna Ni Onchú

SCOTTISH

Carmag Mac an t-Sionnaich
Gràinne Ni Fearghal
Iasg
Mòrag Ni Artair
Ruairidh Mac Carmag

OTHER

Apollo Lykaios (Greek God, Lord of the Wolves)
Aulus (Roman)
Dionysius (Greek)
Decimus Augustus (Roman)
Gaius (Roman)
Mars (Roman God)
Apollo (Roman God)
Pytheas (Greek)
Tisiphone (Greek)
Locations

Ériu (Ireland)

Abhainn Na Siúire (River)
An Bhearú (River)
An Charraig Dhubh (Mountains)
Bod Carraig (Mountains)
Caher Conri (Headland fort)
Carn Tigherna (Hillfort)
Clárach (Hillfort)
Cnoc Duíginn (Hillfort)
Cnoc Uisnigh (Hillfort)
Chrúachain (Rathcroghan)
Curràghatoor (Hillfort)
Emain Macha (Navan Fort)

Na Comaraigh (Mountains)
Niúig (Settlement)
Ráth Na Conall (Hillfort)
Ráth Na Niúig (Ringfort)
Ráthgeal (Hillfort)
Sliab Crocta Cliac (Galty Mountains)

Gaelic Afterlife
Mag Mell (Warriors' Heaven)
Otherworld (Gaelic Hell)

Gaul (France)
Aremorio (Northwest Gaul/France)
Dún-an-Rí (Conall and Mórrígan's fort)
Lugudunon (Lyon, France)
Massalia (Marseille)
The Great Sea (The Mediterranean)

Iberia (Spain)

Northern Albu (Scotland)

The Mounds
Aes Sídhe home

ABOUT THE AUTHOR

Author David H. Millar was born in Belfast, Northern Ireland. He is an internationally published and award-winning author. David is the founder, owner, and author-in-residence of A Wee Publishing Company. He writes historical fantasy with a Celtic twist.

David is the author of the five-volume *Conall Series* set in Ireland, Scotland, France, and Italy, and the series spin-offs *The Dog Roses* and its sequel, *The Dog Roses: Resolution*, and *The Blood Queen* and its sequel *Brianag*.

Resident in Houston, Texas, David is an avid reader, armchair sportsman, and Liverpool Football Club fan. He lives with his family and tuxedo kittens, Beau and Stiletto.

Facebook: aweepublishingco.com
Twitter: @DavidHMillar
Goodreads: www.goodreads.com/author/show/8248581.
David_H_Millar
BookBub: @DavidHMillar
Instagram: author.davidhmillar

www.ingramcontent.com/pod-product-compliance
Lightning Source LLC
Chambersburg PA
CBHW032005310726
48972CB00002B/281